My Friend Flicka

Ken loves his life on the ranch in
Wyoming but the thing he dreams
about most of all is having a
colt of his very own. Then one day,
whilst riding the range, his dreams
come true – he sees the filly he has
always wanted – his Flicka.

The three 'Flicka' books are:

MY FRIEND FLICKA
THUNDERHEAD
GREEN GRASS OF WYOMING

MY FRIEND FLICKA

Mary O'Hara

Illustrated by C. E. Tunnicliffe

MAMMOTH

First published in Great Britain 1943
by Eyre & Spottiswoode (Publishers) Ltd
New edition published 1974
by Methuen Children's Books Ltd
Magnet paperback edition published 1978
Reprinted 1979, 1981, 1983, 1985 and 1988
Published 1989 by Mammoth
an imprint of Mandarin Paperbacks
Michelin House, 81 Fulham Road, London SW3 6RB
Reprinted 1990, 1991

Mandarin is an imprint of the Octopus Publishing Group

ISBN 0 7497 0051 3

A CIP catalogue record for this title
is available from the British Library

Printed in Great Britain
by Cox & Wyman Ltd, Reading

Chapter One

High up on the long hill they called the Saddle Back, behind the ranch and the county road, the boy sat his horse, facing east, his eyes dazzled by the rising sun.

It seemed like a great personage come on a visit; appearing all of a sudden over the dark bank of clouds in the east, coming up over the edge of it smiling; bowing right and left; lighting up the whole world so that everything smiled back.

The snug, huddled roofs of the ranch house, way below him, began to be red instead of just dark; and the spidery arms of the windmill in the gorge glinted and twinkled. They were smiling back at the sun.

'Good morning, mister!' shouted Ken, swinging his arm in salute; and the brown mare he rode gave a wild leap.

To keep his seat, riding bareback as he was, he clapped

5

his heels into her sides, and she leaped again, this time with her head down. Stifflegged and with arched back she landed; and then bucked.

Once, twice, three times; and Ken was off, slung under her nose, hanging on to the reins.

She backed away and pulled to get free, braced like a dog tugging at a man's trouser leg.

'No you don't!' gasped Ken, sitting up to face her and clinging to the reins. 'Not that time you didn't—'

She jerked her head viciously from side to side. Ken's teeth set in anger. 'If you break another bridle—'

This thought made him crafty and his voice fell to a coaxing note. 'Now Cigarette – be a good girl – thatsa baby – good girl—'

Responsive to the change of tone, one of her flattened ears came forward as if to peer at him and see if he spoke in good faith. Reassured, she stopped pulling and moved up a step.

Ken got warily to his feet and went to her head, still talking soothingly but with insulting words.

'Thatsa girl – stupid face – whoa, baby – jughead – no sense at all—' and this last was the worst possible insult on the Goose Bar Ranch where a horse without sense was a horse without a right to existence.

Cigarette was not wholly deceived but stood enjoying the stroking of Ken's hand and awaiting developments.

'D'you think I'd ever ride a ornery old plug like you if I had a horse of my own like Howard's?'

The frown faded from his face and his eyes took on a dreamy look. 'If I had a colt—'

He had been saying that for a long time. Sometimes he said it in his sleep at night. It was the first thing he had thought when he got to the ranch three days ago. He said it or thought it every time he saw his brother riding Highboy. And when he looked at his father, the longing in his eyes was for that – for a colt of his own. 'If I had a colt, I'd make

6

it the most wonderful horse in the world. I'd have it with me all the time, eating and sleeping, the way the Arabs do in the book Dad's got on the kitchen shelf.' He stroked Cigarette's nose with the unconscious gesture of an automaton. 'I'd get a tent and sleep in it myself, and I'd have the colt beside me, and it would have to learn to live just the way I do; and I'd feed it so well it would grow bigger than any other horse on the ranch; and it would be the fastest; and I'd train it so it would follow me wherever I went, like a dog—' At this he paused, struck through and through with bliss at the thought of arousing such devotion in a horse that it would follow him.

There was no warmth yet in the level rays of the sun, and the dawn wind was cold on the mountain side, so that Ken presently began to shiver in his thin dark blue cotton jersey. He turned to face the wind, tasting something of freshness and wildness that went to his head and made him want to run and shout – and ride and ride – to go on all day – as fast as he could and never stop—

He was hatless, and the wind made a tousled mop of his soft straight brown hair, and whipped colour into his thin cheeks that had not yet lost the whiteness of winter school-days. His face was beautiful with the young look of wildness and freedom, and his dark blue dreaming eyes.

He must get on Cigarette again.

The moment this thought passed through his mind, Cigarette knew it and turned her head a little to look at him. Her whole body got ready. Not exactly resistant, but waiting.

First he had an apology to make. In all fairness, he must tell Cigarette that the fault had been his own. He had put his heels into her.

He knew exactly what his father would say if he told him about it.

'Cigarette bucked and tossed me.'

'What did you do? Put your heels into her?'

7

'Yes, sir.'

He and Howard had to say Yes, sir, and No, sir, to their father because he had been an Army officer before he had the ranch, and believed in respect and discipline.

Gathering up the rein, slipping it over Cigarette's head, Ken was humming, 'Yes, sir— No, sir— Yes, sir— No, sir—' and this seemed to have a soothing effect on Cigarette.

When his father had mounted Cigarette, to show him how, she stood like a statue; never started or jumped; and then had moved off slowly and comfortably like a well-behaved horse in a park. But when *he* mounted her, like as not she would toss him four or five times running, all because he couldn't help trying to grab on with his heels the moment he straddled her. That she wouldn't stand; and that he couldn't help doing.

He turned her so that, on her left side, he was up the hill from her. She was not a tall horse, but even so, the jump from the ground for a boy was a long one, and sometimes his arms didn't pull strongly enough. Last summer he hadn't been able to do it at all, but when he had no saddle must always mount by a fence or from a rock. So far, this summer, he had missed it only a few times.

He took hold of her withers and back, jumped and pulled, landed well up against her, held stiffly there by his arms, then carefully swung his blue-trousered leg over; and slowly, just like his father, settled to her back, legs hanging straight down.

Cigarette was calm. He tightened his rein, squeezed the calves of his legs a little, and she moved off.

One of the exciting things about coming up from school in Laramie to the summer vacation at the ranch, was the weather. Always something doing. Winds and rainbows and calm sunny days, then an electric storm; or frosts or even blizzards. People said it was because of the eight thousand foot altitude.

Now, all the clouds in the sky had caught the sunrise colours, and there was a mingling of pink and red and gold and a keen blue, like electricity, and a wind that was boisterous, like someone scuffling with you, and it played and rippled over the greengrass and made it look like watered silk—

'Greengrass – greengrass—' he chanted, cantering along, thinking how different the greengrass of the range was from the green grass in the little square lawns before the houses down in Laramie, because, on the range, it stretched as far as you could see, and there were jack rabbits hiding in it that sprang up and sailed away over it, riding on the wind with great leaps, as big as small deer. And on the range you called it greengrass, all in one word; and it was important. They read out of the newspaper, 'Greengrass in Federal County already,' early in the spring. Everyone said, 'Have you got greengrass yet? We have.'

It was in the spring that it was important, after the last big snow storm in May when all the horses and cattle were so thin and weak from the long winter that it seemed if the greengrass didn't come soon, no one could stand it any longer; and it came first like just a tinge of pale green on the southern and eastern slopes; and the cattle picked and mouthed at it; and soon it was like green velvet; and then, at last, in late June, like this. A sea of rippling grass.

Ken topped the hill and stood staring. From here he looked west over a hundred miles of the greengrass; and south across the great stretch of undulating plateau land that ran down to Twin Peaks, and beyond that across broken crags and interminable rough terrain, mysterious with hidden valleys and gorges and rocky headlands, all the way to the wide farm valleys of Colorado. Beyond them the Neversummer Range stood wrapped in snow winter and summer.

He put his head back and sucked in the smell of the

cleanness and the greenness and the snow and the windiness – all so sharp and heavenly.

This was what he had been waiting for. All through the last unbearable months of school, the endless classes, the examinations—

At this an uncomfortable feeling gripped him. His and Howard's reports had arrived in yesterday's mail with a letter from the Principal of the school addressed to their father, Captain McLaughlin. And McLaughlin had slung them on the desk with some papers and bills to open later. By the time Ken got back to breakfast surely his father would have opened them. There was that examination – Ken knew he hadn't done very well—

He wondered what time it was now. He looked down at the ranch.

From his high point of vantage the ground fell away to the north in broken undulations and steppes. Just before it reached the low level of the stream and the meadows a mile away, there was a little gorge in the low hills, bounded by a cliff on the eastern side, and, on the west, a steep hill, both of them covered with thick black pine. In the gorge were cottonwood and young aspen. A stream bed with a thread of water and a road wound through, leading from the stables and horse corrals on the near side, out into a V-shaped clearing beyond the gorge. This, grass covered and studded with young cottonwood trees, his mother called The Green.

Right in the gorge, stretching silver arms up above the trees, and set to catch every stray current of air that sucked through the gully even on windless days, stood the windmill.

On beyond that, in a convenient elbow of the hill to the left, was the bunk house, almost invisible and wonderfully sheltered from winter storms. Farther on down the left side of the V, the long rambling stone ranch house followed the downward slope of the ground by dropping a step from kitchen to dining room, from dining room to living room, and from living room to study.

Its length was marked by the criss-crosses of the peaked red roofs, by the long, grass-covered terrace along its eastern face, and the low stone wall which upheld it.

There was no sign of life about the place. Too early yet, thought Ken. Wait – there's smoke coming out of both chimneys. Gus has made the kitchen fire for mother and now he's getting breakfast in the bunk house.

He fastened his eyes on the cow barn. It was the lower boundary of the Green, a vast structure, sinking into the earth to a depth of four feet or more, the gently sloping peaked roof hooding it so closely it left only a ten or fifteen foot strip of whitewashed wall to be seen.

Yellow Guernsey cows were standing about the gate of the corral in the Calf Pasture, to the east. They were waiting for Tim to come and let them in. After they were milked he would let them out of the gate to the north, where they could wander across the meadow to the stream and stand during the heat of the day under the tall cottonwood trees which had their roots down deep under the stream bed.

Far beyond, across the meadows and the hills that sloped up from them, a long freight train was chugging on the railroad tracks. Two toy locomotives, and a toy train. It seemed hardly to move. It was climbing up from the east, going west, soon would cross the top of the Rocky Mountain Divide, and then it would drop its extra locomotive and start down towards the Pacific, and gather speed – and tear along—

An echoing whistle pierced the silence. The train was approaching the Tie Siding crossing.

The cows were moving into the corral – that little black post was Tim, fastening the gate back.

It wouldn't be long before breakfast. Everybody was awake. Going downstairs, his mother would call, 'Time to get up boys!' His father was sitting up in bed with his hair rumpled, pyjamas rumpled, hand reaching out for a cigarette.

Gosh – if his father had read the reports! And that wasn't all, there was the saddle blanket too, the lost saddle blanket.

He turned from looking at the ranch house and let his eyes sweep the hillside. Saddle blanket, saddle blanket – every time he asked his father for a colt, McLaughlin said, I'll give you one when you deserve one – not before. It might be caught on a shrub, on a rock – or lying in a gully. Lucky I woke up early. Howard will be sore that I didn't wake him. He always wants to go along. He can never wake up, but I can—

A jack rabbit sprang up almost underfoot. Cigarette jumped, but Ken sat tight, and as the rabbit sailed away, he gave a yell and chased after.

Cigarette loved a good run.

Leaning back as Rob McLaughlin had taught his boys to do, feet forward and out, reins free, Ken rode like a steeple chaser.

Rabbit, pony and boy disappeared over the crest of the Saddle Back.

Chapter Two

Nell McLaughlin pulled the drop-leaf cherry table out from the corner, opened the leaves so that it would comfortably accommodate four people and flung a red-checked cloth over it.

The roomy kitchen was full of bright sunshine from the windows which opened on the front terrace. It made squares of gold on the painted apple-green floor; and in front of sink and stove and baking table there were hooked oval rugs with gay flower patterns. A little brown cat sat by the stove washing her face.

Neither motherhood nor the hard living at the ranch had deprived Nell of her figure or her maidenliness. At thirty-seven she looked not much older than when she had won a silver cup, at Bryn Mawr, for being the best all-round athlete of her class.

Of medium height, with a long slender waist, her curves

were held where they belonged by trained muscles, and, as she walked, there was a lightness about her which came partly from natural vigour and partly from the way her narrow head lifted from the shoulders to face whatever was to be faced, a danger, a storm, a loved one, a hope or a fear.

Her skin was tanned to a light fawn colour, not dry and weather beaten, but smooth and with a lustre that came of persistent care; and the thin lips of her rather wide mouth, with clear cut, sensitive curves, were only faintly pink. Her satiny hair, of the same soft fawn colour, fell in a bang over her forehead; the rest was just long enough to be brushed back in shining smoothness and fastened in a little bun in her neck. Riding, she often pulled out the few pins that held it and let it go wild in the wind; and then, with her pale forehead and her dark blue eyes with their wide free look, hers was the face from which Ken's had been copied.

Ken was late to breakfast.

Coming in, he looked first at his father to see if he had opened the reports.

Then he said, 'Good morning, Mother, good morning, Dad,' pulled out the one empty chair – a green-painted ladder-back chair with seat woven of rawhide thongs – and sat down. His heart was beating hard because his father's face had its glaring look and Howard was smug. Howard always got good marks.

The two boys looked at each other across the table.

Howard was considered the handsome one of the two. His hair was black, like his father's, with a meticulous centre parting; and the straight lines of mouth and brows and the bold and somewhat arrogant carriage of his head, made him seem formed and already possessed of a definite character, whereas Ken was unformed, his face sometimes falling into lines of poetic wistfulness and beauty, sometimes like something accidentally assembled – of doubtful promise.

Ken was afraid to look at his father. His blazing blue

eyes were hard to meet. They glared at you out of the long, dark face with its jutting chin. Often Ken felt his own eyes reeling back from an encounter, and he would turn away or look down.

McLaughlin picked up a card and a letter which was lying open beside his place. 'I suppose it will be no surprise to you to hear that you have not been promoted,' he said. 'You might like to see your marks.'

He tossed the card over to Ken.

Nell McLaughlin handed Ken a blue bowl full of oatmeal covered with cream and brown sugar and said, 'Let him eat his breakfast first,' but Ken took the card and tried to focus his eyes upon it. He hated so to look, it was hard to see anything at all.

While he studied it there was a silence, Howard eating his bacon and smiling. Nell's face was troubled. She looked down, buttering her toast.

Ken read his marks through and finally came to the English examination.

He looked up and met his father's eye.

McLaughlin leaned forward. 'Just as a matter of curiosity,' he said, 'how do you go about it to get no marks in an examination? Forty in history? Seventeen in arithmetic! But a *zero!* Just as one man to another, what goes on in your head?'

'Yes, tell us how you do it, Ken,' chirped Howard.

Nell shot a swift look at her oldest son. 'You eat your breakfast Howard,' she snapped.

Ken had no answer. His face burned, and he bent over his plate and began on his oatmeal.

McLaughlin pushed away his plate and took out his pipe. There was silence while he filled and lit it, then he picked up the letter and read it aloud.

My dear Captain McLaughlin:
It is with regret that I must tell you that Kenneth's

*examination marks, averaged with his daily work, do not
bring his grades up to passing mark. This is particularly
disappointing as his failure is due to carelessness and
inattention rather than lack of ability. If he had done
even a fair amount of work consistently throughout the
school year he would have been promoted into the sixth
grade. As it is, he will have to repeat the fifth.
With kind regards to Mrs McLaughlin and yourself,
Very sincerely,
Leonard Gibson*

McLaughlin put down the letter and looked across the
table at Ken, then at his pipe which had gone out.

'Fortunately,' he said, reaching for a match, 'there are
almost two and a half months before school begins again.
You'll do an hour a day on your lessons all through the
summer to make up this work.'

Nell McLaughlin saw Ken wince as if something had
actually hurt him, and his eyes went to the wide-open
window with a despairing look.

'Well,' said McLaughlin, his voice like the crack of a
whip. 'Speak up. What have you got to say for yourself?'

'I dunno,' answered Ken.

'What were you going in that English exam? What were
the questions you missed?'

'We were supposed to write a composition.'

'What did you write?'

'I didn't get started.'

'Didn't write a word?'

Ken shook his head.

'Couldn't you think of anything?'

'Yes, I had it all planned. I was going to write the story
about how you lost your polo mare. How the Albino stole
her from Banner—' Ken's eyes went to his father's. 'We
could write anything we wanted, it had to be at least two
pages—'

'Well, what happened to you?'

'I – I – got to thinking about it. Thinking about Gypsy and the Albino – and what it was like, when he took her away – where he took her to – and all the wild horses in his band – and where they were all that time. All of that. I thought there was time, I thought the hour had just begun, and then the bell rang—'

'And you never even started?'

Howard said, 'He was looking out the window all the time. I saw him.'

Tears were crowding at the back of Ken's eyes. He wished his father would stop looking at him.

There was a knock at the back door and McLaughlin shouted, 'Come in.'

Gus, the Swedish foreman, came in, carrying his big felt hat in his hand. His thickset body bent in a sort of bow aimed respectfully at Nell, and he looked first of all at her as he said, 'Gude mornin', Missus,' and then, 'Mornin', Boss.'

He did not come clear into the room, but propped himself by a hand on the door, leaning there in his shy manner, a little smile like a child's turning up the corners of his mouth. His round pink face was framed in a mop of tight grey curls.

'What's today, Boss?'

Ken and Howard stopped eating to listen.

Only Gus, or perhaps their mother, could ask their father his plans and get an answer. When they asked him, he just said, 'Wait and see.' Or perhaps would not answer at all. And as every day of the summer was packed with events as thrilling as a circus, they lived much of the time in such suspense that they were ready to burst, dogging their father's steps, trying to be everywhere at once so as to be sure not to miss anything.

Weather always entered into the plans. So before McLaughlin answered, he glanced out the window, noting the clear deep blue of the sky, and that the big white cumulus clouds were sailing across at a rapid pace.

'There's a wind high up in the pines,' said Nell. 'Heard it the first thing this morning – like surf – a roaring.'

'And the windmill's goin' lickety split,' said Howard.

'Clear for today and mebbe tomorrow,' said Gus, 'but a big cloud bank in de soudwest. Storm cookin' up.'

McLaughlin sat in thought and puffed at his pipe, not at all embarrassed by the fact that four pairs of eyes were watching him and four people waiting for his words.

Finally he said as if to himself, not looking at Gus, 'A good day to move the horses.'

'*Ja*, Boss. It's time de horses were off de meadows. De grass is growin' an' we should have water on 'em soon.'

Howard couldn't keep still. 'Could I help you move 'em this year, Dad?'

Ken didn't ask because he had no hope.

McLaughlin turned to look at Howard, but he wasn't thinking of him and did not answer. He smoked and Gus waited. At last he said, 'Yes. We've got a month before Frontier Days. I've to get four of the older horses in shape to rent for the Rodeo. That means foolproof. And those three-year-olds will have to be broken. I can't let them go any longer.'

'You're not going to break them yourself, Rob?' said Nell in a loud alarmed voice.

Her husband didn't answer.

'You promised last year!' exclaimed Nell.

'It's my own fault for letting them go so long.'

'It's not your fault or anyone's. You haven't time. You haven't help enough to take care of twenty horses, let alone a hundred.'

'Well, I can't let them go any longer.'

'You shan't do it!' The dark blue of Nell's eyes turned almost black with the widening of the pupils.

'Why, Nell—'

'I can't stand it.' Her smooth brown face flushed. 'You fighting the horse, and the horse fighting you. Yells and falls and dust and sweat – it makes me sick to see you.'

Gus suggested. 'Dere's sure to be some good bronco-busters in town 'bout dis time, waitin' for de Rodeo.'

McLaughlin frowned. 'No bronco-buster is going to break my horses.'

'But Rob—'

His voice rose. 'It ruins a horse!' He was shouting. This was one of his pet tirades. 'He loses something and never gets it back. Something goes out of him. He's not a whole horse any more. I hate the method, waiting until a horse is full grown, all his habits formed, and then a battle to the death, and the horse marked with fear and distrust, his disposition damaged – he'll never have confidence in a man again. And if I lose the confidence of my horses—'

'But they're only three-year-olds,' persisted Nell. Howard and Ken looked at her in astonishment. There was a soft look about her fawn-coloured hair and smooth, un-lined face, but nothing soft about the determined look with which she faced her husband. How could she be so fearless in the face of their father's anger and shouting!

'Besides,' she said, 'they *have* been handled a little, re-member; it's not as if they were broncs that had just been pulled in off the range.'

McLaughlin sat for a moment or two without reply, then he turned to Gus. 'All right, Gus—'

'Can I help you to move 'em, Dad?' said Howard again.

'No,' roared McLaughlin. 'It's tough enough for one man to move a hundred horses, half of them broncs, or loco, all of them fresh as hell after a winter out, without a kid along to be popping his head up somewhere at just the moment to stampede the bunch!'

'Couldn't I even open the gates for you going down?' said Howard, crestfallen at the thought of missing the long day's riding, the close inspection of all the new spring colts, the exciting trip up on to the summer range on number Twenty with Banner, the big stud, and his band of brood mares.

His father ignored the question and turned back to Gus. 'You and Tim had better spend the day on the irrigation ditches then. They'll have to be in shape before we turn the water on the meadows.'

'*Ja*, Boss.'

'And catch up Shorty and saddle him for me. I'll be up at the stables in a half hour or less.'

'*Ja*, Boss.'

Gus went out.

McLaughlin put down his pipe and pulled his coffee cup towards him. There was a moment's silence, then Howard asked Ken, 'What horse did you ride this morning, Ken?'

'Cigarette.'

McLaughlin looked up. 'You've been riding Cigarette?'

'Yes, sir.'

'Did you manage to catch her and tie her up without her breaking anything?'

'No, sir."

'What did she break, a bridle?'

'No – that is – not today. She broke a bridle yesterday.'

'What did she break today?'

'The metal catch on the halter rope.'

'Haven't I told you you can't tie that mare with one of those? That you have to put a lariat on her?'

'Yes, sir.'

'Well, why didn't you?'

'I thought – I thought—' Ken's voice failed him. There weren't any words. He gulped his milk.

'You thought! Trouble is, you don't think.'

McLaughlin's voice was gentler.

Howard spoke again. 'Did you find the saddle blanket, Ken?'

'What saddle blanket?' asked McLaughlin, on the alert again.

'I lost a saddle blanket out on the range yesterday after-noon when we were riding,' said Ken.

'Oh, you did?' His father was sarcastic again. 'Rode with a saddle, I suppose, and didn't cinch it properly?'

'Yes, sir,' said Ken doggedly, 'but I found it this morning.' There was a quiver in his voice.

'Anything the matter with it?' snapped McLaughlin.

Ken was desperate. 'Well, it got a tear; got caught on the barbed wire—'

McLaughlin roared. 'What am I going to do with you? You're the stupidest kid for losing and busting and forget-ting—'

Ken stared at his plate and felt the heat rising to his face and a lump choking his throat. 'Dad – if I only had a colt—'

'What's that got to do with it?'

'Howard's got a colt. He was only nine when you gave him Highboy; and he trained him. I'm ten and even if you did give me a colt now, I couldn't catch up with Howard because I couldn't ride it till it was a three-year-old, and then I'd be thirteen.'

Nell laughed. 'Nothing wrong with that arithmetic.'

But McLaughlin answered. 'Howard never gets less than seventy-five average at school. And he pays attention to what I tell him and doesn't lose equipment or break it or get it spoiled somehow.'

Ken had no answer to any of this, and kept his eyes down.

'Did Cigarette toss you?' asked Howard cheerfully.

'Yes,' answered Ken.

'Did you clap your heels into her?' demanded his father.

'Yes, sir,' said Ken automatically.

'Did you rub her down?'

Nothing for it, it was all going to come out. He turned to his father drearily. 'I – no, sir, she got away from me.'

'Got away from you? Where?'

'Just at the County Road gate, as I was closing it, coming into the Stable Pasture.'

'How did it happen?'

'Well, I had the rein in my hand, and I was standing there—'

'What for?'

'Nothing. Just locking around – looking back at the range – and after a while, she wanted to graze and she just gave a little jerk, and she was loose, and then she knew it, and I couldn't catch her. She ran away.' Ken felt he might as well tell it all and be done with it. 'And she got her foot in the rein and broke it.'

'Thought you said you didn't break a bridle today.'

Ken hedged, 'Well, this wasn't exactly the bridle, it was the rein.'

His father unexpectedly made no comment, but looked thoughtfully at Ken. 'What were you thinking of when you were standing there by the gate – just standing?'

'My colt.'

'*Your* colt! You haven't got a colt.'

'The colt I've got in my mind,' explained Ken.

'Oh, so you've got one in your mind?'

'Yes, sir.'

'Well, you better keep it there where it won't run away.'

Howard laughed loudly, and McLaughlin knocked the ashes out of his pipe, stuck it in the pocket of his leather vest, and got to his feet.

Ken said desperately, 'Won't you give me a colt, Dad?'

McLaughlin paused a moment and looked down at his small son. 'You're going to have to buck up, Ken. I don't know what to do with you. You never have your wits about you. Always wool-gathering. You lose a saddle blanket the first time you go riding—'

'But I found it again—'

'Yes, found the blanket and lost your horse. Trouble is, you don't try.'

'I do try.'

'I'd like to see some proof of it. Come, Howard. You can ride with me as far as the meadows and open the gates.'

Ken pushed his chair back too. 'Can't I help?'

'Certainly not. You have your study to do. Every morning right after breakfast. Remember that.'

McLaughlin's scarred boots and heavy spurs clattered across the kitchen floor. Howard strode after, nobly refraining from casting a patronizing glance at Ken.

Nell got her apron and tied it over her short blue-and-white-checked dress. Her bare legs had a smooth coat of sunburn and her small bony feet were neatly shod in brown Mexican huaraches.*

Ken stood in a daze, looking at the door that had closed behind his father and Howard.

He felt his mother's hand on his head. She moved it gently, straightening his part. 'Kennie,' she said, 'you can ride any horse on the ranch. Why are you so set on having a colt?'

'Oh, Mother, it isn't just the riding. I want a colt to be friends with me. I want him to be mine – *all my own*, Mother—'

As she looked down into the upturned face, her heart misgave her at the passion and intensity of his longing, but she understood. Yes, she, too, was like that – *all my own* – and she turned away and began to clear the table.

Nell's cat was mewing beside her, begging.

'No, Pauly, this is for the dogs.' Nell had some scraps and corn meal mush on a big plate. She handed it to Ken.

'Take it out and feed the dogs, Ken.'

Chaps, the fat, curly black cocker, with long hairy chaps on his front legs, was out there, drooling with eagerness. The yellow collie with the white ruff around his neck and the sad brown eyes stood one side, polite and patient, waving his brush of a tail as he looked at Ken.

* sandals

23

Ken put down the plate and went slowly back into the kitchen.

His mother was bustling about. She put a plate of food near the stove for Pauly, whipped the cover off the table and shook it, let down the drop leaves, and pushed the table over into the corner of the room by the window.

She picked up the little bright oval rugs. 'Here, Ken, you might take these out and shake them for me—'

She went to the sink and ran hot water into the dishpan.

Standing there she could look out of the door and watch him shaking the rugs slowly – making a game of it – trying to scare the dogs; and it took her back suddenly to when she was a little girl and her mother had made her shake the rugs out of doors after breakfast. That was at the Cape Cod cottage when it had begun to be too hot to stay in Boston—

The water filled the dishpan—

She used to shake them very slowly, one by one, looking around, sniffing the salt tang in the air, listening to the soft boom of the breakers on the beach until her mother's voice inside would call to her to hurry with those rugs—

The hot water was running over and burning her hands—

'Hurry with those rugs, Ken.'

He brought them in. 'If I could have a colt,' he said, like an automaton.

'You go up and do your study now, Ken, and get it over with.'

'Where will I put the rugs?'

'Lay them on that chair. I have to sweep the floor yet.'

Ken obeyed and walked reluctantly to the door of the dining room. 'Where'll I study?'

'Where are your school books?'

'On the shelf in my room.' He went out of the door and she could hear his steps dragging up the stairs.

She sighed. Now all summer, it'll be the colt, she thought. I wish Howard wouldn't tease him so much. No use speaking to Rob about it, he upholds him – says Ken has to take it – I'd make Howard shut up – wish Rob would give him a colt—

She dried the dishes rapidly and put them away.

There was no kindling, and she ran out to the woodpile behind the house, and seized the hatchet, swinging it as lustily as if it had been a racket on the tennis court.

It's a good thing Gus isn't around, she thought. The other day Gus had caught her cutting wood and had gently taken the axe from her hand. 'T'ree men on de place and you cut your own wood, Missus? No – no, not wile old Gus is here—'

It had amused Nell at first to be addressed as the *Missus*, but it had not taken her long to learn that, here in the West, it meant 'the woman', with all that the word signified of gentleness and motherliness. Here, in her world of men, husband and sons, hired men, haying crew, horse buyers, to be the *Missus* meant to be that before which they could remove their hats, and bend their heads. In the cities a woman could turn into a driving machine, or harden herself to meet difficulties, but the Missus on a farm or ranch, though she might be milker of cows or trainer of horses, must be more and not less woman for all that, or she would rob the men around her of something which was as sweet to them as the sugar in their coffee.

She carried in her kindling, filled the basket beside the stove, and took up the broom. Through the window she caught sight of a great tumbleweed bounding across the Green, and stood still, watching, her lips parted and her eyes alight. She heard the jack pines roaring – like surf, she thought, yes, like the sea. She could see them bending and swinging in the wind. It was a day when she wanted to be outdoors, riding on the range, where the wind would whip her hair and drive her the way it drove the tumbleweed across the Green.

But first, sweeping, bed-making, cleaning, the noon dinner— She began to sweep, singing,

Oh, the ship she sailed,
Across the sea,
Good-bye, my lover, good-bye—

Chapter Three

When Ken left the kitchen the alarm clock on the wall shelf beside the spice closet pointed to twenty minutes to nine. He wondered if he should time himself right from then or from the moment he went into his room, or from when he set his books on the table. This was a very important point, but as he could not decide, he went upstairs as slowly as he could, just in case it was all part of the hour.

He paused on the landing in front of the picture of the duck. If he stood there looking at the duck picture he could get into another world. He knew how to do it. To get into another world you had to make yourself the same size, in your mind.

When he put his face down to the little pools in the stream and stayed there a long time, pretending that he was one of the little crabs that scuttled from rock to rock, or a baby trout smaller than a minnow, pretty soon he was right in that world under the water and could almost know why they moved about and went up so seriously to meet each other, talked a moment, then hurried away.

It was one of the most exciting things, to get into another world than your own regular world, especially at a time when the regular world or the things you had to do in it bored you. Like now.

But he felt misgivings, standing there. His mother would hear, from the kitchen, that he hadn't gone all the way upstairs. He went on up, down the hall, into his room, and noisily closed the door. Possibly she would time him too.

He looked at the alarm clock that stood on his dresser – almost ten minutes to nine – funny—

He stood a few moments looking around. He and Howard each had a small room to himself.

Ken loved his room. The walls were white-washed, and there was a big window opening out to the front over the terrace and the Green. He could see everything from it. Sunshine poured in.

Best of all, Ken loved his little walnut bed, because that was really home. Everything was home in a way except school. The United States of America was home and he could feel it when they sang *The Star-Spangled Banner*. And the ranch was home. The house was home. But most particularly the bed was home. It was like friendly arms close around him every night when he got into it.

It wasn't very tidy. He and Howard had to make their own beds, and he had made his in a hurry, before he went out riding. Now would be a good time to straighten it up. That was a good dutiful deed – about as good as studying – it probably could be counted in the hour. The quilt, which was light green with sprigs of pink and blue flowers on it, was crooked and humped over the bedclothes underneath. He threw it back, then paused, his eyes on the wall at the head of the bed.

28

There were these pictures – one on each side – about eight inches square, with a flat wooden frame an inch wide.

And inside the frame—

He dropped the quilt, moved up to one picture and stood minutely examining it. What people! Peasant people, his mother had told him, probably Swiss.

They were dressed very oddly. The man had a white shirt, embroidered suspenders, a tilted hat with a feather in it, short pants to his knees, and a flute in his hand!

The woman had a white waist, laced black bodice, full skirt, a handkerchief over her head, and she was sitting on a ledge which jutted into a stream with her bare legs and feet in the water. She was leaning over, reaching her arms to hold a little naked boy who stood in the stream and leaned against her, frightened, it seemed, and lifting one foot out of the water because a big duck with a flock of baby ducks was paddling about, cruising close to his legs. Under the boy's mop of hair, exactly the same yellow as the ducklings, his face looked around, quite frightened. His eyes were very blue and his cheeks fat and red. His mother smiled indulgently.

His father, behind them, seemed protecting them, and sat watching and ready to play the flute.

Ken had never been in such a world as that.

He climbed across the bed and looked at the other picture which was another peasant picture, but inside a house.

Down at the end of his room was the strangest picture of all.

Ken went to look at it. There was a verse written in the corner which he knew by heart.

> Intreat me not to leave thee,
> Nor to return from following after thee.
> For whither thou goest I will go,
> And where thou lodgest I will lodge.

It was a picture of a desert land. And a man stood as if waiting to go, looking at the maiden for whom he was waiting. But she had run back to throw her arms around a woman, and there they stood, arms about each other. And the verse in the corner was what she was saying. They were dressed in long, draped, brightly coloured shawls.

'Intreat me not to leave thee,' he murmured, liking something about the way the words made his voice rise and fall. Besides, there was something in this picture that the other pictures did not have, something completely grown-up and mysterious and a little exciting.

'Intreat me—' He jumped and ran back to the bed when he heard quick steps across the kitchen floor below. Outside the kitchen door his mother's voice called, 'Here, Kim— Here, Chaps—'

This time he really finished the bed and smoothed the quilt. It looked very nice. He stood regarding it, thinking that now he must take down his books.

His desk was in the corner near the window. It was just a table with a few drawers, and over it hung a wall bracket with three shelves. The study books were not the only books on it. There were some fairy books. There was 'Castle Blair' – and what a world that let you into – a whole gang of children that lived in a castle in Scotland. Ken knew it as well as they did. And there was 'At the Back of the North Wind'. And there was—

He was just scanning the titles. He sighed deeply. He didn't feel very well and wondered if perhaps he was going to be sick.

Resolutely he picked out his arithmetic book, sat down, opened it and began to think.

Shorty – ugly brown Shorty with mops of hair on his hoofs and his forehead, and legs so short his father had said he was built like a dachshund—

But he always rides Shorty when there's something hard to do, thought Ken. Howard's got Highboy. Wonder if they're saddled yet. Bet I could do a round-up all alone if I could have Shorty. He does it just about all himself, he always knows better than anybody else where the horses are when you're hunting for them – wonder how he does that, smells them I guess – and he knows which way they're headed, and he takes a short cut and gets there ahead of them. Wonder why he likes to do that? He's a horse too, and he ought to be on their side and not help catch them – guess it's like playing tag. Dad says Shorty's the smartest horse on the ranch, but I don't like him. He's kinda mean. I like Banner better—

Ken's eyes took on a vacant look as in imagination he pictured the big golden chestnut stallion who sired the yearly crop of twenty colts. All the youngsters, three-year-olds, twos, yearlings, and now the little foals, were his.

Banner was like a king. He had never been ridden, but he and Rob McLaughlin were friends and understood each other. Nell said that until she had come to the West she had never known how nearly human a stallion could be.

Ken had seen his father and Banner standing close, facing each other, Banner's ears taut, his nose stretched out with nostrils distended as they tried to breathe in the very essence of the man they reached for, and his legs stiff and trembling a little. He didn't like to get too close to people.

His father's legs were stiff too and braced apart, the way he often stood, and his arms were folded, and his round head with the tight curled black hair tilted back and he talked in a low, even voice that no one but Banner could hear, as if they were making plans.

Banner and his father together ran the ranch.

Suddenly Ken heard the sound of horses coming near the house and started up so quickly that the leg of his chair tangled with the leg of the table and he went sprawling on the floor, then scrambled up and over to the window. There they were. Chaps was along too. Chaps and Shorty were crazy about each other. Shorty always liked to have

Chaps along. Chaps had so much sense. Kim wasn't there. Locked up, probably. He made trouble. He looked like a coyote and some of the colts were afraid of him. Chaps was jumping up and down right under Shorty's nose, practically under his feet. When he did that, it always looked as if he was nipping his nose. Shorty didn't mind. Perhaps that was their way of kissing. But Banner minded – Chaps had to keep away from the stallion.

Ken leaned out of the window as far as he could to see the last of them as they went down the Green, just jog-trotting, and disappeared around the end of the house—

'Ken!' Nell's voice came floating up from the open window below. 'What are you doing?'

He scurried back to the table and made it true before he answered, 'I'm doing my arithmetic.'

'What was that crash?'

'My chair fell over.'

'What made it fall over?'

'It just fell over—'

Nothing more from Nell, and Ken summoned all his energy and frowned at his open book. He must make a plan. He would do cancellation over. He liked cancellation. It was fun crossing out the figures above and below the line and turning everything into nothing.

He hunted for his pad, opened all the drawers, and found it.

Then he heard Nell coming up the stairs, and she opened his door.

She had some fresh bureau scarves over her arm, and came in briskly and went to his chiffonier to change the scarf.

'I was thinking, Ken, it would be a good idea if you spent your study hour on that composition.'

'The composition?'

'Yes, the one you didn't write. If you wrote it nicely we could send it to Mr Gibson and tell him how it was you came not to write anything – that you were thinking about it – and he might let you have some credit for it.'

'The one about the Albino,' said Ken, and his eyes went thoughtfully to the window. 'How would I begin it?'

'Have you got paper there?'

'Yes.'

'Well, just pretend you're telling someone about it – someone who doesn't know. Me, for instance. Perhaps I've forgotten. Who was the Albino, anyway?'

Ken grinned, and said, 'A big white stallion – just a bronc – who came over the border from Montana when they had a drouth there. Dad called him a big ugly devil but a lotta horse—'

'That's fine,' encouraged Nell. 'And what did he do?'

'Stole everybody's mares, and when they had a spring round-up six years later they caught him and the whole bunch of mares and everyone around here found some mares they had lost, and the Albino had taken Gypsy—'

'Who was Gypsy?'

'Dad's polo mare that he had in the Army and he had put her in the brood mare bunch and he was counting on getting a lot of good colts from her—'

'Yes?'

'But the Albino stole her, or she ran away to him. And when they caught them both in the round-up, Gypsy was there too, with four colts, and Dad brought 'em all back to the ranch. And the colts were beauties, and fast and strong, but wild as anything. And Dad sold the two horse colts and put the fillies in the brood mare bunch, but he never could break them. He said the Albino was bad blood. Loco. Rocket's one of them. She was the best of the four.'

'And what about Gypsy. Is she still alive?'

'She's twenty-three years old, and she hasn't got many teeth and she's kinda poor now 'cause she can't chew so well, but she has a colt 'most every year, and good ones too.'

33

'Now you see, Ken, that would make a very good composition. And you could call it "The Story of Gypsy." '

She came to the back of his chair and stood there.

'You begin it now, dear.'

'The hour is nearly up.'

'You can finish it tomorrow.'

Ken sighed deeply, and wrote, 'The Story of Gypsy', carefully at the top of the paper.

Nell went out of the room and he heard her open the door of the upstairs closet and take the carpet sweeper out of it, and go into her own room and begin to sweep the floor.

He lifted his head and listened for sounds that came from farther away. How far had they got down the road? How would Banner behave with Shorty around? Stallions didn't like geldings – didn't like anything but mares – Banner—

The hovering pencil drew a long horse face – two sharp ears on the alert – and began on a wind-tossed mane.

Ken tore down the road. He'd take the short cut. They'd been gone almost an hour and they were on horseback. He'd meet them about halfway coming back maybe, and see the whole bunch moving. He'd find a good place and hide so his father wouldn't see him.

He trotted along in the irrigation ditch. It was dry because the water hadn't been turned in yet. This way he would avoid the road and the gates. Howard might be stationed at any one of the gates.

He kept a sharp look-out. Not a horse in sight anywhere. Now if I had my horse, I'd be riding. We could canter along in the ditch here.

A tangle of briars and chokecherry bushes grown over the ditch blocked his way and he fought his way through. When the ditch was crossed by the barbed wire fences he got down on his hands and knees and crawled under.

He was winded. He always lost his breath easily when he first came up to the ranch after the winter in Laramie. He slowed down and plodded along. It seemed a long way.

He left the ditch and climbed up a hill. From here he could see Gus and Tim working in the ditch in the Crooked Meadow and could hear their voices. Tim was swinging a pick; the sound of the blow reached him after he saw the pick land.

And a mile or more away he could see Castle Rock, the great beetling rock, jutting up seventy feet high, with peaks and parapets and turrets shaped like a castle. It overhung the aspen grove at the far end of the meadow.

That was where they were, down there near the rock. His father was rounding up the mares with their foals, getting them out of the woods, bringing them back through the meadow slowly. He never ran them. He'd keep them walking slowly all day, let them stop to graze. He said scornful things about riders who galloped and yelled and drove horses on the run.

Ken ran down the hill and headed for the big rock. He ran as far as he could and then stopped to get his wind again and make a calculation.

From where he was now, on the grazing land which sloped down to the barbed wire fence around the meadow, he could see the wide gate open and fastened back. That was so the mares could come through up to where he was. There was a sort of road here, and the mares would follow it naturally and stay right on it. It curved north and then east across the grazing land, and then merged with the road that led from the Lincoln Highway to the ranch. Probably his father would take them that way, through the Green and the Gorge up to the stables and give them all a feed of oats there before he took them on through the Stable Pasture and out on to the Saddle Back.

If he could hide somewhere near here, where he could keep his eye on the gate, he'd see them pass quite close.

35

He looked about for shelter. Here and there was a jagged outcropping of the pink granite which underlay the soil, here and there a small clump of wild currant bushes.

He chose the bushes, dropped down behind one and sat panting. He could get his wind now.

What a lot of time they were taking. He put his head around the bush and looked and listened, but there was not a sound, nor could he see any of the mares down in the meadow. They must all be in the aspen grove at the end, hidden by the trees and big rocks.

He drew back behind the bush and lay down and suddenly felt very tired and very happy. The report and the saddle blanket and the study – all the unpleasant things – were behind him; and the grass he was lying on smelled sweet; and he was going to see his father and Banner bring the brood mares and foals up from the meadow. The sky was close, and the blue curved over him – up here at the ranch you could always see the curve – it wasn't flat. The clouds were solid looking, with definite strange shapes, and the wind was driving them across the sky – in a moment he was sound asleep.

He woke with a jerk, coming up from such a deep place that it seemed he must have slept for fours.

He was bewildered and sat up, trying to gather his wits. Then he remembered and scrambled to his feet – would he be too late? – they might have passed while he was asleep – he ran out from behind the bush – head on into the bunch.

The mares were coming up from the meadow, almost noiselessly on the grass, McLaughlin in the rear, and Banner offside in the middle. They were walking as quietly as the cows coming in for milking.

In the lead was a powerful, long-legged mare with a shiny black coat. She carried her nose in the air, her wild, staring eyes ringed with white. Rocket, the loco mare, daughter of the Albino.

As Ken shot out from behind the bush, almost colliding

with her, she snorted in terror and went straight up on her hind legs.

For a moment Ken was under the dangling black hoofs of her forelegs and smelled the heat of her body, then she twisted to one side, made a great leap and shot away, and it seemed to Ken that it was a hundred horses that leaped and scattered after her, instead of just twenty.

The foals were terrified. They wheeled and galloped beside their mothers, holding themselves close as if any invisible cord bound them.

Ken could see nothing but the legs and bodies of horses pounding past him, and the smaller, shadow-like shapes of the foals. Then he heard his father shouting, and the long-drawn cry, 'Whoa – whoa – whoa there—' that carried so far and had such power to quiet the horses, but this time it was as if they did not hear him.

Ken ran to a pile of rocks and scrambled to the top so he could see all that happened.

Rocket had gone off at an angle to the line of march and was on a dead run, stretched out like a race horse, with the whole bunch after her. She was heading for the Rock Slide, a place where the grazing land broke down to the lower levels of the next pasture over a long curving hill of sheer rock. To go down it on foot, he and Howard had to sit and slide. No horse, not even the most sure-footed, could negotiate that drop. If she went over she'd go head over heels, she'd roll and bounce to the bottom, and all the others too, if they followed her, the whole band of mares and colts pitching down, somersaulting, rolling, crashing—

'Whoa – there – whoa – whoa—' McLaughlin's voice rang out on a note of desperation. He was galloping as fast as he could to head off Rocket, but she had a long lead and Shorty was slow.

Ken groaned. The Rock Slide – that black fury, Rocket – *running fool* – and for once his father's voice powerless—

Then Ken saw the big stallion, Banner, shoot out of the

crush. His bright chestnut coat was like flame in the sun-light. His feet thundered.

'Oh, go it, Banner – go it!' shouted Ken in agony, dancing up and down on his rock.

Banner's ears were flat back, his head dropped low to the ground and elongated so that it seemed an extension of his neck. He had a look of fury. Nothing made the stud so mad as to have a mare break out of the bunch when he was in charge. If he could catch Rocket he'd half kill her—

The two horses were running at an angle to each other, Banner gaining. They converged near the Rock Slide. Banner's head was suddenly right over Rocket's, his golden mane mingled with her black mane, his mouth open and his big teeth bared.

Suddenly his jaws snapped and Rocket gave a furious squeal and stopped with a jar. Banner whirled and lashed and his heels struck her side with a ringing smack. The other mares telescoped up against them.

Then Banner was everywhere at once, biting, driving, wheeling and kicking the mares back. As they milled around he dropped his head again and charged them, swinging back and forth in long semi-circles, until he had got them turned and moving in the other direction, back up the grazing land towards the road.

Not one single mare lost – not a colt hurt or crushed – Rocket herself, panting and foam flecked, walking meekly back towards the road—

Ken's terror was now for himself. If his father should see him! He might not have. Might have thought it was something else that scared them, a coyote, or perhaps just Rocket's craziness.

He slid down the rock and sat hunched up at the base of it. He was fairly well hidden there, rocks and currant bushes all around him.

His hands were cold and trembling with the awfulness of what he had done and of what the loss of the brood mares, or even a few of them, would have meant to his father.

He could hear the pounding of the horses' hoofs going farther away and he began to breathe more easily. Then a shadow fell on him and he looked up and saw his father sitting there on Shorty.

After one look into the blazing eyes under the down-drawn brim of the Stetson hat, Ken dropped his head and sat silent.

'I – I just came to see the horses,' he murmured at last.

McLaughlin said nothing.

Ken looked up again and the look on his father's face made him burn all over.

He cried out sharply, 'I didn't mean to do it, Dad – I didn't mean to scare them—'

He wanted to go on and explain that he had fallen asleep and then run out to see if they had gone – and Rocket was right there. But there wasn't time. Without a word of answer or blame, McLaughlin wheeled Shorty and went cantering away after the mares.

Ken felt as if he had been put out of the ranch, out of all the concerns that Howard was in on. And out of his father's heart – that was the worst. What he was always hoping for was to be friends with his father, and now this, so soon after getting home— His despair made him feel weak. He put his head down on his drawn-up knees and his hands were clenched tight.

After a while he slid down flat and slept again; a deep exhausted sleep this time that made up the hours he had lost riding so early that morning.

It was long after noon when the faraway cry of a hawk, harsh and sad, drew him up to wakefulness; and he opened his eyes directly into the blue of the sky and saw the hawk wheeling against it.

The wind had gone down. The hawk circled and cried again. Ken yawned deeply and lay there, watching the hawk, his arm lying in the currant bush.

At last he sat up against the rock. His eyes wandered, taking in everything with an absent, unconscious look.

Not twelve feet away the long neck and head of an ermine came up through a gopher hole at the foot of a rock. The soft fur was dun-coloured, like the earth. Except for the little movement, and unless you had been looking right there, you could never have seen him. It was like a miniature periscope. Neck and head were the same size, as if there were eyes and an infinitesimal pair of ears on the neck itself. As it looked around the whole neck rotated. Presently it was looking right at Ken, seeing him. After a moment's calm inspection it withdrew its head and disappeared.

Ken sat, gathering up the threads that stretched from the events behind him to the events ahead. He would have to meet his father and everyone; they would all know that he had almost stampeded the mares over the Rock Slide.

Of course, now, he couldn't get to be friends with his father.

And he wouldn't get a colt this summer.

The hawk circled lower and cried again, but Ken didn't hear it. It swung down close, spreading six feet of brown feathered wings, curled talons reaching for the rock.

As the shadow fell on him, Ken looked up and gave a great start, and the hawk flapped its wings violently, and slid off sideways.

Ken got to his feet and started home.

If he couldn't have a real colt, at least he could have a make-believe. His eyes changed expression. Maybe one like Rocket – black and shiny with her nose up in the air and her tangled mane and tail streaming, and the very wickedness and wildness of her—

Or Banner – the gloriousness of his rush after Rocket – the way he made all the mares mind him – the long snaky head, the blazing gold of his hide – as bright as the coals in the stove—

Ken's mouth opened a little, smiling.

Chapter Four

Banner had got his name when he was a two months' old colt, on the day that Nell first saw him.

She was riding alone on the Saddle Back one August afternoon, cantering easily, twirling a short strip of soft leather in her right hand. The prevailing southwesterly wind of the Rocky Mountains sang in her ears and moved like a veil between earth and sky; her white silk shirt filled and ballooned; her hair was loose and blowing; and the grass on the hillsides leaned and rippled and sprang erect again with an incessant murmuring sound.

Hay was being cut somewhere, and the strong aromatic scent of it – the late summer scent of hay and mint and pine and snow – had a keen edge of sweetness to it that hurt her lungs. Miles away, a rancher was shouting at his horses, and the sound drifted to her like an echo, made musical and poignant by the distance. Lost in delight, she twirled her quirt, swaying a little to the rhythmic thud of her pony's hoofs; and she had such a sensation of lightness it seemed to her that on this high peak of the Divide, the world was curled in a wave – herself carried on the rolling crest of it like foam.

Suddenly the grey gelding she rode pricked his ears. She was approaching the brood mares. Around the shoulder of a hill she came upon them, already on the alert, facing towards her, heads up nervously. Nell stopped her horse and sat watching. Some of them galloped away – the colts clinging to their mothers' sides – then stopped at a distance and turned to stare again.

A rich dark chestnut colt, fearless and adventuresome, broke out of the bunch and came towards her with a long, springing trot. There was a very fury of curiosity and expectation in his lifted head and flaring nostrils. His cream-coloured tail was lifted high, pluming out on both sides of him, and with the full tossing light mane, he seemed to float on the wind, hung with banners.

And so he got his name, and was duly registered and raised to be the stud of Goose Bar Ranch. Banner, out of the Arab mare El Kantara, by Hamilcar.

With the passing years, his dark chestnut coat had grown lighter, and the blond tail and mane darker, so that now in full maturity, the stallion was a bright red-gold all over. The name still suited him. He had lost nothing of his wild grace and ardour, and, trotting, still came on the wind, full sail set, head up, and the high, free springing step.

When the moon rose that night, after the long journey with the mares up to the summer range, the stallion was standing, as he often did, on the sharp rocky peak of one of the hills of the Saddle Back, slanted as if on a stair, with fore-feet solid and close together on the summit, his long gleaming body sloping down, his lofty head and reaching ears the very picture of kingly power.

Round about him and beneath him on all sides was a wider world than even his swiftness could ever need or use; the same world of hills and plains, plateaus and headlands, mesas and mountains that Ken had filled his eyes with that morning.

Within a radius of a few hundred yards below him were his twenty-odd mares and their foals, now weary from the day's long trek up from the meadows. Some of them were grazing, some lying flat on their sides in an ungainliness of abandon which was grotesque in the mares, but in the foals had a charming helplessness. Cushioned on the springing greengrass, earth and horse as close as two hands with palms pressed together, they lay sleeping under the eye of the watchful stallion.

A sudden thunder of hoofs pulsed on the air and drifted away again. Instantly Banner's head turned and his ears pointed. A mile or more away the band of yearlings was on the run. Something had startled them; or with their crazy high spirits they were just tearing around, turning night into day.

Closer by, a frightened little whinny shrilled out, not much more than a squeal of alarm. A foal, grazing too far from his mother, had come to with a start, alone and terrified, his world shattered.

Banner calmly watched the long-legged youngster while he galloped to one mare after the other, sniffed them, and squealed his disappointment.

At last the placid mother lifted her head from her grazing and called him. The little one halted in mid-gallop, wheeled, nickered, and ran to her side, thrusting his head immediately beneath her.

And at last Banner twisted his massive neck and looked in another direction – down at the ranch where lived his god.

Oats.

The smell of the big, hard, muscular hand that held the bucket.

The harsh voice that pierced his vitals.

All this went with the greatest goodness that he had ever known. His world went no further. Together, he and Rob McLaughlin ran the ranch. In the fall the two would separate the spring colts from their dams and Banner would bite and kick and drive the mares away while McLaughlin penned the colts. In the worst of the winter blizzards, Banner would bring the mares home from five or ten miles away, knowing that McLaughlin would have been before him to open gates and doors and fill the manger of the feed shed with hay. Now and then Banner had to do or endure something he could not understand. This too he accepted. When Rob McLaughlin's blazing blue eyes commanded, Banner looked no farther.

Now, smoke was coming from the chimney of the ranch house.

Banner saw it and smelled it. It was a familiar, good smell. His ears quivered, taut and listening. Often voices, shouts, barking of dogs, the piano, the radio, reached him in a medley of sounds, all good. All Rob, and shelter and food and companionship. But tonight, no sound but the chug of the windmill pump.

Banner swung his head back again and stood straight, facing the moon. The golden fire that was in his eye when he was alert died down and his lids half closed.

Nell too was watching the moon rise.

She was standing at the living-room door, looking out across the terrace and the Green.

It was a Dutch door, cut horizontally in half, like a stable door; and Nell's elbows were propped on the top of the lower part. Leaning over a little she rested her smooth sunburned cheeks in her hands.

She had been riding that afternoon, and was still in her black jodhpurs and white silk shirt.

Dead tired, as she often was at night, she told herself that she had letters to write, and she must set the sponge for tomorrow's baking; but she just stood there, leaning, and looking across the Green.

She was thinking about Ken and what he had done that day and how furious Rob had been.

Nothing had been said about it to Ken.

Howard always took his cue from his father, so he too ignored Ken. They talked about the mares, the colts, and how long the grass was, and which mares had not yet foaled, and the old piece of lariat that was still tied around Rocket's neck, from the time, more than a year before, when Rob had tried to get Rocket in the chute and Rocket had broken three lariats in succession. Nell had had to drive into town to buy new ropes, until, in Cheyenne, they were asking, 'What kind of an outlaw is the Captain trying to break?'

The reason McLaughlin had given up trying and had let her go was because she had kicked to pieces the little wooden coop which led into the chute, and had so injured her hocks and legs that he was afraid she would be ruined.

'I've always worried about that noose around her neck,' Rob said at supper. 'It might choke her someday. Get caught in a branch or wire. Never turn an animal out with a rope or ever a halter on – not if it's to run wild for a long time.'

'What if it did choke her?' asked Howard. 'You always say she's no use to you.'

'There's a responsibility we have towards animals,' said his father. 'We use them. We shut them up, keep their natural food and water away from them; that means we have to feed and water them. Take their freedom away, rope them, harness them, that means we have to supply a different sort of safety for them. Once I've put a rope on a horse, or taken away its ability to take care of itself, then I've got to take care of it. Do you see that? That noose around her neck is a danger to her, and I put it there, so I have to get it off.'

Ken had not talked at all but ate his supper in silence.

At bedtime, when he came to kiss his mother good night, she put her hand on his head, and he pressed his forehead against her for a moment, then kissed her quickly and went to kiss his father. Then up to bed.

Something's simply got to be done, thought Nell. I wish Rob would give him a colt.

Across the Green, the Hill was a black silhouette against a luminous fan of moonlight that was spreading behind it.

The pines were motionless. It was a calm, brooding night. The line of the Hill climbed to the right and became the cliff overhanging the Gorge. To the left it ran down to nothing and joined the Calf Pasture. The young cottonwoods on the Green, about a dozen of them that Rob had planted, were swaying. They were never quite still. The round sphere that the mass of their leaves made floated on the air with a faint whispering sound. They were a lighter green than anything else, like a girl's fairness against the black-bearded Hill.

What tons of water it had taken to make them grow. They had carried water in buckets – dozens, hundreds of buckets of water from the spring – and poured on their roots. And even so, many of them had died and new ones had to be put in. Rob was always having to put in new little cottonwoods. They would never have been there if it hadn't been for his determination. In the fall their leaves turned pale gold and drifted off the trees, and whirled about on the Green in little cyclones and curling eddies.

I'm glad I've got the Green, she thought. Like the village Greens home in New England. This is really like the East. No, not the East. The East is cosy. There is never the distance, the fat, empty distances – the wide loneliness. Miles and miles before you come to another house. Just animals. Grass and animals and sky. You can smell the loneliness. No – it's the emptiness you can smell. Of course, you can smell that. It is empty. Other places, the land is full of houses and factories and towns and people

46

and people's doings. But this is almost desert. And it has this sweet, fresh, singing, wildness – you can breathe it in, the very moment you wake in the morning. And it lifts you. You could just float out of the window into the blue of the sky, young and new like the country.

It's just the house that's like the East. A New England country house made of pink stone. Not like the western ranch houses. They're like ugly workshops. Untidy. Old wrecks of machines dumped anywhere. Tumble-down buildings leaning together. No time, I suppose, not an ounce of energy or a minute of time left over from the awful, hopeless struggle to make a living. Sun in the wrong place where it scorches and burns and exhausts you. Black shade where you want sun and warmth. No comfort. The buildings lie in a heap, as if they'd been thrown there – and there they stay.

She raised her head and sniffed. The flower border below the terrace wall was crammed with iris and forget-me-nots and larkspur and lilac and petunias. It was the lilac scent that drenched the evening air. Fancy lilac as late as this – in New England it would have been over long ago.

She felt two tiny paws against the leg of her jodhpurs. Pauly gave a little pleading meow. When Nell paid no attention she proceeded to climb up her leg, hooking her claws into the cloth. At about the belt line, Nell, in self defence, caught hold of her and lifted her to sit on her left arm. This was the cat's favourite seat. She looped her right arm around Nell's neck, holding on with a velvet paw which never permitted the tip of a claw to emerge.

Nell straightened up with a sigh, leaned her cheek against Pauly and smoothed the soft fur. Then she got her sewing basket and Ken's torn saddle blanket, and went to sit close beside Rob's desk in his study, where he was working at his accounts.

Chapter Five

The big gasoline lamp on the top of Rob's desk laid a circle of brightness on the gloom of the room and enclosed them both.

Nell sat with one foot under her. Her fine, narrow head was bent over her work and her hair shone like fawn-coloured satin in the lamplight. She had been careful of her hands with their long pointed fingers and almond shaped nails, and they were as smooth as the brown eggs that came from the Rhode Island Red hens. When she talked, she gestured with them, and they had that artless look, the lack of any clutch or grasp, the question in the bent back, reaching finger tips, which always suggests a poetic nature.

Rob often watched them, thinking that they moved like something that was helpless, seawood floating – Ken had the same hands. They didn't take hold. But now, weaving the blue wool in and out the torn saddle blanket, Nell's hands were quick and deft.

Between stitches she glanced at her husband, his round head, with the tight cap of black hair, had the hardness of a profile on a coin. Presently she said, 'Rob – give Kennie a colt.'

Rob made no answer. He might not have heard. Sitting at his desk, before him a pile of bills and a scratch pad on which he was jotting figures, he was silent and absorbed.

Bills, thought Nell. I wonder which one, particularly. He's worried these days. Always figuring, always accounts, he hates it too, hates figures as much as Ken hates 'em – never used to do it.

This thought escaped into speech. 'You never used to keep so many accounts, Rob.'

This got an answer, as his pencil jotted down a total and scored a heavy line. He leaned back with a short laugh.

'Never knew I'd have to.' He stretched wearily, then reached for the pipe lying on the ashtray, and opening his pen knife, he began to scrape it out.

'Are we broke?'

'We're – just two jumps ahead of—' His voice trailed into silence, and Nell's eyes flitted wildly for a moment, as if she would find the pursuing menace lurking in some dark corner of the house.

'But haven't we always been? Is it any worse?' she asked.

He grinned a little. 'For a long time I didn't know it,' and he took out his tobacco pouch.

'Know what?'

'That each year I was worth less money, instead of more.'

'Is it really like that, Rob?'

'It is. A rancher or a farmer can't know whether he is operating at a profit or a loss unless he makes a very careful yearly inventory. I read that in a Government Bulletin once. That's what pulled me up. You can see why it's true. Equipment deteriorates, buildings run down, there are stock losses, indebtedness increases; but it's all so gradual,

49

almost imperceptible, a man doesn't notice it. He drifts along, thinking that things are about as they always were. You see it all around here. Some poor devil trying to renew a loan, or get a new one he badly needs, and finding out he hasn't got anything left that the banks will lend on. He's been on the down grade for a long time – and never knew it. It hits him all of a sudden. He's a bankrupt – and the day before, he thought he was a capitalist. Well – I take the trouble, now, to know where I stand.'

'And is it? Are we on the down grade?'

'We are.'

'But we're more and more careful all the time. We spend less; don't have as much help – why, we're actually stingy—'

'In the beginning I still had some capital – what was left over when I bought the ranch. I was going to save that – should have. It would have sent the boys to college. But now that's gone. Of course I thought that when I got the horses well started – when they were of an age to sell, I'd make it all back and more, but expenses always keep ahead of me. With so many pure-bred horses, for instance, and more coming all the time, there are such walloping taxes.'

This always made Rob angry. 'It's a cock-eyed law – to put high taxes on registered stock – it ought to be the other way around. They ought to tax out of existence this run-down mongrel stuff that Wyoming is full of. It would be better for the state if they did. I wish I had nothing but registered horses. These colts of Gypsy and the Albino have put a bad strain into my stock.'

He sat scowling for a moment, and then said, 'The worst thing of all is, I can't sell my horses at a profit. Not even at cost, most of the time.'

This struck a chill through Nell. Everything depended on the horses.

'Perhaps the markets will get better—' she said, but her voice reflected the fear in her heart.

Rob struck the back of his hand angrily on the desk. 'A thing like this – Doc Hicks' bill – this gets me. He can't help it. I'm not blaming him, but here it is. Three visits at fifteen dollars each, and even then the mare died—'

He leaned back and puffed at his pipe and Nell darned in silence.

'Bad enough to pay veterinary bills when they get well, although you don't know if you'll ever sell the animal for enough to pay you back for all he's cost. But when they die! By God, I'll not do it again. Sick or well they can take their chances. They get well when you do nothing for them, and give them up; they die when you get the vet and nurse them.'

Often, when Rob talked like this, a tide of fear rose in Nell's heart. It was almost panic. Oh, Rob, Rob, what'll we do? If you'd only stayed in the Army – if you'd only never bought the ranch – but you would have it – you're like Ken. When you set your heart you can't give up – just because you were so crazy about horses, and such a fine rider at West Point—

Her eyes were hidden from him. Lids down, she watched the thread weaving in and out of the blue blanket, and there was no tremor of her hands to show him that she was frightened – had been frightened for years—

'Doc'll have to wait for his money,' said Rob. 'I'll owe it to him – and some more added to it. I've got nine two-year-olds for him to geld.'

'When's he coming?'

'Sometime this week. I told him to come any day. I've got the colts in. Poor devil, I don't see how he lives. Nobody pays him. Nobody can afford to.'

'Rob, doesn't *anybody* make money ranching?'

He shook his head slowly. 'Not any more. Used to, when there weren't any fences, no taxes to pay – when they ran their beef on public lands – the big beef barons of the early days. That's when the fortunes were made in cattle. Not any more.'

'But Charley Sargent? Surely he makes money with his race horses?'

'Now and then a killing, perhaps. A lucky break. But by and large, he's spending money, not making it. He inherited his money. Now he's spending it the way he likes the best – raising race horses.'

'What about sheep?'

'There's money in sheep, if you have the right sort of land for it. In the good years, that is, and when the market is right. But it's a big gamble. You can make a lot, and you lose a lot. The ranchers that are raising sheep now – they're a new bunch. Came in with fresh capital. I met Summerville in the Stockgrowers' Bank – we got to talking – he said nobody in Wyoming makes money any more except the Dude ranchers. And *he knows*,' added Rob grimly.

'Then why – why–' said Nell, and hesitated to finish her sentence. Again she felt the panic rising.

'Why are we here, trying it?' said Rob. 'Well I still think horses are the best bet.'

Like Kennie, thought Nell. One idea in his head, and he'll never give up—

'A well-bred, well-trained, registered four-year-old horse is worth at least twice as much as a prime steer – perhaps four times as much. It's true that a horse eats twice as much; on the same piece of land you can only run half as many horses, but – if there were decent markets for highbred stuff – you might make money. Trouble is, the markets.'

'The Army seems the only sure market—'

'Sure; but they don't pay enough. At the Army Remount Depots, it costs them nearly a thousand dollars to raise a colt to four years. They pay us ranchers one hundred and fifty, or one hundred and seventy-five. You can't even get back the cost of production at that figure.'

'Polo then—'

'Polo's the only hope. For a well-trained polo pony you

can get anywhere from two hundred to two thousand. But you've got to sell them as individuals – under the saddle, not in carloads. And I haven't any connections – no one to show them and promote sales.'

'When the boys grow up—'

'That's it. Howard and Ken. With the start they've got, they'll be crack riders, they can be polo players – show and sell – and then, Nell—'

Rob turned his eyes to her. They had such burning intensity, she almost expected to see them glow in the dark, like cats' eyes.

She gathered up her sewing to put it away, and the little brown cat, squeezed down by her side in the armchair, moved, stretched and turned over on her back, mewing.

'What's your hurry?' asked Rob.

'I've finished my mending.'

'Stick around. I've just got a little more to go over here.' He laid down his pipe, picked up his pencil again, and Nell leaned back in her chair.

Pauly, on her back, closed her eyes. Nell's hand sank into the soft cream-coloured fur on her belly.

Nell began to fall asleep. She was going down, floating deeper. Delicious— She roused herself with an effort.

Rob put out his hand and clasped her arm. 'Don't go.'

'I'll be asleep if I don't. And I've got to set the sponge for tomorrow's baking.'

'I wish you wouldn't bake. Do as all the other country people do. Eat out of cans. Buy your bread at the Safeway in town.'

'That stuff! Made of sawdust blown up – no taste – you could blow it across the room.'

'I don't want you to work so hard.'

'It isn't much. The boys love it.'

'And so do I.'

'And I do myself.'

53

'But you do too much. Bad enough for me to be slaving – not you—'

Nell got up and Pauly hit the floor with a little grunt. 'You come in when you've finished.'

She went into the kitchen where one kerosene lamp was still burning, hung on the wall by the big black coal stove.

Rob finished his figures, closed his book, put it away and leaned his head on his hand, tapping with his pencil absent-mindedly on the blotter. He had caught a frightened look on Nell's face, when she was sitting there sewing, and it haunted him. And I didn't tell her the half of it, he thought. I shouldn't ever have done it. What a life for her. Damned if I won't quit. I quit the Army. Now the ranch . . . No. Not licked yet, not by a damned sight. Boys growing up . . . Howard's a help already. Ken . . . Ken . . . now what am I going to do with that little son of a gun? Could have shaken the teeth out of his head today. Never can be where he ought to be, run an errand and get back on time, do a little job right, or remember what he's told. Give him a colt, Nell said. Give him a colt because he damn near stampeded the whole brood mare bunch over the Rock Slide. If it hadn't been for Banner— Great Guns! What a horse. Ahead of me all the time. If he passes it on to the colts, that kind of head work, and the heart and the courage, what polo ponies I'll have. That's one thing that's gone right. The blood in my horses . . . all but the Albino strain. That loco brute Rocket – always out in front with her nose in the air looking for trouble, and the three others. She's the worst. Not one of 'em really broke. I ought to shoot 'em all. I would, too, if they weren't so damned fast. Now I wonder what she meant by that give him a colt. I'd like to. Got to get closer to the kid some way. Every time I'm all set for a get-together session with him he hands me a facer like this thing he pulled today. I want to give him a colt and he makes me give him a bawling out. He doesn't mean it. Wants to please me, I can see that. Looks to me sometimes as if he was afraid of me. Don't like the way he turns his head away and looks down. Never comes to me for help. That's bad. He ought to turn to me . . . my fault somehow . . . or else he's just at an impossible age . . . but Howard wasn't . . . got to get friends with him . . . maybe this summer . . .

Rob got wearily and stiffly to his feet, stood in thought a moment, then put out the gasoline desk lamp and walked into the living room.

He called through the dining room to Nell, 'I'll be there in a minute – don't go away – I've got to go up to the bunk house,' and went out the front door and turned to the right.

Overhead the sky was clear, but in the southwest the heavy bank of clouds was spreading. Unless the wind rose again and scattered it, they'd have a storm.

As McLaughlin approached the bunk house he could see light burning inside. He pushed open the door with a clatter and crossed the dark kitchen to the living room. Here, Gus and Tim were seated at the long table, on which burned two kerosene lamps.

Gus was mending a bridle; Tim was drawing a picture, copying from a poster propped on the table. Before him was a bottle of Indian ink and in his hand a drawing pen. Tim's ambition was to be a sign-painter. The picture was of a voluptuous-hipped young woman, sitting on the end of a bench, looking coyly sideways at a youth on the other end. The room was already lavishly decorated with Tim's drawings, all of them, apparently, images of the same seductive female in different poses.

'Hello boys.'

'Hello, Boss.'

'I was just thinking,' McLaughlin paused. His eyes were fixed absently on Tim's face, which was a rich dark colour, from dirt or sunburn or both, and wore its habitual expression of comic mystification. Tim was always expecting a laugh, but never knew why.

'What's that bridle, Gus?'

'De one Ken busted dis mornin',' said the Swede.

'I left Rocket in the Stable Pasture. She broke away from the gang just there at the gate to the County Road – raced along the fence hell for leather. The rest of them were going through nicely and for once none of them followed her and she was out of sight in a minute.'

'Dot mare!'

'I closed the gate and went on with the bunch. Left her inside. It's just as well. I've got to get her into the chute and get that noose of rope off her neck, or she'll hang herself one of these days – I can do that tomorrow and then put her out and she'll find her way up to the bunch alone. See that the gates into the Home Pasture and the corrals are kept closed. I don't want her to get out. Where's the mare Ken was riding this morning?'

'Cigarette? I caught her up and put her into the Home Pasture,' said Tim. 'Thought Ken would be wantin' her agin.'

'That's all right then. Good night, boys.'

Rob went back to the house. Nell was still in the kitchen. He sat down in the corner at the table, and took out his pipe.

'Well – what about Ken and the colt?'

Nell wet a clean cloth at the faucet, wrung it out, folded it in a big square, laid it over the yellow bowl with the sponge and set the bowl on top of the warming oven. Then she seated herself on the edge of the table, clasped one knee and looked at Rob.

'I want you to give him a colt.'

'He doesn't deserve one.'

'What's that got to do with it? Aren't you ever going to give him a colt?'

'Sure I am. I've been expecting to.'

'Well, why don't you then?'

'I told you – he doesn't deserve it.'

56

'But Rob, he never will.'

'Why won't he? Howard did.'

'Ken's different. He's so far behind now, it's hopeless. If you wait until he catches up, and he really has it coming to him, he just won't get one at all.'

Rob ruminated. 'If he attends to his studies this summer—'

'That's another thing, Rob. That isn't going to get anywhere.'

Rob's expression of shock and consternation was almost comical. 'Not going to get anywhere! For God's sake! That's what I'm counting on – why won't he?'

'He really can't study. He hasn't the habit.'

'Didn't he study today?'

Nell laughed. 'He exposed himself to his books—'

Rob got up and walked up and down the floor. 'But my God – I've told him to. I've given the order—'

Nell kept discreetly quiet. Of all the manoeuvres that were difficult for Rob, a right about face was the most difficult.

After a while she said, 'Let's try a different method. Ken needs to succeed at something. Howard's too far ahead of him. Bigger and smarter and his wits about him, and—'

'Ken doesn't half try; doesn't stick at anything.'

'But he's crazy for a colt of his own. He can't think of another thing.'

'But Nell, it's all backwards. You can't bribe children to do their duty.'

'Not a bribe—' she hesitated.

'No? What would you call it?'

She tried to think it out. 'I just have the feeling Ken isn't going to pull anything off.' She looked across at Rob. 'And it's time he did. It isn't the school marks alone, but I just don't want things to go on any longer with Ken never coming out at the right end of anything.'

'I'm beginning to think he's just dumb.'

'He's not dumb—'

'This thing he pulled today – stampeding the mares—'

'You know he didn't mean to—'

'That's just the point. It's stupidity and carelessness. Nothing I say to him makes any impression. He still goes around wool-gathering, not knowing where he is or what's going on around him.'

'Maybe a little thing like this would turn the trick. If he had a colt of his own, trained him, rode him—'

'But it isn't a little thing. It's not easy to break and school a colt the way Howard has schooled Highboy. I'm not going to have a good horse spoiled by Ken's careless ways. He never knows what he's doing.'

'If Ken could really accomplish something like this, it would make a big difference in him.'

'That's a big *if*.'

'Rob, it's important. He's got to get square somehow. The way he looked tonight. Hang-dog – sullen almost. He's in everybody's bad graces. What he needs really is—'

'To snap out of it.'

'Well, if you want to put it that way. I was going to say he needs to grow up a little.'

'How will having a colt make him grow up?'

'Well, *you* know, something of his own. Responsibility. You see, he'd have something real, in flesh and blood, that he cared about more than all the things he goes mooning about. If he achieves anything with the colt, I think it'll show in everything he does next year. He'll be more of a man.'

She took off her apron.

They put out the kitchen lamp, went down the step into the living room and Rob called, 'Here Kim, here Chaps!'

Reluctantly the dogs rose from their mats, stretching themselves; yawned, and followed Rob and Nell out on to the terrace.

Four dark horse shapes took fright and leaped away

from the fountain, galloped off a little, then turned and stood, watching curiously.

Rob and Nell led the dogs away around the corner of the house and put them into the tool shed. Returning, they sat down on the coping of the fountain.

The horses were coming back, a few steps at a time, their ears pricked.

'Which are they?' asked Nell.

'The three-year-old broncs.'

Nell said nothing. The fact that they had been left here, in the Home Pasture, which was just a ring of barbed wire fence about a half mile in area, enclosing a section of woods, hills and fields around the ranch buildings, meant that they were at hand for use. He was going to break them. 'But not if I know anything about it,' said Nell to herself.

'Four of the mares haven't foaled yet. I think Rocket's dry this year,' Rob said.

'I thought Rocket had foaled already. A black horse colt. The other day when I was down in the meadow, there was a black horse colt that I thought was hers. A little new one.'

'I thought so too. But when she made that break away from the bunch today there was no colt following her.'

'But I saw it nursing—'

'Must have been nursing on one of the other black mares. This time of year, when their coats are so rough, it's hard to tell them apart.'

'Rob, I'm sure it was Rocket—'

Rob suddenly got to his feet. Nell knew the thought of a colt left down there in Castle Rock meadow, perhaps hidden somewhere in the aspen grove at the far end, perhaps hurt – would worry him.

'But I rode all through the aspen grove,' he said. 'I didn't leave any colts behind. Besides, if she'd had a colt, Rocket wouldn't have left it. You never can get her away from her colts.'

He sat down again on the coping and watched the

59

horses that were coming towards him, step by step. 'I'll drive down to the meadow tomorrow and take another look.'

The four horses kept their eyes fixed upon him. They knew him. The smell of him, the look of him. At the sound of his voice, if it came from half a mile away, every horse on the ranch stopped in his tracks and looked around. They stood in a half circle in the moonlight facing him.

'They want oats,' said Rob. 'I haven't got any oats, you beggars!' He raised his arms, flapped them, yelling, and the horses leaped and galloped away into the darkness.

Rob and Nell laughed.

The moon was well up, huge and theatrical above the black pine branches on the hill. The Green was in shadow, just the tips of the cottonwoods catching the light. They sat in silence, watching the moon climb. More and more of the cottonwoods rose into the light, floating softly.

'They're like ballet girls,' said Nell, 'dancing on the Green.'

The horses were returning. Very slowly they came close, and made a ring, watching Rob.

In the bunk house Gus yawned and put away his work.

'Give us a tune, Tim, while I finish my pipe. Den I'm turnin' in.'

Tim wound the little gramophone, inspected the records carefully, chose one and put it on.

Seated again, his chair tilted against the wall, Tim leaned his head back and both men were silent.

The tune spun out on the clear night air, and reached Rob and Nell sitting on the coping of the fountain.

It was an old song, with all the childish pathos of the melodies that are loved on the plains, or born there; and seemed to come from a voice singing far away.

> Dar-ar-ar-ling I am growing o-o-old,
> Si-il-ver threads among the go-o-old,

60

Shine upon my brow today-ay-ay,
Life is fading fa-a-ast away.

The song ended.

Gus sighed. The needle spun round and round, finally grinding on the record, and Tim got up and turned it off.

Chapter Six

The mile-square Stable Pasture, so called because it was
nearest to the stables, was a terrain of startling wildness
and beauty. A broad runway of level grass went along the
County Road fence on the south. North and west, it ran
into low hills, with a sparse, erratic growth of large twisted
pines, and the soil here was a shallow layer over a mountain
crag which broke through everywhere in cliffs and sharp
stone teeth. Out of the rock-clefts grew pines and junipers.
At the base of the cliffs were caverns in which were skeletons and piles of bones, remnants of wild animal orgies.
The cliffs overhung fragrant little dells where mushrooms
and larkspur and strawberry plants pushed up through the
loam and pine needles. Going north, the hills and cliffs
became steeper; and at last, in a series of broken, wooded
steppes, plunged down to the level of Deercreek, the
mountain stream which formed the northern boundary.

The Stable Pasture was an endless field of exploration for Howard and Ken. Just to find a new path up or down the Steppes, without getting pocketed somewhere from which there was hardly a way out, was a day's delight. Nell loved to wander in it, or to take a book with her for a whole afternoon in some small secret dell. Here, all summer long, the mysterious shapes of the deer stole like shadows across the shafts of sunlight. One couldn't sit very long, quiet and still and watching, without seeing the slow determined movement of a porcupine, or the serpentine undulations of a pretty, white-striped skunk, or the awkward plunges and playful tumbling dashes of whistling pigs, or the continuous soft movement of gophers, cottontails and jacks. If there was no meat for dinner, Nell or either of the boys could take a twenty-two and spend an hour in the Stable Pasture in the late afternoon and bring home half a dozen tender young cottontails.

That night Rocket had the pasture all to herself. She had made the rounds of it several times.

She stood now at the closed gate which opened on the County Road and looked across at the grassy slopes of the Saddle Back. They shone a bright silvery grey under the moon. Suddenly she lifted her hind leg like a dog, swung her head savagely around and tried to butt her bag. It was hot and bursting. She turned again and stood motionless, looking up at the range, her ears pricked.

She started off on a fast trot along the fence. With long thrusting strides she made the ground run away from her. Her big haunches crinkled with each piston stroke; her head was high, nose reaching up, her sparse irregular mane fell untidily, part on one side, part on the other side of her neck. The frayed piece of lariat was knotted about her neck and hung under the mane. A fine line of white ringed each eye. She had an angry, crazy look.

She stopped at the corner of the pasture where another barbed-wire fence came in at right angles. Standing there, throwing a far, piercing gaze into the distance, her ears moving incessantly, she trembled to every sound that drifted on the still air. Suddenly she started off again, following the cross fence.

All in through the rough and varied terrain of the Pasture ran threads of paths. Rob had found a way down to Deercreek for the automobile. The horses knew it from birth and covered it all, clawing their way up, leaping from ledge to ledge, sliding down on their haunches, sure-footed as mountain goats.

For an hour Rocket scoured the pasture, crashing down the Steppes to Deercreek, forcing her way through the thicket on the other side of the stream, standing at the northern fence, sniffing.

Far over yonder were the hay meadows. Castle Rock Meadow farthest of all.

It was the breeze that played over Castle Rock Meadow, the aspen grove at the far end, that she wanted to smell.

But for all her searching and listening, there was no little whimper for her ears, nor the touch of fumbling warm tongue and lips upon her bag, nor the closeness of a nimble little shape running at her side.

After a moment or two she continued her way along the fence, going at a long swinging trot; then turned another corner and began to climb and finally had made the complete round of the boundaries of the pasture once more.

She came out of the pines, cantered down the hill, went past the stables and pulled up at the County Road fence. Standing here she sent a loud ringing neigh into the night, hurling it like a fierce accusation.

A mile or more away on the Saddle Back, Banner heard the neigh and pricked his ears. He appeared to appraise the importance of it, dismiss it as making no immediate demands upon him and swung his head back again.

The cry was heard, too, by the band of yearlings grazing quietly on the other side of the crest. A little golden filly, who might have been Banner in miniature, raised her head sharply and stood alert, listening.

The loud angry neigh came again, and the sorrel filly neighed in reply and flung herself into a gallop. On the crest of the hill she stood, looking down at the County Road and the Stable Pasture.

Rocket's head was lifted and her ears strained forward. She had heard the whinny of the little sorrel, and a shuddering took her. She began to prance up and down inside the fence, then turned and galloped away from it, in the direction of Castle Rock. She had cried for her foal – there had been an answer, and one that touched her maternity, but still, not the voice of the little one who so lately had been part of herself; and she was confused, and in bewilderment galloped towards the dark woods that lay between her and Castle Rock.

The yearling filly neighed again and plunged down the hill towards the road. The voice tore at Rocket. She stopped; turned; an answering neigh broke from her; and suddenly, indecision left her, and she reversed her direction and galloped towards the fence.

Very few untrained horses are jumpers, and a western mustang will always break through a wire fence rather than leap it, but the joy and eagerness in Rocket's heart gave her wings, and she made a beautiful clean jump over the wires and the two horses rushed to each other, pressed their cheeks together, intertwined their heads and necks, with loving, excited whinnies.

Rocket wanted more. Her bursting bag – this colt, as well as the little one she had lost, surely this yearling child of hers could take the milk that was causing her agony.

Her voice coaxed. She turned herself in the proper position to the little sorrel and whinnied again. But the yearling had been on grass for six months; the instinct to nurse was dead. It stood, unresponsive, head turned back towards the hill, where now it heard its comrades running.

Rocket whinnied again in desperation. She swung her haunches close against the colt. The youngster answered with a sensitive and affectionate neigh, and turned to rest its head on top of the mare's haunches. Rocket moved closer, the golden head slipped down and sideways, at last it was there, reaching under, fumbling for the teat. Rocket stood motionless, her head turned over the haunch of the nursing yearling.

An hour later, the black mare and the golden yearling were cantering side by side; they had left the ranch and the Saddle Back far behind them. Ahead of them were the broken headlands of the Colorado border, and in their nostrils the smell of the snow from the faraway mountains of the Neversummer Range.

Chapter Seven

Even before he opened his eyes next morning Ken knew that something was wrong, and he pushed away the moment of complete awakening. He lay facing the window and saw that the pines on the hill were quiet. No wind today.

Then he remembered. He had stampeded the mares.

He had a feeling that it was late. For some time he had been half hearing all the early morning noises. Gus opening the kitchen door. The only reason his steps across the kitchen floor and the shaking down of the ashes and the making of the fire didn't wake everyone was because they were so used to it. There had been steps going down, too, and his mother's voice saying, Time to get up, boys—

He slipped out of bed and went to the window, hitching up his pyjamas. Howard was on the terrace right underneath, and Ken could see the top of his head, black and smooth, with the part exactly in the centre. He had on blue jeans, and a clean chambray shirt and a red bandana.

Howard looked up. 'Hi.'

Ken stared at him without answering.

Howard's black eyebrows and his thin mouth were straight lines across his face. He was smiling a little but his eyes were watching craftily.

'Mad at me, ain't you?'

'Tattletale!'

'I didn't tell on you.'

'Yer a liar.'

'All I did was ask if Cigarette tossed you, and if you found the blanket.'

'You started it – you knew I'd get it in the neck—'

'That's not lying.'

'Yer always gettin' me in trouble – you want to—'

'Say, let's make up, Ken – we could go down to the swimmin' pool – it's gonna be hot.'

Ken glowered.

'We could start on the colts—'

'What colts?'

'Our summer colts. Dad left four of 'em in the Calf Pasture yesterday. We gotta halter-break them, like we did last year. I get first choice he said.'

'Do you choose one and then I choose one and then you and then I? Or do you choose both yours first?'

'Well he said I could choose both first—'

'I betcher lyin'—'

'Tell you what, Ken, if you'll make up, I'll choose just one and let you choose next.'

Their father's voice came loudly, 'Didn't I tell you to watch that sprinkler, Howard?'

Howard hastily changed the sprinkler.

McLaughlin was coming from the tool house. He had let out the dogs and they were jumping around him frantic with joy, as if they were afraid, every night, there would never be another letting out or another morning.

McLaughlin had a shovel in his hand and went about the Green cleaning it of the manure the horses had left and shouting to Howard about taking an interest in the grass that had been so hard to start and was still hard to keep green.

The red Rhode Island hen that had stolen a nest followed him, clucking and picking at the manure spots, and the hatch of cheeping yellow chicks swarmed around her, tiny feet twinkling at her call, and wing-fluffs beating the air.

Ken faded back into the room and hastily began to dress.

The smell of coffee filled the house.

Howard watched his sprinkler, moving it, little by little, down the terrace, and planned his day. Ken would be all right now, he thought, he was never hard to manage – they might have fun in the swimming pool – or go shooting—

'Breakfast!' sang out Nell's voice. She ran out on to the terrace. She had on a green dress with a zipper all the way down the front and a sash across the back. She clapped her hands and yelled for them to come, and Rob dropped his shovel and ran at her, and Ken stopped tying his necktie to watch. His mouth was open and there was a smile on his face because it was always fun when his father and mother started playing. She dodged and ran around the fountain, and her husband chased her and reached out a hand and caught her sash and undid it, and she screamed and ran for the steps, and both dogs ran in between them barking and almost tripped him up.

They'd gone in. Ken hurried to finish but he hated to go down, he felt so out of things. On the way downstairs he stopped before the picture of the duck. It was a big black duck with white breast and legs and white bars on his wings. He was fierce and handsome standing on his rock, just about to launch himself into the waves of the grey, choppy lake. There was such a reaching in his eager beak and one lifted foot and the forward tilt of his body, Ken felt

69

as if it dragged him in too. In another second he would feel the icy sting and shock of the water, the bitter cold, sharp, up-pricked waves, and the greyness of the misty air hanging over it, full of fear and loneliness. His skin went gooseflesh.

At the breakfast table his father was waiting to hear Ken clatter the rest of the way downstairs.

'I bet he's looking at the duck,' said Howard.

'What duck?'

'On the landing. He looks at it for an hour sometimes.'

'Howard,' reproved Nell, 'he never looks at it for an hour.'

'Well, a long time – seems like an hour.'

'In God's name!' McLaughlin's voice was rising. 'What duck on the landing?'

'My Audubon print,' explained Nell quickly. 'The one that hangs under the clock. Ken likes to look at it.'

'Ken!' roared his father; and hastily Ken's sturdy shoes clattered the rest of the way down the stairs, and he came into the kitchen, his hair meticulously parted and slicked down, and his face sullen.

'What did you stop on the landing for?'

Ken opened his napkin and looked down, embarrassed. 'I was looking at the duck.'

'The duck! Out the window?'

'The duck in the picture there.'

There was a little amused glint in Nell's eyes as she helped Ken to oatmeal.

'Didn't you know we were at breakfast?'

'I – I—'

'Didn't think,' finished his father for him.

Ken didn't look up or make any reply. He had known it would be like this. He poured cream on his oatmeal and reached for the brown sugar.

'Ken,' said his father, 'I'm going to take back an order I gave you yesterday. I'm going to remit your hour of study.'

Ken looked at his father in astonishment – his mouth opening in relief and pleasure.

'I've got other plans for you this summer,' McLaughlin continued pompously, and Nell tucked her face down to hide her smile. How often had she heard Rob order a baulky horse to *Whoa!* or seen him spur and lash a runaway!

'And,' continued Rob blandly, 'I'm going to give you a colt.'

Ken shot out of his chair. Spoon and dishes went clattering.

'A – a – spring colt, Dad? Or a yearling?'

McLaughlin was taken aback, but Nell dropped her eyes again. If Ken got a yearling colt, he'd be even up with Howard.

'A yearling colt, your father means, Kennie,' she said smoothly. 'Sit down and eat your breakfast – look what you've done to your porridge.'

Ken gathered up the china and silver he had scattered, replaced them and sat down again. Colour had rushed to his face.

'I'll give it to you a week from today,' said his father. 'Between now and then you can look them over and make your choice.'

'I can have any yearling colt on the ranch that I want?' asked Ken.

His father nodded calmly, pushed his chair back and took out his pipe.

Speechless, Ken turned to look at Howard and the two boys eyed each other.

Even up, at last.

'Does it have to be a yearling colt, Dad?' asked Howard. 'Could it be a spring colt if he'd rather have a spring colt?'

'It could be anything foaled on the ranch since a year ago,' said McLaughlin. 'There are eighteen yearlings. So

71

far, thirteen or fourteen new colts; a few to come yet.'

'Will you take a yearling or a spring colt, Ken?' asked Howard.

In answer, Ken turned upon Howard an exaggerated pitying sneer, copied from the movies, and mastered only after much practice.

But his father asked the same thing. 'Yearling or spring colt, Ken?'

Ken answered, 'A yearling.'

'Horse or filly?'

This stopped him. His eyes lost focus as mental images crowded. Rocket was a mare. But there was Banner. And the Albino, mustang hero. There emerged from the confusion a definite sense of the superiority of the male.

'I'll take a horse colt.' His voice was final and authoritative. An imperceptible glance passed between Nell and her husband.

McLaughlin said, 'That narrows it down. Let's see – how many horse colts were foaled last year?'

'Ten fillies and eight horse colts,' said Howard. 'You've got eight horse colts to choose from, Ken.'

Things were moving very fast for Ken, horses crowding him—

'Which were they?' said Nell. 'I've got them all down in the Stud Book. I left it up at the stables the other day, in the tack room. Ken, run up and get it, and we'll look over the list.'

'I'll go too,' said Howard, sliding out of his chair; and both boys rushed out of the door.

Ken tore ahead. A colt – a colt! His own!

His mind was full of images. A little foal just born, almost knocked down by its mother's tongue licking it . . . Banner rearing, his great forefeet beating the air, his big light belly, his fierce face and arching neck – a little yearling running . . . a black . . . a chestnut . . . his colt was all of them . . .

He dropped his head back and yelled; he pranced and galloped.

Howard caught up with him and said, 'You crazy!'

'My colt, my colt,' sang Ken. He ran in a circle, pacing, racking. He stuck his elbows out, said, 'Whoa, there! Hi!' He tossed his head and shook his mane.

'You goofy!' exclaimed Howard, watching him.

Ken rushed at him with fists up. Howard fell into position and they sparred. Ken didn't care what happened to him. His arms went like flails. Howard blocked his blows easily.

Ken broke out of it and went flying up to the stable. He had a sharp consciousness of change and new importance. Things had begun at last. Things could be real now.

They found the Stud Book and ran back with it.

As Nell read out the list of yearlings and the names of their dams Ken began to feel queer. These were definite flesh and blood animals; named, described, tagged, in a book; not the colts that had kicked their heels and played and tossed their manes in his dreams. He felt the sense of loss which every dreamer feels when the dream moves up, comes close, and at last is concrete.

'I haven't named them all,' Nell was saying. 'There were some I never saw. They had run off somewhere when I went up on Twenty to look them over and put them in the book.'

'The bronc bunch,' grunted McLaughlin, referring to the progeny of the Albino. 'They're always missing when they're wanted.'

'Ken and I trained four of these yearlings ourselves,' said Howard.

Every summer the two boys had the job of handling and halter-breaking four of the spring colts.

'The colts the boys trained last summer were Doughboy and College Boy and Lassie and Firefly,' said Nell, studying the book. 'Two horse colts and two fillies.'

'Say, Ken,' said Howard eagerly, 'why don't you take Doughboy? He was one of yours. And when he grows up he'll be sort of twins with mine, in his name anyway. Doughboy, Highboy, see?'

But Ken looked scornful. Doughboy would never have half Highboy's speed. Last summer McLaughlin, looking over the colts, had said, 'He's a chunk. We'll name him Doughboy. He might turn out a heavy hunter. Look at the big legs on him!'

'Lassie then,' suggested Howard again. 'If you want speed. She's fast as anything, and she's black as ink. Like Highboy.'

'I said I was going to take a *horse*,' said Ken. 'Besides, Dad said Lassie'll never go over fifteen hands.'

'Remember one thing, Ken,' said McLaughlin. 'You can't tell much about a colt when it's new-born, and not always much more when it's a yearling. Blood's the thing. The prepotency of blood—'

They had heard this term often, for whenever McLaughlin got talking about horses he used it.

'That's the trouble with this stuff I've got from the Albino. He had prepotency. That devil passed on his traits. They don't wear out. Must have had some magnificent blood strains somewhere in his ancestry. Arab probably. Put enough Arab blood into a line and it gives prepotency – to the traits you don't want as well as to those you do. Lots of Arab blood in these western mustangs. Comes from the Arab and Barb horses the Spaniards brought over—' McLaughlin got up, went to the shelf beside the spice closet, and took down one of his favourite books on the genealogy of the American horse. He turned the pages, looking for a certain passage, found it, sat down again and began to read. The boys exchanged a glance of agonized impatience as the familiar lecture started.

Suddenly Howard jerked his head around. 'Car coming!' he exclaimed. Rob stopped reading. They heard a car rattle

74

over the cattle guard at the Home Pasture fence, come up the low hill behind the house in low gear and whizz past. The boys darted to the pantry window and saw the rear of the car as it disappeared over the crest of the hill on its way to the stables.

'A big, dusty, black car,' announced Howard.

McLaughlin closed his book. 'Might be Doc,' he said.

'The vet?' exclaimed Nell. 'What for?'

'To geld the two-year-olds. Boys – run up to the stables and see if that's Doc Hicks.'

Ken and Howard slammed through the kitchen door and vanished.

'But those two-year-olds are still out on the range,' said Nell. 'I saw them just the other day.'

'I brought them in. They're in the Six Foot Pasture.'

The Six Foot Pasture, about a quarter of a mile square, was so named because it was fenced with barbed wire to a height of six feet, the highest and tightest fences McLaughlin had on the ranch. The near end of it adjoined the corrals, the far end, the County Road.

Nell stopped eating. 'Rob – don't let the boys see the gelding.'

'They might as well,' said Rob. 'They have to know, sooner or later.'

'They know already. But so far they've never actually seen it. You've always had it done before they got home from school.'

'Won't hurt 'em.'

The boys burst through the door. 'It's Doc Hicks and his assistant.'

'I thought so. Run back and tell Gus to get a fire started up there and get some water boiling.'

'He's already up there. He's got the fire lit.' They turned to dash away again. Nell called Ken back.

'You haven't finished your breakfast. Drink your milk and eat every bit of that ham.'

75

A moment later Gus appeared at the door. 'If we cude have an old sheet for clean rags, Missus?'

Nell brought an old sheet, clean and folded, from the linen closet.

Ken gulped the last swallow of milk, wiped his mouth, said excuse me please and darted out. Gus was walking away, the sheet over his arm.

'Dad's given me a colt, Gus! Any colt on the ranch up to a year old!'

Gus looked down at him. 'You gonna train it and take care of it yourself, Ken?'

'You bet!'

Gus made no comment but his head tilted in a speculative manner.

Rob and Nell, left alone, had a last cup of coffee together; then Nell rose to clear the table and Rob lit his pipe. There was an odd expression on his face. 'Did you notice his voice when he said that?'

'Said what?'

'*I'll take a horse colt!*'

They looked at each other and Rob gave a sudden guffaw of laughter. He went to the door, took his big hat from the hook and pulled it on, dragging it down to his eyebrows. 'He's never talked or looked like that in his life before.'

Nell suddenly laughed too.

Rob added, 'Now if he just picks a good one—' and the door slammed behind him.

Nell stood for a few moments, the laughter fading from her face, then she went to the sink and began to draw the water.

'A bloody day,' she sighed. 'I just hope they all get through—'

It was considered by many breeders that it was better and certainly safer to geld colts at the age of a year or a year and a half, but Rob wanted to retain as long as possible the young stallions' endowment of furious power.

76

The nine two-year-olds, clustered now at the far end of the Six Foot Pasture, near the County Road, were well grown and fleshed, their necks thick and strongly arched. The hairs of their manes and tails stood out with a separate vigour of their own, and their hides shone so brightly that the early morning sun, blazing down, struck glints from the round haunches and bulging neck muscles.

Like schoolboys, they wrestled and punched.

A couple shot out of the bunch, whirled and lashed with hind feet. The others leaped and scattered. A golden sorrel dropped his head, stiffened his legs, twisted his body and began to buck. When he finished he stood looking about as if for applause, shook himself violently, then ran at another horse with head stretched out, ears laid back and teeth bared.

Two big blacks rose on their hind legs and began a make-believe fight, coiling and uncoiling inside the floating fringes of their long black hair. They struck at each other with their forefeet, then curved away only to meet and charge again. One head rose over the other to nip at the back of the neck. The other twisted out, reared higher and counter-attacked.

This shadow-boxing was brought to an abrupt halt when the sound of a long trilling whistle reached them from the direction of the corrals. Every horse faced around, pricked his ears sharply and became motionless.

It took them a little while to think it over, watching the corrals with their near-miraculous eyesight which brought the scene, a quarter of a mile away, as close as if with a telescope.

The whistle came again.

They began to move, slowly at first with nodding heads, then faster, until the leaders broke into a canter and the rest followed.

They swept down on the corral in a bunch, propped and stopped.

Nervous and curious, with ears straining forward, they

77

watched the men moving within the enclosure as if demanding to know why they had been called.

Ken perched on the high corral fence, almost choked with excitement. 'I've got one too!' he exulted. 'Oh, you beauties! In a year, my yearling will be a two-year-old like you!'

Longing to be closer to them he slipped down from the fence and ran to his father. 'Dad, can I bring them in?'

'Don't have to bring them in – just get me a bucket of oats.'

Rob opened the corral gates and when Ken brought the bucket went through to the colts and offered it, talking to them gently, allowing each one to dip his nose in the bucket for a delicious mouthful.

When he returned to the corral, they followed close, jostling him.

Ken shut the gate and mounted the fence again.

Doc Hicks was pulling on his clean white overalls.

Doc, six feet two and built like a Hereford steer, never wasted time. A day's work often meant two or three such jobs as this, perhaps a hundred miles of Wyoming roads to cover in his big high-powered car, piled full of boxes and satchels, instruments, serums, bottles, lariats, ropes and halters.

Old Bill Sims, lantern-jawed and sad, worked with him, never saying a word, never smiling. Bill took charge of the equipment, sterilized and laid out the instruments, swung the lariat when the colt had to be thrown, cleaned up afterwards.

They worked fast.

It was not yet dinner time and the sun was almost directly overhead when Bill carried the gear to the car again and packed it in. He and Doc took their places in the front seat, the engine started, the car pulled away. The job was done.

Ken watched the car coast down the hill to the cattle

guard, then pick up speed on the long curving road which led out to the highway. When it disappeared around the shoulder of the hill Ken made for the pine woods that were up behind the house and flung himself face down on the warm pine needles.

Next year it would be his own colt who would be struggling on the ground with Bill sitting on his head, who would crowd into the corner when it was over and stand there motionless, shocked, taking no notice when Rob went to him with oats and pats and comforting words – *pretty tough old fellow – pretty tough—*

Oh, he knew all right that you couldn't have more than one stallion on a ranch – stallions were bothersome, they were even dangerous and fought and killed each other – but – but—

Ken pounded with the toe of his boot on the earth.

He heard a match stuck close by and raised his head to see his father standing there, lighting his pipe.

McLaughlin sat down beside his boy, put out an arm, and drew him against him. 'Kennie—'

'Oh, my colt, Dad! My colt.'

Rob's arm tightened. Ken pressed against it, crying bitterly.

Chapter Eight

At dinner, McLaughlin said the first thing he was going to do was to get Rocket into the corrals, and into the chute, cut the piece of rope off her neck, then drive her out of the Stable Pasture and out on to the range with the other brood mares.

'Until I get that done,' said he, 'I can't turn the gelded colts into the Stable Pasture – she'd get mixed up with them and I'd have the hell of a time cutting her out again.'

'How long will you keep the colts in the Stable Pasture?' asked Nell.

'About a week. I've got to keep my eye on them. They'll have to be exercised daily. After that, they can go out on to the range with the others. You boys can give them a hard run every day. Ride 'em like hell. This is your chance to whoop it up and yell and act like cowboys.'

'Why?' asked Howard.

'If there should be an infected one amongst them – which is always possible – he'd just stand around till he dies. Make him run. That causes drainage of the wound, stirs up circulation. If they're left alone, they'll stand around and mope and won't eat enough to keep up their strength.'

Ken hadn't wanted his dinner. Even the smell of the food tightened the flesh at the base of his nostrils.

Nell was looking at him. She said, 'You can leave the table if you want, Ken. Put up my hammock for me. I may want it later.'

Ken went out to the terrace. Over one part was a lattice roof, made of aspen poles. It had been built to hold a canvas and make shade against the hot summer sun. To Nell it was the Pergola, and she was training vines to run up the corner poles. Some day they would grow all over the lattice and make shade enough without any canvas, and the sunlight would filter through, and the green leaves would hang down, and underneath it would be a cool green and gold light.

Ken stood looking up. The canvas had not yet been spread and the direct glaring light hurt his eyes.

Ken got the hammock, hung it near the Pergola and lay down in it on his back, with feet and hands dangling over the sides, giving little shoves against the ground.

The lilac bushes in the angle near the stone steps and the flowers of the border gave off a strong fragrance in the heat. There were horses on the Green, some of them drinking at the fountain, some cropping the grass, some just standing looking at the house. There were no stallions there, just mares and geldings.

Nell came out with her apron tied around her and her coffee cup in her hand and stood looking at the sky.

'Golly, it's hot!' she said. 'It's time we had the canvas up.'

She looked over at Ken, as she stood stirring her coffee,

and then sat down in one of the hickory chairs beside him.

'It doesn't really do them any harm, Ken,' she said.

Ken wasn't surprised. She could always read his thoughts.

'Doesn't it, Mother?'

'No. It has to be done. Don't feel badly about it, dear. It isn't nice to watch. I was sorry you had to. In a week, they won't know that anything ever happened to them.'

'Won't they?'

'Just look at Highboy. And all of the great racehorses.'

'All gelded, Mother?'

'Most of them. A few are stallions, but more are geldings. Ken, you know the world is full of unpleasant things. Pain and operations and sickness and discomfort. You mustn't mind. That's just the way life is. Besides all that, there is health and goodness and soundness and fun and happiness, too, for horses as well as boys – much more of the good things than the bad—'

He turned his face to her, beginning to smile; and she put out her hand and pushed the damp hair back from his forehead. 'Take the bad with the good. That's the way grown-up people do. You've just had a little bit of growing up today.'

'I really do feel an awful lot different, Mother,' he said. 'When I got up this morning and didn't even know I was going to have a colt seems awful far away.'

'People grow up that way,' said Nell. 'In spurts. All of a sudden, they are years older.'

Ken's face became thoughtful. 'Besides, I can have a filly instead of a horse colt. Dad rides a mare.'

McLaughlin's voice, laughing loudly, came out of the kitchen window, and the horses on the Green raised their heads, looked at the house and walked expectantly towards it.

McLaughlin appeared in the doorway. 'Look at the beggars. Beggin' for oats—'

82

He disappeared again. There was always a bucket of oats hanging on a hook in the enclosed porch outside the kitchen door. He came out with the the bucket and went down on the Green to the horses. They crowded around him.

On such occasions he insisted on their good behaviour. This meant observance of rules of fair play and turn about. A horse that stuck his nose into the bucket and would not take it out would get a good smack on the side of the head. If they whirled and lashed each other in their jealousy and greediness, he put the bucket behind him and delivered a lecture, the tone of his voice expressing such surprise and indignation that they would hang their heads and all but promise never to do it again. Sometimes he would be completely surrounded and hidden and a scrimmage would start. Big bodies wheeling, rearing, heels lashing this way and that, hoofs pawing the air. One would think he must be down and trampled. But always he would emerge, swinging the bucket in one hand, smacking the nose of this or that horse angrily with the back of the other hand, his voice rising in harsh reprimand. And gradually the horses would calm down again and follow him meekly.

'Ken,' said his father, 'run down and open the gate into the Calf Pasture. I left the four foals with their dams in there yesterday. The ones that you and Howard are to halter-break this summer. Let them come in here with the bunch.'

Ken ran down the Green to the gate beside the corral of the cow barn, which opened into the Calf Pasture, and hooked it back, but no mares were in sight.

Rob gave his trilling whistle which, standing close beside him, you could hardly hear, but which carried a great distance.

Presently there appeared the sharp head of a horse around the shoulder of the hill which was at the upper end of the pasture. Then another and another. Three little colts came out with their free dancing steps – as if they had springs under their hoofs. Soon all four mares with their foals were trotting towards the gate. They slowed up as they came through and walked slowly on to the Green.

'Oh, look at Highboy and Tango!' exclaimed Nell.

Highboy, who had wandered some distance away and was nosing for clover on the side of the hill, had suddenly spied the mares, and something had excited him.

A pretty black mare was looking at him, standing in a pose of excited recognition.

Then with loud neighs, the two rushed towards each other, and when they met, they touched their faces, pressed their cheeks together, and at last Highboy rose lightly, standing close beside her, and flung one foreleg over her neck.

Nell and Rob and the boys were laughing.

'Reunion,' said Rob. 'They were born the same spring and have always been sweethearts, and they were separated all through the winter while I had the mares down in the meadow.'

Nell said, 'Exactly the way I used to be with my best little girl friend when we'd been away from each other for the summer.'

'The most affectionate animal in the world,' said Rob. 'You don't see the young ones leaving their mothers if they can help it. They stay in the family group. You'll often see a mare on the plains with a four-year-old colt, and a three-year-old, and a two, and a one, and a foal. All together. They don't break up unless something happens to make them. And they never forget.'

Highboy and Tango wandered away together. Tango's little black colt, about a month old, following and trying to nurse.

'It's her first colt,' said Rob. 'Looks like a good one. Howard, hand me the bucket. This is a good chance to give the colts their initiation.'

He fed the mares first and then offered it to the colts.

They would have been terrified, but seeing that their mothers were enjoying it, they nosed the bucket, gave it a sniff, and, hating the metal and the human smell of the hand, wheeled and pranced off. At a safe distance they turned, stood watching, and at last edged up again.

Rob never missed a chance to instruct the boys in horse psychology and the right approach to training.

'This is the beginning,' he said, 'of their getting used to human beings. It would have been better to start with these little fellows when they were just a few days old, as soon as they got their legs, and started out on their careers of being horses. They've been alone and free down in the meadow since they were born a few weeks ago, and that's time lost. Worse than lost, for they learned a world in which there are no human beings – just horses, grass, running water, trees, perhaps the strangeness of a wooden fence post and a wire fence – nothing more. And now they've got to change their minds about the world. It's different from what they've learned. It's a world where humans take the first place. Human beings master them. They have to obey. Humans are the most important of all. But they'll soon learn.'

'They're learning already,' said Howard. 'You can see them.'

'They learn from their mothers. They copy. They do everything their mothers do. That's why it's practically impossible to raise a good-tempered colt from a bad-tempered mare. That's why I never have any luck with the colts of the wild mares I get. The colts are corrupted from birth – just as wild as their mothers. You can't train it out of them.'

The light changed suddenly, and McLaughlin looked at the sky. The heavy cloud bank in the southwest had engulfed the sun and a coolness came into the air.

'It's going to rain,' he said. 'Will you ride this afternoon, Nell?'

'Later,' she answered. 'I've got to bake my bread now before the fire goes down.'

'I'm going for the mail – anything you want?'

'Two cakes of Fleischman's yeast, and Gus wanted tobacco – Rough Cut – the next time anyone went to the store.'

She went back into the house and the boys ran to the big red Studebaker, where it stood on the hill behind the house. Howard got in the front seat, and Ken in the back.

Just about to let in the clutch, McLaughlin paused and looked at Howard.

'By the way, Howard, when did you ride Highboy last?'

'Yesterday afternoon.'

'I was noticing his legs – you turned him out with dirty legs.'

'I groomed him,' Howard wriggled.

'Yes, down to his knees.'

'He kicks.'

'And whose fault is that?'

Howard sat in silence.

'This would be a good time,' said McLaughlin, 'to take him up to the stables and groom him. He's right there where you can easily catch him.'

'Can't I go with you to the store first?' asked Howard.

McLaughlin sat looking around at the weather signs, as if he had not heard.

Just like his father to wait until a little fun was up and then choose that time to make him groom Highboy.

He got out slowly. Ken climbed into the front seat.

'Take out the stone from in front of the wheel,' said his father.

Howard obeyed and the car slid down the hill, the gears gripped, the engine started, and it rattled over the cattle guard and was off down the stretch of straight gravel road over the little stone bridge that spanned Lone Tree Creek, on up and around the shoulder of the wooded hill, and out of sight.

Chapter Nine

There were two miles of winding road with a fine hard-packed surface of reddish decomposed granite; then a sharp turn under the big sign that said GOOSE BAR RANCH, and out on to the Lincoln Highway.

'Dad,' began Ken.

'Yes?'

'I hate the gelding.'

'I do too, son, but it's got to be done.'

'To all of them?'

'Yes, if they're to be any use.'

'Are they really just as good after?'

'Well, something's gone out of them, but it's something that's no use to men, except in a stud. You can see the difference. The life in the tail that makes it lift and plume out, the curve in it, the curve in the neck, the thickness and power of the neck, the carriage of the head, the look in the eye, the expression of the face. I like to ride a stallion myself if he's well trained. I often have. They use more stallions in Europe and Asia than we do here, but it has its disadvantages. Only the best blood should be passed on. And where you get wild horse colts growing up without gelding, there's indiscriminate breeding, and the stock runs down. That's why the mustangs have deteriorated on the plains in the West here. Only occasionally do you get really fine specimens, and then it's due to luck.'

Ken sat thinking about it. Especially about the race-horses that were gelded and still were big and powerful, still ran races.

His spirits were rising. He felt that he was catching something of his father's attitude about it. He could even think back to what happened in the morning without sharpy stinging feelings in the palms of his hands. All the same—

'Dad, I've decided to take a filly instead of a horse colt,' said Ken.

McLaughlin laughed. 'O.K. But don't take it too seriously, Ken.'

Ken sat thinking about his colt. He had a week to choose. He would ride up to the Saddle Back every day, look over the yearlings—

'Something I want to say to you, Ken.'

Ken looked up. The man-to-man way his father spoke to him made him feel they were almost friends already.

The car sped across the over-pass.

A train with two locomotives was passing underneath, and when they reached the highway again, was running parallel with them. It whistled shrilly, the smoke drifted across the road and shut down on them like fog. McLaughlin didn't speak until they had passed the train and the smoke and noise had gone.

'It's this, Ken. I'm giving you a colt. Any colt you want. And yet, I'm not satisfied with the performance you've given this spring. You know that. Maybe you think it's funny I give you the colt when what you deserve – for

88

flunking all your exams and pulling that stunt yesterday –
is a good hiding.'

Ken's face sobered, and he looked straight ahead.

McLaughlin continued. 'I don't want you to think I'm
letting you off. I'm not. I haven't gone soft – don't get that
into your head. I expect just as much of you as I ever did.
And this isn't any reward, because you haven't won a
reward.'

'What is it?'

'It's a partnership. I'm going to need the help of both of
you boys, and you have to be trained so you'll know how to
give it. You're going to train the yearling. I'll give you a
little help just with the first breaking, but you'll train her,
and she'll train you. I want you to make a good pony out of
her. I want her to make a man out of you. Get me?'

'Yes, sir.' Ken looked up with a wide smile lighting his
face.

'But that's not all,' said his father. 'You've got other
duties. You can give some time to your colt – not all your
time. You've got two of these foals to halter-break—'

'Yes, sir.'

'You've got to help exercise four horses for the Rodeo;
run the gelded colts every day for half an hour for this
whole week; help with all the ranch work the way you
always do. I don't want to find you welshing on work because you're playing with your colt—'

'No, sir.'

'This giving you the colt is a kind of bargain between us.
I give you the colt, you give me more obedience, more
efficiency, than you ever have in your life before. Is it a
bargain?'

'Yes, sir.'

McLaughlin slapped his hand on Ken's knee, and a
flush coloured the boy's cheeks.

They were silent for a while and Ken's eyes drifted
across the landscape, then came back to the wide highway

89

that ran, he knew, from the Atlantic to the Pacific sea-board, three thousand miles of macadam road, nearly straight. Some of the western roads he had been on with his father were empty of traffic. They cut the plains, straight and flat as far as the eye could see. The cars that used them went at top speed, boring like bees into the distance, only a few in a day. Sometimes for hours, perhaps whole days, the road was empty. But the Lincoln Highway was alive with traffic. Each of the cars they passed told its story, or a brief word from his father gave Ken the clue. The trans-continental traffic looked it. Big, expensive-looking cars, covered with dust, loaded with luggage so that the rear ends hung low, spieling along at eighty miles an hour, going somewhere fast; miles to eat up before nightfall. Tourists, perhaps from New York or Boston, headed for some Dude Ranch or National Park for a vacation. As they flashed by, you could see, inside, the heads of women and girls tied up in bright handkerchiefs.

They passed a big truck, loaded with straight pine poles. 'Poles from Pole Mountain,' said McLaughlin. 'Some-body's building a barn.'

'Do they buy the poles?'

'Pole Mountain is a Government Reserve. You can get the poles free but you have to cut them and transport them. It costs money to get a load.'

There was some local traffic; second-hand cars in none too good shape, of nearby ranches; a few big cars of business and professional men running from Cheyenne to Laramie; some hard-worked roadsters and sedans of travelling men; one long caravan – 'snake' they called it – of new cars being hauled from the East for sale in Cali-fornia, saving railroad transportation costs by using the Lincoln Highway.

As they arrived at Tie Siding, there drew up from the opposite direction a sample of the type of conveyance which is to be seen on every mile of the western highways.

It was a Ford sedan, bulging and sagging like an old washer-woman. The top of it was piled with mattresses, chairs, tables, bedding. The rear end was festooned with bundles and boxes tied on with knotted lengths of clothes line; an old rusty stove, half covered by a bed quilt, was roped to one bumper. Humanity of all ages packed it from floor to roof, and poured out when the door opened. Their faces were dry and wind-beaten and strained. Girls and boys alike wore faded, soiled denim pants. The small children and the baby looked both sick and sad. Their eyes were drawn up, there were deep lines on each side of the colourless mouths. One small youngster was bawling, not with fret or anger, but with a persistent despair.

McLaughlin turned off his engine and they sat a moment, watching.

'Where are they going to?' asked Ken.

'Just moving on. Poor people trying to find a way to live. They try the towns, can't make the grade, think the country would be easier, manage to get a homestead, or buy some land from someone else who has failed—'

'How can they pay for it?'

'They don't – they promise to pay, or give a share of the crops – or maybe they rent. And, of course, they get the worst land with little or no water, impossible for anyone to make a success of. And then they fail there too, and move on. The country is dotted with rotting barns and houses. And the land, that was good grass land once, is ruined, ploughed up, the native grass killed.'

'But won't it grow again?'

'In about ten years. It's a crime to break ground in this country of high winds. The Indians knew that and they found a better way. Early in the spring or after the seed had fallen in the fall, they'd burn the old grass. Then there'd be new grass springing up unchoked, and no top soil ploughed up to blow away like dust with the first dry summer.'

Mrs Olsen, wife of the man who ran the combination

Post Office and store, came hurrying out in her neat white pants and jacket.

'Hello,' she said cheerfully.

She had a trim, close-cropped black head, a great deal of rouge on her cheeks and lips, and a quiet, efficient way of going about things.

'I'll take two gallons,' said the tall, oldish man who had climbed out of the sedan, and he stood over Mrs Olsen as she put the hose into the tank and the petrol began to pour.

Others of the family scattered around both sides of the store to the rest rooms. Several of the children crossed the road to stand watching a pair of brown bears that were in a big cage of woven steel wire. Ken and his father got out of the car and went to the store, in which a number of men were making purchases or sitting about.

Other cars were stopping for petrol, and Mrs Olsen came running in and out to make change.

A truck stopped, and the driver came in for tobacco, while Mrs Olsen filled his tank.

'What's your load?' asked McLaughlin.

'Dead calves.'

'Dead calves!' said everyone.

Olsen said, 'From Morrison's place, north across the highway, I'll bet—'

'That's right.'

'I heerd they wuz cartin' the dead calves away in truck-loads from his place – hundreds of 'em—'

'That's right.'

'Sure tough luck for Morrison,' said Olsen. 'If he don't find a way of clearin' his herd of abortion, don't seem likely he can keep goin'—'

Ken went out and climbed up on the sides of the truck and looked down at the load of corpses; dark red bodies, white faces, good Hereford calves. They smelled pretty bad already.

The driver was getting back in.

Ken jumped down again and went back to the store.

'Government's takin' a hand in clearin' the state of abortion,' said Crane, over in the corner of the store. 'Specially dairy stock. But it's my guess if they forbid milk to be sold, over the whole country, unless the cows it comes from are free of abortion, they's goin' to be one hell of a big milk shortage.'

The dry farmer family had finished their buying – two gallons of petrol and a lollipop apiece. They packed themselves into the sedan and rattled off to the west.

'Why don't you come over to our turkey shoot this Sunday?' asked Olsen of McLaughlin.

'Your wife gets all the prizes,' kidded McLaughlin.

Olsen wagged his head proudly. 'She's pretty good. But you have the name of bein' a fine shot yourself, Captain. You'd better try. There's always some officers from the Post comes out—'

Old Reuben Dale, their neighbour on the west, asked, 'Any sign of mountain lions on your ranch this summer, McLaughlin? I've lost two calves out of the pasture on my place down near your Castle Rock Meadow, and I've got a notion it's a lion. Bert heerd a cat scream the other night when he went out to bring the cows in.'

'Cats,' said McLaughlin slowly. 'No. I haven't seen any. Haven't heard any either, but I think I'm short a colt—'

'They love horse meat,' said Reuben, grinning.

As Ken and his father left the store with the mail and the yeast and tobacco and three lollipops and a peppermint patty for Nell, Ken looked up at his father. 'What colt, Dad?'

McLaughlin didn't answer, and they got into the car. Ken asked again, 'What colt are we short?'

'Rocket's. I think she had a foal. She hasn't got it now. Before I drive her out of the Stable Pasture, I'm going down to Castle Rock Meadow to take a look around.'

Ken felt excited. He thought of the aspen grove, of

Castle Rock, as big as an hotel, with all the caverns and passages and tunnels underneath it, and the skeletons and bones that lay in them. Wildcats—

McLaughlin was driving a little faster. Kennie glanced at him and saw that he had something of his hard angry look. His father was worried.

'What gun will you take, Dad?'

McLaughlin didn't answer for quite a long time, then said, 'I'll take the Winchester. But I won't use it, Ken. The time you come on wildcat is the time you haven't got your gun with you.'

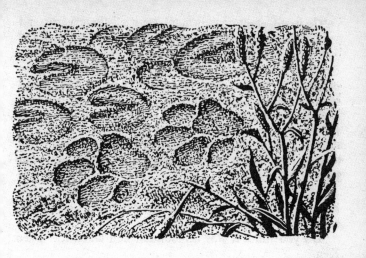

Chapter Ten

Blow flies rose, buzzing, as McLaughlin and the two boys stood looking down at all that was left of Rocket's foal. The hide was not yet dry; particles of flesh still clung to teeth and tiny hoofs; the hair of tail and mane lay in a swirl over the skeleton.

It was in one of the caves at the base of Castle Rock that Howard had come upon it, and after the first triumphant cry which called his father and Ken to him, they had stood without speaking, and there was no sound except for the angry humming of the flies that finally settled again on the carcass, shining, greenish, and busy.

'It was black,' said Ken, stirring with his foot the little tail that was swirled over the bones.

Death, now. This might have been *his* colt. Gelding and death – what else?

'That's why Rocket wouldn't leave, isn't it, Dad?' said Howard.

'Guess so, son.'

'Didn't she know it was dead?'

'She knew and she didn't know. Mares are funny about death. A mare won't hang around a dead foal or pay any attention to it. I've often thought they really don't recognize it or understand at all, but when they get far away from it, then they remember and begin to hunt and whinny for it.'

McLaughlin squatted down and began to examine the carcass. The spinal cord was severed in two places at the base of the neck.

It had not been entirely eaten, the hide was intact on the haunches, the head crushed, parts of the bones of the legs scattered some distance around.

'Do you think it was a mountain lion killed it?' asked Ken.

'I think so. A wolf would have picked it cleaner. It didn't die of itself, that's sure, or it wouldn't have been in this cave. Something dragged it here. Plenty of game has been dragged in here to be eaten.'

The place was a charnel house of bones, as were all the caverns under Castle Rock.

'Take a look around, boys, we'll see if we can figure out what killed it and how it happened. The ground here in the cave is too hard to show any prints.'

Ken was glad to feel the air on his face as he emerged from the cave, and to get away from the smell, and the sound of the blow flies.

The day seemed to have changed and between the high bank of light grey cloud and the earth was a scud of tattered dark clouds, racing from one mountain top to another.

'Going to rain,' said McLaughlin.

Howard gave a shout. 'Here's blood, Dad—' He pointed to a long red smear on a flat rock some distance from the cave.

McLaughlin grunted. 'Dragged it across.' The line from the rock and cave led down to the stream. On the strip of sandy beach where the stream had eaten under the bank they found four clear, round prints.

'There it is,' said McLaughlin. 'Mountain lion, really, though they call them wildcats around here. Look at the size of him.'

The prints were as big around as flapjacks.

Close by was the much trampled watering place of the horses, and here too, amongst the hoof prints, they found more of the prints of the lion.

Howard said excitedly, 'Bet he killed it when the horses came here to water – jumped from the bank right on it—'

McLaughlin lit his pipe in his leisurely way, and then shook his head. 'Wrong.'

'Why?'

'Use your wits. A foal of that age – perhaps a week old – doesn't drink water.'

'Well then, when Rocket came down to drink—'

'Rocket's a wildcat herself. If it had jumped her foal when she was close by she'd have attacked it. The cat would have been on the ground – she'd have cut it to pieces. What puzzles me is, where was Banner? If he'd seen the cat first, or smelled it, there'd have been a dead cat, not a dead colt. Banner must have been up at the other end of the meadow – Rocket off alone down here with the foal, and the cat was too quick for her – killed it—'

They reconstructed the scene. Rocket grazing. The colt separated from her, perhaps lying on the grass asleep – the sudden attack, the colt's scream – and Rocket rushing to the rescue when it was too late – the cat's escape – the mare sniffing, hanging over the dead foal, then in bewilderment wandering away to hunt elsewhere.

'And then,' said Howard, 'when Rocket had gone away, the cat came back and dragged it away into the cave to eat it.'

97

'And I guess that's the end of the mystery,' said McLaughlin.

'But it's not the end of the mountain lion,' said Ken. 'Where is it, Dad?'

McLaughlin took out the little steel measuring tape he always carried, and measured the space between the prints of forefeet and hindfeet. 'Five feet three,' he said, putting the tape away. 'A big fellow.'

Both boys eyed their father, ready to take their cue from him. He seemed serious but not worried.

'That's what I'd like to know, Ken,' he said, standing thoughtfully, puffing at his pipe, and looking all around, over at Dale's fence line, off at Castle Rock, and closer by through the aspen trees. 'I'm glad I've got the brood mare bunch out of this meadow.'

'Will the wildcat get others, Dad?'

'There's nothing here now for him to get. Everything's out on the range or up by the house. If the cat gets game enough here he'll stay here. Let's hope he will.'

'What do they eat?'

'Everything that's alive. Even mice and gophers. They like a fresh kill, but they'll kill anything that moves, for fun it not for hunger.'

'Can they get the horses and colts when they're on the range?'

'Not so easily where there's no cover. They hide and sneak up. Their only chance would be a surprise. If a horse saw them or smelled them first it could get away, because a cat's got no speed – legs too short. Now and then, if there's one horse off alone, a wildcat will attack it. They leap from the ground then, land on its neck, bite the spine through. A quick kill.'

Suddenly there was an ear-splitting crash of thunder, and the rain poured down as if the explosion had burst a reservoir. The big round footprints of the wildcat melted and ran off in a slide of water.

As McLaughlin and the boys raced for the Studebaker, standing tilted on the hillside, Ken wondered if the cat was lurking somewhere near. He cast a glance backwards at Castle Rock. On those high battlements and ledges were no end of hiding places. The cat might be crouching there, watching all they did.

They got into the car and started off.

Castle Rock was a sinister and fascinating place. Ken and Howard had explored it from top to bottom many times, crawling through the underground passages, counting and studying the bones and skeletons in the caves, climbing up outside all over the high parapets and ledges, and still could not feel that they knew its secrets. On one of its ledges there trembled a huge boulder, as big as a locomotive, as smooth as a pebble. They had strained and heaved at it, convinced that a strong enough push would send it crashing off the ledge and caroming down.

One morning, soon after dawn, Ken, standing on top of the great rock, had seen five coyotes organize themselves into a relay race and run down a rabbit in the meadow. They had stationed themselves at five points in a big circle, and had functioned in perfect team work, one coyote taking up the chase where the other dropped it, until the rabbit was exhausted, and had begun to bleat and squeal, making little futile dashes in this direction and that. Then the pack of coyotes had flung themselves on it like football players in a scrimmage; there was a moment's fierce nosing, biting, shoving; then the coyotes had come out of it and trotted off, and there were only a few bare white bones left on the meadow grass.

McLaughlin drove the Studebaker across the creek to the southern side of the ranch and went back over the hills which led down to Deercreek and into the Stable Pasture, thinking to find Rocket and drive her out of the pasture without leaving the car.

Howard said, 'The way she goes through fences or

jumps them – even if we do get her out the pasture, she can come back in, can't she?'

'She can, and she does. That's the hell of having such a horse on the place.'

'Then why do we do it?'

'It may hold her. Sometimes she minds the fences, sometimes she doesn't – just as she fancies – the thing is to get her up to the brood mares— Banner'll keep her there. He's the only one can manage her.'

It was still raining hard, and as they cruised about through the woods, up and down the little trails through the Steppes, the boys could see that their father was losing his patience. The rain streamed down the windows of the car. Lightning split the skies and thunder came in peal after peal.

Rocket was nowhere in the Stable Pasture. They mounted their horses at last, Nell and Gus and Tim joined the hunt, and protected from the driving rain by oilskins they all scoured the woods and Steppes for an hour, but there was no sign of the mare, not even the usual clue she left behind her, a broken fence.

'For once, she's gone over the fence and not through it,' said McLaughlin bitterly. 'I'd like to know which way.'

He sent Tim and Gus to do the milking and their evening chores, Nell and the boys to the house to get dry clothes on, and himself rode out on to the Saddle Back. If Rocket had joined the brood mare bunch of her own accord, there was nothing more to worry about; if not, she must be found.

The rain had stopped. The wind was sweeping all the clouds away and a perfect rainbow spanned the sky, framing the hill. Colour had come back to the ranch, the strong electric blue of the sky that in contrast made the roofs so red and the range so green and the pines so black.

McLaughlin, mounted on his big, nervous blood-bay

mare, Taggert, galloped up the Saddle Back into the strange light that blazed down from the rainbow.

He had no idea where the mares were. They might be close at hand hidden in one of the depressions of the rolling land which were invisible to the eye at a little distance, or miles away. Suddenly he was amongst them. They were quiet, watching him. They had known someone was coming – one rider, Rob McLaughlin.

Banner was waiting for him and came forward immediately to meet him.

Taggert pricked her ears. Rob spoke to Banner, and sat quiet, looking about, counting the mares, searching for Rocket, while Banner and Taggert had a small interchange of civilities tinged with flirtatiousness, Banner asking impertinent questions, Taggert telling him to keep his distance.

A second rainbow shone out, almost as strongly coloured as the first, and the space between the two filled with a bright brown colour. There came the hint of a third rainbow.

Rocket was not there.

McLaughlin turned his mare and rode out of the bunch. Banner galloped behind him for a mile, then circled away and returned to his responsibilities.

When he had unsaddled, Rob gave orders to everyone to look for Rocket until she was found. The daily rides of Nell and the boys were to be directed to that end. Gus and Tim were to keep a look-out, wherever they happened to be working.

Rocket must be bred immediately, if possible on the ninth day after she had dropped her foal, so that she would foal early next season. A colt born late in the summer had not the strength or growth enough to meet the early winter storms.

'And after that,' said Rob, 'I'll get that piece of rope off her neck.'

He seemed to have lost his annoyance now that the day's work was done. He stamped about the kitchen, sniffing at the smell of fresh bread that filled it, but Nell, glancing at him, saw on his face the implacableness that she dreaded.

She got the bread knife and cut off the warm, crusty end of a loaf – smeared it thick with fresh sweet butter and handed it to him, smiling at the size of the bite that went into his mouth. But she was thinking of that bit of rope. What it was going to cost, measured in time and violence and fury, to get it off.

Lying beside Rob in the big walnut double bed that night, Nell had almost dropped off to sleep when she heard his voice.

'Nell—'

'Yes, dear?'

'This wildcat business – and the boys – what do you think?'

Her back was to him, but she could hear by his voice that he was wide awake and uneasy. He was up on one elbow.

'I know. I was thinking too. It scared me to death.'

After a silence, 'To tell them to be on the lookout – to get heavier guns for them – the twenty-twos would be no good—'

She finished for him. 'It would just spoil the whole summer, wouldn't it?'

'They'd have to take their guns whenever they went out—'

'Yes.'

'And even so—'

'That's it.'

Silence again for a few moments. 'There's probably hardly a chance of danger – only a chance in a hundred.'

'Do they attack people, Rob?'

'Attack anything if they want to. They're incalculable. Cats, you know—'

'Can they really kill?'

'They can kill anything they can get the drop on – horse, cow, man – anything.'

'But only when they're hungry, I suppose. And there's so much small game – and the horses too–'

'Horseflesh is their favourite meat. Nell, I think I'll say nothing to them. I hate to put fear into them.'

'They're mostly on horseback anyway, Rob.'

'Yes.'

Nell lay thinking it over. It did not seem to her an imminent danger. Just one more of the hazards of the mountain life. There was not a day that they were not in danger from something– Oh, God, watch over my boys – my three boys–

'Nell–'

Rob's voice was lower, and he moved closer, leaning over her. 'There's *you* too–'

'Me?'

'You go out. Up in the Stable Pasture to read or walk – all afternoon alone–'

'Yes.'

'And fishing. Hours off alone. In Deercreek, you walk along the stream there – trees overhead–'

'Yes–'

'Nell, I can't let you.'

'Oh, Rob, I can't stay in – I have to go out – I have to feel free–'

'Not under the trees, Nell.'

'They jump from trees, don't they?'

'Yes.'

'Damn the thing – what a nuisance.'

'Promise me, Nell–'

She reached a hand back and patted him. 'I don't want you to be worried, dear – you have enough on your mind – but I'm really not a bit afraid.'

'I know, but that's no help. Chances are, sooner or later,

one of us will get a shot at it – if it comes up this end of the ranch, But meanwhile, don't go fishing in Deercreek. Fish in the meadows where the stream runs in the open and there are no trees.'

'All right, dear.'

'Promise?'

'I promise I won't fish in Deercreek.' She laughed and closed her eyes again.

Always at night her fatigue was a positive pressing thing. She could feel it all through her, a heavy, sweet aching. And yielding to it was like sinking into a sucking depth.

Her thoughts began to scatter into grotesque formations like pieces of broken glass. She felt Rob's cheek on her hair. He was kissing her softly, all over her cheek and temple and down to the corner of her mouth.

He thinks I'm asleep, she thought, and breathed more evenly and deeply, her eyes closed. *So – dead – tired* – the deep place drawing her down into unconsciousness— Rob getting her all into his arms and the the curve of his body – something moving in the thick foliage of the trees over Deercreek – a branch stirring gently – shadows – wind rushing through with a sound—

Chapter Eleven

The week that followed during which Ken was to choose his yearling was a busy one for everybody.

It rained every day out of one big purple cloud which drifted away at night, so that the mornings came in hot and clear, but by noon it was over the ranch again, and would start to rumble, then shiver and crack with lightning; then the downpour of rain, while the horizons all around were calm and blue, with fleecy white clouds motionless upon the hills.

Nell called it the Goose Bar sprinkling system. It brought out the strong, fresh colours of the flowers; dark salmon geraniums in the ultramarine blue window boxes, and red, pink, purple and white petunias in the flower border. The roofs of the buildings were red and clean, with no dust on them, and the grass as green as a billiard table.

The boys were riding Lady and Calico and Buck and

Baldy, the horses that were being trained to rent for the Rodeo.

'When you're hunting for Rocket and looking over the yearlings and chasing the geldings you might well be training these plugs,' said McLaughlin.

'Which shall we ride?' asked Howard.

McLaughlin, stretched out in a chair on the terrace with his pipe just before supper, gave this careful thought. 'Now, let's see. Lady's nervous and she runs away. Went over backwards with Tim last week. Baldy, stubborn brute, argues with you but he's always right. More sense than a man. Calico, a running fool. Never knows when to stop. Wears himself out. Howard, you take Calico, and don't forget for a moment that he hasn't got sense. He'll be in a lather over nothing. Too willing. His mouth's hard. Don't encourage him to lean on the bit. Hold him in but don't carry his head. Talk to him a lot. He'll quiet down for the voice better than anything else. Ken, you take Lady. I'm giving her to you because most of the time you don't know where you are. You sit like a sack of meal, almost forget to hold the reins – she'll not know you're on her back. I've noticed when you're on her, she's never gathered. Goes about as if she was grazing. It's a good thing. Good for that mare, anyway. Eases her down. But watch out for her running away. Just don't let her get going too fast. When she does, it suddenly comes to her that she'll take the bit and run away; kind of goes to her head. I want to break her of that habit this summer. She's a fine horse.'

'I'll help with Lady too,' said Nell. 'She always behaves well with me. I love to ride her. We understand each other.'

'O.K. As a matter of fact, you could ride any of them, and it would be a good thing to change about. Any of you could ride Buck and Baldy. No use telling you what to do with Baldy, he'll do what he pleases, but it'll usually be the right thing. He won't object to orders unless they're unreasonable. And Buck needs a lot of suppling and he's not as bridle-wise as he should be. Take them down into the practice field and do figure eights on them for an hour every other day. Just get them a bit quicker at answering the aids; more up and coming. Practice starts on the trot and the canter. Use saddles. Groom them before and after. Now remember, boys, this will be a daily duty for you, don't forget it, or neglect it, and I don't want to have to watch you or bother about it. You can keep the four of them in the Calf Pasture, they'll be handy to get at and won't get mixed with the other horses. Give them all the riding you can.'

A Colorado buyer, Joe Williams, came to see if McLaughlin had any horses to sell. He came once or twice every year, collecting horses that he afterwards sold at the local auctions; but the prices he offered were so low that his appearance at the ranch was always the signal for Rob McLaughlin to lose his temper.

Williams offered thirty-five or forty dollars for an old brood mare with her spring colt; twenty or thirty for an old gelding broke for saddle and work provided his teeth were good enough to keep him in flesh; but as he paid cash down, and the only other way of getting anything at all for horses that were not fit for good markets was to ship them to the glue factory in a carload of old plugs and wild broncs dragged in off the range, McLaughlin, after hours of argument, loud words and insults, usually made a deal with him. Nell always urged him to. 'After all,' she said, 'they're only getting older, and it's hard to keep them in condition, and he can get eight or ten of them into his truck, and even at his prices, that means a couple of hundred dollars.'

On this occasion McLaughlin said that he'd get in some horses that were useless to him from his outlying pastures, and they'd make a deal; and Williams drove away, promising to be back inside of a week with his truck.

Jingo, one of the two-year-olds, died.

McLaughlin never allowed anyone to show, or even to feel, any grief about the death of the animals. It was an unwritten law to take death as the animals take it, all in the day's work, something natural and not too important; forget it. Close as they were to the animals, making such friends of them, if they let themselves mourn them, there would be too much mourning. Death was all around them – they did not shed tears.

But Jingo – the way he would come up behind you, nipping your shoulder, asking for attention— Ken could not forget him easily.

Gus tied a rope to the dead horse's head and fastened it to the back of the little Ford truck and hauled him away across the ranch to the shaft of the abandoned mine on the hillside, three hundred feet deep—

The really big event of the week was that McLaughlin engaged a bronco-buster to break the three-year-olds.

Ken saw the man first when they were coming down from the stables just before supper one evening, and the bronco-buster was standing on the Green talking to Nell.

He was very small and neat. His legs were thin and bowed in tight blue jeans that were rubbed to light blue inside the thighs and on the seat. His waist was not much larger than Ken's and was belted snug. His small face was bright red and blank-looking. His blue eyes were so direct they made other eyes seem shifty.

Nell introduced him, just saying that this was Ross Buckley who was going to ride in the Rodeo and had a couple of weeks of free time right now, waiting for the Rodeo, and thought he would put it in breaking some horses.

'I heerd you-all had some hot-bloods up here,' said Ross in a pleasant drawling voice. 'Thought I'd like to have a try at 'em, if you've got any that need breaking.'

Nell said, 'Come on, Howard and Ken – time to clean

up for supper,' and walked away with the boys, leaving McLaughlin there talking to Ross.

Ross had arrived in a Ford sedan piled to the roof with saddles and bridles and blankets and lariats, and when Nell had talked to him and found out what he wanted, she kept him there until McLaughlin came down from the stables.

McLaughlin engaged him, and took him up to the bunk house and introduced him to Gus and Tim, and every day since he had been working in the corral at the broncs.

And in addition to all this, hours had been spent every day, looking for Rocket; but no one had seen hide nor hair of her.

Ken had not yet been able to decide on his colt.

Rocket had her filly hidden away with her in a little valley near the Colorado border.

There was deep meadow grass in the bottom, timothy and red-top; there was gamma grass on the sides of the slopes that shut them in; there was, best of all, high clover at the base of the hill above where a spring burst through the ground in a dozen bubbling holes.

The water loitered in winding runlets, and at last joined to make a little stream, and the stream made a bed of moist earth for a copse of cottonwoods and aspen, and the shade and moisture made food and cover for a thicket of raspberry and gooseberry bushes and wildflowers; bluebells with yard-long stems as fine as hairs, white Mariposa lilies with pansy dark hearts, and the wild forget-me-not blossoms like tiny seeds of turquoise, and larkspur – pink, white, and blue – death to cattle and horses.

The filly nosed the larkspur, breathing in its scent, then blew out her breath, snorting, and moved over to the clover and feasted. She stood shoulder deep, green stems and yellow blossoms sticking out on either side of her mouth as she chewed, her head up, looking around contentedly.

She had only nursed a few times. Rocket was not so

imperative now that the first agony was relieved and the milk drying up. The two horses – big black mare and little orange one, grazed side by side in the meadow, and drank at the springs, and cantered on the hill-sides, standing now and again on the crests with eyes alert and ears sharply pointed.

They were not alone in the valley. In the copse twittered wild canaries and bluebirds. Half a dozen handsome black and white magpies argued noisily in the cottonwoods; a flock of goldfinch swooped across the valley, warbling; swung upwards, circled around, and disappeared over one of the hills, only to appear from a different direction and make the round again. Small game moved in the grass; in the sky were a pair of hawks on the watch; and two antelope were feeding in the valley, curious and dainty as porcelain figurines.

On the day that her foal would have been nine days old, Rocket cantered up one of the hills and stood at the top, looking over.

When the filly came up beside her, the mare bared her teeth and nipped at her. The filly moved away, and Rocket continued her searching of the wind and the plains.

The filly lay down and went to sleep.

Rocket made the round of the hilltops, at a gallop. On one crest she stood and neighed loudly.

It was the northerly outlook that held her eyes the longest. The ranch lay due north. *Banner* was north . . . Before evening she and the filly had left their valley and were working north, pausing to graze and water, not hurrying.

Chapter Twelve

Ken wakened one morning in the dark and turned to face the window, and when it showed faintly grey outside, he got up and stood watching the dawn brighten in the east.

Ken never dreamed at night. He often wondered why, and asked his mother. 'Howard dreams, and you and Dad; and I heard Tim telling about a crazy dream he had – why don't I ever dream?'

His mother had looked at him oddly and said, 'When you dream, it's dreams of another sort – at a different time.'

'Why?'

But she didn't seem to know why any more than he did.

He stood with his face at the screen, shivering a little and feeling excited, because he was going to go out. He could see that the weather had changed.

There were small, tattered, low-flying black clouds, as if

the one big cloud had been torn to pieces; there were a few stars going in and out between them; and behind all the clouds a greenish glow spread upwards from the horizon.

There wasn't enough light yet for him to see anything clearly. It seemed a world of near-darkness, in which vague outlines appeared and vanished, floating and shadowy. His thoughts were like that, too. He groped for familiar footing in his mind, but everything was changed. Something new had come into him so that he was different. Even Tim said that he had grown an inch since his father promised him the colt, and Howard treated him as if he was important. But something had gone out of him, too; and sometimes he wanted it so that he was in a panic.

It was a place he used to play and be happy in; quite secret, no one knew he was there; and safe, because he had everything his own way; pleasant, because there were no unhappy endings. In the real world just about everything had an unhappy ending or tripped him up somehow, but *there*, there were no endings at all – dreams don't end – one piles on another – dreams just drift, like a picture or a view with mist over it, and then, in the mist, another picture taking shape – always one putting the other out – never an end.

He had been, in a way, trying to get back to this place all week, as if it was his last chance—

But now he was outside. The door was shut. It was windy and dangerous outside— The colt – he began to dress hurriedly. Today or tomorrow he must choose his colt. He would ride up now on to the range and look at the yearlings again.

It was still dark when he stole out of the front door and felt the terrace grass under his feet. No one had heard him. That was good. He didn't want Howard along. Going out in the early morning was almost like going into the underwater world, or the world of a picture, or in a dream. Not quite so safe as a dream because he did have to watch his horse, or, if he was climbing on Castle Rock, he had to be careful of his footing, but still nothing like the ordinary world of the daytime.

He walked softly across the Green to the Calf Pasture to get his horse.

Ken had been a night wanderer ever since he had learned to walk alone and to climb over the edge of his crib. Nell would wake, hearing a sound in the hall or living room, would find the baby's crib empty and go searching for him.

She'd find him somewhere in the dark, crawling or standing unsteadily on the tail of his nightgown and would pick him up and carry him back to bed.

She tried tying the bottom of his nightgown in a knot with his feet inside, but he merely became more expert at balancing. Then she hobbled him with a soft diaper, but he learned to swing both feet together over the side of his crib, hang with little monkey hands, drop down, and shuffle instead of walk.

When he was older, sometimes he'd go outdoors in the night.

Often Nell did that herself. Restless or unable to sleep, she would slip from her bed, tie a robe around her, take pillow and blanket and go down to her hammock, and lie with her face to the sky, watching the stars.

Ken found Lady just inside the fence of the Calf Pasture, and when he held out his hand and spoke to her, she didn't move away but let him take hold of her halter and lead her out.

He had been riding Lady all week when he was exercising the geldings and looking for Rocket and inspecting the yearlings. He had gone to look at the yearlings every day, and yesterday his mother had ridden out with him. They hadn't been able to find them anywhere, until suddenly, from a high place, they heard the thunder of hoofs.

'They sounded like a regiment,' said Nell, telling about

it at supper. 'And we looked down and saw them, a stream of colour flying down the draw. It was beautiful to watch them! They shone in the sun – sorrel and black and bay and roan – the flowing movement – so gay, so free, so frolicsome!'

And then they had ridden down to the yearlings and dismounted among them, and Nell exclaimed upon the way their first year of life changed their appearance – dark chestnuts turned to sorrels, a pink roan changed to a blue, blacks lightened to brown, odd spots and marking vanished completely; and conformation altered almost beyond recognition.

'They look stunning,' she told Rob. 'Smooth and sleek and glossy, their little hides so full and taut they look as if they would burst.'

Ken himself had been dazed by the beauty of them. The rich feeling – one of them his own, but which? He wanted them all, and until he chose, in a way, they were all his.

Ken led Lady up the little path through the Gorge, into the corrals, and then into the dark stable, put the catch on her halter, poured a measure of oats in the feed box in the manger before her, and began to groom her. Dad said use saddles – can't see why – better do it anyway—

Lady was a big red roan with a black tail and mane. She moved quickly, her head had a proud, high carriage; her dark eyes were full and intelligent.

Ken slid around her, close to her haunches, one hand on her tail, and then gave her a whack and said, 'Get over!'

The mare moved over with her quick strong step and Ken rubbed down her other side. He put on the saddle blanket, then the saddle, and cinched it as tight as he could, remembering the blanket he had lost; lastly the bridle – she had finished her oats. He led her out of the corral and shut the gate. There was a rock there upon which he often stood to mount the tallest horses. He led Lady up to it. First he tried the cinch again. Loose! She always blew herself up when she was being saddled. That was what he had forgotten to do the other day with Cigarette. He took the cinch up three more holes, mounted, and moved off.

The four broncs that Ross was breaking were grazing in the Stable Pasture close by the corrals, and when they saw him, they trotted over to him, and Ken drew rein and stood there, letting them come up and sniff and nicker at Lady; and she nickered back. When he went on they followed for a little while, and then turned back to the corrals – waiting for their oats, he thought. Ross always gave each one a measure of oats before he worked them. Their names were Gangway, Don, Rumba and Blazes.

Sometimes, Ken thought, as he cantered towards the County Road gate, the names his mother gave the colts in their first summer didn't stick, because the colts changed so. There had been Irish Elegance, so smooth and classy-looking the first summer that Nell said she was naming him after a beautiful, copper-coloured, California rose. But the second summer he had turned into a little mick, so they dropped the *Elegance* and just call him *Irish*.

Ross was having a tough time breaking Gangway, a big blood bay out of Taggert, the tallest and handsomest of the four. Yesterday Ken and Howard had sat on the corral fence watching Ross working with him. Gangway was bucking, and Ross had called to Howard to open the corral gate and let him out. The horse bucked out of the gate with him, and Ross swung his quirt, and spurred him, and Gangway sun-fished and cork-screwed and jack-knifed. Ross sat with a little grin and his quirt going all the time, and when he came past Ken, exploding in great grass-hopper leaps, he said, 'Might's well keep him goin' and git it outen his system.'

When it was over and he had ridden Gangway back into the corral and dismounted, Ross went over to the fence and stood hanging on to it, vomiting.

Ken had to dismount to open the gate to the Country

Road. He was careful to hold the rein tight as he led Lady through and closed the gate behind him. He found another rock to mount by and started up the Saddle Back.

All the clouds had turned pink, and behind them the sky was a faraway, fiery blue.

The higher he climbed the wider the sky was, and the farther stretched the fleet of tattered clouds. They were getting more colour every minute, some of them blazed crimson. All the stars had disappeared except one, which shone between two clouds, bright gold.

Lady wanted her head.

There was a strong current of sympathy between the boy and the mare. When he wanted to stop and look around she understood perfectly and stood with ears pricked and head turning, absorbed in contemplation just as he was. And at exactly the moment when he had had enough, she knew it, and would move forward without the signal.

Today she was excited by the colour and the electric quality of the air and the feeling of movement in the grass and the sky, and she kept asking for a free rein. When Ken gave it to her, she stretched out her nose and went up the steepest part of the Saddle Back at a gallop.

Ken looked for the yearlings where they had been yesterday but there was no sign of them. He rode around for an hour, thinking that Shorty would have taken him right to them, but Lady didn't have that much sense, she was just excited and wanting to run in any direction. All the sunrise colours had gone now, and the torn shreds of clouds were purple and grey and stormy looking.

Ken rode up to the highest peak of the Saddle Back so that he could look all around for dozens of miles; but the range was empty; not a head of stock anywhere. Still, he knew they could be hidden in the folds of the hills and never show an ear – but which fold? Which hill?

He rode on, and suddenly, coming around a curve, he

saw Banner standing out in front of the brood mares, intent and alert, gathered for action.

Ken had barely time to turn his head when he saw Rocket and a sorrel filly cantering towards the bunch, and then he saw Banner trot out to meet them with lowered head and an expression of irresistible intention in his whole body.

Rocket and the young sorrel halted together. Rocket whinnied. Banner screamed. His head snaked along the grass. He reached them and circled around them both. Rocket began to gallop away. Banner pursued, first on one side of her then on the other. The sorrel colt clung to its mother's side, whinnying nervously. She got in Banner's way. He gave a vicious, snarling neigh, plunged at the little one and bit it in the ribs. It screamed and fled, Banner pursuing.

Lady was taut and trembling with excitement, as Ken was himself. The brood mares, too, were motionless, watching the chase.

The filly showed Banner a clean pair of heels. How she could run!

Rocket trotted nervously up and down near the brood mares. The filly made a big circle, with Banner thundering after her. She came back to the mares, and as she passed them Banner swerved and went for Rocket. The filly fled past Ken. He saw frightened eyes in a tangle of streaming hair and slim legs, and a pang went through him. For a fraction of a second she had looked at him, and it was like an appeal. He wheeled his mount and followed her, turning in the saddle to look back at Rocket.

Rocket was cantering away again with Banner close beside her and before the curve of a hill shut them from view, Ken saw her come to a stop, and the great body of the stallion rear over her. For a moment the two of them, twisted into one shape, were sculptured against the stormy sky.

When Ken turned and looked again for the filly she was nowhere in sight. He pulled Lady up short. The range was empty, with no movement but the clouds and the grass, and no sound but the panting of the mare he rode and the thud of his own heart beating.

Rocket's colt – a yearling, a filly – and *his own*. He hadn't had to choose one after all. She had just come to him. His own because of that second's cry for help that had come from her eyes to his; his own because of her wild beauty and speed, his own because his heart burned with him at the sight and thought of her; his own because – well, just his own.

Then, from far ahead of him came an excited whinny – another and another. The filly appeared from nowhere, a tiny shape, running on a ridge in front of him, tail streaming against the dark tattered clouds; she plunged over the ridge, he heard more whinnies, he kicked Lady in the ribs and gave her her head, and in a few moments stood on the ridge, looking down, and saw the beautiful filly rejoining the band of yearlings, who welcomed her with excited chatterings as school-children welcome each other at reunion in the autumn.

Ken rode down the mountain in a daze of happiness. No dream he had ever had, no imagination of adventure or triumph could touch this moment. He felt as if he had burst out of his old self and was something entirely new – and that the world had burst into something new too. So this was it – this was what being alive meant— Oh, my filly, my filly, my beautiful—

Chapter Thirteen

'For once you're back to breakfast on time,' said Rob, as Ken took his seat at the table.

Nell filled Ken's bowl with oatmeal and passed it to him.

Ever since she had read in the Government bulletins that all prize stock was raised on elaborate formulas of mixed grains – *or ground oats* – and had noticed that the dogs, when they were hungry, squirmed through the wire fence into the calves' corral and ate the ground oats from the feed boxes, oatmeal had a place on her breakfast table. If you can raise good calves and colts on it, I guess you can raise boys, she reasoned. And McLaughlin, with a long line of oat-eating Scottish ancestors behind his brawn and toughness, agreed.

With the oatmeal there was always a big pitcher of yellow Guernsey cream and a bowl of brown sugar. Nell, smiling, pushed them towards Ken, noticing the unusual colour in his face. The boy flashed a glance at his mother; his eyes were dark with excitement. His whole face was lit up – transfigured really – and she felt a slight sense of shock. What had happened? He had been different all week, more sure of himself, more alert and happy, but this—

Rob McLaughlin was looking at Ken too, not missing a thing. Something had happened that morning on the range—

'What horse did you ride?' he asked.

'Lady.'

'And where is she now? On her way to the border?' jocularly.

'I put her in the Home Pasture. She's out there at the fountain now.'

'Was she hot?'

'No, sir, I cooled her off coming home.' There was a little smile of pride on Ken's face, and Nell thought, all the right answers, so far.

The examination went on. 'Did you give her a good workout?'

'Yes, sir.'

'Then don't ride her again today. Take Baldy if you want a horse.'

'Yes, sir.'

'Break anything? Lose anything?'

'No, sir.'

Rob laughed. He leaned over and patted Ken on the head. 'Good work, young man – coming along!'

Ken burst out laughing. He was so excited it was hard to sit still and answer properly. He wasn't going to tell about his colt yet – not till tomorrow when the week was up. But it was hard to hold it in, hard not to jump up and run around the kitchen, shouting and crowing. Anyway – he could tell about Rocket—

'I didn't *lose* anything, I *found* something!' He boasted, shovelling in big spoonfuls of oatmeal. 'I found Rocket. She's back.'

'Where?' demanded Rob and Nell and Howard all together.

'With the brood mares.'

'Good,' said McLaughlin. 'Let's see – what day would this be after her colt, Nell?'

'If the colt was less than a week old when she lost it,' calculated Nell.

'Yes – and then this past week – yes, somewhere between the ninth and fourteenth day. That's about it,' McLaughlin grinned. 'So the wild woman came back of herself.'

'She came up from the South, and Banner went out to get her. She's bred already.'

'I'll say she is,' said McLaughlin.

Nell went to the stove, lifted the bacon out of the hot fat and laid it on a platter. 'Orders, please,' she cried.

'*Two on a raft and wreck 'em!*' shouted Rob jovially, with his big, white-toothed smile.

'*One, looking at you!*' shouted Ken hilariously.

Howard jumped up. 'I'll do yours *over and easy,* Mother—' No one could do Nell's egg to suit her like Howard. She liked it lightly fried on one side, then lightly on the other, not broken. It had to be flipped. Rob could flip them but he made a big to-do about it and tossed them high and many a one landed on the stove or the edge of the skillet. Howard poured a little of the hot bacon grease into a one-egg skillet and broke an egg in. While it crackled and spat, he salted it carefully, and in a moment loosened the curling brown edges, then with a smooth motion of his wrist, gave the pan a lift and a thrust, and the egg rose a few inches into the air, turned a slow somersault, and slid back into the fat.

Carrying the hot plates with holders, Nell distributed the eggs, and set the bacon on the table. She was still thinking about Ken, and kept looking at him. Every time he caught her eye, he smiled blissfully. He was all excited –

there was something he was not telling – something he had seen out on the range that morning – the colt, of course, the colt—

'Nell,' said Rob, 'are you very busy this morning?'

'Nothing special – no baking or cleaning – why?'

'How'd you like to break a bronc for me?'

Nell looked up quickly. 'One of the four? That little mare, Rumba?'

'Yes.'

'I'd love to!'

'Why doesn't Ross do it?' asked Howard.

'Ross is too tough.' Rob's face looked grim. 'I'm not going to let him monkey with her. I've stood all I can with the other three – I wouldn't be surprised if Don's knees are damaged.'

'Not permanently?' cried Nell.

'Well, it'll take a long time for the swelling to go down. He threw himself about so. And, all tied up the way Ross had him, he kept falling on his knees. I had to walk away – couldn't look at it. Don't like to interfere with a man when he's been hired to do a job and is doing it his own way, but I couldn't stick it. The little mare – why her feet would fit in a tea cup, as dainty as a fawn. And her forelegs—' he picked up Ken's arm, 'about as big round as Ken's wrist.'

'She's a very funny, special little mare,' said Nell. 'I remember her last summer when you brought her in to halter-break her. She fell in the water trough on her back and wouldn't get up.'

Ken remembered too, laughing, 'Yes – she stayed there all afternoon with her feet sticking straight up.'

Howard persisted, 'Then why don't you do it, Dad?'

'I'm far too heavy, Howard. I've been on her and taught her a bit, and she's used to the saddle all right but she needs a light rider; and she's afraid of Ross – even if I didn't let him tie her up. She shakes every time she sees him.'

'Could I ride her?' asked Howard.

'You're light enough, but it isn't only the actual weight. There's something a bit heavy handed about you, Howard. I saw you give Calico's head a bad jerk the other day.'

Howard scowled. 'He was swinging his head up and down. I hate that.'

'So you punished him?'

Howard nodded. McLaughlin said quietly, 'Sometimes one has to punish a horse. Calico's got a bad habit with his head, but you gave him more than he needed. Little Rumba couldn't take anything like that at this stage of her training. It might start her bucking, and I don't want her ever to buck. She needs to be reassured and just held nicely, and sort of coaxed.'

'What about me?' demanded Ken.

McLaughlin laughed. 'Why you'd go off into a dream and the horse could run away with you and you wouldn't know it until ten miles later you'd wake up and wonder where you were. What you've got, Ken, is fine hands, but no control. Rumba needs someone with authority. Your mother's got that, and hands like yours, and she's lighter in the saddle than any of you – not pounds, but balance; seat. I want you both in the corral when your mother rides Rumba. You'll learn something.'

When Nell walked up to the stables she was dressed in well-cut jodhpurs made of carefully softened and faded blue-jean denim. Suitable clothes for her ranch life had been hard to find. She hated to be untidy – hated to be constrained; boots and breeches she found too heavy and binding, so she had her white linen jodhpurs (from Abercrombie and Fitch) copied by a local tailor in blue-jean material. She had half a dozen pairs of these; they were nearly indestructible, light enough to be cool, washed perfectly, and were very becoming to her slender, free-moving body. A darker blue jersey polo shirt with very short sleeves left her brown arms bare; she wore pigskin gloves, a round blue linen hat with a narrow brim to pull down over her eyes and stick on against the Wyoming winds – (it was said by the local wits that, in Wyoming, you can tell a stranger from a native because the stranger, if his hat blows off, will pursue it) – and on her feet, under the straps of her trousers, soft tan jodphur shoes with small chainless spurs set into the leather of the heel. Even so, long before the day was done she was weary of the denim and leather, and was glad to get back into light cotton dresses.

Rumba, saddled and bridled, was waiting, tied to the post. Ross came riding into the corral on Gangway, and dismounted.

'Mornin', Missus,' he said to Nell, managing to convey both gallantry and deference in his slow drawling voice; and Nell again thought, with a little glow of pleasure, that *Missus* was a royal title in the West. Ross, by the very tilt of his small body as he faced her, put himself at her service.

'How's the pony this morning?' asked McLaughlin.

'A bit spooky and a little stiff – but travellin' all right.'

'Mother's going to ride Rumba,' said Ken.

Ross's eyes moved quickly to Rumba, then to McLaughlin. He busied himself loosening the cinch on Gangway, and said quietly, 'She ain't ready to ride yet. She ain't been sacked out with her feet tied, like I done with Gangway and the others.'

McLaughlin said quietly, 'Rumba's feet are too small and her legs too delicate to tie up.'

'I wouldn't ride her myself,' insisted Ross, 'lessen I was in a Rodeo and paid to. Them hot-bloods is worse than broncs if once they git to buckin'.'

'I think she'll be all right,' said McLaughlin. 'Mrs McLaughlin's about the right weight; she's a little timid, but she won't have any trouble.'

'Timid!' marvelled Ross. 'I put my wife on a ole plug once that was broke pretty fair, and it got to runnin' a little,

124

and she busted out cryin' and came back bawlin'. Did I get it!'

'You don't look old enough to have a wife, Ross,' said Nell.

'I got a wife and two kids 'bout half as big as Howard and Ken,' said Ross grinning. 'I'm twenty-five. My brother's twenty-six.'

Ross rolled himself a cigarette and sat down against the corral fence. Howard and Ken climbed up and sat on the top railing. Nell walked over to Rumba, and Rob stood beside Ross talking to him, and pretending not to watch.

Rumba became taut, her ears forward, looking at Nell, her head up as if she was on the point of rearing, and her hind legs crouching. Nell held out a hand and talked to her reassuringly, but when the hand touched her head, Rumba jerked up. Nell kept stroking her and talking to her until at last the mare was quiet and her trembling and crouching stopped. Nell turned her back to her, leaning against the post, and stood there talking to Rob and Ross, to give the mare a chance to get used to her body and her voice. Under the eye of a human being an unbroken horse is in terror.

'Is your brother a bronco-buster too, Ross?'

'No, Ma'am, he ain't got the heart. You just gotta have the heart fur it.'

'Do you do a lot of it, Ross?'

'Sure do, Ma'am – all summer long. All over the country, wherever there's a show. One summer I made a thousand dollars. As soon as one Rodeo's over, I'm itchin' to git to the next. Everyone says I'll git killed, but, hell, what's the difference? Better than work at that—'

Rumba, feeling more free now because no eye was upon her, reached out her nose and Nell felt the soft muzzle against her back between the shoulders. She paid no attention, but Rumba, as if alarmed by the smell of her, jumped back.

Ross was talking about the Rodeo Riders' Union, called

COWBOYS' TURTLE ASSOCIATION, to which he belonged. At a Texas Rodeo, they struck for a share of the gate receipts in addition to the prize money. This held up the show for a couple of hours, but they won out.

Rumba tried again. This time she was bolder and took a long breath, drawing in the very essence of the human being who, she knew in advance, was going to mount her. Nell knew that if a horse hates the smell of a person it is hardly possible to make friends. On the other hand, if he likes it, friendship is only a matter of time and patience.

Obviously Nell passed the test, for Rumba rested then, with her nose touching Nell's arm, her eyes and ears directed to the men who were talking, indulging her natural curiosity. Rob did not want the little mare to feel she was the centre of attention. He said horses were like people – no one liked to feel all eyes upon them except show-offs, like Gangway, who always expected to be watched.

'Don't you ever get hurt, bronco bustin'?' asked Howard, his feet dangling over Ross's head from where he sat on the fence rail above him.

'I'll say,' was the laconic answer. 'Last summer I hurt myself in every show I was in—'

'Break anything?'

'Ribs, collar bone – back hurt – knee wrenched. Spent most of my time in hospital. When I went in fur the third trip last summer, I was broke. They waan't goin' to let me out till I'd paid my bill. I says, You might as well let me out for I ain't got no way to make money layin' here in hospital, I got to git ridin' before I kin pay you off. Well, they wouldn't. An' they was arguin' with me, and I says, You call up the Rodeo Committee here, and tell 'em about me not bein' able to pay my bill. Well, I guess they did, for they let me out, and I never heard nuthin' more about the bill, neither.'

Nell turned around to Rumba and saw that the mare had accepted her. She no longer shivered, but kept her eyes on

Nell without fear. Nell gathered up the rains, still stroking her and talking to her. She went to the side, put both arms on top of the saddle and leaned there, now and then lifting her knee up under the mare's belly as if she was going to mount.

Rumba showed no alarm. Her head was turned a little, one eye back watching Nell.

Now Rob joined her and held Rumba's head. Nell put her foot in the stirrup, mounted very slowly, swung her leg over the haunch, got her seat, and Rob untied the halter rope from the post and adjusted the stirrups.

A little pressure of the legs, a little urging with voice and hands, and Rumba started off slowly. Nell was careful to hold the reins fairly short so that, in case the mare took a sudden notion to buck, she could not get her head down. They made the round of the corral several times, then Rob opened the gate, he and Ross mounted Don and Gangway, and all three rode down to the practice field for a morning's work.

Chapter Fourteen

When Ken went to bed that night, he kissed his mother, and then threw his arms around her and held her fiercely for a moment.

Smiling, she put her hand on his head. 'Well, Kennie—' her violet eyes were soft and understanding.

He went upstairs, smiling back at her over his shoulder, having a secret with her. He knew that she knew.

He lit the candle in his room and stood staring at the flickering light. This was like a last day. The last day before school is out, or before Christmas, or before his mother came back after a visit in the East. Tomorrow was the day when, really, his life would begin. He would get his colt.

He had been thinking about the filly all day. He could still see her streaking past him, the wild terrified eyes turned to him in appeal – the hair blown back from her face like a girl's – and the long, slim legs moving so fast they were a blur, like the spokes of a wheel.

He couldn't quite remember the colour of her. Orange – pink – tangerine colour – tail and mane white, like the hair of an Albino boy at school. *Albino* – of course, her grandsire *was* the Albino – the famous Albino stud. He felt a little uneasiness at this; Albino blood wasn't safe blood for a filly to have. But perhaps she hadn't much of it. Perhaps the cream tail and mane came from Banner, her sire. Banner had a cream tail and mane too when he was a colt; lots of sorrel colts had. He hoped she would be docile and good – not like Rocket. Which would she take after? Rocket? Or Banner? He hadn't had time to get a good look into her eyes. Rocket's eyes had that wild, wicked, white ring around them—

Ken began to undress. Walking around his room, his eyes caught sight of the pictures on the wall – they didn't interest him.

The speed of her! *She had run away from Banner.* He kept thinking about that. It hardly seemed possible. His father always said Rocket was the fastest horse on the ranch, and now Rocket's filly had run away from Banner.

He had gone up to look at her again that afternoon; hadn't been able to keep away. He had ridden up on Baldy and found the yearlings all grazing together on the far side of Saddle Back. And when they saw him and Baldy, they all took off across the mountain.

Ken had galloped along the crest above them watching the filly. Footing made no difference to her. She floated across the ravines, always two lengths ahead of the others. Her pinkish cream mane and tail whipped in the wind. Her long delicate legs had only to aim, it seemed, at a particular spot, for her to reach it and sail on. She seemed to Ken a fairy horse. She was simply nothing like any of the others.

Riding down the mountain again Ken had traced back all his recollections of her. The summer before, when he and Howard had seen the spring colts, he hadn't especially noticed her. He remembered that he had seen her even before that, soon after she was born. He had been out with Gus, one day, in the meadow, during the spring holiday. They were clearing some driftwood out of the irrigation ditch, and they had seen Rocket standing in a gully on the hillside, quiet for once, and eyeing them cautiously.

'Ay bet she got a colt,' said Gus; and they walked carefully up the draw. Rocket gave a wild snort, thrust her feet out, shook her head wickedly, then fled away. And as they reached the spot, they saw standing there the wavering, pinkish colt, barely able to keep its feet. It gave a little squeak and started after its mother on crooked, wobbling legs.

'Yee whiz! Look at de little *flicka*!' said Gus.

'What does *flicka* mean, Gus?'

'Swedish for little gurl, Ken—'

He had seen the filly again late in the fall. She was half pink, half yellow – with streaked untidy looking hair. She was awkward and ungainly, with legs too long, haunches a little too high.

And then he had gone away to school and hadn't seen her again until now – *she ran away from Banner*— Her eyes – they had looked like balls of fire this morning. What colour were they? Banner's were brown with flecks of gold, or gold with flecks of brown— Her speed and her delicate curving lines made him think of a greyhound he had seen running once, but really she was more like just a little girl than anything – the way her face looked, the way her blonde hair blew – a little girl—

Ken blew out the light and got into bed, and before the smile had faded from his face, he was asleep—

'*I'll take that sorrel filly of Rocket's; the one with the cream tail and mane.*'

Ken made his announcement at the breakfast table.

After he spoke there was a moment's astonished silence. Nell groped for recollection, and said, 'A sorrel filly? I can't seem to remember that one at all – what's her name?'

But Rob remembered. The smile faded from his face as he looked at Ken. '*Rocket's filly*, Ken?'

'Yes, sir.' Ken's face changed too. There was no mistaking his father's displeasure.

'I was hoping you'd make a wise choice. You know what I think of Rocket – that whole line of horses—'

Ken looked down; the colour ebbed from his cheeks. 'She's fast, Dad, and Rocket's fast—'

'It's the worst line of horses I've got. There's never one amongst them with real sense. The mares are hellions and the stallions outlaws; they're untamable.'

'I'll tame her.'

Rob guffawed. 'Not I nor anyone, has ever been able to really tame any one of them.'

Kennie's chest heaved.

'Better change your mind, Ken. You want a horse that'll be a real friend to you, don't you?'

'Yes—' Kennie's voice was unsteady.

'Well, you'll never make a friend of that filly. Last fall after all the colts had been weaned and separated from their dams, she and Rocket got back together – no fence'll hold 'em – she's all out and scarred up already from tearing through barbed wire after that bitch of a mother of hers.'

Kennie looked stubbornly at his plate.

'Change your mind?' asked Howard briskly.

'No.'

'I don't remember seeing her this year,' said Nell.

'No,' said Rob. 'When I drove you up a couple of months ago to look them over and name them and write down their descriptions, there was a bunch missing, don't you remember?'

'Oh, yes – then she's never been named—'

'I've named her,' said Ken. 'Her name is Flicka.'

'Flicka,' said Nell cheerfully. 'That's a pretty name.'

But McLaughlin made no comment, and there was a painful silence.

Ken felt he ought to look at his father, but he was afraid to. Everything was changed again, they weren't friends any more. He forced himself to look up, met his father's angry eyes for a moment, then quickly looked down again.

'Well,' McLaughlin barked. 'It's your funeral – or hers. Remember one thing. I'm not going to be out of pocket on account of this – every time you turn around you cost me money—'

Ken looked up, wonderingly, and shook his head.

'Time's money, remember,' said his father. 'I had planned to give you a reasonable amount of help in breaking and taming your colt. Just enough. But there's no such thing as enough with those horses.'

Gus appeared at the door and said, 'What's today, Boss?'

McLaughlin shouted, 'We're going out on the range to bring in the yearlings. Saddle Taggert, Lady and Shorty.'

Gus disappeared, and McLaughlin pushed his chair back. 'First thing to do is get her in. Do you know where the yearlings are?'

'They were on the far side of the Saddle Back late yesterday afternoon – the west end, down by Dale's ranch.'

'Well, you're the Boss on this round-up – you can ride Shorty.'

McLaughlin and Gus and Ken went out to bring the yearlings in. Howard stood at the County gate to open and close it.

They found the yearlings easily. When they saw that they were being pursued, they took to their heels. Ken was entranced to watch Flicka – the speed of her, the power, the wildness – she led the band.

He sat motionless, just watching and holding Shorty in when his father thundered past on Taggert and shouted, 'Well, what's the matter? Why didn't you turn 'em?'

Ken woke up and galloped after them.

Shorty brought in the whole band. The corral gates were

closed, and an hour was spent shunting the ponies in and out and through the chutes until Flicka was left alone in the small round branding corral. Gus mounted Shorty and drove the others away, through the gate, and up the Saddle Back.

But Flicka did not intend to be left. She hurled herself against the poles which walled the corral. She tried to jump them. They were seven feet high. She caught her front feet over the top rung, clung, scrambled, while Kennie held his breath for fear the slender legs would be caught between the bars and snapped. Her hold broke, she fell over backwards, rolled, screamed, tore around the corral.

One of the bars broke. She hurled herself again. Another went. She saw the opening, and as neatly as a dog crawls through a fence, inserted her head and forefeet, scrambled through and fled away, bleeding in a dozen places.

As Gus was coming back, just about to close the gate to the County Road, the sorrel whipped through it, sailed across the road and ditch with her inimitable floating leap, and went up the side of the Saddle Back like a jack rabbit.

From way up the mountain, Gus heard excited whinnies, as she joined the band he had just driven up, and the last he saw of them they were strung out along the crest running like deer.

'Yee whiz!' said Gus, and stood motionless and staring until the ponies had disappeared over the ridge.

Then he closed the gate, remounted Shorty, and rode back to the corrals.

Walking down from the corrals, Rob McLaughlin gave Kennie one more chance to change his mind. 'Better pick a horse that you have some hope of riding one day. I'd have got rid of this whole line of stock if they weren't so damned fast that I've had the fool idea that someday there might turn out one gentle one in the lot, and I'd have a race horse. But there's never been one so far, and it's not going to be Flicka.'

'It's not going to be Flicka,' chanted Howard.

'Maybe she *might* be gentled,' said Ken; and although his lips trembled, there was fanatical determination in his eye.

'Ken,' said McLaughlin, 'it's up to you. If you say you want her, we'll get her. But she wouldn't be the first of that line to die rather than give in. They're beautiful and they're fast, but let me tell you this, young man, they're *loco*!'

Ken flinched under his father's direct glance.

'If I go after her again, I'll not give up *whatever comes*, understand what I mean by that?'

'Yes.'

'What do you say?'

'I want her.'

'That's settled then,' and suddenly Rob seemed calm and indifferent. 'We'll bring her in again tomorrow or next day – I've got other work for this afternoon.'

Chapter Fifteen

Ken lay face down on the pine needles under the trees on the Hill over the Green. His chin was propped in his hands. Looking down, he could see the Green and the house. Now and then he could hear voices from the kitchen. Howard was in there with their mother – he was telling her about what had happened when they brought Flicka in.

They were getting dinner. It wouldn't be long before it was time to eat. He wished he didn't have to go down at all. Howard would watch him. His father would ignore him or glare at him. And if he looked at his mother, that would be the worst of all—

The dogs were both on the terrace. It was a hot, sultry day, and Tim and Gus were putting the awning over the Pergola. Nell had been saying for several days it was time to put it up – the sun was getting too strong. Ken watched them working at it, Tim up on the roof, Gus on the terrace, pulling it and straightening it over the lattice, Tim nailing it on. Ken couldn't figure out what was going to happen. Was he going to get the filly? She was his. No one had questioned that – but would they be able to get her? Would there perhaps be several more efforts like this morning's, and then would they give up, and would his filly be forever out there on the range? Wild, alone, free – not friends with him at all? And his father not friends either? Everything a mess – the summer spoiled – Howard with Highboy, crowing over him more than ever?

There was the sound of a car coming, and looking off between the trees, Ken saw a long grey smart-looking car coming around the bend of the road. It tooled along, over the bridge, finally across the cattle-guard and up behind the house.

He wondered who it was. His father was already coming out of the front door on to the terrace, and now, around the end of the house, the visitor appeared – Ken couldn't make out who, a very tall man (not a rancher) with a wide felt hat; and his father held out both hands and gave him a loud and noisy welcome. Perhaps it was an officer from the Army Post.

Nell came running out of the house with her apron on, and there were very jolly greetings again, and then Howard came and Ken could see him introduced and shaking hands.

They talked for a while, then pulled up chairs on the terrace and sat down. His mother went back into the house. Gus and Tim had finished putting up the canvas, and went towards the bunk house. Howard sat on the terrace wall, close enough to hear what they were saying, and played with the dogs.

Ken felt very out of it all— He wondered if the stranger was going to stay to dinner, then forgot him again thinking about Flicka. He put his head down on his arm. There was a fly somewhere near, one of the summer 'racing' flies. They raced and raced around you in circles – never went very far away. They were always there underneath the pines. Though they weren't really nice, the sound of them made you happy because they went with summer, and hot sun, and pine needles.

He poked with a stick at the pine needles, digging a little hole. There were some ants running in and out of the needles, very busy. He put his stick in the way of an ant, and watched the ant crawl over. Then he shook it off, put the stick down again, and again the ant crawled over. He could keep on doing that all morning, he thought, and a hundred times the ant would crawl over the stick and still not be getting anywhere.

Flicka – how was *she* feeling? Would she remember them? Would she hate them all, himself too? People always said horses never forgot. She had a lot of bad things to remember – Banner chasing her, and biting her; then being driven into the corral, and the way she got hurt and scratched when she crawled out.

The bell was ringing. He roused himself and looked down. Nell had sent Howard to the spring house to ring the big locomotive bell which hung in an iron frame in the very top of the peaked roof of the spring house. His father had bought the bell from the Railroad – it was bright brass and lined with scarlet, and a wire was attached to it, which hung down over the roof to the ground. There was a little wooden handle on the end of the wire. You could ring the bell by holding the wooden handle, getting a good swing going with your arms, and pulling rhythmically, and when the bell got going it sounded all over the ranch, up at the stables and down in the meadows.

Howard was ringing for him. They didn't know where he was. Ken got up, ran down the hill, crossed the Green, and went in through the kitchen so he could wash his hands and slick his hair down.

His mother was there and she seemed a little excited.

'Mr Sargent is here, dear, he's going to stay for dinner, and we're eating in the dining room – you boys will help me—'

In a moment Ken was on the terrace shaking hands with Charley Sargent, and his father's arm was across his shoulder and he was saying, 'And here's the other one – I've got a couple of jockeys, you see—'

And Charley Sargent, whom he remembered now, was shaking hands with him warmly, and he was looking up into the long, humorous face under the big sombrero; and suddenly he felt much better, because everyone seemed to have forgotten about Flicka, or that he was in disgrace again.

They had a fricassee of some cottontails he and Howard had shot yesterday evening, and his mother had cooked them with a border of fluffy white rice, and a sauce of mushrooms and cream, and Charley Sargent kept raving about the bread and asking for more and more of it, and saying he never got anything but bakery bread at home, and had thought bread baking was a lost art in Wyoming.

Howard and Ken didn't say very much, but the three grown-ups talked; and it was very interesting, because everything Charley Sargent said, he said in a funny way that made them laugh. They were talking about something very exciting – the shipping of a carload of horses from Sargent's ranch down to Los Angeles, for a man there to sell on assignment to a polo club. There was space enough in the car for four more horses, and Sargent wanted to know if McLaughlin wanted to go in with him on the deal, pay part of the shipping expenses and ship four horses.

Ken looked at his father and could see that he was in the best humour – his eyes blue and flashing, and his big white teeth laughing in his dark face; and his mother was happy too, her hair brushed so smooth and sleek down over her forehead, and her eyes, that were the same colour as the dark purple iris in the bowl on the centre of the table, wide open and smiling – and dimples in her cheeks – and she had a funny, gay remark to make to everything Charley Sargent said; so, soon they were all shouting, the boys laughing too.

After dinner McLaughlin took Sargent into his study, and Ken and Howard cleared the table while their mother washed the dishes and tidied up the kitchen, and it was while they were doing that, that they heard their father talking about Rocket.

The men were sitting with tall glasses and a bottle of Scotch, and McLaughlin was shouting.

'I'm telling you! With all your race horses, you've got nothing like this. A bronc, unbroken – nobody's been able to break her, but I can show you that she-devil running like nothing you've ever seen – twenty-five – twenty-eight – thirty miles an hour—'

Ken carried a tray of plates in to his mother, and said to her, 'Dad's telling him about Rocket—'

Nell went to the door and stood listening a moment, her dish towel over her shoulder and a dripping glass in her hand. Rob and Sargent were both laughing and shouting now – 'You're crazy—'

'I'm telling you!'

'There ain't no such animal!'

'What'll you bet?'

'If I could get a mare that could do twenty-eight without training—'

'If you can break her she'll make a fortune for you on the track.'

'I've got a bronco-buster can break any horse that was ever foaled.'

'Except Rocket! But if you can't break her, you can get race horses out of her—'

'Jake can break her, I tell you – if she's worth breaking—'

139

'Worth it! Didn't I tell you?'

'Can she really do thirty an hour?'

'I'll sell her to you cheap.'

'How much?'

'Five hundred I'm asking—'

'How fast did you say?'

'Got a stop watch?'

'I've got a speedometer—'

Everything was forgotten except running Rocket and timing her, and before Nell had finished going over the dining-room rug with the carpet sweeper McLaughlin was out shouting for Ross and Guss, and they were all up at the stables saddling up to bring in the brood mares.

'Bring 'em all—' said McLaughlin. 'I won't take the chances of bringing her in alone— I need Banner to help me.'

Sargent, in his smart tweed business suit, and his tan Oxfords, and a big sombrero on his thin grey hair, rode Shorty; as luck would have it the brood mare bunch were not very far away on the Saddle Back, and before the afternoon was half over, they were all in the corrals, milling around, Banner very curious as to why they were in, keeping his eye on McLaughlin. Rocket was wild-eyed and jumpy as usual, especially when she found herself singled out, separated from the others, and all alone in the small corral.

'Why the necklace?' said Sargent. 'Is that a mark of special distinction?' But while he spoke, he was walking around the mare, eyeing her shrewdly, noticing the great width of chest, the wide flaring nostrils, the long, springy hocks – she was a little too high in the haunches and too long in the body. He didn't like her eyes or the way she held her nose up.

Rob was ashamed of the old piece of rope around her neck. 'I've been intending to get that off her—'

'Now's a good time—'

Rob laughed. 'I've told you she's a hellion. I'm likely to lose my life trying to get that rope off— I'd rather sell her first—'

McLaughlin decided to run Rocket in the Stable Pasture, along the strip of level grass just inside the fence of the County Road. He went down to the house and everyone got into the big Studebaker, Nell and the boys in the back, and Sargent beside Rob in front. They drove back up to the stables, and Ken got out and opened the gate into the Stable Pasture, the car waited for him until he had closed it, and he hopped in again. Gus was waiting inside the corral, and when McLaughlin called to him to let Rocket out, he opened the gate, and the big mare walked slowly out alone, and stood looking around, as if wondering why the others were not coming too.

McLaughlin had stopped the car. Now he started it heading for Rocket. She moved off in the right direction; the Studebaker followed; she broke into a trot, and her head came up, and her ears pricked with excitement. McLaughlin's foot pressed heavier on the throttle; the mare gave no sign of making increased effort but kept her distance easily.

Suddenly she shied out to the side; McLaughlin swerved and circled, to drive her back to the fence, but she had another idea in her head. She shot off to the woods with such speed that in a moment or two she disappeared from sight.

McLaughlin cursed freely, but followed, dodging in and out of the trees, and finally taking one of the little trails that led down to Deercreek. They caught sight of the mare again as the car forded a shallow place in the stream. She was emerging from the aspens on the other side, and soon, on the hillside, came up against the fence which was the northern boundary of the pasture. She turned and trotted along beside it.

McLaughlin, noticing the way she kept hesitating, and

looking over the fence, said, 'She's thinking about Castle Rock Meadow again—'

The mare came to a pause and McLaughlin stopped the car, watching her.

Suddenly the mare lifted her forefeet, and without taking the trouble to jump, crashed through the fence, tearing the wires, plunging on in spite of the barbs caught in her hide. In a moment she had disappeared in the woods on the other side.

At such a time McLaughlin drew on the store of profanity accumulated during his years of service in the U.S. Army.

Charley Sargent was laughing.

'She's on her way back to Castle Rock Meadow,' said Rob. 'She lost a colt there a couple of weeks ago, and can't get it out of her head. She'll go through every fence, the bitch. More work for Gus or me tomorrow. Here Howard, get out and mend that wire—'

He pulled a pair of pliers and wire cutters from the pocket of the car and handed them to Howard.

The boy jumped out, hunted around the fence posts until he found a loose piece of wire, cut it to the needed length, drew up the broken ends and fastened them together with the short piece.

'Now,' said Rob, 'we'll surprise her by meeting her at the aspen grove. She'll be there ahead of us. Hold tight, everybody!'

They bumped through the woods, following narrow paths that bored through what seemed impenetrable greenery, growing lush and thick down here by the stream. They twisted around tree trunks and stones, finally emerging from the woods on an open hillside covered with low scrub and sage, and ran along this at so tilted an angle that the car seemed about to turn over.

But when they finally reached the aspen grove, Rocket had made her investigations, and put the matter from her mind. She was grazing calmly on the range above the meadow; she had gone through or over three fences to get there.

McLaughlin was elated. 'She's not far from the road that leads home over the north range. It's the flattest ground anywhere around. If she decides to go back to the corrals she's likely to take that way.'

He circled up slowly behind the mare. She paid no attention. He tooted the horn. Rocket hated the horn; she looked nervously around for a moment, then headed for home with the car behind her.

It was perfect ground for a workout. No one in the car spoke now, they were intent on watching the mare. She had at last broken into a canter. Every reach took her much farther than the reach of most horses, but the astonishing thing about her was the complete lack of effort. She seemed to float along. Ken remembered, with such inner rapture that it almost choked him, that Flicka had the same effortless floating gallop. Where was this hidden power in them? Perhaps the too high haunches – the slight extra length of body.

Ken and Howard and Nell were all hanging over the back of the front seat.

'Great guns!' muttered Sargent. 'She's like a locomotive – does she always run with her nose up in the air like that?'

'Yes,' said Rob, 'Star-gazer—'

'Get going,' said Sargent. 'She's not half trying.'

'Look at the speedometer,' said Rob.

'Jumping Jehoshaphat!' said Sargent.

The car went faster, the speedometer touched thirty. The mare appeared to be trying no harder, but kept her distance easily.

When Rocket reached the road which led in from the highway, she turned, going towards the house, McLaughlin after her.

'One more burst of speed, now,' cried Charley Sargent.

'If that speedometer goes over thirty I'll buy her!'

'Without even trying!' scoffed Rob, pressing his foot on the throttle, and hitting the horn. At the sound of the horn, the mare bounded forward. Sargent kept one eye on the mare and one on the speedometer. It was climbing – thirty – thirty-one – thirty-three – and was wavering just short of thirty-five – as she thundered over the little stone bridge and started up the last stretch towards the Green.

'The cattle guard, Dad!' yelled Howard.

McLaughlin did not abate his speed. Nor did Rocket. When she came to the cattle guard her reach was longer, her body rose higher, but still apparently without effort, she floated over the fifteen-foot broad jump as if it had been the creek.

Rob and Sargent went to have some more drinks, and an hour later the bargain was concluded – he would buy Rocket for five hundred dollars; delivered at his ranch, sound in wind and limb.

'And just how you'll do *that*, me lad,' he said grinning, 'is anybody's guess.'

'Leave it to me,' said Rob boastfully.

Also, Rob would complete the breaking and training of the four three-year-olds, and have them ready to ship in ten days to Los Angeles in Sargent's carload of green polo horses. And so the profitable and exciting afternoon ended, and Sargent drove away.

At supper every incident of the day was talked over, even the cottontail fricassee, and Nell's bread, and how pretty the table looked with the purple iris in the centre bowl, and the way Charley Sargent looked at Nell and paid her compliments and kidded Rob.

After supper the boys went out with their twenty-twos to get more cottontails, and Rob and Nell sat on the terrace and enjoyed the evening.

There was a magical clear light over the world that seemed to emanate from the soft indigo of the sky. Right over the Hill opposite the Green was one golden star. It twinkled coquettishly, and not very far off in the sky a single coiled mass of white cloud winked back. The cloud was full of lightning, and went on and off like an electric light. For as long as ten seconds it would flash into illumination, filled through and through with rose and gold light, then would blink a few times and go out, rumbling softly. The star twinkled merrily back. Nothing else in all the twilight world moved; it was as if everything watched the little play between the star and the cloud.

At last the sky was crowded with stars, and the cloud, grumbling and flashing intermittently, moved off and disappeared behind the hills.

'The boys went down to the meadow, didn't they? Castle Rock Meadow?' asked Nell.

'Yes – went down to get some more cottontails.'

Nell said nothing. A little breeze had sprung up and played through the pines on the Hill with a sound that was like a sigh. The earth and the pines seemed very black under the starlit heavens. In the darkness between twilight and moonrise, with the boys not returned from Castle Rock Meadow, Nell and Rob were uneasy and found nothing to say.

They were both glad when two dark shadows appeared on the Green and Howard's voice said, 'Rocket's colt's been mauled again, there's not a speck of flesh left now – it hardly even smells.'

'Maybe the mountain lion was back at it again,' said Ken.

'We hunted around for tracks, before it got dark, but we didn't see any.'

'What about cottontails?' asked Rob. 'I thought you went out hunting.'

The boys each held up two.

'Well – get on up to the spring house and skin 'em and clean 'em – it's about bedtime—'

The boys disappeared in the direction of the spring house, and presently Rob said, 'Nell—'

There was no answer. He leaned over to look at her and saw that her head had fallen sideways as she sat reclining in the long canvas chair. She was sound asleep.

Chapter Sixteen

Rob had his work cut out for him next day. Banner and the mares had been driven out soon after Sargent left. Rocket, uneasy and restless in spite of a good measure of oats poured into a feed box and set on the ground, was kept alone in one of the corrals.

'The noose?' said Nell at breakfast, pouring cream in her coffee. 'Are you going to bother to take that off before you load her?'

Rob looked outraged. 'Do you think I would deliver her with that old string around her neck?'

Howard and Ken looked at each other. That meant getting Rocket in the chute. Rocket was to be got into the chute, then she was to be got into the truck!

'Who'll drive the truck?' asked Nell.

'I'll drive it myself. I'll take Gus along – might need him.'

Breakfast was eaten quickly. McLaughlin hurried up to the corrals. Gus was told to fill the truck with petrol and oil and get it ready for the trip. Tim was to help in the chute.

They moved Rocket through the corrals without much trouble, but when she was once more in the small coop which led to the chute, and the heavy gate closed behind her, she began to snort and rear.

The narrow passage into the chute was open before her, but even though they urged her, and yelled at her, and flapped blankets and quirts over the fence on her back, she was too wise to go in. She could see through and at the far end, a heavy door blocked escape.

'It's that door,' said McLaughlin. 'She sees that there's no way out through the chute. We'll have to open that door, and let her see daylight through. Then perhaps if I rush her from here, I can drive her through. Ken, you get up there on top of the chute wall, close by the door. Open the door. If she rushes in, you slam the door shut. It's going to take quick thinking and quick action. You can lean down and handle the door from the top – it's not easy – mind you don't fall down into the chute. The doors swings from inside out – if you get it three-quarters shut and she crashes against it, she'll shut it the rest of the way herself.'

Ken climbed up on the wall of the chute, unsteady with excitement. McLaughlin, blanket on arm, climbed a few bars of the fence of the coop.

'Ready, Ken? Open the door.'

Ken leaned over and hauled the door open, and at the same moment Rob gave a yell and flapped the blanket on Rocket's haunches. Rocket saw the daylight at the far end of the chute and plunged through. Ken closed the door again – just in time – the mare crashed against it.

She was right under him, and as he pulled back, she reared and her great head and wild eyes were in his face.

'Pole, Tim!' shouted McLaughlin, and Tim, standing ready, thrust through both walls of the chute a heavy pole to cut off her backward escape. It was at the height of the mare's haunches, too high for her to get her feet over, and not so high that she could back under it.

When she came down on all four feet again, and felt the pole behind her, she began to fight.

McLaughlin climbed the wall of the chute, opposite Ken, and struggled to get hold of the frantic creature's head. She reared again, and this gave him a chance to grasp the rope with both hands. She shook her head and tried to tear loose. He hung on and was almost dragged over the wall. She screamed, thrust out her head with teeth bared. McLaughlin ducked and she dropped again, breaking his hold. She put her head down on the ground and kicked. Her legs struck the wall of the chute and one got over the pole; but in the wild fury of plunges which this caused, she got it free.

Then she reared again, and McLaughlin had another chance at her head. Ken watched the look of hot anger combined with implacable determination on his father's face. He had the clippers in his right hand, waiting his chance.

Suddenly Rocket dropped to the earth and stood quiet a moment, her sides heaving with breaths that were almost groans; and McLaughlin reached his hand down, clipped the rope, and it fell free. But at that instant the mare reared sharply again, McLaughlin could not draw back quickly enough, and the top of her head struck him in the face.

Ken saw the blood spurt from his father's eye as Rocket's foam-flecked head described a complete backward arc, and she crashed to the ground, breaking the pole behind her.

For a moment McLaughlin clung to the wall, swearing, one hand to his face, while the mare fought madly below him, her feet thundering on the walls, her great body flinging itself from one side to the other.

McLaughlin got down and put his bandana to his bleeding face. One eye was swelling rapidly. 'That's that,' he said going around into the corrals.

Rocket, screaming and grunting, was struggling desperately to right herself. She had fallen so far backward that her head and neck were almost in the coop. This gave her forelegs more freedom, and by vigorous writhings and twistings, pushing and kicking with her legs, she forced herself out of the chute and into the coop, and immediately scrambled to her feet.

'We're all set now, Gus,' said McLaughlin. 'Bring the truck in there, back it up against the far end of the chute. Tim, you get the runway and set it in the chute. We'll drive her right through the chute up the runway and into the truck.'

'Better fix dot eye, Boss,' said Gus, looking at Rob's face, 'und de cheek – dot's bad cut – split wide open. Let Missus fix up for you.'

Rob held the handkerchief over his eye. He looked down at himself. He was spattered with foam and blood. He frowned.

'Yes, I'll go down and clean up. Gus, I don't want any more trouble with that mare. You can never tell what she'll do. Once she's in the truck, we're pretty safe, but to get her there is the trick. Better saddle Shorty. I'll ride him through the chute and up the runway, and there's a chance she might follow him into the truck.'

While Tim and Gus manoeuvred the truck until its back was flush against the door of the chute, Rob went down for first aid.

'I think it really needs stitches, Rob,' said Nell, examining it closely, having washed her hands in hot water and soap, and laid out all her first-aid kit on the kitchen table. 'It's on the cheekbone, below the eye, really a wide cut.'

'Deep?' asked Rob.

'Not so very deep.'

'Fix it with tape then.'

Nell held the lips of the wound closed until the bleeding had nearly stopped, then made little bridges of narrow adhesive tape across, and finally a dressing over all.

Then she put both arms around his neck and laid her cheek against his, holding him closely. He felt a slight tremor through all her body.

'Don't worry, honey,' he said. 'It's nothing.' He patted her on the shoulder – suddenly his arms held her hard and he kissed her, then he went upstairs to change into spotless whipcord riding breeches, polished boots, and tailored jacket.

Back up at the corral again, the loading was accomplished with comparative ease. Shorty was ridden up the incline into the truck, Rocket followed. Shorty was ridden down again, and before Rocket could follow, the back of the truck was closed and escape was shut off. She was neatly enclosed in the six-foot walls of the truck, made of sturdy two-by-fours bolted together. She reared, she clawed at the rails, she neighed wildly, she plunged and leaped until again and again her feet slid out from under her and she crashed to the floor, then scrambled up to begin all over. But there was nothing she could do. No one paid any attention to her any more. Rob picked the old piece of lariat triumphantly out of the chute, and draped it around his own neck. He and Gus got into the box of the truck, and the boys begged to ride along as far as the turn on to the highway.

They passed the house, the boys hanging on the steps of the truck, shouting good-bye to Nell, who came out to wave to them.

But Rocket's story was not yet ended. Where the ranch road turned off from the Lincoln Highway, was the sign of the ranch. Every rancher is proud of his ranch sign, under which all visiting cars must pass, and exercises great ingenuity in thinking up something striking and effective.

McLaughlin's sign was a high square arch. On the broad horizontal board which was the span of it, he had painted GOOSE BAR RANCH, in red letters against a blue ground. To each side were reproductions of his brands.

As they reached the sign, Rocket's wild eyes were upon it – this strange bar, bearing down upon her from the skies – and she reared to meet it.

Standing astretch on her hind legs, her head up, the sign caught her a blow on the top of the brow. There was a great crash in the truck; McLaughlin glanced back anxiously; he pulled up, and they got out and climbed up over the sides; but Rocket lay motionless. Rob got into the truck, against Gus's anxious warnings, but there was no danger, for Rocket never moved again.

The men stood about the truck, not daring to speak until McLaughlin made a move. The colour was flooding up into his face all round the swollen purple part, and there was the look of blazing fury in his eyes which Ken expected. To be baulked or beaten – to lose something he prized – this always put McLaughlin into a rage.

He laughed harshly. 'Well, there we are,' he shouted. 'I'm glad of it. No more trouble with *that* God-damned old bitch – wish I'd shot her and all the rest of her tribe years ago— Gus, take the truck up to the old mine and dump her in – I'll walk home.'

Another truck was turning in off the highway. It came abreast of them and drew up – Williams, come back, as he had said he would, for a load of cheap horses.

'I'll sell you a carcass!' McLaughlin joshed, as Williams climbed out of his truck. They explained what had happened. Williams climbed up the side of McLaughlin's truck and looked in.

'God! What a piece of luck,' he said. 'A fine, big mare— But I've seen things like that happen before – a little bit of a blow can kill a horse, provided you land it in the right place—'

'I've got a load of horses for you, Williams,' said McLaughlin with a strange look in his eyes. 'A bunch of broncs—'

'Bring 'em on,' said Williams, jocularly, 'if we can load 'em, I'll buy 'em—'

'All the kith and kin of this mare,' said McLaughlin, savagely.

'Ought to be some good horse-flesh, if they're anything like her. How many?'

'Hardly know myself. They're all over the range. We'll have a time rounding 'em all up.'

'I've got all day.'

'I'll send Tim back to help you, Gus,' said McLaughlin, and rode back to the ranch in Williams's truck.

When Tim came, he and Howard and Ken rode up to the old mine with Gus to see the last of Rocket.

The boys lay on the ground at the edge of the deep shaft, their faces hanging over, while the men backed the truck close to the hole, fastened ropes to Rocket's hoofs, passed them around a tree opposite, and with this leverage were able to drag the carcass to the very edge of the open back of the truck.

They removed the ropes, got in the truck, and using poles as levers, shoved and pushed at the inert black mass. She moved slightly – she was sliding – suddenly she was over.

The boys saw the great body plunge, caroming from side to side, the hoofs turn up, the mane and tail whipping and winding – then the darkness swallowed her. Nothing – and a long silence before the jarring thud three hundred feet below, that shook the earth they were lying on.

Sitting at dinner in the kitchen Williams said, 'If I may be so bold, why do you wear the piece of lariat around your neck, Captain? Someone been roping *you*—'

Everyone laughed but Nell. Her face coloured up – she reached over and pulled the rope from Rob's neck, went to the stove, and lifting a lid off, dropped it into the fire.

The rest of the day was spent rounding up horses of all ages, descendants of the Albino.

At first no one had believed that McLaughlin really meant what he said – that every single one of the Albino's blood, no matter how beautiful, how fast, or how promising, was to be sold. But as the hours went on, and one after the other was gathered into the corrals, and still they went out on horseback to gather more, with Nell busy with the stud book and names, it became apparent that he was in earnest.

Ken and Howard were kept at the gates, opening and shutting them as the different bands were brought through, taken down to the corrals, the one bronc picked out and held, the others sent out again. Gus and Tim and Ross were all riding.

'And that's every last one of them,' said Nell at length, closing the book. Her voice was regretful.

She and Williams were in the stable, looking out into the corrals, over the top of the Dutch door. The two boys were perched safely on the corral fence, Rob and the men in the corral with the milling broncs.

'Except Flicka,' murmured Ken, and he looked across the corral at his mother and caught her eye. She was looking at him too, thinking he knew, the same thing. He had not been exactly worried about Flicka. After all, she was his own, his father had given her to him, she couldn't be sold without his consent.

'Nine of them,' said McLaughlin, counting, and Williams went out of the stable into the corral.

Now began a long period of bargaining. With the horses under their eyes McLaughlin and Williams argued until the watchers were tired.

'I could get ten in the truck,' said Williams. 'Haven't you got another to throw in?'

'I might have,' said McLaughlin, 'but let's settle the price of these first.'

They did some figuring on bits of paper, and finally the deal was closed.

McLaughlin walked over to Ken, called him down from the fence, and walked away with him.

'Ken,' he said quietly, 'I'm going to give you a chance to do a sensible, manly thing. I want you to choose another colt, and let me sell Flicka to Williams with the rest of this hell's brew.'

A wave of heat rushed all over Ken's body. He looked down, dug with his toe in the gravel of the path, and shook his head.

McLaughlin was quiet and persuasive. 'You've seen for yourself – what can you expect? It's for your own sake I'm asking, as well as to save myself the trouble and unpleasantness of trying to help you do something which is impossible. What's the use of having another Rocket on your hands? You've seen what end she came to – and no one could have tried harder with a horse than I tried with her—'

'But I'm going to *tame* Flicka,' whispered Ken. 'Sometimes bad horses get tamed.'

McLaughlin's voice rose angrily. 'Look up!'

Ken looked up and was more frightened than ever. His father's face looked appalling. It was swollen out of all shape, one eye was closed by purple and black lumps above and below, and the white dressing on the cheekbone was surrounded by an inflamed, angry circle.

'Are you going to be a bull-headed little simp or a sensible boy?'

Ken said stubbornly, 'Dad, I have to have her – she's mine.'

He really meant, *she's me*. It felt as if his father were asking him to be torn apart.

'For me, Ken, then; and for your mother – let's have a pleasant summer. Let's have *something* turn out right—'

Ken shook his head, and suddenly felt his father's hand

on his shoulder, gripping with such strength it hurt him.

'I'd like to shake the teeth out of your stubborn head—' said McLaughlin savagely; then turned around and strode back to the stable. Ken followed, his heart pounding, but triumph singing within him. Flicka was his. She couldn't be taken.

'That's all,' shouted McLaughlin. 'Nine of them. Now we'll load 'em.'

With the assistance of Shorty, the broncs were driven through the chute into the truck and penned in.

The truck stopped at the house, while Williams made out a cheque to Rob. Though it wasn't as much of a cheque as he would have got for Rocket, yet it was big enough to bring a little satisfaction into his one open eye.

'Want to ride out to the highway in the car?' Rob asked Nell. 'And see the last of them?'

They all got into the Studebaker, and followed Williams along the road, watching the struggles of the horses in the truck. Although they were tightly packed, several of them, frantic with fear, were being troublesome.

One of them kept rearing, and got his forefeet over one side. The truck tilted going along the side of the hill, and suddenly the impossible happened. The bronc clawed up the side of the hold, got his body across it, and toppled over.

It was a tremendous fall, as the hill sloped down forty feet or so, and the bronc went bounding, rolling, somersaulting to the bottom.

Rob brought the Studebaker to a stop. They all jumped out and stood watching, while Williams halted his truck and got down from the box.

When the bronc hit the bottom of the hill, he leaped to his feet and stood, apparently unhurt, looking around in a comical surprised fashion. Everyone began to laugh.

Williams came back to McLaughlin. 'It'll make me too late if I go back and load him again.'

Rob took his cheque out of his pocket. 'Here's my fountain pen – make me out a new cheque – take the price of him off–'

Williams hastened to do so as he knew that, once the bronc had been loaded in his truck, and his cheque given, the loss should have been his and not McLaughlin's. He said jocularly as they exchanged cheques, 'I'll let you feed him for a year and I'll buy him from you on my trip next summer.'

McLaughlin said, 'On your way! You want to get to the border before dark, and by the way – drive *around* the sign out there by the highway – *not under*!'

'You bet. Well – so long.' Williams climbed into his truck and drove away.

The bronc was running about the meadow, looking around in an odd startled fashion as if he didn't know where he was. Suddenly he began to gallop hard, then his head went down, he turned head over heels, lay still a moment, got up and again began to gallop.

The boys looked at their father trying to read in his face the explanation of this strange behaviour. The bronc was certainly acting in an unnatural manner. Nell knew, with a sick feeling in her heart, that the beautiful young thing was injured.

McLaughlin's face was set and hard, his eyes narrowed. They stood in silence watching the colt going through the strange gyration over and over, galloping, turning head over heels, lying still a moment, then getting up and galloping again.

At last, McLaughlin said, 'Is the Winchester in the car?'

'Yes,' said Howard promptly. 'You put it in the back when we went to look for the wildcat, remember? And told us to leave it there.'

'Get it.'

McLaughlin took the gun, then said, 'Nell, you go on home with the boys.'

'Oh, can't we stay?' said Howard.

'No. Bad enough to have to shoot him. This isn't a show.'

Nell drove away with the boys, and McLaughlin took a careful position on level ground and raised the gun to his shoulder.

He wanted to be sure—

There was a long wait, until the colt came to a pause in his gambols. When at last he did, standing in the same comical, surprised fashion, as if asking what was going to happen, there was the sharp crack of the Winchester. The bullet whined, the echoes came thundering back softly from the hills, and the colt went gently down in the deep grass of the meadow.

'And that's the last of them,' said McLaughlin, as he lowered the rifle and stood a moment watching, to see if there was any movement in the grass. Then he ejected the empty shell and added savagely, *'Except Flicka.'*

Chapter Seventeen

Several days passed before McLaughlin found time to make another effort to bring Flicka in, days in which he seemed to care nothing about what had happened or was going to happen. He was concerned only with his work. He drove the men hard, and Nell, too, had all she could do working with Rumba as well as attending to her housework. He ignored Ken.

The four three-year-olds were coming along nicely. The daily routine of oats, grooming, exercising, filled out their muscles and put a fine sheen on their coats. They had reached the point where they pricked their ears and pranced gaily when their trainers whistled them into the corral in the morning. Gangway had stopped his bucking, and McLaughlin put the four of them through a daily workout down in the practice field, which included the swinging of polo sticks and whacking at the ball.

On Sunday the family went to church in Cheyenne.

There was the usual argument before going. Rob, who wanted to spend the morning sitting on the terrace reading the funny papers, said he thought they ought not to go because some officers might come out from the Post. 'There's always a chance, you know, that someone might buy a pony.'

'Not Sunday morning,' said Nell firmly. And then she added with the one deep dimple in her right cheek showing, 'But you don't have to go, dear, your face isn't healed up yet. That's a good excuse. I'll go and take the boys.'

McLaughlin said, 'Right-o.' Fifteen minutes later, when Nell was ready to go and Howard and Ken were dressed in their long grey flannel trousers and white shirts and small round white linen hats with narrow brims, he came running upstairs and roared indignantly, 'Do you think I'll let you go to town and sit in that pew without me by your side?'

As they waited for him to dress, the boys fidgeting, Nell explained to them that Army Officers are trained to be very particular how they look for the sake of their prestige, so they must all wait patiently.

At last McLaughlin came down looking clean and handsome in his light grey flannel suit, with a soft felt hat tilted at just the right angle on his black hair and nothing but a small piece of adhesive on his cheek bone.

Nell was in a dark green print, with turban and high-heeled pumps. Tim had washed the car, and the maroon paint and shining nickel was as bright as anything they had passed on the Lincoln Highway.

McLaughlin's habitual pace was sixty-five miles an hour. Today, with a slight feeling of pressure in him, he edged it up to seventy, but as usual they were late, and made a commotion as they were ushered up the aisle of the church, with everyone seated listening to the first lesson being read.

They dined in town, with the Bartletts; and by the time

they got back to the ranch, a number of visitors were there; and from then on the pleasant sociabilities of Sunday afternoon kept the place alive with cars coming and going, trays of bottles and glasses being carried in and out, and much talk and laughter.

Children love to hear the conversation of their elders, and Howard and Ken stuck close to their father and mother, and the group of officers and officers' wives; and listened to the story of Rocket's violent death told again and again; the loco bunch described; and the Albino's prepotency and intractability discussed and commented upon.

Loco was a word Ken had heard ever since he was born. *You're loco* meant the same as, *You're crazy!* or *What a goof!* But the way it was being talked about now was different, very serious somehow . . . he didn't get it . . .

He sat on the low stone wall of the terrace, his legs dangling over the flower border, and watched a big bumble bee boring into a purple petunia blossom, while his elders gossiped.

Gus and Ross and Tim had been talking about loco animals too.

Last night Howard and Ken had spent an hour in the bunk house before bedtime, as they often did, listening to the men swap yarns, and the talk was all about what made animals loco in the first place.

Tim told a tale of a little black colt who was chased by a pack of coyotes; the mother defended it bravely. But all through the night the mare and the foal were in terror of their lives. They fought and ran, and turned to fight again. And by the morning the colt's hair had turned pure white, and it was loco.

The bronco-buster had a story to match that.

He'd been talking about the horses he had on his own ranch. He had built up a band by catching wild mustangs, breaking them, now and then trading for a good mare. 'But to tell the truth there waan't a real good horse on the place. Them catch colts – they're hard as hell to pull in. I'd go out a-huntin' and mebbe see a bunch strung out on the sky line – ridge runners – they git up on a high place where they kin see you comin' a mile off – and like as not you never catch sight of 'em again – if you do git a few and git 'em broke, you ain't not nuthin'.

'My top horse was one of them catch colts. He waan't no good. Cold-mouthed, couldn't feel the bit at all, just didn't savvy. I made up my mind I'd get a real good colt, bred right, and raise him to be Top Horse.

'Waall, I had a good mare and I paid ten dollars for service by a Government stud.'

'Service comes free from Government studs,' said Gus.

'The ten bucks was the cost of hirin' a trailer and transportin' my mare. A year later, she dropped a foal, and he grew up a beauty. Long straight legs and eyes as soft as a woman's. Smart little feller too. When he was a yearlin' I rode his mother out to a homestead I had put under fence out by Centennial, and the colt come along with us. You know that country up there? Them old cock-eyed mountains goin' straight up into the sky – and nary a house or a road or a human being as fur as you kin see. I had set my fence the summer before; but that ole wind got-a-whippin' and a-pullin' it and laid it down for half a mile. I had a week's work cut out for me. It was while I was havin' a smoke after dinner one day that I seen this big mountain lion jump the yearlin'. The yearlin' was off there a ways, a-grazin', clost to a hillside; and that cat came a-shootin' down through the air and lit on top the colt. Ever see one of them lions? Stand as high as a new born colt – an' scream like a woman – enough to curdle your blood. Lie in the trees, on tops of rocks, leap on colts or horses as they go by.'

'How can they kill a horse?' demanded Howard.

'It's a real neat trick. Leap up on top the neck, and bite

in at the base of the spine and hang on with their front claws. The rest of 'em's a-swingin' under the horse's head and neck, with the hind feet hooked under the horse's chin, clawin' agin it. The weight of the crittur twists the horse's head plumb around and breaks its neck. Down it goes and the rest is pickin's.'

'Did it kill your colt?'

'Nope. He screamed and went down and rolled, an' the ole lady was grazin' not so very fur away, and she come on the run and went for the cat. Cats ain't brave – don't put up much of a fight. They'd ruther run if they don't get the drop an' kill with the first leap. It took to the tall timber, and by the time I got my gun and was a-lookin' for a shot, there waan't a sign of it. But the colt could never stand no one on his back after that. When he got older, I did my best to break him, but he'd keep a-lookin' round at me, shakin', jumpin' – never did git him broke. He ended up plumb loco.'

All of this talk drifted hazily through Ken's mind, while he watched the bumble bee boring its way into a half opened petunia bud. The bee was completely hidden and the weight of it bowed the blossom almost to the ground. Ken waited to see it come out again. What a world that must be to get into, the very heart of a little flower – if he was a bumble bee now—

Behind him on the terrace, the Major's wife was teasing Rob and Nell to come to a dance next Saturday night at the Post. 'We never see you two in town,' she said. 'Not that I blame you— If I had a place like this—'

'Remember last time we went to a dance at the Post?' said Rob grinning.

'Do I!' exclaimed Nell. 'Last fall. And there was a flood while we were away.'

'I remember,' yelled Howard. 'The water was over the bridge coming back, and you couldn't drive over!'

Ken remembered too; it had been an exciting night. Just

163

before bedtime, when he and Howard were sauntering home after a stroll with Gus, there had been a great roar, and a wave of water came down Lone Tree Creek and left a wide river in the meadow where there had only been a creek before. The dogs rushed down and barked at the water and it covered the stone bridge that led up the cattle guard, and the parapets of the bridge, too.

'There we were about four in the morning,' said Rob, 'driving in from the highway, and my headlights picked up water in front, where there should have been a road, and we got out to see what had happened, and there was a river between us and home.'

'For mercy's sake,' screamed Mrs Gilfillan. 'What did you do?'

'You should have seen us. The parapets of the bridge were only about one foot under water. So we took off our shoes and stockings, I rolled up my trousers, Nell picked up her skirts, and we waded across on the parapets – left the car where it was till morning—'

'Did you say a party at the *Post*?' kidded Lieutenant Grubb. 'And anyone going home sober enough to walk a couple of tight ropes over a river—'

There was one of the jovial roars of laughter from everyone that made Howard and Ken join in without exactly understanding what the joke was.

The bumble bee came out of the petunia and circled around, tasting several flowers in succession, then found one it liked and bored in again.

Ken saw Paul sitting over a gopher hole at the far side of the Green. She was waiting for the gopher to stick its head out. She sat as still as a little brown statue, braced on her front paws, her eyes down into the hole. She would wait there ten minutes – fifteen – twenty – and at the last the gopher wouldn't be able to stand it any longer and he'd stick his head out to see if she'd gone away—

They were talking about Rocket again.

Major Gilfillan said, 'No reason, of course, why there shouldn't be inherited insanity among animals just as there is among human beings, but—'

Lieutenant Grubb interrupted. 'How could you ever be sure what it is? There are all sorts of temperaments. Just sheer intractability, or too high spirits, would give you the same type. And that's not necessarily insanity, nor is it a bad thing. Take humans – for instance, a youngster too spirited to control—'

'It *is* a bad thing,' interrupted the Major. 'And you might as well call it insanity, for it amounts to an inability to adjust to environment.'

'But when that type *does* adjust, you've got something super.'

'How many of them ever do? Most of them beat their heads against the wall until they beat their brains out.'

'Even so, I maintain that it's not insane for a freedom-loving individual man or beast, to refuse to be subdued.'

Tim and the little bronco-buster sauntered down the Green, going to find the cows and bring them in for milking.

Colonel Harris said, 'My experience has been that the high-strung individual, the nervous, keyed-up type – is apt to be a fine performer. It's the solitary, or the queer fellow, that I'm afraid of. Show me a man who plays a lone hand – no natural gregariousness, you know – the *lone wolf* type – and I'll show you one who's apt to be screwy.'

Pauly was still sitting motionless over the gopher hole. Suddenly she made one smooth, lightning stroke of her paw across the opening, and then she crouched, struggling with something that was alive. Her head was turned sideways, she was crunching. Presently it wasn't alive any longer, and Pauly stood up, lifted her head with the dead gopher hanging from her jaws, and slowly trotted up the Hill into the woods.

165

'... in some cases, an actual psychosis, no doubt about it,' said the Major.

The words danced in Ken's brain. He didn't know what they meant, but it didn't matter. He was too happy. That morning in church, he had suddenly nudged Nell, and when she looked down into his beaming face, she realized the minister had just read the words *beautiful upon the mountains*. Ken's lips silently formed the word *Flicka*, and Nell smiled back. All week he had thought of nothing but Flicka. She got into his conversation – he would be talking about *she* this, and *she* that – and his father would suddenly roar, 'What *she*?' His father was grim and angry with him, but not even that worried him.

Every night when he went to bed, he lay awake thinking of Flicka as long as he could. He would see her floating over the ravines, flattened in a leap, her long slim legs stretched forward and back until she seemed just a slightly curved line, suspended. And he would see her face as if it was close to his own. In reality he had seen her close to, only once. That was the first time when she had fled past him, terrified, and had cast him a glance. Then her face had been so close he could almost have leaned over and touched it. Some day, he thought, he would. He'd stroke her face, he'd brush out that untidy bang of hair, he'd put it neatly between her eyes, he'd put his own cheek right against her soft nose.

At odd moments, a very ecstasy of possession filled him. Now, sitting on the terrace wall, his heart sang, and he hung his head for fear everyone could see the pride and joy shining out of his eyes ...

Behind him they were all shouting with laughter again, and he turned to see what it was about. His mother was telling something that made them laugh. She was saying that the reason Rob had looked so rakish driving to church that morning was the way he wore his hat.

'It's the whole thing—' she said, 'the way a man wears

his hat. It can make him look like a – a – respectable gentle-
man—' (there were shouts at this) 'or a rake,' she went on
('Bring him on,' giggled Mrs Gilfillan) 'or a pompous
ass—' (the Major whacked Colonel Harris on the back and
said, 'Get up and bow, Colonel') 'or very, *very* careful—'
finished Nell, and the Lieutenant said, 'I never can be
good, so I'm just careful.'

Then they got trying on hats in different ways.

Ken and Howard tried on hats too, strutting about; and
Mrs Gilfillan and Mrs Grubb put on the boys' little white
linen hats and sat there with them perched on their blonde
heads.

Later in the afternoon, McLaughlin stuck a tin can on
the tip of one of the branches of a pine tree on the Hill
opposite and the officers took their revolvers and practised
target shooting, standing on the terrace.

Their father told the boys to get their twenty-twos and
give an exhibition of marksmanship, and at last he brought
out the big guns, the Express rifle, and the Winchester, and
the officers all tried shooting with them, and the long shells
went crashing across the valley, chipping off pieces of the
cliff half a mile away, until Tim came up from the barn, his
face darker and redder than usual, saying that he couldn't
milk the cows, with the big guns booming over the barn –
they'd kicked over two buckets already.

Then Mrs Grubb and Mrs Gilfillan said they wanted to
ride out and see the brood mares, so they all crowded into
two automobiles, and McLaughlin led the way.

When they found the brood mares, they stopped some
distance off and got out, and McLaughlin promised that
Banner would come out to meet them and do the honours.

'How do you know he will?' asked Mrs Gilfillan.

'He always does.'

The mares stopped grazing and stood, alert, curious,
and ready to run. Banner was amongst them.

His head topped them all, and even from a distance,

the men and women watching could feel the penetration of his eye.

Suddenly the big stallion moved towards them, ears pricked, inquiring eyes wide and fearless, and began to trot, his legs alternating in high, free, curving steps, his mane streaming, his tail up.

'Flying all his flags!' cried Nell.

A roar and a cheer burst from the officers as the stallion, without breaking his trot, increased his pace and came down the wind to them like a bugle call.

Banner halted ten yards off and stood looking the group over. His golden coat blazed in the sunshine.

'What an intelligent face!' exclaimed the Colonel. McLaughlin, still in his grey suit and rakish hat, went forward to the stud, apologizing gravely for not having brought a bucket of oats in the car.

Lying in bed that night, Ken remembered the way Banner had looked. Banner, the Sire of Flicka – Flicka was the same, the same burnished gold, the same beauty, the same flags flying— Oh, *mine* . . . my colt . . . my own . . . my *very* own . . .

He wondered when his father would bring her in again.

He had been wondering that every day when Gus put his round pink face in at the kitchen door and said, 'What's today, Boss?' But his father had planned other work. Meadows to be taken care of, water to be turned out of one ditch and into the other. Endless hours of work on the three-year-olds that must be ready to ship in just a few days now. A new cattle guard being built at one of the railroad gates.

But next morning, when Gus said, 'What's today, Boss?' McLaughlin gave the order for the day's work and then said, 'And I think—' and paused.

Ken looked down to hide his excitement; he clenched his fists under the table.

McLaughlin went on, 'Tomorrow we'll get the yearlings in again, Gus, and cut out Ken's filly. I want to do that before Ross leaves. We may need his help.'

Tomorrow . . .

Chapter Eighteen

When Ken opened his eyes next morning and looked out he saw that the house was wrapped in fog. There had been no rain at all since the day a week ago when the wind had torn the 'sprinkling system' to pieces and blown all the tattered clouds away. That was the day he had found Flicka. And it had been terribly hot since then. They had hardly been able to stand the sun out on the terrace. They had gone swimming in the pool every day. On the hills, the grass was turning to soft tan.

Now there were clouds and they had closed down. After a severe hot spell there often came a heavy fog, or hail, or even snow.

Standing at the window, Ken could hardly see the pines on the Hill opposite. He wondered if his father would go after the yearlings in such a fog as this – they wouldn't be able to see them; but at breakfast McLaughlin said there would be no change of plans. It was just a big cloud that had settled down over the ranch – it would lift and fall – perhaps up on Saddle Back it would be clear.

They mounted and rode out.

The fog lay in the folds of the hills. Here and there a bare summit was in sunshine, then a little farther on, came a smother of cottony white that soaked the four riders to the skin and hung rows of moonstones on the whiskers of the horses.

It was hard to keep track of each other. Suddenly Ken was lost – the others had vanished. He reined in Shorty and sat listening. The clouds and mist rolled around him. He felt as if he were alone in the world.

A bluebird, colour of the deep blue wild delphinium that dots the plains, became interested in him, and perched in a bush nearby; and as he started Shorty forward again, the bluebird followed along, hopping from bush to bush.

The boy rode slowly, not knowing in which direction to go. Then, hearing shouts, he touched heels to Shorty and cantered, and suddenly came out of the fog and saw his father and Tim and Ross.

'There they are!' said McLaughlin, pointing down over the curve of the hill. They rode forward and Ken could see the yearlings standing bunched at the bottom, looking up, wondering who was coming. Then a huge coil of fog swirled over them and they were lost to sight again.

McLaughlin told them to circle around, spread out fan-wise on the far side of the colts, and then gently bear down on them so they would start towards the ranch. If the colts once got running in this fog, he said, there'd be no chance of catching them.

The plan worked well; the yearlings were not so frisky as usual, and allowed themselves to be driven in the right direction. It was only when they were on the County Road, and near the gate where Howard was watching, that Ken, whose eyes had been scanning the bunch, as they appeared and disappeared in the fog, realized that Flicka was missing.

McLaughlin noticed it at the same moment, and as Ken rode towards his father, McLaughlin turned to him and said, 'She's not in the bunch.'

They sat in silence a few moments while McLaughlin planned the next step. The yearlings, dispirited by the fog, nibbled languidly at the grass by the roadside. McLaughlin looked at the Saddle Back and Ken looked too, the passionate desire in his heart reaching out to pierce the fog and the hillside and see where Flicka had hidden herself away. Had she been with the bunch when they first were found? Had she stolen away through the fog? Or hadn't she been there in the beginning? Had she run away from the ranch entirely, after her bad experience a week ago? Or – and this thought made his heart drop sickeningly – had she perhaps died of the hurts she had received when she broke out of the corral and was lying stark and riddled with ants and crawling things on the breast of one of those hills?

McLaughlin looked grim. 'Lone wolf – like her mother,' he said. 'Never with the gang. I might have known it.'

Ken remembered what the Colonel had said about the Lone Wolf type – it wasn't good to be that way.

'Well, we'll drive the yearlings back up,' said Rob finally. 'No chance of finding her alone. If they happen to pass anywhere near her she's likely to join them.'

They drove the yearlings back. Once over the first hill, the colts got running and soon were out of sight. The fog closed down again so that Ken pulled up, unable to see where he was going, unable to see his father, or Ross or Tim.

He sat listening, astonished that the sound of their hoofs had been wiped out so completely. Again he seemed alone in the world.

The fog lifted in front of him and showed him that he stood at the brink of a sharp drop, almost a precipice, though not very deep. It led down into a semi-circular pocket on the hillside which was fed by a spring; there was a clump of young cottonwoods, and a great bank of clover dotted with small yellow blossoms.

In the midst of the clover stood Flicka, quietly feasting. She had seen him before he saw her and was watching him, her head up, clover sticking out of both sides of her mouth, her jaws going busily.

At sight of her, Ken was incapable of either thought or action.

Suddenly from behind him in the fog, he heard his father's low voice, 'Don't move—'

'How'd she get in there?' said Tim.

'She scrambled down this bank. And she could scramble up again, if we weren't here. I think we've got her,' said McLaughlin.

'Other side of that pocket the ground drops twenty feet sheer,' said Tim. 'She can't go down there.'

Flicka had stopped chewing. There were still stalks of clover sticking out between her jaws, but her head was up and her ears pricked, listening, and there was a tautness and tension in her whole body.

Ken found himself trembling too.

'How're you going to catch her, Dad?' he asked in a low voice.

'I kin snag her from here,' said Ross, and in the same breath McLaughlin answered, 'Ross can rope her. Might as well rope her here as in the corral. We'll spread out in a semi-circle above this bank. She can't get up past us, and she can't get down.'

They took their positions and Ross lifted his rope off the horn of his saddle.

Ahead of them, far down below the pocket, the yearlings were running. A whinny or two drifted up, and the sound of their hoofs, muffled by the fog.

Flicka heard them too. Suddenly she was aware of

danger. She leaped out of the clover to the edge of the precipice which fell away down the mountainside towards where the yearlings were running. But it was too steep and too high. She came straight up on her hind legs with a neigh of terror, and whirled back towards the bank down which she had slid to reach the pocket. But on the crest of it, looming uncannily in the fog, were four black figures – she screamed, and ran around the base of the bank.

Ken heard Ross's rope sing. It snaked out just as Flicka dived into the bank of clover. Stumbling she went down and for a moment was lost to view.

'Goldarn—' said Ross, hauling in his rope, while Flicka floundered up and again circled her small prison, hurling herself at every point, only to realize that there was no way out.

She stood over the precipice, poised in despair and frantic longing. There drifted up the sound of the colts running below. Flicka trembled and strained over the brink – a perfect target for Ross, and he whirled his lariat again. It made a vicious whine.

Ken longed for the filly to escape the noose – yet he longed for her capture. Flicka reared up, her delicate forefeet beat the air, then she leaped out; and Ross's rope fell short again as McLaughlin said, 'I expected that. She's like all the rest of them.'

Flicka went down like a diver. She hit the ground with her legs folded under her, then rolled and bounced the rest of the way. It was exactly like the bronco that had climbed over the side of the truck and rolled down the forty-foot bank; and in silence the four watchers sat in their saddles waiting to see what would happen when she hit bottom – Ken already thinking of the Winchester, and the way the crack of it had echoed back from the hills.

Flicka lit, it seemed, on four steel springs that tossed her up and sent her flying down the mountainside – perfection of speed and power and action. A hot sweat bathed Ken from head to foot, and he began to laugh, half choking—

The wind roared down and swept up the fog, and it went bounding away over the hills, leaving trailing streamers of white in the gullies, and coverlets of cotton around the bushes. Way below, they could see Flicka galloping towards the yearlings. In a moment she joined them, and then there was just a many coloured blur of moving shapes, with a fierce sun blazing down, striking sparks of light off their glossy coats.

'Get going!' shouted McLaughlin. 'Get around behind them. They're on the run now, and it's cleared – keep them running, and we may get them all in together, before they stop. Tim, you take the short way back to the gate and help Howard turn them and get them through.'

Tim shot off towards the County Road and the other three riders galloped down and around the mountain until they were at the back of the band of yearlings. Shouting and yelling and spurring their mounts, they kept the colts running, circling them around towards the ranch until they had them on the County Road.

Way ahead, Ken could see Tim and Howard at the gate, blocking the road. The yearlings were bearing down on them. Now McLaughlin slowed up, and began to call, 'Whoa, whoa—' and the pace decreased. Often enough the yearlings had swept down that road and through the gate and down to the corrals. It was the pathway to oats, and hay, and shelter from winter storms – would they take it now? Flicka was with them – right in the middle – if they went, would she go too?

It was all over almost before Ken could draw a breath. The yearlings turned at the gate, swept through, went down to the corrals on a dead run, and through the gates that Gus had opened.

Flicka was caught again.

Mindful that she had clawed her way out when she was corralled before, McLaughlin determined to keep her in the main corral into which the stable door opened. It had eight-foot walls of aspen poles. The rest of the yearlings must be manoeuvred away from her.

Now that the fog had gone, the sun was scorching, and horses and men alike were soaked with sweat before the chasing was over and, one after the other, the yearlings had been driven into the other corral, and Flicka was alone.

She knew that her solitude meant danger, and that she was singled out for some special disaster. She ran frantically to the high fence through which she could see the other ponies standing, and reared and clawed at the poles; she screamed, whirled, circled the corral first in one direction, and then the other. And while McLaughlin and Ross were discussing the advisability of roping her, she suddenly espied the dark hole which was the open upper half of the stable door, and dived through it. McLaughlin rushed to close it, and she was caught – safely imprisoned in the stable.

The rest of the colts were driven away, and Ken stood outside the stable, listening to the wild hoofs beating, the screams, the crashes. His Flicka within there – close at hand – imprisoned. He was shaking. He felt a desperate desire to quiet her somehow, to *tell her*. If she only knew how he loved her, that there was nothing to be afraid of, that they were going to be friends—

Ross shook his head with a one-sided grin. 'Sure a wild one,' he said, coiling his lariat.

'Plumb loco,' said Tim briefly.

McLaughlin said, 'We'll leave her to think it over. After dinner we'll come up and feed and water her and do a little work with her.'

But when they went up after dinner there was no Flicka in the barn. One of the windows above the manger was broken, and the manger was full of pieces of glass.

Staring at it, McLaughlin gave a short laugh. He looked

at Ken. 'She climbed into the manger – see? Stood on the feed box, beat the glass out with her front hoofs and climbed through.'

The window opened into the Six Foot Pasture. Near it was a wagon-load of hay. When they went around the back of the stable to see where she had gone they found her between the stable and the hay wagon, eating.

At their approach, she leaped away, then headed east across the pasture.

'If she's like her mother,' said Rob, 'she'll go right through the wire.'

'Ay bet she'll go over,' said Gus. 'She jumps like a deer.'

'No horse can jump that,' said McLaughlin.

Ken said nothing because he could not speak. It was the most terrible moment of his life. He watched Flicka racing towards the eastern wire.

A few rods from it, she swerved, turned and raced diagonally south.

'It turned her! it turned her!' cried Ken, almost sobbing. It was the first sign of hope for Flicka. 'Oh, Dad, she has got sense, she has! She has!'

Flicka turned again as she met the southern boundary of the pasture, again at the northern; she avoided the barn. Without abating anything of her whirlwind speed, following a precise, accurate calculation, and turning each time on a dime, she investigated every possibility. Then, seeing that there was no hope, she raced south towards the range where she had spent her life, gathered herself, and rose to the impossible leap.

Each of the men watching had the impulse to cover his eyes, and Ken gave a howl of despair.

Twenty yards of fence came down with her as she hurled herself through. Caught on the upper strands, she turned a complete somersault, landing on her back, her four legs dragging the wires down on top of her, and tangling herself in them beyond hope of escape.

'Damn the wire!' cursed McLaughlin. 'If I could afford decent fences—'

Ken followed the men miserably as they walked to the filly. They stood in a circle watching while she kicked and fought and thrashed until the wire was tightly wound and tangled about her, piercing and tearing her flesh and hide. At last she was unconscious, streams of blood running on her golden coat, and pools of crimson widening on the grass beneath her.

With the wire cutters which Gus always carried in the hip pocket of his overalls, he cut the wire away; and they drew her into the pasture, repaired the fence, placed hay, a box of oats, and a tub of water near her, and called it a day.

'I doubt if she pulls out of it,' said McLaughlin briefly. 'But it's just as well. If it hadn't been this way it would have been another. A loco horse isn't worth a damn.'

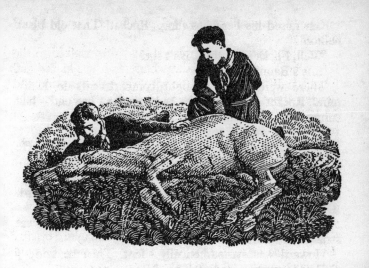

Chapter Nineteen

Ken lay on the grass behind Flicka. One little brown hand was on her back, smoothing it, pressing softly, caressing. The other hand supported his head. His face hung over her.

His throat felt dry; his lips were like paper.

After a long while he whispered, 'I didn't mean to kill you, Flicka—'

Howard came to sit with him, quiet and respectful as is proper in the presence of grief or mourning.

'Gee! Highboy was never like that,' he said.

Ken made no answer to this. His eyes were on Flicka, watching her slow breathing. He had often seen horses down and unconscious. Badly cut with wire, too – they got well. Flicka could get well.

'Gosh! She's about as bad as Rocket,' said Howard cheerfully.

Ken raised his head scowling. 'Rocket! That old black hellion!'

'Well, Flicka's her child, isn't she?'

'She's Banner's child too—'

There were many air-tight compartments in Ken's mind. Rocket – now that she had come to a bad end – had conveniently gone into one of them.

After a moment Howard said,

'We haven't given our colts their workout today.' He pulled up his knees and clasped his hands around them.

Ken said nothing.

'We're supposed to, you know – we gotta,' said Howard. 'Dad'll be sore at us if we don't.'

'I don't want to leave her,' said Ken, and his voice was strange and thin.

Howard was sympathetically silent. Then he said, 'I could do your two for you, Ken—'

Ken looked up gratefully. 'Would you, Howard? Gee – that'd be keen—'

'Sure I'll do all of 'em and you can stay here with Flicka.'

'Thanks.' Ken put his head down on his hand again, and the other hand smoothed and patted the filly's neck.

'Gee, she was pretty,' said Howard sighing.

'What d'ya mean – *was*!' snapped Ken. 'You mean she *is* – she's beautiful.'

'I meant when she was running back there,' said Howard hastily.

Ken made no reply. It was true. Flicka floating across the ravines was something quite different from the inert mass lying on the ground, her belly rounded up into a mound, her neck weak and collapsed on the grass, her head stretched out, homely and senseless.

'Just think,' said Howard, 'you could have had any one of the other yearlings. And I guess by this time, it would have been half tamed down there in the corral – probably tied to the post.'

As Ken still kept silent, Howard got slowly to his feet. 'Well, I guess I might as well go and do the colts,' he said, and walked away. At a little distance he turned. 'If Mother goes for the mail, do you want to go along?'

Ken shook his head.

When Howard was out of sight, Ken kneeled up and looked Flicka all over. He had never thought that, as soon as this, he would have been close enough to pat her, to caress her, to hold and examine her. He felt a passion of possession. Sick and half destroyed as she was, she was his own, and his heart was bursting with love of her. He smoothed her all over. He arranged her mane in more orderly fashion; he tried to straighten her head.

'You're mine now, Flicka,' he whispered.

He counted her wounds. The two worst were a deep cut above the right rear hock, and a long gash in her chest that ran down into the muscle of the foreleg. Besides those, she was snagged with three-cornered tears through which the flesh pushed out, and laced with cuts and scratches with blood drying on them in rows of little black beads.

Ken wondered if the two bad cuts ought to be sewn up. He thought of Doc Hicks, and then remembered what his Dad had said: 'You cost me money every time you turn around.' No – Gus might do it – Gus was pretty good at sewing up animals. But Dad said best thing of all is usually to let them alone. They heal up. There was Sultan, hit by an automobile out on the highway; it knocked him down and took a big piece of flesh out of his chest and left the flap of skin hanging loose – and it all healed up of itself and you could only tell where the wound had been by the hair's being a different length.

The cut in Flicka's hind leg was awfully deep—

He put his head down against her and whispered again, 'Oh, Flicka – I didn't mean to kill you.'

After a few moments, 'Oh, get well – get well – *get well*—'

And again, 'Flicka, don't be so wild. *Be all right,* Flicka—'

Gus came out to him carrying a can of black grease.

'De Boss tole me to put some of dis grease on de filly's cuts, Ken – it helps heal 'em up.'

Together they went over her carefully, putting a smear of the grease wherever they could reach a wound.

Gus stood looking down at the boy.

'D'you think she'll get well, Gus?'

'She might, Ken. I seen plenty horses hurt as bad as dot, and dey yust as good as ever.'

'Dad said—' But Ken's voice failed him when he remembered that his father had said she might as well die, because she was loco anyway.

The Swede stood a moment, his pale blue eyes, transparent and spiritual, looking kindly down at the boy; then he went on down to the barn.

Every trace of fog and mist had vanished, and the sun was blazing hot. Sweltering, Ken got up to take a drink of water from the bucket left for Flicka. Then, carrying handfuls of water in his small cupped hands, he poured it on her mouth. Flicka did not move, and once again Ken took his place behind her, his hand on her neck, his lips whispering to her.

After a while his head sank in exhaustion to the ground . . .

A roaring gale roused him and he looked up to see racing black clouds forming into a line. Blasts of cold wind struck down at the earth and sucked up leaves, twigs, tumbleweeds, in whorls like small cyclones.

From the black line in the sky, a fine icy mist sheeted down, and suddenly there came an appalling explosion of thunder. The world blazed and shuddered with lighting. High overhead was a noise like the shrieking of trumpets and trombones. The particles of fine icy mist beating down grew larger; they began to dance and bounce on the ground like little peas – like marbles – like ping-pong balls—

They beat upon Ken through his thin shirt and whipped his bare head and face. He kneeled up, leaning over Flicka, protecting her head with his folded arms. The hailstones were like ping-pong balls – like billiard balls – like little hard apples – like bigger apples – and suddenly, here and there, they fell as big as tennis balls, bouncing on the ground, rolling along, splitting on the rocks.

One hit Ken on the side of the face and a thin line of blood slid down his cheek with the water.

Running like a hare, under a pall of darkness, the storm fled eastwards, beating the grass flat upon the hills. Then, in the wake of the darkness and the screaming wind and hail, a clear silver light shone out, and the grass rose up again, every blade shimmering.

Watching Flicka, Ken sat back on his heels and sighed. She had not moved.

A rainbow, like a giant compass, drew a half circle of bright colour around the ranch. And off to one side, there was a vertical blur of fire hanging, left over from the storm.

Ken lay down again close behind Flicka and put his cheek against the soft tangle of her mane.

When evening came, and Nell had called Ken and had taken him by the hand and led him away, Flicka still lay without moving. Gently the darkness folded down over her. She was alone, except for the creatures of the sky – the heavenly bodies that wheeled over her; the two Bears, circling around the North Star; the cluster of little Sisters clinging together as if they held their arms wrapped around each other; the eagle, Aquila, that waited till nearly midnight before his great hidden wings lifted him above the horizon; and right overhead, an eye as bright as a blue diamond beaming down, the beautiful star, Vega.

Less alive than they, and dark under their brilliance, the motionless body of Flicka lay on the blood-stained grass, earth-bound and fatal, every breath she drew a costly victory.

Towards morning, a half moon rode in the zenith.

A single, sharp, yapping bark broke the silence. Another answered, then another and another – tentative, questioning cries that presently became long quavering howls. The sharp pixie faces of a pack of coyotes pointed at the moon, and the howls trembled up through their long, tight-stretched throats and open, pulsating jaws. Each little prairie-wolf was allowed a solo, at first timid and wondering, then gathering force and impudence. Then they joined with each other and at last the troop was in full, yammering chorus, capering and malicious and thumbing noses and filling the air with sounds that raise the hair on human heads and put every animal on the alert.

Flicka came back to consciousness with a deep, shuddering sigh. She lifted her head and rolled over on her belly, drawing her legs under her a little. Resting so, she turned her head and listened. The yammer rose and fell. It was a familiar sound, she had heard it since she was born. The pack was across the stream on the edge of the woods beyond.

All at once, Flicka gathered herself, made a sudden, plunging effort, and gained her feet. It was not good for a filly to be helpless on the ground with a pack of coyotes near by. She stood swaying, her legs splayed out weakly, her head low and dizzy. It was minutes before balance came to her, and while she waited for it her nostrils flared, smelling water. *Water!* How near was it? Could she get to it?

She saw the tub and presently walked unsteadily over to it, put her lips in and drank. New life and strength poured into her. She paused, lifting her muzzle and mouthed the cold water, freshening her tongue and throat. She drank deeply again, then raised her head higher and stood with her neck turned, listening to the coyotes, until the sounds subsided, hesitated, died away.

She stood over the tub a long time. The pack yammered again, but the sound was like an echo, artless and hollow with distance, a mile away. They had gone across the valley for hunting.

A faint luminousness appeared over the earth and a lemon-coloured light in the east. One by one the stars drew back, and the pale, innocent blue of the early-morning sky closed over them.

By the time Ken reached Flicka in the morning, she had finished the water, eaten some of the oats, and was standing broadside to the level sun-light, gathering in every ultra-violet ray, every infra-red, for the healing and the recreation her battered body needed.

Chapter Twenty

Everybody went out to see Flicka right after breakfast and she stood against the fence as far away from them as she could get, while they discussed her injuries and her points, and whether she was more like Banner or Rocket—

Every remark made about her went through Ken as if it had been made about himself, if, but he too wanted to get a verdict and said, 'She's got wonderful points, hasn't she, Dad?'

McLaughlin glared at Ken. 'You've bought her, Ken. She's signed, sealed and delivered. Always choose them first, set your heart on them, buy them, and study their points afterwards – that way you'll be a first-rate horse-man.'

Ken's face got red and he looked away. Flicka, as if she felt the shame of her position, urged herself weakly along the fence in one direction, then turned and went in the other, trying to escape.

'*I* think she's a perfect little beauty,' said Nell, who was there in her riding clothes, ready to give Rumba her work-out.

'I want her moved down to the Calf Pasture,' said McLaughlin. 'There's shade there, and grass, and the running stream of water. I'll be needing this pasture for the other horses.'

'But the Calf Pasture's got only three strands of barbed wire,' said Ken uneasily. 'She might jump it and get away.'

His father cast him one of his withering glances. 'She won't jump it, Ken. She won't jump anything. Not for a long time yet.'

'Besides,' said Howard, 'down there she'll have company. The calves and our colts with their mothers. She won't be alone.'

'She'll be alone, all right,' said McLaughlin with a short laugh; and Ken remembered the remark about a loco horse always being a Lone Wolf. 'She'll keep to herself.'

Nell and Ross went down to the stable to begin the work on the polo ponies, and the rest of them spread out in a fan behind Flicka and gently urged her towards the gate which Gus had opened into the Calf Pasture. She went a few steps at a time, then stopped to rest with her head hanging weakly.

McLaughlin looked angrier than ever. Finally she was in the Calf Pasture and the gate was closed after her. Gus and Tim went off to their work and McLaughlin said, 'Come on, Howard, no use standing here looking at a sick horse all day.'

Ken was glad she was in the Calf Pasture. It was here the boys trained their colts, here the milch cows grazed at night and the calves in the day-time. And it was nearer the house. From the Green, from the terrace, from Ken's window, a great deal of the Calf Pasture could be seen, and it comforted Ken to think that Flicka was close by even when he couldn't be with her.

187

When the sun grew hot, that first day, she made her way with slow tremulous steps to the shade under the three pine trees that stood in a row on the hill. She hadn't yet gone down to the brook. It would be too far for her, Ken thought, so he carried the tub into the Calf Pasture and filled it with fresh water, and set the feed box with a measure of oats beside it – food and water, sun and shade, all within a few feet of each other. She barely touched the oats, blew out more than she took in, and didn't graze at all. Ken thought that perhaps it hurt her to move about, grazing – he must ask his father for hay.

After dinner the men were loading the four Rodeo horses, Lady, Calico, Baldy and Buck, into the truck for McLaughlin to drive into Cheyenne.

Ken hurried to catch his father before the truck started, and found him in the cab.

'Dad!'

McLaughlin looked down. 'Well?' he barked.

'Could I have a few forkfuls of hay for Flicka? She doesn't graze, I think she can't move around much.'

Being asked for hay was like being asked for his right eye. McLaughlin's rule was, never feed hay when there's greengrass growing.

He roared, 'I told you you cost me money every time you turn around.'

'Could I, Dad?' repeated Ken unflinchingly.

'All right,' said McLaughlin. 'Just for a few days.' He leaned out the window of the truck, shouting for Gus, and Ken dashed away.

'All set, Boss,' said Gus, coming around from the back of the truck. He got in beside McLaughlin, and the truck started off, with the horses prancing uneasily at first, but soon settling down to enjoyment of the ride, with their heads peeping over the high sides, looking curiously at the moving panorama.

Ken carried the hay out to Flicka on a pitchfork. Every

step he took for her was a joy. When Flicka saw him coming she tried to run away, and Ken said, 'Oh, no, Flicka, don't run away, don't be afraid of me. *I am Ken.* And this is hay. You like it, Flicka – come and get some hay.'

He stood some distance off, having placed the hay near the tub of water, and presently Flicka came limping back, smelled at it, and began to eat.

Ken lay with his elbow on the ground and his head propped on his hand, looking at Flicka. Now and then she would raise her head and look back at him, munching. She was getting a little bit used to him.

He knew she was better, her wounds were not bleeding today. They were swollen, and where the flesh had been pink and wet yesterday, today it was darker and dry. The scabs were forming.

Howard was doing his colts for him today too. Ken hated to leave Flicka even for an hour.

At milking time Tim went down to the cowbarn, carrying the milk pails. The bronco-buster, as usual, was with him, walking stiffly on his high heels, his thin legs in their pale blue jeans so bowed that a dog could have run through them.

They made a detour into the Calf Pasture to take a look at the filly.

'I'll be doggoned,' said Ross calmly, with no expression at all on his small face, 'she's beginning to look right pert.'

He sat down on a rock, took out his cigarette papers and a bag of Bull Durham, and expertly rolled himself a cigarette.

Tim stood there with two milk pails on each arm and the usual surprised grin on his comical Irish face. 'Well, Kennie,' he said, 'how do you like trained-nursin'?'

'All right,' said Ken, shamefacedly.

'When I seen her go for that fence,' continued Tim, 'I didn't really believe she'd try it – then I sez to meself, *crazy people you c'n lock up in asylums – crazy horses you gotta let kill themselves.'*

Ken slowly lifted his head and stared at Tim's dark red grinning face.

Suddenly all the odds and ends of thought which had confused him came clear in his mind. *Loco* – it wasn't just loco, the way you said, *Oh you're nuts*. It meant wrong in the head – lunatic asylums – crazy people – *Flicka wasn't right—*

Horror went through him like zig-zags of lightning.

'She sure is a wild woman,' said Ross seriously.

Ken looked from Tim to Ross. 'Do *you* think she's really—' The word that had always been so easy to say now stuck in his throat. He brought it out with difficulty – 'loco?'

'She sure is.'

'Did you ever break a – loco – horse, Ross?'

'Wa'al, now and then I git an outlaw handed me to break.'

'What do you do?'

'Break it if I kin.'

The bronco-buster flipped away the butt of his cigarette and rolled himself another.

'Last spring I had an outlaw to break – never worked harder with a horse in my life, but I didn't lick him, he licked me – just plumb wore me out.'

'Where was he?'

'Jock Heely got me to go down with him to a ranch where he'd bought a horse. Said I could break it out and ride it home through the Badlands. I oughta known better. He talked me into it. Got down there, found a wild, ten-year-old bronc, never been ridden. Jock, he'd always pass up a real good horse, buy the worst and the oldest. When you git 'em broke – if you do – you ain't got nuthin'.'

'Wa'al, I worked with him for three days straight. Got him so's I could ride him some. We started home through the Badlands. He'd git to turnin'—goldarned if I could make him go straight. An' I lost my sense of direction, 'cause when the sun set it set in the east. Yes, sir, I was turned plumb around and head back where I come from. Wa'al, I tied the bronc up to a tree, and lay down and went to sleep. In the mornin' I tried it agin, but he'd turn and turn till I was dizzy. Couldn't make him go straight nohow. Beat him till my arm give out. I quit him at last, left him go, and hoofed it to the nearest town with my saddle on my head.

'Now and again, I see Jock – an' he tells me I owe him a bronc. I tell him I owe him a good bit less than nothin'—'

'Could you break a filly like this?'

'Wa'al, if I was a-breakin' her, I'd not give her no oats – not much of anything till she was broke. Yer Dad now, he makes me feed these broncs oats while I'm workin' with 'em – that makes 'em too spooky and lively. I'd have had 'em broke long before this if he'd let me lay off the feed. With her, I'd git her weak-like, then tie up her feet so's she couldn't run, then sack her out till she was wore out fallin' down and gittin' up, then git on her back and give her the quirt. That way you kin git a horse to knuckle under, but Ken, you have to keep it up so long when they're loco, or a real outlaw, and treat 'em so mean, that there ain't much left when you git through with 'em. T'aint wuth it.'

Ken hardly knew when they left. The doors of the air-tight compartments in his mind had opened up and the events of the past fortnight unrolled like a piece of film. The bronco jumping out of the truck, rolling down the hill – the crack of the Winchester that sent it to its knees in the grass – Rocket going down the hole – the sound she made when she hit bottom like a muffled bass drum – *plunk* – before that, when she reared up in the truck and brained herself against the sign – when she fought in the chute and almost put out his father's eye – loco – *loco*.

But he remembered Banner too, and that made him feel worse than when he remembered Rocket. Banner – and how the officers had cheered, and his mother had cried, 'All his flags flying!'

Flicka ought to be running on the upland too, *her* flags flying in the wind, golden and beautiful like Banner — *not the hole* . . . if he could have undone it all then, and put her back on the range, free and alone, he would have.

Chapter Twenty-one

When Nell finished working with Rumba she changed
from riding clothes to a flowered print house dress. After
dinner she did the housework she had not finished that
morning, then went out on the terrace. She sighed when
she looked at the window boxes and the flower border, with
the blossoms beaten to shreds by the hail of the day before.
That was the way, up here on top of the world – such
things came down out of the sky! Rob, last night at supper,
was telling about a hailstorm where the blocks of ice were
so large, a man couldn't lift one; couldn't get his arms
around it. And a band of sheep had been cut to pieces.
People drove out in their automobiles from the nearby
towns to see the sheep that were lying around, killed by the
huge chunks of ice that fell out of the sky. The dead
animals made a stench for miles around. And she herself
had been in Cheyenne one Fourth of July when there was a

bad hailstorm, and the plate-glass roofs of all the greenhouses in town had been shattered; and every automobile which was in the path of the storm had its top cut to pieces.

Nell found her gardening gloves and her trowel and shears and went about clearing the broken flowers and leaves out of the boxes.

No more fresh home-grown lettuce for the table this summer ... the lettuce bed was cut to pieces ... too late now to start it again ... the glass over the hot-bed broken ... Rob'll have to get some more and fix it up ... he'll be wild ... what a stew he's in about Ken ... it was I that started it ... I said give him a colt ... and now look ... Ah-ah-ah – this geranium ... ruined ... might as well cut it back to nothing ... what for supper ... the cold meat loaf and creamed macaroni and cheese ... the oven'll be right for that when I've made the cookies ... make enough this time ... how these men go for sweets ... and Rob'll bring back the fresh tomatoes and lettuce and peaches when he comes home with the truck ... just look at this mess here ... what a storm ... four of the little Rhode Island Red chicks killed ... couldn't get under Mamma's wings quickly enough ...

When she had done what she could to put the boxes and flower borders in order, she went to the kitchen, built up the fire and began to mix the cookies, remembering with amusement how she had evolved this cookie recipe.

Rob had asked for doughnuts, made very rich and crisp as he had at some time or other in his childhood eaten them.

Nell studied doughnut recipes in several cook books, decided that to make them extra crisp, she should use more shortening; she settled on a composite of the different recipes, with generous quantities of rich Guernsey butter.

When the dough was made – a great mound of it, yellow with butter – she heated the fat in the iron kettle, cut out the first doughnut and dropped it in the fat to test it.

Watching, she was surprised to see the doughnut separate into two halves, then into quarters, then into eights, then into crumbs, finally vanish altogether.

Nell was in dismay, looking at the mound of yellow dough destined to melt into nothingness in the hot fat.

Changing her plan, she rolled it out into thin sheets, spread it on cookie tins, then with a sharp knife criss-crossed it into diamond shapes, put it into the hot oven, and presently took out a batch of the crispest, richest brown-edged cookies she had ever tasted.

This became the special cookie recipe of the Goose Bar Ranch, and whenever Nell was requested to make them, they told her to 'Start to make doughnuts.'

Now the oven was ready, and when she had nearly finished mixing the dough, Ken came into the kitchen. He leaned against the table, his elbows propped, his chin in his hand. A little red bandana was tied around his neck. His soft brown hair was in wild disorder.

'If Flicka's really loco, Mother—'

His appearance shocked Nell. The look in his eyes was direct, almost staring – nothing like Ken. He was looking at her now to drag facts from her.

'Well, Kennie?'

'If she's loco?'

'It's a bad lookout for her, then, isn't it?'

There was a long silence. He struggled. 'If she *really is*, Mother—'

'If she really is, Ken, then not all the king's horses and all the king's men—' Nell didn't finish, but flung the dough out on the table, floured the rolling pin and began to roll it out.

Ken watched her, hooked on that terrible IF.

'Mother, is there anything you want – *terribly?*'

Nell paused, looking out of the window, then began rolling the pin lightly over the dough again.

'Kennie, there's something I've wanted – *terribly* – for a long time.'

195

'How long?'

'Since a few years after you were born.'

'But Mother! I didn't know you *wanted* anything!'

'Most everyone wants something, dear—'

'But not *you*, Mother. You're grown up, and married and you've got Dad and us – why, you're *finished*—'

Nell laughed. 'And I shouldn't be wanting still then, if I'm finished, should I? But people do, Kennie.'

'Everyone? Always, Mother? Don't you ever get really finished?'

Nell again put down the rolling pin, and stood with a far-away look in her blue eyes. 'I wonder. Sometimes for a minute of two.'

That brief experience of peace and fulfilment that came, she thought, now and then unexpectedly and unaccountably. Why should one, at a certain moment, be held in the stress and ceaseless striving and wanting? And the next be almost swooning in desireless bliss – open, drinking, basking—

'Mother—'

'Well?'

'*Do* you? *Will* I?'

'Will you what?'

'Get through wanting?'

'What do you want now, Kennie?'

There was a feeling in his chest that his breath was too much for it and crowded it.

'Mother, I do so *want* Flicka to be all right and not loco.'

Nell looked at him, rolling the dough thinner and thinner.

In his eyes she saw a question. He was asking if it wouldn't come true, if he wanted it hard enough; and his face was strained in anguish.

Right now, she thought, narrowing her eyes against the tears that came so quickly, stinging them, *right now* – to let him know, once for all, that wanting, and wishing can't buck a fact.

'Perhaps she isn't loco, dear, we don't know yet for sure. But if she is, Ken,' her words came slowly, '*wanting* won't change it.'

Ken turned away and walked out of the kitchen with his chin tucked down into his neck.

'Come back when the cookies are baked, dear,' she called after him. 'There'll be some hot, crisp, brown, crumbly ones—'

She went on rolling out the dough, cutting the cookies, putting them on tin sheets in the hot oven. But she had really gone away with Ken, up the Hill, into the woods, face down on the pine needles, hands clawing at the ground, salt tears burning—

'No, Kennie – not all your love and longing – not all the wishing and wanting—'

But she didn't know that Ken was seeing the deep hollow shaft of the mine on the hillside, with a horse going down into it – not Rocket.

He couldn't stand it. There must be a way out . . . there always had been . . .

Ken turned over on his back and looked up at the sky. It was close, it was a deep blue, but not opaque; it looked as if you could go into it, farther and farther . . . Thinking this way, just drifting, he began to feel better. There were well-trodden paths in his mind that led out and away from the real, and on and into limitless worlds of fancy. He stopped thinking about Flicka. Stopped thinking about anything real. In that other world of fancy, there were colts and fillies too. He wanted the make believe colt that couldn't hurt itself, that could fly over six-foot fences, that needn't be broken and trained, *that couldn't be loco*, that would carry him on its back as easily as a bird carries one of its own feathers . . . He began to feel comfortable and free . . . this was the way . . . this was the way . . .

The boy lay motionless, his eyes wide, his gaze straight upwards into the blue. The lines of strain on his face relaxed. His mouth was slightly open, his expression faintly smiling.

An hour slid by. The light changed, the shadows lay long and flat over the world. A bird began to cry on an insistent anxious note but Ken did not hear or move. His breathing was regular and deep, but there was a pause between breaths, as with a person sleeping.

The insistent clanging of the supper bell roused him, and he sat up, startled. How could it ever be supper time already?

He turned in the opposite direction and looked to Flicka's place near the three pine trees in the Calf Measure. She was lying down, not very far from where he had put the tub of water and the feed box.

Something about the weariness of her body, prone on the grass, the utter stillness of it, wrenched at his heart. He had forgotten all about her, and had been off by himself, having fun— Supper – he mustn't be late!

He ran down the Hill, across the Green and into the kitchen and washed his face and hands and slicked his hair.

All his agony was back. Flicka – why, she might be dead out there – lying dead instead of just asleep – one couldn't tell – and if she was, it would be his fault, because he had really deserted her when he was thinking about all those other make-believe colts – he had turned his back on her. Perhaps his disloyalty might have broken the slight hold she had on life. Perhaps, somehow, she had known it, had known what he was doing, that he didn't want her any more; and perhaps she had felt more and more tired and weak, and at last had lain down, and . . .

After supper he hurried out to see her. She was standing up again, and this time barely moved away at all at his approach. He sat down before her on the grass, clasped his arms around his knees, and made his vows to her.

198

'I didn't mean it, Flicka . . . you're the one I want . . . I won't leave you again . . . never, Flicka, I don't want those other colts. *They're nothing, just nothing at all*. And you're my responsibility. That's what Dad said. I pulled you in from the range where you were free and wild and could take care of yourself, and I've made you so you can't; so you're my responsibility to take care of.'

Flicka stood looking at him. Her large eyes were dull and not fully opened. All her hair was very untidy. Her legs were not quite straight under her, but a little splayed out. But her ears were forward, she seemed to be listening, to be paying attention, and she was not frightened.

Chapter Twenty-two

Nell, with a dark blue silk kimono belted around her slender waist, was brushing her hair for the night. It lay loose upon her shoulders in a soft, wavy, tan mass; and as she brushed, she walked around the room, putting clothes away in the closet, opening the bed, bringing out Rob's pyjamas, and talked to him about Ken.

'I wish you'd be nicer to him, Rob.'

'Why? He's gone against everything I told him to do.'

'I think he's suffering deeply.'

'Suffering! So am I. And what's it all for?'

Rob, seated in the low arm chair, reached out a booted foot and dragged the boot-jack close. He planted one foot upon it, and set the other heel in the notch, continuing, 'If he was going to have a horse to break and train as Howard did Highboy, it would have taught him something, made a man of him. But what can he do with this poor little filly? Not a damned thing. He'll sit in that pasture and watch her all summer, and neglect his work. Howard has been walking his colts for him for two days.' He pulled hard against the jack, and drew one foot out of the long worn, brown boot.

'Give him a little time, Rob,' pleaded Nell. 'He's all torn up.'

'So am I. I'm *burned* up.' He pulled off the other boot and pursued his thought. 'There isn't a thing he can do with her in this condition. Couldn't put a halter on her. She's got no strength, even if she should pull through – which I doubt. Frighten her once more, drive her into a corner and rope her and halter her, and she's through.'

'But Rob, you don't see! It's already *done* – much of it. Ken is changed already. *He's* learning even though he can't train *her*.'

'Learning what? Learning to lie on his tummy under a pine tree?'

Nell sank down on a stool before Rob's chair and folded her arms on his knees. The week of heat and the hours of daily training and riding of Rumba had burned the end of her nose and brought colour into her face which was usually the shade and tone of pale, waxed pine.

Rob leaned back in his chair, and out of his dark face, his vivid, burning blue eyes looked at her without softening. 'Learning that it pays to be bull-headed?'

'No! He's learning to face facts. And that's the whole thing, isn't it?'

'Face facts! I don't see any sign of it,' he said harshly. 'And the kid looks like hell. If this goes on all summer he'll be in fine shape to go back to school in September.'

Nell felt rebuffed and got up and went about in silence.

Rob stood up, picked up his boots, kicked the boot-jack back into the corner, went over to Nell, and with the boots hanging in one hand, put the other arm around her.

'Love me?' he asked.

'I knew you were going to say that!' she exclaimed

angrily. 'When you've just made me mad, that isn't any time to say things like that.'

His one arm squeezed and shook her a little. 'Love me?' he repeated.

'I don't feel the least bit loving.'

'Love me?'

The one deep dimple in Nell's right cheek appeared in spite of herself and she turned her face away. 'Oh, *yes*, then, have it your own way!'

She made her voice insulting, but it was an irritating habit of Rob's to be satisfied with outward obedience, as if, once that was granted, by his own persistence and violence, he could drive people the rest of the way.

'That's all right then,' he said; and with his hard bullet head, pressed her face around until he could kiss her mouth.

'But Rob – Ken—'

'Don't talk about him,' he roared, dropping his arm. 'I've had all I can stand of him.' He went out the room, slammed the door, and stamped down the hall to the bathroom.

Nell climbed into bed, turned up the kerosene lamp that stood on the bedside table, took her book from beside it, and began to read. Her dimple had disappeared and her lips were very set and prim.

Next day Rob planned to drive to Sargent's ranch to make final arrangements about shipping the four polo ponies. Nell was to go with him, and they would be away all day.

When, at breakfast, Howard and Ken heard about it, Ken said, 'Would you have time, Dad, to come out before you go and look at Flicka and see how you think she is? She looks better, and she's eating some oats.'

'No, I wouldn't,' roared McLaughlin. 'I don't want to see her or to think about her.'

There was a heavy silence. Everyone ate rapidly, eyes

down. Presently McLaughlin's gaze swung over again towards his younger son and noted the circles under the child's eyes.

'Did you go swimming with Howard yesterday?' he asked.

'No, sir.'

'Why not?'

'I didn't want to leave Flicka.'

'Now I've had enough of this! Howard does your work, and you're all set to spend the summer under the pine tree watching Flicka. Do you suppose that's good for you? What sort of shape will you be in when it's time to go back to school? This is the hottest weather we'll have all summer. Your swim is good for you. You take a dip with Howard today and do your work too.'

'Yes, sir.'

Presently Howard said, 'Remember what you said, Dad? That Flicka would stay alone and not go near the other horses? You were right. She stays alone in the corner by the fence, or under the pines. Why does she? I thought horses liked company.'

McLaughlin made no reply, and Kennie came bravely out with the answer, 'Because she's a Lone Wolf.'

McLaughlin turned to Ken, surprised, and the boy looked back at his father. Rarely had he been able to face those hard eyes for so long a minute. He did it now for Flicka. If she was a Lone Wolf, then he was a Lone Wolf too. He had to fight her battles. He was with her, the same as her – and it gave him courage.

Matching his stare with Ken's, Rob said to himself, 'Well, I'll be damned. The little son-of-a-gun. Nell was right – facing facts – he's taking it on the chin.'

McLaughlin turned his head away and asked for another piece of toast. Nell jumped up and turned the piece of homemade bread which was lying on the edge of the coal stove. It was toasted a delicate brown. She brought it, hot and crusty, on the tin burner, and slid it on to the edge of Rob's plate.

Rob was thoughtful as he took a slab of the fresh unsalted butter and spread it on his toast.

'Ken,' he said presently, 'that isn't what I meant when I said Flicka would keep to herself. It's because she's sick. A wounded or sick animal always stays alone.'

Ken's dark blue eyes, confiding and full of hope, clung to his father's face, and McLaughlin felt an emotion within his breast.

'Oh,' said the boy. He would have liked to ask if Flicka was not a Lone Wolf after all, but it seemed wiser not to press his father's sudden kindness.

After a moment McLaughlin said, 'Has she salt, Ken?'

Ken's face showed such consternation that it was comical. Both Rob and Nell turned away their heads. 'No,' said Ken, guiltily, staring at his father.

'I've got a piece of iodized salt up in the stable,' said McLaughlin frowning.

'I won't be ready to leave right away, Rob,' put in Nell. 'If you want to go out to Flicka – I've a few things to do—'

'All right, Ken,' said his father. 'I'll bring the salt out to her, and give her the once-over.'

Joy coloured Ken's face and Nell emitted a faint breath of relief.

Ken rushed out to Flicka. He had already seen her that morning. Soon after sunrise he had presented himself, and standing before her, said, '*I am Ken.* Do you know me? Are you getting to like me? My name is Kenneth McLaughlin.' He put his fist on his chest. 'And your name is Flicka. That means Little Girl. We're going to be friends.'

Now he ran out to her again and said, 'Dad's coming to look at you, Flicka. Now you be a good girl and don't run away.'

As if she had understood him, Flicka stood quietly at a

204

little distance when McLaughlin came out and set the chunk of iodized salt down near the pine tree. Then he took out his pipe and lit it, and examined the filly, while Ken watched his father to read the verdict on his face.

Finally McLaughlin said, 'She's so sick and hang-dog – it's hard to tell a thing about her now.'

'Do you think she's – loco?'

Rob growled, 'I would have sworn it, by the way she's behaved ever since she was born, but as a matter of fact, we've never seen her except when she was scared out of her wits.'

Ken thought back. Even the first time he had seen her, when she was running away from Banner, and her eyes had looked like balls of fire, then too, she was terrified. Yes, and when she was brought in the first time – and the second—

'Every horse looks wild in the eye when it's terrified,' added McLaughlin.

Ken forced himself to mention the one worst piece of evidence against her. 'She tried to jump that fence – she knew she couldn't.'

McLaughlin said, 'You must remember she's had the worst possible bringing up.'

'How?'

'She's been brought up by a crazy woman, hasn't she?'

'Oh—'

'Besides,' said McLaughlin with a little grin, 'anyone – even you or I – can try the impossible once. You know the saying. *It couldn't be done but the darn fool didn't know it and went ahead and did it.* Horses *have* jumped six feet and more – trained jumpers. Maybe Flicka thought she could do it. So we'll forgive her that. Point is, will she learn? *Can she* learn? Rocket couldn't learn.'

'Dad, if she is – loco – like Rocket, couldn't we put her back out on the range?'

'Why?'

'So she could be like Banner was, Sunday – not like Rocket—'

Rob looked at Ken's face. It was so desperately earnest, so direct, that again the man felt an emotion. *Facing things*—

'Now let's think that through, Ken. Banner's on the range because he has work to do in life, isn't he?'

'Yes, sir.'

'What work?'

'Breeding the mares and taking care of them and the colts.'

'And what's a mare's work?'

'To have the colts – or be ridden.'

'Exactly. But if she's loco, her colts are no good. You saw that bunch I sold last week. Only reason I could sell them is because they're beautiful horses, and there's always some fool ready to take a chance on a horse, loco or not. Someone is breaking them now, or trying to. Some of them are dead or dying, or fatally injured. It would have been better if I had put a bullet into every one of them.'

'Better—' faltered Ken, his eyes going to Flicka.

'Better for them in the long run. But I needed the money.'

There was silence for a moment, and McLaughlin's teeth bit into his pipe stem grimly. 'Only place for a loco horse, or one who can't be subdued, is on the wide-open range; and far away from civilization too, where no man can see them and pull them in. If anyone sees them, and if they're beautiful and fast too, there's no hope for them. Someone's going to have a try at them, and that's the end.'

Ken could not speak.

'You've seen how the bad blood carries on,' McLaughlin continued. 'As for training them for the saddle, remember how hard I worked with Rocket.'

'Oh, Dad!' breathed Ken in dismay. 'Maybe I'll never get Flicka trained!'

'For God's sake! What have I been telling you? Warning you?'

Ken stood in a stupor.

'Didn't you understand?' asked his father. 'What did you think *loco* meant?'

'Oh, just goofy—'

'And when did you tumble?'

'Yesterday. Tim said, you could put crazy people in lunatic asylums, but you had to let crazy horses kill themselves.'

Rob gave a short, exasperated laugh. 'Well, thank God for Tim.'

'Dad—'

'Well?'

'When you said she'd been so frightened, always, when we'd seen her – did you mean that maybe she isn't loco?'

Before answering, Rob eyed the filly thoughtfully and drew several long puffs of smoke through his pipe. 'She's got a very intelligent face,' he said at last. 'Much better than Rocket's. Fine, delicate mouth, lovely eyes set far apart, that light tracing of veins all over. But we can't really know until we see how she responds to training.'

'How can I train her? What shall I begin on?'

'You can't do a thing with her now. All you can do is win her confidence. That's the most important thing anyway. There's one thing that will help you, Ken.'

'What?'

'Her sickness and misery. When you take away everything, freedom, friends, home, habits, happiness, from a living creature, almost life itself, it will turn, in sheer need and desperation, to the one thing that is left. And that's *you*.'

'*Me*.' Ken had never felt so important.

'Yes. You are her whole world. Make her like it.'

It was a serious moment for Ken; he was thinking about himself in a way he never had before, and he paid close attention to all his father was saying. McLaughlin took his time, as if there was nothing to do but examine Flicka and explain to Ken what must be done with her. He stood with one arm folded across his belt, the other elbow resting on it and the hand holding the bowl of his pipe. His legs, in their whipcord riding breeches and dark brown boots which were polished for the trip to Sargent's ranch until tints of ox-blood showed in the folds of the leather, were braced apart.

'I've been trying to breed fear out of these western horses for years. Flicka has been frightened. Only one thing will ever thoroughly overcome that, and that is, if she comes to trust you. Even so, some bad reactions of the fear may remain. This does not mean that you must not master her. You must. She will have many impulses that must be denied because you forbid the actions that rise from them. But that's discipline – that will come later – if she gets well. Meantime . . .'

'What can I do right now?'

'Not a thing in the nature of discipline. Give her love, give her companionship, give her your voice. Talk to her.'

'I do, Dad, all the time.'

'That's right. Make her grow so dependent on you, so used to your coming and going, *always with some good thing for her* – hay, oats, fresh water, or just talk and friendship – that she can't help turning to you.'

McLaughlin paused, his thoughts going farther afield. 'I have read stories of wild animals in circuses – vicious, untamable individuals – who became gentle and tractable because they fell ill, or got hurt, and some human being tended them and cared for them kindly. It has often happened. That's why I say Flicka's weakness makes your opportunity. *You* don't have to restrain and discipline her, because her wounds are doing that already. And you are on her side, against her weakness and pain. You help her.'

Flicka had come closer and was licking at the salt.

The lecture went on. 'Remember, a horse can tell you a lot of things, if you watch, and expect it to be sensible and intelligent. Pay attention to all the little signs – the way it moves its body, the ears, the eyes, the little whinnies – that's its way of talking. There is the neigh of terror, the scream of rage, the whinny of nervous impatience (that's a very funny sound), the nicker of longing or hunger or friendliness or delight or recognition. She'll talk to you, and it's for you to understand her. You'll learn her language, and she'll learn yours – never forget that *they can understand everything you say to them.*'

'*Everything*, Dad?' This was really exciting.

'Everything. And when you once realize that, friendship with an animal begins to be quite a different thing. Communication, see?'

When the red Studebaker, as clean and shining as if for a trip in to church, had taken his parents over the cattle guard and around the bend of the hill, Ken hurried back into the Calf Pasture. Now that he knew Flicka could understand him there were some more things he wanted to tell her. How sorry he was—

He would stand in front of her and say, '*I am Ken.*' (That was important for her to know.) 'And I am your friend, Flicka. I am so sorry, so – very – sorry, you are hurt, and I hope it doesn't hurt you much any more. I'm going to give you everything you need and I'll be with you, so you won't be very lonesome— I'll have to leave to go swimming in a little while, and I'll have to walk my colts, but that won't be long—'

But Flicka wasn't near the pine tree. As Ken stood, looking for her, he heard her neigh, and his heart gave a leap. It was as if she was speaking to him. It was the first sound she had made since her terrible screams in the stable the day she was caught. Then he saw where she was standing, at the southern fence, her head stretched over it, looking off to the Saddle Back. Her ears were pricked, she was listening, and Ken heard the faraway sound of hoofbeats — the yearlings were galloping on the upland.

Flicka neighed again, and by the lift of her head, and the way she was turned, and the sound she made, Ken knew she was heartsick for the freedom she had lost ... it was the *Neigh of Longing* ...

Ken's head dropped on his chest; there was a burning behind his eyes; he turned away and walked slowly back to the house.

Chapter Twenty-three

Ken found a nicer place for the filly.

A fence ran from the corrals of the cowbarn, straight
north, dividing the Calf Pasture from the practice field; a
path led along this fence, and, about three hundred yards
from the corrals, reached a spot where several cottonwood
trees made a wall of foliage. Under the boughs of the trees,
the path sloped sharply down for ten feet or so to a flat area
of beautiful green turf, through which Lone Tree Creek
ran.

When the creek was in flood, all this flat part was
covered; but now, in summer, it was dry, and the grass
such a vivid green that, coming upon it from the dryer land
roundabout, it was startling to the eye. Golden sunlight lay
upon part of it; part of it was dark and pleasant with the
shade of the cottonwood trees that hung over the hill and
sent their roots winding down its face to bore underground

for water. Here, without having to hunt for it, Flicka had rich grass to eat and running water to drink; there was both sun and shade.

Ken called the place *Flicka's Nursery*, and each morning and evening he walked down the little path carrying a can of oats to empty into the wooden feed box which he had set near the roots of the cottonwoods.

Standing as tall as she could at the foot of the bank, Flicka could just see over the top of it and catch sight of Ken coming. He could see her too. It made him tingle all over, the first time he saw her head – just the pretty face, with the blonde bang over her forehead and the dainty pricked ears framed in the down-hanging branches of the cottonwoods – and realized that she was looking for him and waiting for him.

Ken bragged about it that night at supper, but Howard said, 'Nuts! She's lookin' for her oats, not for you.'

McLaughlin answered sharply, 'Oats, or the bringer-of-oats, in the long run it gets to be the same thing.'

And Nell added dryly, 'Are human beings any different?'

No doubt about it, Flicka did love her oats. As Ken stooped over to empty the can into the feed box, she would be close beside him reaching her nose in; but when he put out his hand to stroke her, she pulled back. She would not let him touch her.

Ken still had work to do; work in the corrals when the brood mares were brought in with their colts and the colts were branded; work on the fences when Tim was sent out with the small Ford service truck, full of fence posts that had been cut the summer before, dried, and dipped in an asphalt mixture to protect them against ground-rot; work on the ditches and the meadows which must be given every possible chance to grow hay in these last weeks before the cutting. Now that the Rodeo horses had been taken to town, the two boys were riding Cigarette and Highboy again, and every few days must ride the boundaries of the ranch to spot any breaks in the fence, any strange animals that had got in, any gates open that should be shut. Fishermen came in from the highway, opened the gates to drive their cars through so they could get down to the stream to fish, and sometimes drove out again without closing the gates. One day Ken and Howard found a hundred head of yearling steers that had got in on the McLaughlin land and were gorging in the meadow and trampling the grass. The boys galloped home to give the alarm; McLaughlin and his men rode out, drove the steers off and then McLaughlin, in a rage, wired up the gates and planted posts across so that they couldn't be opened again.

There was also the daily work of halter-breaking and training the four little spring colts. McLaughlin had taught Howard and Ken just how to do it, and for the first day or two he helped them himself.

First, the colt must be penned. The little one came running beside its dam, and the mare came for oats. Once in the small pen, the colt – not much frightened because it was standing by its mother – was held forcibly and the halter put on, and a long lead rope slipped into the halter ring.

Now the colt was hauled away from its dam out into the larger corral to the hitching post. The rope was looped several times around the post, one of the boys was given the end to hold and placed himself behind the post, so that the colt thought he was being held by the boy – not by the post.

Invariably, the colt pulled and fought against the rope. He shook his head from side to side, he braced all four feet out straight and stiff. Even grown horses did this, sometimes sitting down like big dogs. Occasionally this pulling and fighting went on for a long time, but as a rule, with a young colt, it was soon over. The sudden surrender was almost always expressed in the same manner. The colt would rear straight up, paw the air a moment, then plunge forward to release the pull on his head. That plunge was a movement *towards* the master – a capitulation; and the colt never forgot it. At the moment of the plunge, when he approached most closely the one who was coercing him, there came the sudden physical easement of strain – a good feeling. If he stood there, trembling, close to his master, there was the comforting voice, the hand patting his head, and he began to feel safe. Sometimes there were tugs of war again, but never so long nor so determined. And in a day or two the habit was formed. At the slightest pull on the halter rope, the colt would follow.

From this point on, Howard and Ken needed no further assistance. The colts became as familiar with the boys as they were with their dams. They would sniff and nip at them, rear up and play, striking at them with their little forefeet.

The last week or so, all Ken and Howard had been doing with their colts was to lead them by the halter around the pasture, saying *Whoa* now and then, at the same time halting the colt; and making them go at different speeds, from a slow walk up to a brisk trot. When they had walked them enough, they took them back into the pens, removed the lead ropes and played with them, patted and whacked them, waved blankets around them, leaned on their backs, fed them oats out of their hands.

Right over the fence from the Calf Pasture, where the boys worked with their colts, was the practice field, and here, for many hours a day, Ken's mother and father and the bronco-buster worked with the four polo ponies, Rumba, Blazes, Don and Gangway.

At last the day came when the work was done. The four ponies were loaded into the truck and McLaughlin drove them to the station to be shipped with Sargent's bunch.

Then the little bronco-buster left. They all gathered around his battered sedan, packed full of saddles and equipment, and said good-bye to him and wished him luck at the Rodeo.

'Don't take chances,' Nell McLaughlin said. 'But I notice you're pretty careful.'

Ross's steady blue eyes looked at her in his direct and respectful manner, and he answered, 'A man that monkeys around wild horses don't kid himself any, Missus. It don't do no good.'

Then he grinned, 'I may be in hospital agin after the Rodeo, but if I ain't, I'll be back to see how Ken makes out with his filly.' He grinned at Ken and Ken grinned back.

Then he took off his sombrero, shook hands all around, climbed into the driver's seat and rattled off.

And the next thing that happened was the Rodeo.

Ken was entirely alone on the ranch that day with Flicka, when suddenly she couldn't get up from the ground.

It was the last day of the Rodeo. The Studebaker had gone into Cheyenne on each of the four days of the big show, FRONTIER DAYS, called by Cheyenne boosters, *The Daddy of 'em All.*

Ken went the first day and saw Lady and Calico and Buck and Baldy in the parade, ridden by four of the City Fathers, all dressed up in ten gallon hats and fringed chaps. He saw the famous bucking horse, Midnight, throw every rider that mounted him. But Ken didn't go in again, not even on this last day when there was going to be the wild horse race, and it annoyed his father; but McLaughlin said it was up to him. If he'd rather be alone on the ranch than at the Rodeo with his family, why, he could suit himself. But one thing was certain, no one was going to stay with him – not Gus or Tim either, because they'd both been promised the day off. Gus would be back on the four o'clock bus to milk the cows, and until then Ken would be alone.

Ken said he didn't mind – he'd have Flicka.

Ken stood by the car to see them off, and, the last thing, his father stuck his head out the window and called to him,

'All right, kid – leaving you in charge! – *it's all yours!*' And the Studebaker, carrying his mother and father and Howard and Gus and Tim slid down the hill, rattled over the cattle guard and bowled smoothly down the road.

Ken stood there, watching it until it disappeared. How different everything was now that they had gone. *All yours* ... He felt the responsibility his father had laid upon him ... he was in charge. The two dogs, Kim, the collie who looked like a coyote, and Chaps, the black spaniel, were standing beside him. They, too, were watching the empty road. They were used to doing that, and they knew the difference – the road with the Studebaker on it, going or coming, the road empty, and silence all around.

Ken went up to his room and stood before his bookshelf. He picked out the 'Jungle Book', then ran downstairs and out, across the Green, into the Calf Pasture, and down the path by the fence to Flicka's Nursery. She was drinking at the brook when he came.

He greeted her with a stream of talk; he visited with her a while, standing as close to her as she would let him. Then he seated himself on the bank of the hill under the cottonwoods and began to read.

Flicka wandered around her nursery. Sometimes she wanted sunshine, and stood under the dappled golden light until she was warmed through, then a few steps took her into the shade of the trees. Ken, glancing up, saw her standing quite near, watching him. He began to read aloud to her, and her ears came forward sharply as if she was listening.

He read her the part that told about Rann, the Kite, seeing Mowgli, the wolf-boy, carried through the tree-tops by the flock of monkeys; and about Mowgli remembering the Master Word of the Jungle that Baloo, the brown bear who was his tutor, had taught him, and crying to Rann, the Kite, 'We be of one blood, ye and I— Mark my trail! Carry word to Baloo of the Seeonee Wolf Pack, and Bagheera of the Council Rock! Mark my trai-ai-ail!'

Flicka's head turned. As Ken's voice went on, she moved over to the empty feed box, sniffed it, put out a long pink tongue and licked up a few stray grains left over from her breakfast. Then she stood quietly, broadside to Ken, switching her cream-coloured tail to keep off the flies.

Now and then Ken stopped reading, put his book down and lay back on the hill with his arms under his head, looking up through the branches of the trees. He could see a patch of blue sky with a little vague half moon floating in it, the daytime moon, called the Children's Moon, because it is the only moon most children ever see. At first he thought it was a little soft cloud.

It was another hot day, but down here it was pleasant and shady. There wasn't a sound, except for the ripple of the stream where it ran over stones and shallow sandy places, now and then the splash of a trout that flipped out and in again, and, all the time, a faint hum, the buzzing of the racing flies that were always in the out-of-doors. It was a sound that went with summer – part of the silence.

Ken and Flicka were all alone in the Calf Pasture. The four colts that the boys had trained, and their dams, had been taken out to Banner on the Saddle Back, because the job was done – and well done, McLaughlin had said – the colts were perfectly halter-broken. It had taken about a month.

Flicka went down to the stream to drink and Ken's eye followed her. Flicka, of course, had never been halter-broken. It was a most important part of a colt's training and should be done as early as possible because it was the beginning of everything. But Flicka was a year and several months old, and she wouldn't even let him touch her. As for flirting blankets around her, or putting a rope on her – the very thought of such a thing made shivers run down his spine – he could imagine her fighting the rope – behaving as she had behaved up there in the corral and the stable – behaving like Rocket – *Loco—*

At this thought Ken drew up his knees, clasped his arms around them and put his head down on his arms, hugging himself against the dread – *he didn't know yet if she was or wasn't*. He *couldn't* know until he began the halter-breaking. He felt sickening tremors inside.

Just a little while ago he had found courage, somehow, to face the possibility of Flicka's being loco, but now his courage was gone – or at least, he could not easily find it. The hope and sweetness of the weeks of caring for her, and the little filly's tentative response to him, had pushed the dread out of the foreground of his thoughts; had almost pushed it into one of those air-tight compartments of his mind. But the doors did not close as tightly as they had before. The boy knew what was behind them. Having faced the horror once, and righted himself after the shock, he would be able to do it again.

A vague sense of this came to Ken before he lifted his head from his knees, and it gave him strength to look forward to that day – and it was a day that was coming soon – when *Flicka would have to be halter-broken.*

Then he deliberately shoved away all these unpleasant thoughts, shut the door on them, and gave himself up to the rapture of contemplating his filly. The little animal was disclosing to him an odd, fascinating personality; whimsical, remote, temperamental. She moved a step or two at a time across the turf. In the sun, her glossy hide shone like gold, the long cream tail swinging to one side or the other. Now and then she stopped and stood motionless, her attention caught by some far sound or movement that Ken could not hear or see at all; and her statue-like pose, the graceful turn of her neck, the delicate, pointed ears, and every line of her body, instinct with life and intelligence, exerted on Ken the fascination that horses have always exerted upon human beings. He had fallen under her spell – a classic spell.

If she could only, *really* make friends with him! He had done his best to win her confidence. He had done all that his father had told him to do. Surely she knew that he loved her and he was there just to serve her and care for her, and still, when he came near, there was that alert turn of her head, the wary look in her eye, and the quick step away. Still – when the colts galloping on the upland were near enough to be heard, she turned to them, and yearned to them, and whinnied in longing. If she had four good legs, and her freedom, thought Ken, he'd never see her again – she'd be just a stream of power and speed – gold and pink – whipping over the range—

He sighed. Well – it was time to eat – he must go up to the house and get his lunch.

Flicka was still standing up when he left. When he came back, running down the path with the dogs at his heels, his eyes were fastened on the spot just over the brow of the hill where he so often saw Flicka's face watching for him, but it wasn't there.

He ran down the hill and saw that she was flat on her side.

As she heard him coming she made an effort to get up and fell back again.

It stopped Ken dead in his tracks. Then he ran to her and fell on his knees beside her. 'Oh Flicka,' he cried, 'what is the matter, Flicka? What's happened to you?'

She was dying . . . she had been dying all along – or, something had happened while he was away at lunch . . . perhaps she'd fallen and hurt herself again . . . perhaps her back was broken . . .

Hardly knowing what he was doing, he patted her face and kissed it. He went behind her, crouched down, put his arms around her head and held it.

Flicka made another effort to get up. Lying on the left

side, when a horse wants to get up, it rolls over on its belly, straightens the forelegs, pushes against them and against the right hind leg, and so gains its feet. The only leg that is not used in the process is the left hind leg upon which the horse is lying.

About to make the effort, lying on her belly with her legs gathered and her head up, Flicka neighed, ending in a few little grunts, and Ken had to smile because he understood just what she was saying. It was not exactly the neigh of nervous impatience of which his father had spoken, but it was a neigh of determination, and the grunts added on were from nervousness – she was going to do it but wasn't quite sure that she could.

Ken stood back to give her the chance. She started the scramble, then collapsed suddenly and dropped her head again.

'Oh, Flicka, Flicka!' he cried, almost certain now that something must be wrong with her back; and again he fell on his knees and took her head in his arms.

She heaved a deep sigh and half closed her eyes, completely relaxed, while Ken's little brown hands went all over her head and neck, smoothing the silken softness of her skin, patting the sensitive curves of her face, straightening her forelock.

She let him! Was it only because she couldn't help herself? Or was it perhaps what his father had said, that now, in her greater trouble and helplessness, the last shred of her fear had gone and she really wanted him and loved him? Whatever it was, it released all the boy's tenderness and longing. He pressed his hands upon her – he laid his head down on hers, and his breath was troubled.

At last he went back to the bank of the hill and sat down, wishing that the afternoon would hurry by and that Gus would come. The bus would drop him at four o'clock out on the highway. It would take him half an hour to walk to the house, change into his blue jeans (he'd be all dressed

220

up in a tight shiny blue serge suit with a ten-gallon hat and fine shoes) and be ready to milk the cows. Ken was to bring the cows in and have them waiting in the corral, and he was to measure out the cow feed and put it in the feed boxes for the cows, so Gus would have nothing to do but drive them in and milk them.

Flicka seemed to have gone to sleep. Presently Ken lay down on the hillside and fell asleep too.

A sound came into his sleep. A loud, distressed crying. It got louder and louder and then was a terrible, anguished bellowing, and Ken was sitting up straight, wide awake, and tense with fear. It wasn't anything to do with Flicka, but she, too, was holding her head up from the ground, listening.

It was a cow bellowing. The sound came from the east, beyond the Calf Pasture. That was Crosby's land. It wasn't one of the Goose Bar cows then.

Ken was frightened and sickened by the sound. Something awful must be happening. What? Ought he to go and find out? (*You're in charge—*) Maybe the mountain lion. His thoughts jumped to the Winchester . . . where was it? . . . in the back of the Studebaker . . . no, no, the officers had been shooting with it and afterwards his father had put all the guns back in the gun-rack in the dining room . . . yes . . . he could get it, could go to see what was the matter . . .

The boy got slowly to his feet. Should he get the Winchester first? Or go to the cow first? Would he be able to use the Winchester? It was heavy . . . perhaps better to get his own little twenty-two . . . perhaps go first and see what was the matter . . .

Indecision paralysed him; then suddenly he came to life, turned and ran eastward. He flew along the edge of the brook, crossed and re-crossed wherever the footing was best. Some places the willows crowded down thick to the edge of the stream and he had to go around. The bellowing continued. Well . . . anyway, if it was the wildcat it hadn't got her . . . she was making plenty of noise . . . maybe it had got her calf.

Ken ran fast so he wouldn't be frightened. He saw the red hide of a Hereford cow – not one of their own Guernseys. She was standing on the edge of the creek where a barbed wire fence crossed it. As Ken rolled under the fence and went around to her, he couldn't see that anything was the matter – then he saw, and it made him sick.

The bottom strand of the wire fence was broken; some other old wires were tangled with it, and the whole web of wire was wrapped around the cow's udder. She had tried to tear away – one teat was hanging almost off – blood was pouring out of it. The harder she pulled, the deeper the barbed wire embedded itself.

Ken put his hand to his hind pocket of his overalls. He had been told by his father, *never let me catch you out without a pair of wire-cutters in your pants pocket.* But the cutters weren't there. He remembered, clean blue jeans this morning, and the cutters lying on the table in his room. He headed for the cowbarn; there would be cutters there. While he ran he was wishing that Gus would come. He wondered if he should wait for Gus to cut the cow loose – (*it's all yours . . .*) No, he'd do it himself.

It took him fifteen minutes to get back to the cow with the cutters. Then he had been running so hard, he had to kneel beside her for a few minutes until his breath came easily and his hands were steady enough to begin work.

The cow, frantic with pain, tried to butt him. Again and again she plunged to tear loose. Ken talked to her and tried to calm her while his small hands, not too expert with tools, struggled with the cutters, clipping the wire here, there and again, drawing out short pieces, pulling the barbs out of her bleeding flesh, until at last she was free.

He had been wondering what he should do with her. That one teat and some of the long cuts should be sewn up. Perhaps Gus would do it, if he could get her into their own cowbarn. But the cow saved him the trouble of deciding. When she found herself free, she started off at a gallop, blood and milk together dripping from the wounds. She was heading for her home barn.

Ken walked slowly back through the Calf Pasture to Flicka. She was still lying as he had left her.

Horror and loneliness settled down on the boy. He went hunting for the cows, found them in Section Sixteen and drove them all in and shut them in the corral outside the milking barn. He measured their feed and put it in the boxes. Then he went out to the roadside, sat down on a rock and fastened his eyes on the place, half a mile away, where Gus would first appear when he came walking in from the highway.

Ken could hear the sound of the trans-continental traffic. A horn tooting, a car changing gears. The light changed. The shadows fell lengthwise on the grass ... he had the feeling of going off into a day-dream and his eyes wandered ... but he pulled himself back. Flicka ... and the cow ... he was caught into the mesh of things ... he couldn't leave them. Way off on the road there was a little black speck – Gus! plodding along, his arms swinging from his wide, bowed shoulders, walking as if his shoes hurt him.

Ken leaped off his rock and shot down the road to meet him. He couldn't stand the lonely waiting another minute.

Chapter Twenty-four

Ken wanted Gus to examine Flicka immediately, but nothing could deter the Swede from getting back to the bunk house and extricating himself from his city clothes without a moment's delay.

As they walked up the road together Ken told of his day – the terrible things that had happened, Flicka down and hurt somehow, and Crosby's cow with her udder torn to pieces, and how he thought at first the wildcat had attacked her. As he talked he kept looking up at the face of the big foreman. Gus's pale blue eyes, with pupils as small as pin points, were always full of light, and when he smiled his lips went up at the corners like a child's. Nothing ever upset Gus, or hurried him. The big, flashy sombrero looked funny on his grey curls.

While Gus changed into blue jeans and elastic sided boots, Ken put the cows in their stanchions.

Even when the milking was finished and the cows driven

out into the pasture, Gus would not go down to see Flicka or eat supper until he had saddled Shorty and ridden over to Crosby's ranch to see about the cow.

Ken got supper in the bunk house, and when Gus returned they ate it together up there; cold beefsteak, boiled potatoes, apple sauce with thick yellow cream.

The cow had gone home. When Gus got there, Crosby was bandaging her udder. Gus helped him and told him how Ken had found her and cut her loose from the fence. They used adhesive tape and bandages.

'Why didn't you sew her up?' asked Ken.

The Swede shook his head. 'She's tru. Dot cow no good for calving nor milking. Crosby goin' to take her to de butcher.'

Gus washed the dishes and Ken wiped them and put them away. Then Gus took out his pipe and lit it, put his old, torn felt hat on his head, and they walked down through the pasture to see Flicka.

Ken carried a can of oats with him, and, halfway down the path, began to call the filly's name and to whistle to her.

Suddenly he clutched Gus's arm and stopped walking. He called again – there was an answering nicker!

'Oh, Gus – she's calling to me!'

'Yee whiz!' said the Swede, his lips turning up in a smile, 'she sure is, Kennie.'

Ken ran ahead, loping down the path and calling, 'Flicka – Flicka – Flicka—' and an eager whinny came again from the little mare.

When Gus reached the nursery, the filly was sitting up, eating the oats which Ken had poured into her feed box.

'Dot's a funny ting,' said the man slowly, standing over her. 'She's got good appetite. Don't seem sick or hurt.'

He sat down on the bank, comfortable again, and glad to be home, and drew peace into his soul with long quiet puffs of his pipe.

'What do you think it is, Gus?' asked Ken anxiously. 'Should we try to make her stand up?'

Gus shook his head. 'Better wait till your fadder come home. It might be her back, but sittin' up like dot – eatin' her oats – I don't know.'

Ken brought a bucket of water and Flicka put her nose in and drank.

'Ay tink dot smart little filly,' said the Swede.

'You don't think she's loco, Gus?' Ken rolled away the bucket and sat down on the grass beside Flicka with his arm around her neck.

'No. Luk at dot face, dot eye. Not white ring around, like Rocket's.'

'But, Gus, she *did* try to jump that fence—'

'Dot's bad mudder. Bad habits. Wid Rocket, she always go tru fences.'

'Yes. Dad said she was always tearing through fences after that bitch of a mother of hers.'

'But Ken, Rocket break 'em, and de filly *go after*. Dot's *right*. Little fillies must go after deir mudders. Now dis time, is different. Flicka try breakin' 'em once herself and she get bad fall, bad minutes lyin' on de ground wid wire cuttin' in lak fire. Mebbe she smart enough to learn lesson. Mebbe she never buck de wire again.'

'I was on Shorty once, and we stepped over a little piece of loose wire lying on the ground, just an old rusty piece not more than ten feet long, and when Shorty's feet touched it, he shook all over.'

'Shorty's smart horse.'

The family did not get home until after ten. Gus had gone to bed long since, but Ken was waiting for the car on the hill behind the house – he and the two dogs watching the empty road. The sky was crowded with stars, and the Milky Way so brilliant that it shed a soft light over woods and fields and stream.

When Ken saw the headlights of the car, a happy glow

went through him. Chaps began to bark, and both dogs got up and moved around restlessly, wagging their tails and nipping at each other.

The car roared up the hill, circled around, came to a stop, and Ken jumped on the running board and stuck his head in the front window.

His mother's face was right there, smiling at him from under her green turban, and everyone spoke at once. She said, 'Hello, darling, here we are – were you lonesome?' while Howard yelled from the back seat, 'Gee, you missed it! You oughta seen the wild horse race – three Indians fell off.' And his father was looking over the seat, handing Tim the keys of the car, and telling him to open up the back and unload the sacks of potatoes and onions.

'Howard, you help Tim unload and put away the provisions,' he added; then turned to Ken. 'Ken. I want to see you.'

'Dad, Flicka—' It was the third time Ken had said it.

'Come on.' His father's hand fell on his shoulder and pushed him down around the end of the house.

'Dad, Flicka—'

'Ken, I'm proud of you.' They were standing on the terrace, and Ken, looking up with his mouth open in surprise, saw his father's face, tired, but showing his big white teeth in a smile of pride.

Ken stared.

'Crosby's cow,' said McLaughlin. 'We stopped at Tie Siding on the way home for the mail. Crosby was there getting *his* mail. He told me how you had cut his cow loose from the wire when her udder was caught and that Gus rode over and told him.'

Ken was getting ready to say, 'Flicka,' again, when his father lifted one of the boy's hands and held the small, helpless, softness in his own hard fist. 'I used to think these hands of yours would never be good for anything. They had as much strength to them as wet spaghetti; but today they manipulated a pair of wire cutters on a cow that was crazy with pain. You never did anything like that before in your life. What made you do it?'

Ken, wondering himself, said, 'Well, she bellered so, you could hear something was the matter – I thought it might be the wildcat after her; and I remembered you said *it was all mine*; and I thought, if it had been Flicka—'

'Flicka, eh?' McLaughlin turned away and walked towards the door, still holding Ken's hand in his. 'Well. Now what was it you were going to tell me about Flicka?'

Ken rapidly poured out the tale of Flicka's injury and helplessness, and McLaughlin listened gravely.

'How do you know she can't get up?' he asked.

'Because she tries. She gets her head up and makes a sort of scramble, and then falls back again. She acts like she's hurt her back,' he added, his eyes devouring his father's face.

'How's she lying?' asked McLaughlin.

'Right on her side, in her place down there,' said Ken, and added, 'Gus and I didn't try to move her or get her up, we thought you'd know how to do it.'

'And I suppose she can't eat,' said McLaughlin wearily.

'Oh, yes, she ate her oats.'

'How?'

'I put the box right by her nose, and she lifted her head up and ate them.'

'All of them?'

'Yes. Cleaned them all up. And then I gave her a bucket of water and she drank some.'

'Can't be very sick then. I'll wait till morning, Ken.'

'Oh, Dad, please—'

'Shut up!' roared McLaughlin going towards the door. 'Can't a man ever have any peace? Time you were in bed too – come on.'

After breakfast next morning Rob went down to the nursery to see Flicka. Nell left her dishes and went too, with the cat on her shoulder. Howard and Ken were already there.

Flicka had eaten her breakfast oats and licked the box clean. She lifted her head with ease, she whinnied now and then, but she would not get up.

Rob's observations were always made rapidly. He said, 'Stand back, all of you— I'm going to roll her over to the other side.'

Flicka was lying on her left side. He went behind her, leaned over, got hold of her left legs, one in his left hand, one in his right, then, backing off, he gently hauled her over until she was lying on her right side.

The filly immediately made a scramble, using her two forelegs and the left hind leg to push with, and got up. Everyone laughed. Flicka stood calmly in the centre of the group, and when Ken went to her head and put his hands on either side of her face, she remained quiet.

'Nothing wrong with her back,' said McLaughlin. 'It's her leg. That right hind leg. She couldn't use it to push with, and, lying on the left side, she couldn't get up without it.'

'But she's *been* using it, Dad,' said Ken anxiously.

'Yes. It was all healed up, but look at it now. It's swollen. That means infection, and it hurts her worse than it did at first. Look, she's not bearing any weight on it.'

Ken's face was distraught when he noticed the swelling above the joint. Everyone knew that the worst danger of wire cuts was the infection that so often followed. 'What do you do for an infection, when it's a horse?' he faltered.

Nell answered cheerfully, 'Just what you'd do if it was a person. Wet dressings; poultices, so that it will open and drain.'

Flicka showed no sign of fear or nervousness. When Ken petted her and smoothed her neck, she looked at him with trust and gratitude.

'Now that she'll let us get close to her,' continued Nell, automatically stroking her cat, 'there won't be any trouble about it.'

'Why does she let us, Dad?' asked Ken.

'Well,' said McLaughlin grimly, 'she's only got three legs – she can't run away, can she?'

He walked off, Howard after him. Ken knew that his father couldn't bear to look at a sick animal. But his mother said, 'We'll get that cleared up in no time, Kennie. I'll help you.'

A load fell from Kennie's shoulders. At least Flicka wasn't going to die. At least her back was not broken. He went back to the house with his mother, and she boiled some meal and put it in a linen bag, and mixed a disinfectant wash and put it in a bucket for Ken to carry down.

When Flicka saw them coming, though Ken carried a bucket and Nell a basin with the poultices and bandages – enough to frighten even a well-broken horse – she showed no fear.

'She *has* got sense, hasn't she, Mother?' muttered Ken, as they prepared the poultice. 'She knows we're helping her, doesn't she?'

'Looks like it,' said Nell, preoccupied with the bandages. 'Now you stand at her head, Ken – she's more used to you – while I do this—'

Flicka raised her leg off the ground while Nell bathed it and bandaged on the poultice. It made a comical-looking white knob above the hock.

Chapter Twenty-five

Ken's nights were no longer dreamless. There was no
peace for the boy. By day his new responsibility, his
passionate hope, his meticulous care of Flicka; and by
night a procession of dream-adventures, sometimes terrible ones. Often his mutterings and cries brought his
mother or father to his bedside. Something was ever – and
ferociously – at his heels.

It was an agony; and his appearance changed in a way
that was noticeable. Both boys usually grew taller during
the summer vacations, and put on weight too, but Ken had
gained no weight this summer, only height; and his face
was strained and anxious.

But through the agony ran a thread of something so
exciting that he was strung like a taut bow. There was the
first, thrilling whiff of real achievement. It was not only his
hands that had changed. All the listlessness of the day-

dreamer, the sliding away from reality, had gone. He looked, stood, moved, eagerly and with determination. He was in love. He was in the very core of life, and he wrestled with it as Jacob wrestled with the angel.

The achievement was Flicka and the winning of her friendship. He had a horse now. He had her in the same intimate sense that Howard had Highboy. He couldn't ride her yet, but she was his because she had given herself to him.

She loved his hands, his touch, his caresses. She loved to have him stand at her head, facing her, his hands lightly holding her cheeks. They looked into each other's eyes as lovers look. He spent all the time with her that he could.

While she stood eating her oats, his hands smoothed the satin-soft skin under her mane. It had a nap as deep as plush. He played with her long, cream-coloured tresses; arranged her forelock neatly between her eyes, She was a bit dish-faced, like an Arab, with eyes set far apart. Ken kept a curry-comb and brush in the crotch of the cottonwood tree, and lightly groomed and brushed her. Flicka enjoyed this. As she moved about her, first on one side, then the other, kneeling down to brush her legs and polish her small hoofs which had the colour and sheen of cream-coloured marble, she turned her head to him, and always, if she could, rested her muzzle on him. Ken grew used to the feel of the warm, moist lips against his shoulder or back, and his mother complained of all the polo shirts he dirtied tending to Flicka.

He spoiled her. Soon she would not step to the stream to drink but he must hold a bucket for her. And she would drink, then lift her dripping muzzle, rest it on his shoulder, her golden eyes dreaming off into the distance, then daintily dip her mouth and drink again.

When she turned her head to the south and pricked her ears and stood tense and listening, Ken knew she heard the other colts galloping on the upland.

'You'll go back there some day, Flicka,' he whispered. 'You'll be three and I'll be twelve. You'll be so strong you won't know I'm on your back, and we'll fly like the wind. We'll stand on the very top where we can look over the whole world, and smell the snow from the Neversummer Range. Maybe we'll see antelope—'

As her leg got better, Flicka took to following Ken around. She came hopping at his whistle or call and turned and kept beside him as he walked. He would have his hand under her chin, or around under her neck and up the other side of her face, hugging her, or just resting on her neck lightly, with a strand of her mane between his fingers.

This was what he had always dreamed of. That he should have a horse of his own that would come at his call and follow him of its own accord.

Now and then, walking down to give her her oats, he stopped and thought about it in a daze of bliss. Just what his father had said . . . she looked for him as if he was her whole life. She didn't seem to think of anything but him. Before breakfast, when he came through the cow-barn corrals, carrying the can of oats, she was waiting at the gate for him, nickering. She nosed for the can of oats. He held it away and hurried down the path, telling her that the proper place for her to have her oats was in her nursery. Flicka hopped along by his side. She knew as well as he where they were going, and when they reached the hill, ran ahead and was standing over the box when he poured the oats in.

After breakfast, when Ken went down again, his mother was with him, and Pauly, the cat, at her heels. And again Flicka knew what to expect, and was waiting at the corral gate. She turned and hopped in front of them, leading the way to the nursery, and when she got there, stood in the accustomed place, holding up her hind leg for Ken to take the bandage off.

All her timidity had gone. Nothing frightened her now. With her acceptance of Ken there seemed to have come to

233

her a conviction that all men were friendly and safe and their queer doings harmless.

Every day, when the bandage was removed, the wound sponged and washed with disinfectant, and the new poultice and bandage put on, Ken made a fire on the other side of the fence in the Practice Field, and burned the old dressings.

All the time Flicka listened to Ken talking to his mother, turning from one to the other, as if she could understand them.

'Dad says she *can* understand,' said Ken. 'Anyway, she can talk. I understand about six of the things she says.'

His mother boasted, 'Pauly can talk too. She can say seven things.'

'What,' challenged Ken.

'She can say, *Oh, good morning, good morning, good morning. I have been waiting the longest time for you!* That's when she's been waiting in the kitchen for me to come down and make breakfast. And she can say, *Oh, please, can't I have it?* And, *All right for you!* And, *Well, what do you want now?* And, *Isn't this a lovely day? Let's do something!* And, *Oh, leave me alone!* That's when she's a nervous woman. And, *I'm just a poor little helpless cat trying to get along in the world.*'

'That's seven,' said Ken.

'She can really say more than that, because she says *something* every time I speak to her – just a word, maybe.'

'What word?' demanded Ken enviously.

'It depends. *What?* or *Yes*, or *Thanks*, or *Oh, the dickens!*' To prove it, Nell looked at Pauly who was lying on the bank, crouched like a Sphinx, her yellow eyes half open, and spoke her name sharply.

Pauly's reply was as quick as the bounce of a ball. A little sharp, questioning, cry. *Well, what do you want?* This, Ken had to admit, was more than he could get out of Flicka.

234

The filly's physical condition was improving. She ran all over the Calf Pasture on three legs. She was up on the hillside near the three pines in the early morning, broadside to the sun, getting what Nell said was her radium treatment; and the first thing when Ken woke in the morning, he looked out of his window and saw her there, standing in profile, motionless as a statue, her head hanging low and relaxed, as all horses stand for their sun-baths.

The poultices drained and cleansed the deep wound above the hock, and the soreness was relieved, so that Flicka had no difficulty in getting up from either side alone. Soon she began to use the leg in walking; and then Nell said it was time to discontinue the poultices.

The achievement which Ken had been getting just a hint of, like the scent of something delicious but far away tickling the nostrils of a hound, was more than a hint now. It was a reality. A victory that filled his lungs and shone from his eyes and gave strength to his hands. Flicka had recovered. Flicka loved him. There was only one more thing . . .

'Dad,' he said at supper that night, 'Flicka's my friend now. She likes me.'

'I'm glad of that son,' said McLaughlin. 'It's a fine thing to have a horse for a friend.'

Ken's face was strained. 'And her leg's better,' he said. 'It doesn't hurt her. So—'

'Well – what?'

'Well – we've got to find out, don't we?'

'Find out what?'

'If she's *loco*.'

'Loco! Oh.' McLaughlin grunted and frowned. 'She's not loco.'

'But you said we wouldn't know until we began her training.'

'Have you had that in your head all this time? That little filly's got as nice a disposition as any horse I ever knew.'

'But Dad, how do we know? She might be crazy – like Rocket – like she was herself up in the stables, if we tried to put a rope on her – and she's *got* to be halter-broke—'

McLaughlin looked at his small son with a quizzical grin on his face. 'Oh, that's what you want, is it? Some help in breaking that wild woman!'

Kennie nodded. Rob's eyes sought Nell's and then he pushed back his chair, took out his pipe and looked out of the window gravely.

'I think we might do that tomorrow,' he said finally. 'Yes, I think I'll have time. Right after breakfast.'

When supper was over, Ken fled from the table and ran to take Flicka her oats. He told her all about it. He stood smoothing her mane, he begged her to be good. He assured her there was nothing to be afraid of in being halter-broken. He told her how he and Howard had halter-broken the colts; that the colts had liked it; they had all had fun together. He begged her – he begged her! *Oh, Flicka—*

He began to think of what would happen if she *wasn't* good. He thought of Rocket, and then the hole – and then he laid his face against Flicka's mane, and stopped talking to her, because he couldn't tell her about those things – she just wouldn't understand.

Nell came looking for him. She liked to pay a little visit every day to Flicka. They walked up through the pasture together. The air was sweet with the perfume of wild roses. In the sunset there were long horizontal bands of deep rose and golden pink with dark blue sky in between. There was a mass of mauve and violet cloud above. A sickle moon rode in the midst of the colour with one star drawn close.

Nell seized Ken by the shoulder and whirled him around before he saw it. 'There's a new moon in the sky, Kennie – look at it over your left shoulder – and that's good luck.'

Ken obediently looked. He didn't want to stop looking. If it was good luck— Oh, if it was good luck—

Chapter Twenty-six

When Gus leaned in at the door next morning and said *What's today, Boss?* McLaughlin began to outline a full day's work.

He was planning the haying. They'd begin in mid-August. The grass was deep and ripe. They could cut early this year. The weather had been so fine that all the ranchers in the neighbourhood were getting ready to cut. Along the roadsides the mowing machines were already laying swathes of fragrant hay flat. The air smelled different. It was said that when hay was cut in Wyoming, the perfume of it was on the wind for hundreds of miles.

The mowing machines with all their small razor-sharp blades must be gone over, bolts tightened, worn parts replaced; harness mended; new prongs put in the rakes; some repairs made on the stackers . . .

Ken sat in an anguish of suspense while his father gave Gus directions that, surely, meant a full day's work.

'And Gus—' added McLaughlin, 'right now, before we begin with all that, Ken is going to halter-break his filly— I want you and Tim on hand—'

Gus's eyes opened in astonishment. He glanced at Ken's scarlet, downcast face. '*Ja*, Boss— Vere vill ve do it?'

'In the Calf Pasture. Call Tim.' McLaughlin rose from the table. 'We'll do it right now, and get it over with.'

Tim and Gus came down from the stable carrying lariat, halter, and a lead rope.

They stood in a group just inside the fence, and McLaughlin walked forward a short distance with Ken, and told him to call the filly.

Ken obeyed. Presently Flicka appeared coming around the shoulder of the hill. She trotted up to Ken.

McLaughlin undid the red bandana from Ken's neck, handed it to him and said, 'Just sling that around her neck and tie it in a loose knot.'

Puzzled by these strange directions, Ken obeyed, and Flicka returned what, apparently, she thought was a caress, nuzzling his neck with her nose.

'And now take your belt off,' said McLaughlin.

'Here,' said Ken, in a complete fog.

'Slip it through the bandana,' said his father.

When Ken had done that, the belt hung in a loop under Flicka's neck. McLaughlin waved his hand. 'Now go down the path – put your arm through that loop.'

Ken did so, while McLaughlin stepped backward, put his arm across his wife's shoulders, and pretended to lean his weight on her. He was thoroughly enjoying himself.

Ken walked down the path and Flicka hopped by his side, close to him. When they reached the cottonwoods on the hill, McLaughlin called, 'Now turn around and come back. Let go the loop. Just hold your hand in the air under her chin.'

Ken obeyed. The leather belt, the bandana, hung loose on the filly's neck. Ken's hand was in the air under her chin. He led her by an invisible bridle, and the filly followed as close as she could.

'I'd call that halter-broken,' said McLaughlin grinning as the boy reached him. Ken was stunned. 'But Dad—' he said, 'but it's not a *halter*, Dad—'

'You take some convincing, young feller,' said Rob. 'But all right. Give us a halter, Gus.' Gus stepped forward and gave him the halter.

'Now put it on her,' said McLaughlin, handing it to Ken.

Ken almost shook. He held the halter in his hands and turned to Flicka but dared not take a step in her direction.

'How shall I put it on her?' he asked, thinking of the way he and Howard had to struggle with the first halter and the colts.

'Just the way I put the halter on Taggert,' said his father.

Ken thought about that. His father walked up to Taggert holding the halter openly in his hands, and Taggert stood there and stuck her head in it.

He summoned all his courage, went to Flicka and held out the halter. Flicka, who loved his hands, and had never felt the touch of them except in gentleness and affection, came closer, and Ken slipped the halter over her head, and hooked it under her throat.

'Now lead her,' said his father.

Ken obeyed and went down the path twenty yards or so – an easy halt and turn – and back again, with Flicka following so close the lead rope was slack.

'But Dad,' said Ken, completely dazed, 'how did she get halter-broken?'

McLaughlin did not answer directly. 'That's all, folks,' he said, turning to the small audience. Gus and Tim were both grinning. 'That's the way we break horses on the

Goose Bar Ranch. I wish Ross Buckley had been here to see that.'

'But Dad,' protested Ken, slipping the halter off of Flicka's head. She stood beside him, nosing at it, nipping at it with her lips.

'Figure it out,' said McLaughlin boisterously as he walked away. 'Come on, Gus, we'll get at those machines—'

At noon Ken went bathing with his mother. McLaughlin and Howard had gone to town to buy new parts for the mowing machines.

It was a good-sized reservoir which McLaughlin had made in the little pasture between two of the meadows, by damming up Deercreek, just before it joined Lone Tree Creek. The pasture was picturesque, with towering rocks, the two streams, sparse wooded patches alternating with grass.

Ken lay face down on the springboard which jutted out over the deep end of the pool. The sun beat down on his small, wet, brown body. It felt delicious. Everything was delicious – outside and inside him. Nothing to dread any more – no doors closed in his mind against thoughts and fears that made him sicken and tremble – it was all good, the sun, the water, Flicka, his father—

Nell was floating as she loved to do, her ankles crossed as comfortably as if she was lying on a couch. Her head, capped in heavy white rubber, was tilted back so that the water came over her ears, and she saw the whole landscape upside down as if she lay in the bottom of a bowl with the trees and hills and rocks walling her in. Close over her face was the deep blue of the sky, with the fleecy clouds drifting across. It was a moment of perfect rest.

Every so often the turmoil of life quietened down. Things that, it seemed, could never turn out right, unaccountably did. Things got done. Worries faded away. Here was Flicka now, getting better; Rob pleased and being nice to Ken; Ken happy as a lark.

Nell turned on her face and long lazy strokes of her arms made her slide through the water. Her brown feet, small and bony and as naturally formed as a child's made short chopping strokes and churned a white wake behind her.

'Look at Pauly, Mother,' shouted Ken. And Nell, turning her head on one side, saw the little cat on the bank, anxious and almost determined to swim out to her.

'Come on Pauly,' she laughed, wondering if any cat would. Pauly longed to She meowed eagerly; she ran up and down the bank; she even stopped, reached out her paws, and tapped at the surface of the water; she crouched and strained forward as if she was going to. But she didn't.

Nell waded to her, held out her hands, and Pauly flung herself into her arms and climbed to her shoulder.

Walking home through the flooded meadow they let Pauly follow, to see how she would manage it.

Perhaps she would leave them and go home over the hills. But Pauly would neither leave them nor be left; nor was she daunted by the water and the deep grass.

She proceeded in a series of leaps, splashing down into the water, shooting up above the grass the next moment to get a glimpse of those she was following, then disappearing with a large splash. Not even a cry came from her. She conserved every particle of energy for the difficult feat of locomotion.

At last Nell picked her up and let her ride on her shoulder.

Pauly promptly began to lick herself, smoothing her soft brown fur that had got wet and mussed.

There were still some loose ends of confusion in Ken's mind that had to be cleared up. He had been haunted too long by the spectre of the pit.

'Mother,' he said, 'is it *absolutely certain now* that Flicka isn't loco?'

Nell stopped and looked down at her small son from under the big shade hat that was on her loose hair. 'Are you still worrying about that?' she asked.

'Well, how can he be so *sure*? She *is* halter-broke – at least, *kind of* – I can see that. But she's not really trained. There's lots to do yet.'

Ankle deep in the warm water, waist deep in the fragrant timothy and red-top, with her kimono over her arm and her brief black bathing suit drying on her body, Nell stood in thought a few moments. She wanted to banish this fear forever from Kennie's mind.

'Of course she's not trained yet,' she said. 'And you're right in thinking that it's not all going to be as easy as this was this morning. Flicka will oppose you – she will struggle – and you will have to master her. That has to be done. But, darling, there won't be any trouble about it at all – it'll be easy as easy – won't either hurt her or worry you—'

'Why not?'

'Well, she loves you, doesn't she?'

'Oh yes!'

'Well, that shows that she's intelligent. And an intelligent horse that has already had some handling will fight *reasonably* – and that's all.'

'Why does it show that she's intelligent?' demanded Ken.

'Well, it's just a way of putting away fear and facing the truth. What would the world be without love?'

Ken was completely at sea.

'Well, what would it be like here at home, on the ranch, if there wasn't any love here?'

Ken said *O*, and his mouth made a crooked oval in the middle of his innocent face, but it did not close.

Nell started forward again, and glancing down, smiled to see that Ken was as unaware of the love as he was of the air he breathed or the earth under his feet. She tried once more.

'If you find *love* – if a person or an animal finds love – it's the same as finding safety, isn't it? It's comfort and friendliness and help. Everyone longs for it – any kind of love. But if Flicka – we'll say – had found it and yet didn't have sense enough to *know* she'd found it – and went on being crazy and silly with fear—'

'Then she'd be loco?' finished Ken as comprehension came. He looked up at his mother eagerly.

Nell nodded. Pauly, sitting on her shoulder, put out her tiny rough red tongue and licked Nell's cheek.

Ken shouted triumphantly, '*Then she's not loco.*'

That night, when Ken came back from taking Flicka her oats, he walked to the terrace where his parents were sitting and said, wagging his head, 'More poultices, please—'

Nell, who was laughing, stopped as she heard Ken's words and turned to look at him. 'What's the matter?'

'Her hock is swelled up again and she holds the leg up.'

Both his parents sat so still and so gravely for a moment, that it made Ken anxious. 'The poultices cured it before – they'll cure it again, won't they?'

Nell got up suddenly. 'I'll go down to look at it, Ken—' McLaughlin went too.

They looked at the wound which was swollen and obviously painful. Her right foreleg was swollen too, all the way from the knee up to the scar of the chest wound.

Ken was alarmed when his father pointed out to him the second infection. 'Can we put poultices on that too?' he said anxiously.

Nell nodded. 'Sure. It won't be an easy place to bandage, but we'll manage.'

Next time McLaughlin went to town he brought back a bottle of serum and gave Flicka a hypodermic injection.

'What's it for, Dad?' asked Ken anxiously.

'For a generalized infection like this.'

'Generalized infection?'

'Yes. She had just one infected place, on her leg. This chest wound was all healed up and never had been infected. Now it's infected. The infection came through her blood-stream from her leg. That's called a generalized infection.'

McLaughlin spoke in a casual, matter-of-fact way, and Ken's anxiety was allayed.

'Will it get her well quick, Dad?' he asked, beaming.

'Hope so, son – sometimes it helps a lot – sometimes they seem to do as well without it.'

'Where'd you get it?'

'I got it from Dr Hicks.'

The name of the vet always made Ken think of money – and it gave him a shock. That thing his father had said— You cost me money every time you turn around—

'How much did it cost, Dad?' They were walking back together.

'It cost ten dollars.'

Ken stopped walking and McLaughlin strode on without him, heading for the tool house, near which Gus was working on one of the mowing machines.

Ten dollars! *Ten dollars* ... when his father crabbed about every penny the boys spent ... about a forkful of hay ...

Ken ran after his father. McLaughlin was already arguing over the blades with Gus. 'Dad,' he began.

'Well?' McLaughlin's head was raised from the machine.

'I – I – didn't know – what you said, you remember—'

'Well, out with it!' roared McLaughlin impatiently.

'That I cost you money every time I turn around. I didn't see how I could, but now, why, Dad! *Ten dollars* .... thanks ever so much Dad—'

'Ten dollars!' shouted his father, with the twisted, sardonic grin on his mouth. 'Why, for you, Kennie, that's nothing. A mere wave of the hand. You're the boy that threw away three hundred dollars just looking out of the window for an hour.'

'Why – why – I never – three hundred dollars—'

'Go on away and let me work,' roared his father, and bent his head again over the machine.

Ken found his mother. She was busy too, sorting the laundry, sitting on her heels on the floor picking over a big pile of shirts, blue jeans, socks and linen.

Ken posed the problem. 'How did I, Mother? I never did, did I?'

Nell laughed and wrote *six prs. blue jeans* on her list. 'Yes, you did. You looked out the window for an hour when you should have been writing a composition. So you weren't promoted and you have to repeat the grade. And it costs about three hundred dollars for one year's schooling for you—'

'*Three hundred dollars,*' breathed Kennie with awe. 'How can it?'

'Count it up, eight months' board at $25.00 a month. A hundred dollars for tuition and books. You wasted all that, you see. If you had written the composition, your father wouldn't have had to pay that over again for you.'

Ken went to the table, sat down and propped his head in his hand, staring down at the red-checked cloth. It could hardly be believed that such momentous things could follow the small misdemeanour of looking out of a window and neglecting to write a composition.

'If I wrote it now, Mother,' he said at last.

'Well, I told you to do that, a month ago,' said Nell. 'Have you done it?'

'No.'

'Have you even thought of it again?'

'No – not since when Dad said he wouldn't make me do the study.'

'You might do it of your own accord,' said Nell, writing on her list. 'He does things for you of *his* own accord—'

245

'I know – that's it. Mother, do you think if I wrote it, Mr Gibson would take me back in my own grade?'

Nell put down her pencil and paper, and sat back on her knees. 'Kennie, you write the composition, *The Story of Gypsy*; and I'll write him a letter, explaining. And we'll send them to him. And perhaps when school opens, he may decide to let you try again.'

She began to crowd everything into the big laundry bags and Ken got down on his knees to help her. When it was done, she said to him,' And you'd better hurry up about it. Before you know it, summer'll be over.'

Chapter Twenty-seven

By the time the harvest moon, as yellow as saffron, rose over the dark sky-line of the eastern horizon, and hung there, trembling behind the pulsations of the atmosphere, there was the smell of autumn on the wind and a blanket of dazzling fresh snow on the Neversummer Range. When the breeze veered to the south, the smell of it blew over the ranch, alien and challenging like the startle of unexpected fingers tapping at the door.

There were different flowers in the dells and along the the streams. No longer the pink and blue and white of spring and early summer – larkspur and delphinium and bluebells. Instead, feathery golden rod; black-eyed susans; asters; everything gold and purple, for the autumn.

The fine weather still held. And because it was due to break any time, McLaughlin decided to hire a crew of six extra men, and get the haying done in three weeks, instead

247

of taking on only a couple of extra hands and letting the work run through September.

Nell had a dozen to cook for, and she was so busy Ken had to wash and disinfect Flicka's legs by himself. The poultices were discontinued. The wounds were hard, but not open any more.

Meals for everybody were in the ranch-house kitchen. No more cooking for Gus to do in the bunk house. Now, when there was a crew of men, Gus's position as foreman of the ranch became more than honorary. After McLaughlin, Gus was in charge, his particular responsibility being the care of the machinery, for which work, like most Swedes, he had an innate ability.

Ken and Howard thought it was fun to eat in the kitchen with the hay crew. The men stamped in at meal time, with clean washed faces and hands, and freshly slicked hair; and the kitchen rang with loud laughter and joshing remarks.

Never a day passed without difficulties or alarms, or some minor catastrophe. To begin with, the hired men were undependable, and for the first week, McLaughlin was kept busy sizing up his crew, firing some, taking them to town, picking up other men. And quite as often as he himself did the firing, they fired themselves for no known reason. Just the laconic statement:

'I'm quittin', Boss.'

'O.K.'

The proximity of the two towns, Cheyenne to the east, and Laramie to the west, made the men restless. They could hear the transcontinental buses out on the Lincoln Highway; and the moment they had a few dollars in their pockets, they were in a fever to spend them.

Other things happened. One day the biggest hay wagon, fully loaded, was turned too sharply by the driver, and tipped over. It had to be completely unloaded, righted, then filled again. Two good hours wasted, and McLaughlin's face as black as thunder.

248

A team of horses, hitched to the rake, ran away and collided with the corner post of the fence, snapping the pole of the rake, and injuring one of the horses.

Another day, when McLaughlin had gone to town, the men tried to get the baler across the creek in Castle Rock Meadow, bridging it by means of a few heavy boards laid across. They foundered the heavy machine in the mud of one of the banks and failed to get it out during a whole morning of sweating and shouting and cursing.

When McLaughlin reached the meadow, at two in the afternoon, he found that the day, so far, had been wasted. Nell, who had driven down to the meadow in the car with him, waited to see how the affair came out.

McLaughlin took charge. He had two teams of horses hitched to the baler. He had the men bring railroad ties and place them as levers behind the wheels which were sunk in the mud, two men on each lever ready to throw their weight on it when he should give the command. McLaughlin himself took the reins and the long whip, and, suddenly giving the command, unleashed enough co-ordinated energy to up-end a house. 'Ginger! Sultan!' The crack of the whip was nothing to the whip-crack in his voice. The men all broke into yells and jounced their weight on the levers; the horses strained and pulled, frustrated by the great weight of the foundered machine. For long, unbearable minutes, McLaughlin lashed the horses with his whip and his voice, while the baler, with the implacable resistance of inanimate things, crouched in the mud. There was no let-up. The terrible striving and struggling was sustained without weakening – kept going by McLaughlin's will and voice and fury – until at last sweat broke out all over Nell. The worst thing to see was the plunging and straining of the four horses.

Suddenly the baler gave up, it tilted out of the mud and climbed the low bank to the accompaniment of yells and cheers.

McLaughlin shouted, 'Whoa!' The horses relaxed, trembling and heaving, and McLaughlin went to their heads and thanked them.

'Good boy, Ginger; good boy, Sultan – well done, old Nellie – Tommy—' Each one got a pat and a word of commendation and their wide, frightened eyes, gazing at McLaughlin, became calm.

McLaughlin explained to the men that the collapse of the bridge was due to the fact that they had laid the boards across the stream at an angle, instead of straight.

Offsetting all the difficulties and wasted hours was the fact that the weather held. McLaughlin had gambled on its holding and for once he played in luck. A fresh wind sprang up every morning just before sunrise, increasing as the day drew on. Much of the raking and gathering of the hay, the loading of the wagons, and the stacking, was done in such a smother of blowing grass that everyone's teeth were on edge. But McLaughlin was thankful. It was the wind that made the weather hold. Storms were gathering all around Sherman Hill, great banks of clouds accumulated and compressed until, driven into themselves, they were formed into coils that were ready to explode in cloudbursts and sheets of flame if they once reached the freedom of the higher areas. When the wind died down at sunset, the edges of these cloud banks could be seen pushing up over the horizon, and during the night they hurried their pace and spread halfway over the sky, gathering themselves for attack, only to be dispersed by the bright strong wind that came with the dawn.

McLaughlin's eye was constantly on the sky. It was not often that a rancher got plenty of water in the early part of summer when the grass was growing, and then dry weather for the haying.

He drove himself and the men.

At meal times, the conversation turned to politics and economics as is the case whenever groups of farm workers are gathered together; and then McLaughlin would remember that a good crop often meant, not wealth, but poverty to the producers, and he would launch himself on a bitter tirade.

'A good crop?' he shouted. 'Yes. So what? So the price of hay goes down till a man can't sell his surplus and break even on the cost of putting it up. I tell you – all this talk of our economic difficulties! – the nigger in the wood-pile is the law of supply and demand. It's cock-eyed!'

'How do you make that out, Boss?' asked Tim.

'Because when you're rich, you're poor. This whole country rich as Croesus – and on relief! Is that cock-eyed? Or is it? Take this county, for example. Suppose we have fine weather, fine crops, all the stock in good shape. Now that's wealth. *Real wealth*. But what's the result? Counted in dollars, we're poor. Sometimes the best crops make a man the poorest. If I should have a good crop of hay here, by chance of freaky weather conditions, as sometimes happens, and everyone around have bad luck – cut their hay at the wrong time, or something like that, then I have to be tickled because I've got the hay when no one else has, and I can boost the price, and charge more and more, when my neighbours are broke, and their animals starving and they have to come to me and buy at my price, and mortgage everything they've got to pay me! That's the year I ought to sell low – but that's the year I sell high! Anything that works out as wrong as that in practice, has to be wrong in theory. Years when we have natural wealth and abundance, we ought to have money in the bank and be able to pay our bills and send our children to college.'

'Do away with the law of supply and demand, and ye do away with a hull lot else,' said old Harvey. 'Ye'd have to have fixed prices, for one thing – no more competition—'

'And no more trusts and monopolies neither—'

McLaughlin pounded his point home. 'The harder you

work, the better you do your job, the more success you have – the worse off you are! Treat a horse that way and what would you make of him?'

It would usually be Gus who would cut the argument short, rise from the table and summon the gang out to their work.

McLaughlin had neither the time nor patience to help Ken with Flicka. Or, thought Ken, was it because she had cost him that ten dollars for the serum that he was so short and irritable?

When Ken bothered him to know what he should do next with the filly, McLaughlin roared, 'Oh, do anything with her you want! Lead her around. Get her used to the corrals and the stables.'

So Ken led the filly by the halter and lead rope. Into the pens and corrals, up through the Gorge into the horse corrals where she had been caught. When he first tried to get her through the door of the stable, she halted, and Ken did not force her. He stood at the door with her, and finally left her there and went in alone and poured some oats into the manger for her. That did the trick. She walked in of her own accord, and when she had eaten her oats, became curious and investigated every corner of the barn. Together they made the rounds, Ken at her head, discussing what they saw.

Everyone on the ranch got used to the sight of the boy leading the little golden mare around. She used three legs, and held up the fourth. The wound on the foreleg was hard and swollen, but did not seem to pain her.

Both the boys had to spend part of each day in the haying field. There were many ways in which they could be of assistance. When the hay was being tossed from the little piles into the hay wagon, to be carried to the big stack and dumped there, the boys could stand in the wagon, tramping the hay down, and distributing it with pitchforks, so that it would load more evenly. There was endless running

of errands and fetching and carrying to be done on Highboy and Cigarette.

'Howard, see this little bolt? Go up to the tool house,
and on the shelf over the window you'll see an old coffee
can, and pick out some more bolts like this, and bring
them—' or

'Ken, ride up to the house and tell your mother to fix up
the dinner and bring it down here in the car to us at noon
time—' or

'Go tell your mother we need some first aid here – a
man's got a bad cut. Tell her to hurry down in the car—'

Howard spent the whole day with the hay crew; but
Ken, when he was let off, hurried back to Flicka in her
nursery.

He was beginning to have a feeling of pressure. Here it
was almost September – school began the fifteenth – only a
couple of weeks more to spend with Flicka. Standing at the
filly's head, so he could talk to her and look into her eyes,
he thought about it and it was appalling. Why, the whole
summer was gone! Back in school soon, *without Flicka*,
living apart from her for many months, not seeing her, not
even knowing what she was doing, how she was looking,
what she was learning – bad tricks or good—

Ken knew that he had to take it like a man. It was part of
the price he paid for Flicka. There was also the composition. He was writing it. He brought his copybook down
to Flicka's nursery and sat on the side of the little hill
between the trunks of the cottonwood trees and worked at
it, and read bits of it aloud to her. It needed to be only a
few pages long. Making it up was not hard, there was
plenty to say, but it was hard to get the spelling right, and
the punctuation. When it was finished, he would copy it at
the desk in his room so that the penmanship would be
perfect.

'This,' he said proudly to Flicka, 'is a three-hundred-
dollar composition, Flicka. Dad gave you to me, Flicka,

and I'm giving him three hundred dollars. So, you could say, I'm paying for you – that's a pretty good price for a little yearling filly – but I'll have to take ten dollars off that, for the shot of serum—'

Sitting nibbling the end of his pencil, his thoughts concerned with *The Story of Gypsy*, his eyes were on Flicka, and it seemed to him that her ribs were showing. It was the first time he had noticed that. She ate her oats, she grazed, but she certainly was thinner than when she had been brought in off the range, thinner even than she had been a week or two ago.

He spoke about it to his father. Rob glared at him. 'Do you give her oats twice a day?'

'Sure.'

'Does she clean 'em up?'

'Yes.'

'All right, then.'

'But Dad – would you come and look at her?'

'God damn it, no! Don't bother me about her!'

Ken went back to Flicka and his copybook and pencil. But when he looked at her, his eyes were troubled. The wounds seemed neither better nor worse; hard and dry and somewhat swollen; but certainly, she had lost flesh.

Everyone is thin, thought Ken, after an illness. And Flicka had been ill a long time. She would pick up gradually, the way grown people did, when her sickness was quite over. Besides the wounds, there was that thing his father had said – an infection of the blood-stream. That means she was sick all the way through. She had a lot to get over.

Chapter Twenty-eight

Nell was counting the days until the hay crop should be in, the haying crew gone, and she would have time to breathe again. She lived in the hot kitchen, or in the car, driving back and forth to town for supplies.

When supper was over and the dishes washed, she had a few hours for herself. She would have a tubful of water waiting for her upstairs; would run up, slip off her kitchen smock and step into the water, then dress in fresh clothes – her cool grey linen slacks and blouse, and wander off alone into the woods for refreshment and solitude.

One night she decided to go up to the Stable Pasture, her favourite haunt. At the last moment, thinking of the meals for the next day, it occurred to her that a fricassee of cottontails would be nice for a change. So she took one of the twenty-twos out of the gun-rack in the dining room, filled the pocket of her slacks with shells, and headed for the Stable Pasture.

An hour later she came hurrying back through the Gorge. Her face was very white and the pupils of her eyes distended. She cast a glance over her shoulder, then stopped and half turned and peered into the darkness that was gathering between the cliffs and under the aspen. Though there was nothing of a frightening nature to be seen she whirled and broke into a run, calling, 'Rob!'

There was a tremor of hysterical excitement in her voice, as with head turning constantly to look over her shoulder her feet flew down the path.

'Rob!' she called again, 'The wildcat!' Then, reaching the edge of the Green, she pulled up short. Rob was standing some distance off, bawling out Tim. He had not heard her, and Nell tried to assume a calmer demeanour. It would not do to appear before Tim in near-hysterics.

She went quietly towards them, anxious to reach Rob, to get hold of his hand, or at least to stand close beside him until he should be through talking to Tim. She was ashamed of her fright but could not control the pounding of her heart or the trembling of her hands. When she had told Rob all about it, she would feel better, she thought.

But she stopped before reaching them, because Rob was shouting, 'When I tell you to pasture the cows in Seventeen I don't mean Sixteen.'

Tim's face was crimson. 'The Missus told me to put them in Sixteen, Captain.'

Nell stood there with the little gun in her hand, looking from one to the other, the wind gone out of her sails.

'Did you tell Tim to put the cows into Sixteen?' shouted Rob.

It was a relief to her taut nerves to whip back at him, 'I did. Any reason why I shouldn't?'

'I say there's a reason,' he bawled. 'I told him to put them in Seventeen. That's why – who's running this ranch?'

Angrily Nell answered, 'One of the cows is coming in heat and I don't want her bred by that Hereford bull over the fence from number Seventeen on Crosby's land. That happened last year. We had a mixed Hereford and Guernsey calf – it's not going to happen again.'

'Whose business is it to give orders to the men?' roared Rob.

'The cows are my job; always have been.'

'You tell me what you want and I'll give the orders!'

Several of the haying crew were seated on the bench outside the bunk house. They could see and hear all that was going on.

Nell's eyes filled with angry tears. 'I'll give any orders about the cows I want!'

She turned and ran into the house, sobbing with fury; because of the fright she had had; because Rob was in a nasty mood and she couldn't tell him about the wildcat; because he had humiliated her before the men; and because she had made the mistake of shouting back at him.

'Never any use,' she muttered as she rushed upstairs, 'just makes him snarl louder—'

She pulled off her slack suit and began to dress for town.

A moment later she heard Rob's voice in the living room, shouting 'Nell!'

She did not answer, but slipped on her green silk print, then zipped it up, stopping to wipe the tears from her face again.

'Nell!'

She perched on the edge of the stool before her dressing table and hastily smoothed and arranged her hair, determined not to answer.

'Nell!'

'What!' Rob could always whip an answer out of her, even against her will.

He came stamping upstairs and stood at the door looking at her. Just because he should have been surprised to see

257

her dressing for town at that hour of the night, he said nothing. She volunteered the explanation.

'I'm going to town,' she said defiantly. 'I can't stand it here another minute. I'm going to a movie.'

There was silence, while she finished arranging her hair. Then Rob said, 'It's quite cold. You'll need a coat. What one will you wear?'

'The light green plaid.'

He went to the closet, hunted in it till he found the coat, took it down from the hanger and was holding it for her when she was ready to put it on.

'Got your hanky? And some money?'

'Yes— Oh, wait. I don't think I've got any money.'

Rob got his wallet out of the coat he had last worn to town and put some bills into her purse.

He followed her downstairs and out to the car, took the whisk broom out of the car-pocket and cleaned the seat before he'd let her get in.

Nell took her seat, her lips set, her eyes determinedly turned away from him. *If he asks me now if I love him I'll slap his face.* She wished he would.

He hesitated at the open door after she had taken her seat and started the engine. Then he stepped back, closed the door and stuck his head through the open window.

'Don't forget to fill up with petrol in town.'

Nell made no reply, waiting, with exaggerated patience, till he should withdraw his head and let her go.

'And don't drive too fast.' He stood back.

Rolling along the Lincoln Highway at about sixty miles an hour, five miles faster than her usual pace, she had a delicious sense of escape.

There was no wind; a high, thin mist dimmed the stars; and the dark plains, full of mystery and melancholy, spread north and south from the highway into infinite remoteness. Now and then her headlights flashed into the eyes of a Hereford steer, standing at the fence of the right-of-way.

She met a train coming up from Cheyenne. Its head-lights blinded her and she slowed down while the long row of windows passed.

In Cheyenne she crept along the streets, marvelling at the Neon lights that outlined the features of every booth, hotdog stand, shop and restaurant. The streets were almost as bright as day.

The crowded, ugly little western town changed her mood. Her own life, the life of the ranch and the outdoors and Rob and the boys, was cut off sharply; as, in putting together the scenes of a moving picture, the film upon which one scene is photographed, is cut with a pair of scissors, and another scene is attached to it with glue.

She yielded herself with relief to this different world, and it played upon her nerves in a stream of soothing, meaningless impressions.

At the theatre, she saw Ginger Rogers and Fred Astaire in a dance-team picture; and here she was lost in delight. Her real life was completely erased. Back again in the days of college proms and holiday dances, she danced the hour through, and came out of the theatre in a daze, hardly knowing where she was, or at what point her life was to be picked up again.

Now she must get home – it was nearly eleven o'clock.

On the highway, she ran into what at first she thought was smoke from a train, then realized it was fog. While she had been at the show, this cloud had crept in from some-where, and now lay upon the road between her and the ranch.

To make that drive through fog even in daytime was hazardous and difficult. At night, it was dangerous. Several times Nell stopped the car, wondering if she would be wiser to return to town for the night. But everything drew her forward – she must get home. She longed to feel the familiar arms of the ranch close around her; she had so much to tell Rob – must tell him about this fog, too. He probably was worried to death. He'd hate to have her driving home alone through the fog late at night.

It took her a long time. She had to open the window, hang her head out, looking down at the front wheel, trying to keep it right on the centre line of the road. It seemed three times the actual distance of twenty-five miles before she turned off the highway and drove in under the Goose Bar Ranch sign.

She wondered if Rob would have gone to bed. At least he'd have left a light downstairs in the living room for her.

Yes – there was the light. She left the car on the hill behind the house, went around to the terrace and looked in the door.

Rob was sitting in the armchair by the radio, absorbed by a playlet he was listening to. One knee was hooked over the arm of the chair. His boots were off, slippers on the heather brown socks that were drawn up over the cuffs of his riding breeches. He was smoking. His brown face looked shadowed and tired. The dark beard showed through on his jaws.

Seeing her he smiled and nodded, then held up a hand for silence, not wanting to miss a word of what he was hearing. 'Mind if I hear this out?' he said softly.

'Not at all,' Nell answered stiffly, and went upstairs to bed.

Half an hour later, he lay in bed beside her, smoking a last cigarette in the darkness. It seemed to him that the walnut bed was vibrating slightly. The tremor emanated from Nell. Lying there, her back turned to him, she was tense from the back of her neck to her toes.

Rob finished his cigarette, ground out the stub in the ashtray on the table, then rolled over and put his arms around her. He held her tight to him, one arm under her neck. With the other hand, he pressed her head against him, smoothed her hair, laid his cheek against it as he so often did, kissing it softly.

It took a long time for her trembling to stop.

When it had; he said quietly, 'What frightened you up in the Stable Pasture?'

She didn't answer.

'Was it the wildcat?'

'Yes.'

'I heard you shoot twice – did you get a shot at him?'

'No – that was cottontails I was shooting at.'

'Did you get the cottontails?'

'I shot them – but the mountain lion got them.'

'What happened?'

'You know the rock up there that I call the Sunset Rock, because I so often climb up it to look at the sunset?'

'Yes – the one in the woods a little way, that comes up out of the earth sharp and jagged – like the top of a mountain poking through.'

'Yes. Well, I had shot the two rabbits, and the light was fading and there were beautiful colours in the sky. I thought there must be a fine sunset if I could get up out of the woods to a high place and see it. So I thought I would climb up the Sunset Rock. It's so steep in places you have to go up on your hands and knees, you know, hanging on—'

'I know.'

'So I set the twenty-two against a pine tree near the base of the rock and tied the legs of the two rabbits together with that narrow black ribbon I had around my hair, and I hung them on a jagged stump of a branch that stuck out of the trunk of the pine tree.'

'How high up?'

'Not very high. Just opposite my face. And then I climbed up the rock and stood up there looking at the sunset. When it was over I came down on the opposite side of the rock, and walked around the base of it to the place I had left the gun and the rabbits, but before I got there I met the lion face to face – not ten feet away – he was coming around the rock, too. And he had my rabbits in his mouth.'

'I'll be damned.'

'We just stood facing each other.'

'Were you scared?'

'Not then. Just so surprised. We neither of us moved for a moment, then he just melted away. It was getting dark – it just seemed as if I blinked my eye and he was gone. I stood listening, couldn't hear a thing. Then I got terribly scared, and started to run home. Then I remembered I shouldn't run – and I tried to walk. I kept looking behind me. I was in a regular panic.'

'I knew he was around here.'

'How'd you know?'

'I saw footprints the other morning.'

'Where?'

'In the corral.'

'*In the corral!*'

'Yes, four perfect prints in that patch of earth that gets the dampness from the water trough.'

Nell was silent, thinking of the cat stalking out from the woods, across the open space to the corrals. She saw it vertical upon the fence bars – the feral shape – crawling over the top, dropping soundlessly down into the enclosure. It went about sniffing, investigating, now and then pausing to listen; and every turn of the head, every attitude, every pause, half crouched, tense, alert, expressed the primal fear in which it had been formed and matured.

'Don't be afraid, honey, don't worry—' Rob's hand held her head against his breast.

'No – but *Flicka*, you know – and if anything happened to her, Ken—'

'Nothing's going to happen. Nell, they've been around before. We've seen the prints. We've heard them scream. They come and go. It's seldom that they hang around close to a human habitation.'

'The Stable Pasture – that's pretty close, Rob.'

'There's lots of game up there, Nell. The woods are full of deer.'

It was true. Several of the hay crew had told of seeing deer when they went up to the Stables early in the morning; and Nell, herself, one day, just pretending that the shape of some twigs and branches and little shrubs were the delicate shapes of deer, suddenly saw that it was true. A group of five does and fawns stood there motionless under her eyes.

'It's strange that the men didn't see the prints of the mountain lion, too.'

'Gus saw them. He was with me. I told him to rake them over. I didn't want the men to see them and talk about it.'

'Because of Ken?'

'Yes. He's gone through enough this summer, without lying awake worrying about the cat, with school only ten days away.'

At that moment they both jumped, and Rob leaped half out of bed. A scream tore the air, rising from the Hill across the Green, going up in a snarling crescendo to a pitch of ear-splitting ferocity, then ebbing slowly away in heart-rending sobs.

Profound silence followed; the deep stillness of the range – as if it had never been broken.

'God!' exclaimed Rob. He struck a match, lit the candle by the bed and turned to look at Nell.

She was sitting bolt upright, her eyes wide and dark, and her lips parted in an expression that was slightly hysterical.

'Did you ever *hear* such a sound!' she said.

Rob shook his head. Then a moment later said, 'Beautiful, wasn't it?'

Nell nodded violently. 'It was gorgeous.'

They sat still, listening, wondering if the cat might scream again, while the flame of the candle flickered and the long shadows danced on ceiling and walls.

Nell slipped out of bed. 'Gimme the candle. I just want to see if that woke the boys.'

She came back a moment later. 'Both of 'em dead to the world. We won't tell them, Rob.'

'Of course not.'

'I wonder if any of the men heard.'

'Not a chance. It's midnight. Listen – what do you say we go downstairs? I can't sleep after that. I'll make you some hot chocolate. I think you should have had something to eat anyway, after your evening in town and the long ride back – what did you see? A good show?'

They belted robes about them, went down to the kitchen and Rob made chocolate; for each cup, one square of bitter chocolate and two spoons of sugar and a cup of milk, cooked together until it boiled – a thick, smooth drink, topped with Guernsey cream.

They sat down at the table to drink, and Nell had a chance to tell about the the show, about the fog, about what she had seen in town. She never felt that she had quite completed an experience until she had shared it with Rob.

When they went up to bed an hour later, all her nervousness was gone, As she blew out the candle, she said, 'Drat that wildcat – he's got my hair-ribbon.'

Chapter Twenty-nine

The afternoon that Ken finished copying his composition, he went over to the Post Office with his mother in the Studebaker, and dropped the long envelope, containing his neat three pages of writing, and his mother's letter, into the mail box.

Driving back to the ranch, he sat silent, aware of peculiar feelings within himself. It was another achievement, something that might amount to quite a good deal in the estimation of his father and Mr Gibson. It was to be kept a secret from his father until Mr Gibson's answer came.

'Of course, he may not answer,' said Nell. 'He may just tell you when you and Howard get there.'

This made school feel very near. And that made Ken think about Flicka. He had never dreamed that at the end of the summer, Flicka would still be lame and half sick. He hated to leave her that way. After he had gone, no one would care for her so devotedly. She would have to shift for herself. She would need her rations of oats for a very long time yet, to put the flesh back on her bones. She had been getting so thin, lately – thinner, it seemed, every day. And her coat was losing its fine colour and sheen.

When they reached home, his mother told him to find Howard and bring him in so that they could both try on their winter clothes. She wanted to find out what new things would be needed before Christmas; what was outgrown; what worn out; what would do; how many new markers she must sew on; how many new socks and pants and undershirts.

She finished going over the clothes, sent the boys out, and went in and made the fire for supper. Then she took her sewing basket and the markers and the underclothes and sat down in a chair by the kitchen window.

She was thinking about Ken and her face was very sad. What would Rob do when he knew that Flicka was wasting away? The men were talking about it already. Gus had said to her only that morning, 'It's de fever. It burns up her flesh. If you could stop de fever she might get well.'

Rob had no eyes and no thought for anything but the haying and the weather. The extra men had gone; Rob and Tim and Gus were storing the baled hay in the barn; stacking the loose hay in long lozenges that gradually took on shape and style, the sides forked down until they were smooth and perpendicular, the tops shaped in rounded ridges to shed rain and snow. Each time they got one stack topped they stretched long strands of baling wire over it to bind it to the earth, and hung heavy railroad ties on the ends of the wire. This kept the wind from blowing the stacks away.

The weather still held; but, each night, the banks of cloud that crept over the sky were heavier, and sometimes thunder rumbled intermittently for hours.

Nell dropped her sewing in her lap and looked out of the window, her brows knotted with anxiety and distress.

The filly won't pull out of it, Rob had said, when the little mare was first hurt; and he was right. Flicka was going to die. If Rob knew – if, perhaps, he had known ever since the generalized infection had poisoned her blood stream and he had given her the shot of serum, he had said nothing; and when the men talked about her he pretended not to hear. But Ken – how could he have failed to see that every day left the little filly with less flesh, less strength, less life? Nell remembered a friend whose baby had been wasting away, and yet, because of the daily care and closeness, the warmth and little smiles and tiny arms still clinging, did not know it until the very end.

Ken did not know.

Soon Flicka began to go down in flesh so rapidly that almost overnight she wasted away to nothing. Every rib showed. The glossy hide was dull and brittle and was pulled over her skeleton as if she was a dead horse.

For convenience of unloading, the big hay wagon was left near the cow-barn corrals every evening; and one morning as McLaughlin and Howard and the men were walking down to it, Gus leading one of the work teams which was to be harnessed into it, Ken was walking with them, carrying the can of oats under his arm. He was going to take Flicka her breakfast.

The little mare was waiting for him at the gate of the corral.

When McLaughlin saw her, he stopped walking, and a look of horror spread over his face. 'What, in God's name, is that?' he shouted.

They all stopped walking and looked at her, and Ken, with a face as white as paper, looked back at his father. 'It's Flicka,' he whispered. 'She's been getting awfully thin.'

'Thin!' roared McLaughlin.

Gus shook his curly head sadly. 'Ay bin thinking she's not goin' to pull out of it,' he said.

'Pull out of it? She's dead already.'

McLaughlin turned to glare at Ken. 'How long has she been like that?'

'She's been going down awful fast the last few days—' faltered Ken.

'It's de fever,' said Gus. 'It's burnin' her up.'

Tim said, 'It's an awful pity. She was a nifty little filly. Hard luck, Ken.'

McLaughlin looked at her again. She was nickering for Ken. Her head was up, looking at him. She was just bones and a dull, lustreless hide.

'That's the end,' roared McLaughlin. 'I won't have a thing like that on my place.'

He walked on to harness the team, and Ken went slowly to Flicka, and down the path to the stream, with the little creature hopping at his heels. He poured the oats in her feed box and she dipped her nose in and ate them.

From the terrace, Nell had seen and heard all that had been said, and she ran down the path to Ken.

As she approached, he looked at her, and she saw his blue eyes sunken into his head, staring.

'She's going to die,' he whispered.

'Oh, Kennie darling—' murmured Nell. She put one arm across the boy's shoulders, and with the other, smoothed the harsh coat of the filly. Her own eyes were filled with tears, but Ken's were dry.

'She still eats her oats,' he said mechanically.

Nell said nothing. She caressed the little mare. 'Poor little girl—' she murmured, and to herself thought, 'Oh, why couldn't it have waited until Ken was away—'

At dinner, Ken ate nothing. Howard said, 'Ken isn't eating his dinner – doesn't he have to eat, Mother?'

But Nell answered, 'Leave him alone.'

Ken had understood what his father meant when he

said, 'I won't have a thing like that on my place.' To allow an animal to die a lingering death was something his father would not do. Flicka was to be shot.

He didn't hear his father give the order to Gus. 'Pick a time when Ken isn't around, Gus, and take the Winchester and put the filly out of her misery.'

'Ja, Boss—'

Ken watched the gun rack in the dining room. All the guns were standing in it. No guns were allowed in the bunk house. Going through the dining room to the kitchen three times a day for meals, Ken's eyes scanned the weapons to make sure they were all there. That night they were not all there. The Winchester was missing.

When Ken saw that, he stopped walking. He felt dizzy. He kept staring at the gun rack, telling himself that it surely was there – he counted again – he couldn't see clearly.

Then he felt an arm across his shoulders and heard his father's voice, 'I know, son. Some things are awful hard to take. We just have to take 'em. I have to, too.'

Ken got hold of his father's hand and held on. It helped steady him. Finally he looked up. Rob looked down, and smiled at him and gave him a little shake and squeeze. Ken managed a smile, too.

'All right now?'

'All right, Dad.'

They walked in to supper together.

Ken even ate a little. But Nell looked thoughtfully at the ashen colour of his face; and at the little pulse that was beating in the side of his neck.

After supper Ken carried Flicka her oats, but he had to coax her and she would hardly touch them. She stood with her head hanging, but when he stroked it and talked to her, she pressed her face into his chest and was content.

He could feel the burning heat of her body. It didn't seem possible that anything so thin could be alive.

Presently Ken saw Gus coming into the pasture carrying

the Winchester. When he saw Ken, he changed his direction and sauntered along as if he was out to shoot cottontails.

Ken ran to him. 'When are you going to do it, Gus?'

'Ay was goin' down soon now, before it got dark—'

'Gus, don't do it tonight. Wait till morning. Just one more night, Gus.'

'Vell, in de morning den, but it got to be done, Ken. Yer fadder gives de order.'

'I know. I won't say anything more.'

Gus went back to the bunk house and Ken returned to Flicka.

He stood by her, smoothing and caressing her as he always did. Usually he talked to her, but he couldn't do that now. There was only one thing in his mind, and he couldn't talk about that. Now and then, as if it came from someone else, he heard a little moan. It was he himself that was moaning.

Below the cottonwood trees, the darkness fell swiftly, and Ken and Flicka were hidden in it together. It folded them around and held them close. He couldn't see her, and she couldn't see him, but he moved around her, and her head turned to follow him so that her muzzle rested against him, as she always did. The darkness pressed them closer together.

At nine o'clock Howard was sent by Nell to call Ken. He stood at the corral gate, shouting.

Again there was the sound of soft moaning. Then Ken pressed a last kiss on Flicka's face, and went up the hill under the cottonwoods.

Flicka was still standing in her nursery when the full moon rose at ten. It was the Hunter's Moon, as yellow as the Harvest Moon, but not so large.

The night was silent, with the profound silence of a sea becalmed. Even the faint roaring of the earth, like the roaring in a shell, was hushed. It waited.

If the mind of a living being – man or beast – is clear, there are forewarnings of the approach of death. The body gets ready. One by one the active functions cease, till, at last, the currents of living force become inverted in a down-whirling spiral into which the creature is drawn, spinning faster and faster towards the vortex.

All of this can be felt; and, feeling this, Flicka knew that her time had come.

Her head hung low. Her legs were slightly splayed under her. Though, from force of habit, she stood by the feed box, she had not touched the oats. Every cell in her body was seared with fierce, burning fever, and sometimes her mind was in a drifting delirium, sometimes in coma, sometimes clear and knowing.

Flicka's wounds did not pain her, but the suction of the down-whirling spiral was an agony felt through every part of her. Now and then her young body found strength to fight against it; she struggled; she lifted her head. She turned it towards the path down which Ken's running feet had come a thousand times that summer. He was all she had, and all she could hope for; but tonight, there was no sound, no step, no help.

For minutes she stayed so, her ears strained for the sound of him, longing and listening, then gradually succumbed to the tug of those inner quicksands, and drooped, wavering, over the earth.

In one of the surges of rebellion, she neighed.

Miles away on the upland, her Sire heard and answered.

Animals call to each other as friends, in passing, or as sentries challenge. *Who goes there?* – and the answer announces a friend or foe. But Banner, knowing that Flicka was one of his own, gave the Master Word as Ken had read it out of the Jungle Book to Flicka – *We be of one blood, ye and I!* And the loud, kingly cry, made into a faint trumpet call by the distance, drifted across the miles, across the roads, across the barbed wire barricades that intervened, and burned a cross-fire of hope into the fever that was consuming Flicka.

She began to prance jerkily, like a marionette pulled by strings. All that was left in her of will and power gathered itself and she trotted downstream along the bank.

She jarred to a sudden stop, standing in terror with head low and feet braced out as if she had come face to face with a phantom. Gradually the terror went out of her, but she held the ridiculous posture as if unable to move. Her head turned again to the ranch house . . . *would he come?*

She was thirsty. The smell of the fresh running water drew her. She waded into the stream and drank, got her fill, lifted her head, turned it again to the house. The cool water rippled against her legs.

There was no sound from the house, no feet running upon the path, and suddenly the last of her little strength was gone. Lunging forward, she fell, half on the bank, half in the water, and lay there, struggling convulsively.

At last she was still.

Some minutes later, from ten miles away on the towering black-timbered shoulders of Pole Mountain, there stole out the most desolate cry in all the world – the howl of the grey timber wolf. It rode on the upper air without a tremor, high and thin, pointed as a needle. Through long minutes the note was sustained, mournful and remote – through long moments it died, with a falling cadence of profound listlessness; and even before it ceased, it had become the very essence of the quiet of the night.

Ken had seen the Hunter's Moon rise over the eastern horizon before he went upstairs, and lying in bed, wide awake, and shaken by a steady fine quivering, he could see it reflected in the opened casement window of his room.

He hadn't completely undressed, but he had the sheet drawn up to his chin, in case his mother or father came in to look at him. He heard them talking together in their room as they undressed. How long they took. It seemed to him hours before the whole house was quiet – as quiet as the night was outside.

He heard Flicka neigh, but he didn't hear Banner answer. Human ears were not keen enough to catch that distant greeting. He knew Flicka was neighing for him. He heard the wolf howl.

He waited still another hour, till everyone was so deep asleep there would be no chance of their hearing. Then he stole out of bed and put on the rest of his clothes.

He carried his shoes in his hands and crept down the hall, past the door of his parents' room, taking half a minute a step.

On the far end of the terrace, he sat down and put on his shoes, his heart pounding and the blood almost suffocating him.

He kept whispering, 'I'm coming, Flicka – I'm coming—'

His feet pattered down the path. He ran as fast as he could.

It was so dark under the cottonwood trees, he had to stand a moment, getting used to the darkness, before he could be sure that Flicka was not there. There stood her feed box – but the filly was gone.

Unreasoning terror swept over him. Something had spirited her away – he would never see her again – Gus had come down – his father—

He ran wildly here and there. At last, when there was no sign of her, he began a systematic search all through the pasture. He dared not call aloud, but he whispered – 'Flicka – Oh, Flicka – where are you.'

At last he found her down the creek lying in the water. Her head had been on the bank, but as she lay there, the current of the stream had sucked and pulled at her, and she had had no strength to resist; and little by little her head had slipped down until when Ken got there only the

273

muzzle was resting on the bank, and the body and legs were swinging in the stream.

Ken slid into the water, sitting on the bank, and he hauled at her head. But she was heavy, and the current dragged like a weight; and he began to sob because he had no strength to draw her out.

Then he found a leverage for his heels against some rocks in the bed of the stream, and he braced himself against them, and pulled with all his might; and her head came up on to his knees, and he held it cradled in his arms.

He was glad she had died of her own accord, in the cool water, under the moon, instead of being shot by Gus. Then, putting his face close to hers, and looking searchingly into her eyes, he saw that she was alive and looking back at him.

And then he burst out crying, and hugged her, and said, 'Oh, my little Flicka, my little Flicka.'

The long night passed.

The moon slid slowly across the heavens.

The water rippled over Ken's legs, and over Flicka's body. And gradually the heat and the fever went out of her, and the cool running water washed and washed her wounds.

Chapter Thirty

The night took a heavy toll from Ken, but for Flicka there was resurgence. At the moment when Ken drew her into his arms and cried her name, the spring of the down-whirling spiral was broken, Flicka was released and not once again did she feel it. The life-currents in her body turned, and in weak and wavering fashion, flowed upwards. A power went into her from Ken; all his youth and strength and magnetism given her freely and abundantly on the stream of his love – from his ardent eyes to hers.

But for Ken, there was, first, the creeping numbness of those parts where the head and neck of the filly pressed. Then the deep chill from the cold water running over his legs, his thighs, almost up to his waist. The mountain stream was fed from the Snowy Range in the North West, and the water was far colder than the shallow, sun-dappled surface looked. Ken's legs were shrivelled and cramped with the cold, and long before the night was over, his teeth were chattering and his body shaking with chills.

It didn't matter. Nothing mattered but that he should hold Flicka, and hold the life in her.

At dawn, when there should have been light, there was, first, a grey gloom, and then persistent twilight. The wind had failed and the clouds had their way at last, forced up from all points of the compass by pressure in the lower areas behind them, Laramie and Cheyenne, both a thousand feet down, and the valleys behind the mountains that were to the north and south.

Often McLaughlin studied the sky, especially the rims of Sherman Hill, and said, 'It's trying its best to storm, but the clouds can't get over the mountains.'

Now they had got over. There wasn't room for them all. They obscured the zenith and then doubled up, one layer below the other.

But Ken knew nothing of the weather – only Flicka; the heat of her body that burned his arms. Towards morning he knew that the heat had gone, and it was not death; when he spoke to her, her eyes still looked back into his. He was full of thankfulness.

As the long vigil neared its end, his senses swam away into a state that was half sleep, half unconsciousness. Often the world swayed. His head sank forward. He heard a commotion; loud bellowing of the cows; snarling cries, some small young animal screamed in terror; and Ken lifted heavy lids to see, across on the hill under the three pines where he had first brought Flicka her oats, a little white and yellow Guernsey heifer – one of the yearlings that shared the Calf Pasture at night with the milch cows – in the grip of a tawny beast.

Ken watched without fear or emotion. The milch cows watched too, gathered in a clump, not too near, now and then bellowing. Several of them pawed and stamped the ground and tossed their heads, turning them as if looking for help. Where was the bull who should have been their

276

protector? Alone, they did not dare attack. They were all de-horned. Though they could lower their heads and make the gesture of goring, they were without weapons. The lion had missed its first hold, and the heifer, rolling and twisting on the ground, by some freak of chance, escaped and ran away with a terrible bleating of fear. The lion pursued, low on the ground, like Pauly stalking a bird; it leaped again, executing an extraordinary parabola in the air and this time Ken saw the 'neat trick' which Ross had described. As the cat curved over the heifer and then fell on its neck, the calf's head was suddenly twisted right around. The mouth pointed upward. Its scream was cut short, and it went down.

There was no more struggling. It was instantly killed. The cat seized the carcass by the shoulder and dragged it a little way, then, excited by the taste of the blood, stretched himself out on the ground, holding the dead heifer between his front paws. At first he tore the abdomen, then one of the plump haunches, the throat—

Ken saw it all as if in a dream. It had nothing to do with him; and long before the grisly meal was finished, his eyes were closed again, and he was floating somewhere, the pain and numbness gone, and a delicious warmth stealing all through him.

Chapter Thirty-one

The alarm clock broke the early morning silence of the bunk house and jangled for sixty seconds.

Before it stopped Tim and Gus were sitting, naked, on the edge of their bunks, yawning and rubbing their heads.

Gus reached for his clothes and began to draw them on; remembering as he did so that something unpleasant was ahead of him. It was a moment or two before it came to him – the shooting of Flicka.

When he remembered he dropped both hands on his knees and sat in silence. Nothing for it, it must be done. The filly might have been left to die of her own accord, but that was contrary to custom on the Goose Bar Ranch – in fact, contrary to custom anywhere. An animal that has no chance for life is put out of its misery. Besides, there were the Boss's orders, and McLaughlin never remanded an order once it was given.

The Swede pulled on his socks and heavy shoes and canvas trousers, then went to the kitchen sink to wash.

Tim was already hurrying out of the door on his way to the spring house to get the milking pails.

Gus finished dressing, made the fire and laid the table for breakfast, thinking that when he had everything ready except frying the eggs and bacon and making the coffee, he'd go down to the Calf Pasture with the Winchester. It wouldn't take a minute. He had the gun with him there in the bunk house. It stood in the corner, still loaded. He'd be back before Tim had finished milking the cows and have plenty of time to make breakfast.

Tim, meanwhile, had gone down to milk, and found the milch cows waiting for him, placid, chewing their cuds, surging through the gate the moment he opened it, in a hurry for their feed. It was just the usual bunch. The dry cows and the yearlings knew better than to be waiting at the gate, for they got no grain rations.

Gus walked down to the ranch house, stood the gun against the house outside, and went into the kitchen to make up the fire.

Gus's shaking down of the ashes every morning was the rising bell for the family. When the kindling had caught, and the flames were licking up around the blocks of coal, Gus closed the back draught and went out. He took the gun and walked slowly across the Green, to the gate of the Calf Pasture.

A few minutes' walk brought him to Flicka's Nursery and showed him that Flicka was not there. He walked down stream and soon found Ken sitting in the water, Flicka's head in his arms.

One look at the boy's face was enough.

Gus crossed the creek, laid down his gun, and seizing the filly by the head, dragged her out on to the grassy bank, as doctors drag infants into the world by the head – never, safely, by any other part.

Ken could not move. Gus lifted him in his arms and again crossed the creek. Ken's head dropped back over the Swede's shoulder, turning to the filly for one last look.

'Good-bye, Flicka.' It was only a whisper.

Rob was standing at his window fastening his belt, when he saw the foreman passing, carrying Ken. He thought, 'Flicka died— I didn't hear the Winchester— Ken's found her dead – fainted—'

He ran downstairs and out, took the boy from Gus's arms, and then noticed the unbelievably shrunken, drawn features, and the violent chills. This was more than a faint. Gus told him how he had found Ken, and Rob carried him in and up to bed.

Rob and Nell put Ken to bed between hot blankets and tried to get some brandy between his lips.

Gus returned to the Pasture to get the gun. Flicka was lying as he had left her, but at his approach held up her head. The man knelt down on the grass by her and felt her head, her neck, looked into her eyes, 'Vell – vell – Flicka, liddle gurl—' He was astonished to feel that her body seemed to have lost its great heat; the fever had gone. He looked at the two wounds. The cuts were clean and all the hard swelling had gone; and he could see by her face that she was brighter, as one can see by the expression in a child's face, even though it is still pinched and wan, that life is coming back.

He stood up, slowly, the gun in his hand, and stood there, hesitating. He had received his orders. He was to shoot Flicka some time soon when Ken was not around. There would never be a better moment than right now.

A minute or so passed, while the Swede stood looking down at the filly and pondering the situation. Then, straightening up, he put the Winchester in the crook of his left arm, raised his eyes to scan the sky and read the weather signs, and his hands automatically fumbled in his clothing for his pipe, tobacco, and matches. A few puffs of his pipe would help him to think this out. That the filly might actually recover was hardly likely. He wondered how long Ken had been holding her – there was no telling – they were all familiar with Ken's habits – he might have been there since dawn.

The big foreman stood pensively, his blue eyes with the far look in them which the eyes of plainsmen have, roving here and there, taking in the weather signs. There was no wind this morning. The sky was clouding over. If the wind did not come up, they'd have rain. Natural enough – the weather was due to break.

In one of the three pine trees there were a dozen chattering magpies. They were flying up and down, circling around the tree, making a great racket. They've got something in that tree, or near it, thought the Swede, rabbit – gopher– His eyes moved on, he noticed the cattle – the yellow and white Guernseys – the yearling heifers and the dry cows, grazing calmly, dotted here and there about the pasture. He noticed their condition – they seemed well fleshed. From there his eyes dropped to the grass. Plenty grass yet in the Calf Pasture – grass was holding out well this year–

He noticed the smoke coming out of the chimneys of the ranch house, and the bunk house. That startled him out of his reverie. Time for him to finish making breakfast – Tim would be up from the milking soon.

He found that his mind had made itself up while he stood there in a reverie. He would not shoot Flicka just yet. Perhaps, by the time Ken had had his breakfast and got warmed up, he might have something to say that would change his father's mind.

The man walked back up the little path, and on to the bunk house.

Chapter Thirty-two

Dr Rodney Scott was six feet three and thin, and in spite of being a veteran of the World War, and bald, had a face like a boy's. He bought a new, high-powered car every year; spent a third of his life on the Wyoming highways, answering county calls at ninety miles an hour – people said Doctor Scott always went on two wheels – another third of his time was spent on the golf links or fishing in the trout streams that had their headquarters in the Snowy Range; and the other third in doing just whatever was the exactly right thing for a doctor to do in order to save human life and alleviate pain and distress.

On this day, which happened to be a Saturday, Rob drove the Studebaker in to Cheyenne, picked up the doctor's trail, and hunted him for many hours and many miles. He found him, at last, at three o'clock in the afternoon, standing in deep contemplation on a rock, casting a long line with a Grey Hackle on the end of it, forty yards downstream to a particular dark streak of water under the shadow of a deep-set rock.

It was two hours later when the two cars, Dr Scott in one, and Rob in the other, roared up the hill behind the ranch house.

Ken's condition had been growing steadily worse. In spite of the hot blankets, chills shook him every few minutes until his teeth chattered. His temperature was 103 when Nell put him to bed. By noon it was 104.

Much of the time he slept, or, at least, thought Nell as she sat beside the bed, holding one of his thin, helpless-feeling hands in both of hers, he was in some sort of unconsciousness.

She had discovered that his pyjamas had never been slept in last night – never unfolded. He had gone to his room at the usual time but apparently had not undressed. She figured out what had happened. It was Flicka's last night on earth – Ken had gone down to her when the house was quiet. He had, doubtless, spent the night just as Gus had found him, holding Flicka in the water.

She wondered if the filly was alive or dead. And then came a deeper wonder, at the way the lives of the two, boy and filly, seemed intertwined.

When Ken roused from his sleep or coma, sometimes he looked at her as if he knew her, sometimes stared at her unknowing. Sometimes he seemed to be listening – turned his head and eyes towards the window, and lay motionless.

'Listening for her—' thought Nell, 'to hear her nicker. Or – listening for a shot . . .'

The day grew darker and more gloomy. Once, there was a sudden sound like the soft rolling of a corps of drums – a mere whisper. Nell went to the window and saw that it was rain. It rolled to a crescendo, then died away in a murmur – not a minute in all. The sky was massed with low clouds.

Standing at the window, Nell heard the sharp excited

barking of the dogs down in the Calf Pasture. They had found something. That was the way they yelped when their hunting instinct was aroused.

Looking in that direction she noticed some chicken hawks swinging in the clouds above the three pines.

She went back to Ken, seated herself on the edge of the bed and leaned over him, examining his face. It was one of the times when he lay motionless, strained, and listening— Was he conscious at all? Or dreaming? His eyes were half open—

'Kennie,' she murmured in a low voice, 'Ken, dear—'

But that was not the sound Ken was listening for, and he did not hear.

Every little while, as time went on, there came again the whispering roll of drums, and then the sigh of the rain ceasing.

The cure of a patient by a doctor is supposed to begin, they say, when the doctor sets his foot in the house.

When Nell heard the men's voices below and their steps on the stairs she experienced an emotion that shook her so strongly that all her hardihood left her, and she covered her face with her hands for a moment. Then she lifted her head and went to the door to greet them.

Ken was tossing and muttering. He did not know the doctor.

As Dr Scott made the examination he was told what had happened. That Ken's filly was ill – dying – and that Ken had gone down to her late the night before and had, apparently, been in the water most of the night, holding the horse in his arms.

'His school opens Monday – day after tomorrow,' said Rob, ending on a question.

The doctor shook his head, said, 'Not a chance,' and put the covers back, parting the jacket of Ken's pyjamas, and loosening the tie of the trousers, baring the narrow brown body, laying his fingers on it, tapping them.

'Perhaps by the end of the week?' asked Rob.

'Not likely,' said Scott cheerfully. 'Sometimes children surprise you; blow up something like this and then get right over it. But his fever is 104. He's got *something* – I don't know what yet.'

'An infection?' asked Nell.

'Of course. You don't run up a fever like this without an infection somewhere.'

'Could he have got it from the filly? He's been with her constantly.'

The doctor shrugged his shoulders as he drew the covers up over Ken. 'That is a statement I wouldn't dare to make. It's possible. Human beings do catch things from animals – anthrax, for instance, which can be caught from sheep. But there's lots of influenza around – more in the country than in town, strange to say. Now I've got to get a look at his throat. Maybe he'll help us. Mrs McLaughlin, you talk to him – they usually hear their mother's voice even when they're way off.'

Rob lifted the boy to the right position, and Nell, in the calm and matter-of-fact voice of mothers, which never failed to fill Dr Scott with humility and respect, talked to Ken, and drew him back, step by step, from that far place where he was wandering, to the little familiar room, and the walnut bed that was like home to him.

He became almost lucid. He opened his mouth and let the doctor look at his throat.

'Nothing wrong there,' said Scott and put the child back on his pillows again. Ken's head turned sideways – and again Nell thought he was listening.

The doctor sat holding Ken's wrist tight clasped in his big strong hand, and looked at the face on the pillow.

For a few minutes there was silence.

The room was getting quite dark. Suddenly it was brightly lit by a shimmering of sheet lightning, and the doctor glanced at the window and said, 'Gonna have some weather.'

In the darkness that followed the lightning came a rush

and a roar of wind that sucked through the Gorge, bent every tree on the Hill and slammed the kitchen door.

Nell lit the kerosene lamp and the doctor stood up and looked down at Ken. The boy's eyes were closed now, and he lay motionless, drawing rapid breaths through dry parted lips.

'He's a very sick boy,' said Scott. 'What *is* this? I saw Ken early last spring. What's happened to him this summer? I wouldn't know him for the same boy – it's not only this cold and fever—'

Nell and Rob looked at each other. It was not an easy question, there was so much to tell.

They went downstairs with the doctor and Rob said, 'It's this horse that he's been breaking his heart about.'

The doctor was puzzled. 'Has he been sick before this?'

'Not sick exactly,' said Nell, 'but on an awful strain, because *she's* been sick.'

Scott could see that Nell was anxious to get back to Ken. He put on his things. 'I won't keep you, Mother (he called all women Mother). You want to get back to him. Rob, he's got to have some medicine right away.'

'I'll follow you into town,' said Rob, 'and bring it back.' He reached for Nell, took her in his arms and hugged and kissed her. 'Now don't worry so, darling, the kid'll be all right.'

'Of course,' said Nell. 'I'll go back to him.'

The doctor gave her some final instructions for Ken's care and went out with Rob.

Chapter Thirty-three

Out in the Calf Pasture, the mangled carcass of the slain heifer lay undiscovered by Gus or Tim or Howard. No one had happened to go just there.

With the threat of bad weather, and the Boss away, Gus had driven the little service truck down to the meadows with Tim, to stretch tarpaulins over the hay stacks, binding them down with baling wire, hanging railroad ties on the corners of them.

Only the dogs had been to the Calf Pasture; they were not hungry for their dinner when Howard put it down for them.

The dry cows and the yearling heifers wandered around the carcass, but returned to their grazing, undisturbed. The mountain lion, lying gracefully along the branch of a cottonwood tree, some distance north of the pasture, was too far to be seen or scented by them. He was gorged to repletion. He would feed again on the carcass of the slain heifer that night, or he would kill again. Mountain lions prefer a fresh kill, and there was plenty here to choose from.

At noon he dropped like a plummet from his branch and went down to the creek to drink. Seeing him, the cows and heifers and calves rushed together and stood facing him, heads low, stamping and pawing with their hoofs.

The lion returned to the place he had come from, crawled through some scrub and rocks to a hollow at the base of a cliff, and went to sleep.

The cattle waited for him to return, but he did not appear again.

There came then one of the sudden, drumming down-pourings of rain. The cattle stood in it gratefully, and moved in a manner that suggested they were loosening their hides and lifting the hair for washing as a bird lifts its wings and opens its feathers.

Gus had gone about his work all day, thinking of Flicka. He had not been back to look at her. He had been given no more orders. If she was alive, the order to shoot her was still in effect. But Kennie was ill, McLaughlin making his second trip to town to buy medicines, and would not be back till long after dark. He did not know just what to do.

After Tim and Gus had their supper in the bunk house, they walked down to the creek. They did not speak as they approached the filly, lying stretched out flat on the grassy bank, just as Gus had left her; but their eyes were straining at her to see if she was dead or alive.

She raised her head as they reached her.

'By the Powers!' exclaimed Tim. 'There she is!'

She dropped her head, raised it again, and moved her legs and became tense as if struggling to rise. The men cheered her on. She rolled over on her belly, reached out her forefeet and scrambled halfway up.

288

'Yee whiz!' said Gus. 'She got plenty strength yet.'

'Hi!' cheered Tim. 'She's up!'

But Flicka wavered, slid down again and lay flat. This time she gave notice that she would not try again by heaving a deep sigh and closing her eyes.

Gus took his pipe out of his mouth and thought it over. Orders or no orders, he would try to save the filly. Ken had gone too far to be let down.

'Ay'm goin' to rig a blanket sling fur her, Tim, and get her on her feet and keep her up. If she's got a chance, that'll help. If she ain't it'll do no harm anyway.'

While they were getting the tools, the post-hole digger and shovel, crowbar, ropes, and blanket, the downpour of rain came again. This time it was persistent. The two men went to the bunk house, put on their oilskins, and brought a couple of lanterns with them when they carried the stuff down to the creak.

Flicka was just as they had left her.

'She's sure goin' to get another drenching,' said Tim.

'Won't hurt her,' said the Swede. 'She bin out in tunderstorms since she bin born.'

It took them an hour to rig the sling. They struck rocks in their digging which had to be prised out. Flicka was lying on a piece of level sward, only a little higher than the level of the creek. To the far side, the ground rose sharply behind her, in a steep hill which, on part of its surface, was a sheer slide of rock – another of the rock slides which were characteristic of the terrain of the ranch.

The men set two tall and sturdy aspen poles deep into the ground on each side of the filly, then rolled her on to the folded blanket. The ends of the blanket were gathered and the rope tied on to them in a knot which, the more weight was on it, the tighter it was drawn. The tops of the posts were notched, and a crowbar laid across them. The end of each rope was passed through a hole bored through the post a few inches below the notch; and when everything was ready, Gus said, 'Altogether, now—' They each pulled on their rope, and the blanket and filly rose off the earth together. When she had reached a height where her feet just lightly touched the earth, they let be, and fastened the ends of the ropes to the crowbar.

So she hung – not in the least disconcerted, and when Tim brought her a bucket of water, put her nose in it and drank.

While the two men were carrying the tools back to the tool house, the heavens let loose.

'We're in for it now,' said Tim. 'I didn't think it could last much longer.'

'I'm glad ve got de tarps stretched over dem stacks,' said Gus. 'De hay's not packed hard.'

When they reached the ranch house, he handed Tim the tools he was carrying. 'I'm gonna stop here, Tim, and see if de Missus need anyting – an' fin' out how de little feller is—'

Tim went on without him, and Gus went into the kitchen, where the oil lamp was hung on the wall beside the stove, and removed his slicker.

Nell heard him stamping about and hurried downstairs.

'Is that you, Gus?'

'Ja, Missus – how is de little boy?'

'Oh, Gus, we don't know yet – he seems pretty sick.' Nell's face was worn and anxious. Standing there, belted in her narrow grey flannel wrapper, she looked slim and childish. Her hair was loose on her shoulders, and she put up a hand and pushed it back with a weary gesture. 'Gus, – is Flicka dead?'

'No'm. Tim and I, we just got tru fixin' her up in a blanket sling. She can't stand alone; but dere's life in her, and she reached for de bucket of vater and drank it down like a good von.'

Nell's eyes sank to the floor, and she stood a moment in thought tapping her foot. 'You didn't shoot her,' she said, just thinking out loud. 'Gus, did he – did Captain McLaughlin say you didn't have to shoot her?'

'No'm, he told me last night to find a time when Ken wasn't around and shoot her. But ven I found 'em like dat dis morning' – I – I —'

'I know,' said Nell quickly. 'I know what you mean. Well – I'll tell Ken. Maybe it'll help him – it'll make him so happy that she's still alive. Gus, now you're here, I want you to set up a cot for me in Ken's room, so I can sleep there and take care of him. It's down in the cellar – you'll have to bring it up.'

'I know vere it is, ma'am,' said Gus soothingly. 'Now you go up to de little boy, and I'll bring de cot up and set it up for you.'

Nell ran upstairs, and found Ken's eyes wide open. He moved every few seconds, turning from one side to the other. His breath was shallow, often with long pauses between.

She sat on the edge of the bed, bent over him and smiled into his eyes with deep, penetrating love. The faintest smile appeared on his lips in answer. She smoothed the hair back from his forehead, then took one of his hands in both of hers and said, 'Kennie – did you know that Flicka seems a little better? Gus has fixed a blanket sling for her, and they've got her up in it, and she drank some water when they held the bucket for her.'

The boy's face changed as if a light had broken over it, and his lips moved, but no words came.

'Maybe – *just maybe*, darling – she'll live after all. We'll do the best we can – but you mustn't hope too hard.'

Ken was trying to move his lips again. At last she heard the words, 'But – Dad – gave – the – order—'

At that moment Gus entered the room carrying the cot. Then he brought the mattress; and as they set it up, Ken's eyes followed their movements.

Gus tip-toed to the side of his bed and looked down at him.

'De filly's up, Kennie – now you be good boy an' soon you be up too—'

'Gus—'

'*Ja?*'

'Did Dad tell you you didn't need to shoot her?'

'No, Kennie, but I ain't done it yet – and maybe he change his mind—'

Kennie's face changed. He closed his eyes and a look of dread and pain was upon his lips.

Gus tip-toed out of the room, and presently Nell heard a whisper from the bed. 'Mother?'

'Yes, darling.'

'Where's Dad now?'

'He went to town, dear, to get some medicines the doctor ordered for you.'

Ken said nothing more. He seemed to be sleeping, and Nell went quietly about the business of making up the cot for the night.

Presently he spoke again. 'Will he be back soon?'

'Any time now, dear, I think.'

Ken lay with eyes closed, but Nell, every time she looked at him, realized that he was tense, listening for the sound of the Studebaker roaring up the hill.

Chapter Thirty-four

The mountain barriers of Sherman Hill were over-ridden at last, and it was not one storm only, but half a dozen of them that rolled up from different points on the horizon and collided.

Masses of purplish black clouds exploded in deafening crashes, or thundered in long, rolling barrages. Glowing balls of electricity ran along the steel tracks of the railroad and the barbed wire fences; swords of lightning slashed down to the ground, one right after the other. It was as if creatures of terrible size and impossible grandeur were struggling in the upper airs, and the earth was spattered with the spent shot and flame.

McLaughlin was on the Lincoln Highway, nearing the ranch, when the full force of the storm struck him.

At the same moment he was finding it difficult to steer

the car, and a sudden bumping and grinding made him realize he had a flat tyre.

Not in the best weather and under the calmest conditions could Rob McLaughlin change a tyre without feeling profane. In such weather as this – and without a slicker—!

Drenched through, half drowned, barely able to keep his footing against the torrents of rain, he bent over the rear wheel; his curses following the ear-splitting cracks of thunder. He boiled with anger. Anger at the car; anger at the storm; anger at Ken who must catch his death of cold sitting in the water with Flicka on his lap just when it was time to go back to school. Anger, above all, against Flicka. Flicka, Flicka, Flicka–that was all he had heard all summer . . . good God, if it hadn't been for Flicka, Ken wouldn't be sick, and he himself wouldn't be here this minute, with streams of water running into his boots and down the back of his neck.

It crossed his mind that by now Gus must have carried out his orders and put an end to the filly, but he wondered. *Had he?* The conviction came to him that Flicka was still alive.

When he reached home and stepped out of the car, Gus was waiting for him, to tell him of having taken the tarps and covered the haystacks.

Rob hurried into the house, Gus behind him, shouting to make himself heard above the howling of the wind and the crashing of the thunder.

They entered the kitchen and stood there, Rob peeling off his wet coat and shaking the water from his hair and eyes. Nell met them.

'How's Ken?' said Rob, before he answered Gus; and hunted in the pockets of the coat he was holding for the package of medicine.

'He seems a little better,' said Nell. 'Anyway, he's been talking. He's not out of his head.'

'Gus,' said McLaughlin, turning to the Swede, 'did you shoot the filly?'

'Boss,' answered Gus, 'I didn't.'

'I gave the order. You've had plenty of time.'

'I – I – couldn't do it.'

Rob picked up his wet coat and began pulling it on again. 'Where's the Winchester?' he said.

'Up in de bunk house.'

'Go get it.'

Gus went slowly out of the door.

Nell clutched Rob's arm. 'Oh, Rob, don't do it. Kennie knows she's alive. He thinks she'll get well. Give him something to hope for.'

'I gave the order,' he said. 'I see no reason for countermanding it. On the contrary, it would have been a lot better if she had been shot weeks ago. It's meant nothing but trouble and misery for all of us. Look what it's brought Ken to.'

'I wish you wouldn't.'

'He needn't know.'

'He'll hear the shot.'

'In this storm? He'll think it's thunder.'

'No, no, he won't. He'll know it's the Winchester.'

'How?'

'He'll know.'

Gus entered the room holding the Winchester in one hand and one long shell in the other.

'Dere's only one shell, Boss.'

'Where are the others? There was a whole box of them.'

'De officers shot 'em all off dat Sunday dey vas here.'

Rob snatched the shell. 'One's enough.'

Gus said, 'You'll find de filly in a sling on de far side de crik. Tim und I rigged it up for her ven we saw she still had life in her.'

Rob got his flashlight from the shelf, and went out. Gus raised sorrowful eyes to Nell's white face. 'Don't take it so

295

hard, Missus,' he said softly. 'De Boss is right. No gude to let sick animals live.'

Nell looked away, pressed one hand to her cheek, and swallowed her tears. Then she turned back to Gus with more composure.

'You go on up to bed, Gus,' she said. 'It's late. Everything will be all right. Don't worry about me.'

'Good night, Missus,' he said humbly, and went out of the kitchen door, pressing his hat on his grey curls.

Nell ran upstairs to Ken. If he was asleep – if only he was asleep – but he was wide awake. He had pulled himself up on his pillows and his eyes were alert.

'That was Dad's car, wasn't it, Mother?'

'Yes, darling, he's home.'

Nell fell on her knees beside the bed, took the child in her arms, and held his head against her breast in such a way that her hand was over his ear.

Rob thrust the shell into the rifle. Holding the gun under his left arm, he used the flashlight with his right. He knew the way as well as he knew the way around his own room, but the light picked out his footing for him.

His anger had passed, but the thing had to be done; and he went through the gate between the Green and the Calf Pasture, and on past the cow-barn.

Going down the path along the fence, he bent his head so the driving rain wouldn't slash his eyes. Where was it Gus said he had rigged the sling? He came to a stop, trying to see through the darkness – listening – waiting for a flash of lightning.

A blinding flash came, and another and another, illuminating the whole pasture, while the skies exploded with thunder. Before the darkness shut the scenes out, Rob had seen three things. He saw the filly in the sling on the far side of the creek, the rock-slide behind her. He saw, down at the end of the field, the cattle bunched together, on guard, frightened, staring. And he saw what they were staring at, something white lying on the ground near the three pines, with a huge mountain lion crouched over it.

Rob stood motionless in the darkness, thinking. He wondered if the mountain lion had seen *him*. The next flash of lightning answered him, for the lion had disappeared.

What was that white thing lying on the ground? Rob wanted to investigate, but he dared not move. Just one shell in the gun—

He stood still for a long time, all his senses strained, listening, trying to see through the darkness, the gun ready in his hands, cocked, half lifted.

The lightning flashes showed the cattle still bunched, watching, and the white thing on the ground with no moving creature near it. Then McLaughlin saw two blazing green eyes fastened upon him. He could not tell whether they were near or far until a flash of lightning showed him that they were in the centre of a mass of shrubs. The lion had hidden himself in those shrubs and was looking out at him from there.

The eyes seemed quite steady. Rob raised his gun, took aim, and fired.

It seemed to him that just before he had pressed the trigger the eyes had disappeared. He lowered the gun and stood warily, listening and looking.

After a while, he strode boldly over to the bushes, shouting and brandishing his gun. With the aid of his flashlight he looked all through them and found, as he had expected, that he had missed. There was no sign of the lion.

Then he examined the carcass near the three pines and saw that it was the remains of one of the yearling heifers. There was little left of it now. It was not a fresh kill. Rob remembered that when he drove in to the ranch with Rodney Scott that afternoon he had noticed hawks wheeling above the three pines.

He wondered if the cat would kill again that night. Was it hungry – or had it eaten? Even that would not mean much, for it would kill on any vagrant impulse – for food, for fear, for fun, or for fury; and here in the pasture were cows and heifers and horse meat – Flicka, so tied up that she could not move even if she had the strength. Rob's ready anger flared up. That was the sort of thing men did to animals. Took away their natural means of protection and then failed to protect them by other means – well – he'd have to stand guard over Flicka all night.

First the cattle must be driven into the cow-barn.

He did this, in a fury of anxiety over the filly. He hurried to her as soon as he had shut up the cows. Flicka welcomed him with a little grunting whinny. He patted her head. 'You win, Flicka.' The blanket had stretched with the rain, and had let her down a few inches. Rob saw that she was bearing her weight on her own feet and he began to think, for the first time, that there was a chance for her recovery.

The storm was passing away, scattered by a wind, high up, which tore the clouds to pieces. Rob suddenly saw a bright star look out from between two clouds, and then disappear.

'Well, we're in for it, Flicka,' he said, stroking the filly's nose. 'A night of it. You're a drowned rat and I'm another. I'd feel better if I had a pocketful of shells – and a drink – and a fire – and some dry clothes—'

In the inner pocket of his shirt he had matches and a pouch of dry tobacco. He lit the pipe. He thought of trying to make a fire but every stick of wood around was soaking wet.

As he smoked, his thoughts traced out a line of probable events. Nell had heard the shot. She knew he had but one shell. She would wonder why he didn't return. She'd remember the wildcat – she'd be worried – and she wouldn't worry long without doing something—

He had barely reached this conclusion, when he saw a light approaching, swinging and bobbing down the path.

'Hey! Nell!'

'Rob! Are you all right? Where are you?'

'Here – on the far side of the brook.' He swung the flashlight.

Presently he saw her anxious face, lit from underneath by the light of the lantern in her hand. Under her other arm she carried the big Express rifle. She was in old khaki pants and a sweater.

'Good girl—' He went to help her across the brook where there were some stones, and took the heavy gun and lantern from her.

'What happened? I heard a shot – was that Flicka?'

'No. The mountain lion.'

'Ah – Did you get him?'

'No.'

'When you didn't come back, that's what I thought of.'

'So you brought a gun. Just what I was wanting. I feel a whole lot better now.'

'Look at Flicka,' said Nell. 'She can't make out what's happening. See how she watches us.'

Nell went to the filly and stroked her face. 'See? She knows me.' Nell turned to look up at Rob. 'She certainly seems brighter. Do you think she has a chance?'

'Can't say. I wouldn't think so, but this bronc blood is tough.'

Nell smoothed the filly's face and murmured to her.

'Rob, I do so want her to get well—'

'Why do you say it that way?'

'Well – Ken. They're so bound up in each other. If *she* gets well, he'll get well—'

Rob's voice rose with a trace of anger. 'Don't say that! He'll get well anyway. Why, Nell, you don't really think he's in danger, do you? He's had lots of colds and fever – they both have—'

Nell was quiet a moment, then shook her head. 'Not like this, Rob. And Rodney's coming again tomorrow. Rodney

299

doesn't make daily calls for nothing. Besides – it's the way Ken looks—'

Rob said gruffly, 'He'll be all right. You'll see. He'll be a different boy in the morning.'

'He heard the shot.'

'How did he take it?'

'Well – *he took it*. Didn't question it. Didn't seem to rebel. I was holding him, trying to shut the sound out of his ears, but just then the thunder wasn't crashing, and he moved a little, and then came the shot – and a gun-shot doesn't sound just like anything else.'

'No. What did he do?'

'His face changed. He pulled out of my arms, sat up, then fell back, put his face in the pillow and didn't speak again. I gave him the sleeping powder the doctor left for him. It's a strong one. He went to sleep. He's sleeping now. That's why I could leave him.'

There was silence for a moment, and then Rob said, 'Nell, if Ken should waken and ask, I think it would be better not to tell him that the filly is still alive. She's been dead and alive and dead and alive so many times, it keeps him on the rack. She *may* be dead by morning. It wouldn't surprise me. And the boy has accepted her death, and he's asleep. With Flicka dead, he'll sleep for a month. If she's alive, he'll be all strung up again.'

Nell agreed. 'I won't tell him.'

Then Rob told her about the slain heifer.

'I knew there was something over there,' she said. 'The dogs were barking in this pasture today, and there were a lot of magpies in the trees.' She looked around uneasily.

'Do you think he's around?'

'I don't think – I know.'

'Can he see us right now?'

'He's got eyes.'

'But is he *watching us and Flicka this minute?*'

Rob laughed. 'Sure, he knows his business, and right now, *that's us.*'

Nell's frightened eyes swept the wall of darkness around them, and she shuddered.

Rob examined the rifle to see if there was a shell in it.

'I loaded it,' said Nell, briefly. 'And here—' She put her hand to the hip pocket of her pants and handed Rob his revolver.

Rob laughed again as he took it. 'You weren't taking any chances, were you? Why – you're an arsenal—' as Nell emptied rifle and revolver shells out of her other pockets.

'I wish he'd show himself this minute,' said Nell, 'and get himself shot. What do you think he'll do?'

'We may never see him again. He's been shot at once, he sees me here, he may make for the woods.'

'Well – if he doesn't – *here is Flicka*—'

'Yes. Well, I'm spending the night with Flicka. I can't get her up to the stables. She can't walk.'

'That's what I thought you'd do,' said Nell. She seized Rob's hand. 'Rob, you're like ice—'

'Well, I'm wet to the skin, and that wind was keen.'

'It's stopped raining now – we could make a fire here and get you dried out.'

'That's what I was thinking – here – where are you going?'

'Back to get some dry kindling and wood.'

'No – no – I won't let you carry all that stuff down – you stay here and I'll get it – no, damn it, you go – and I'll stay.'

They argued as to who should have the lantern, the flashlight, the gun, the revolver – there was danger going – danger staying. Nell went off with the revolver and the flashlight. Rob called, 'And bring some oats for Flicka – we'll see if she can eat.'

Nell returned, laden like a pack animal. She had a sack of kindling and wood on her back, bath towel and dry clothes for Rob over one arm, poncho, pillow and blankets over the other, and a flask of whisky and the revolver in hip pockets.

'It would be fine,' she thought, as she staggered down the path, 'if I met the lion now,' and she was choking with

301

laughter as Rob helped her over the stepping stones of the creek.

'Why,' said Rob reproachfully as she unloaded, 'you forgot Flicka's oats.'

Nell laid her hand upon her bosom, which appeared enormous. 'Is this my natural figure?'

Rob stepped forward gravely. 'What *is* that anyway?'

She pulled up her sweater and produced a muslin salt sack filled with oats.

He grinned as he took it, and carried it to Flicka.

The filly lipped the oats out of his hand and her ears came forward eagerly.

'Well, I'll be damned,' said Rob.

'See?' said Nell, smoothing her nose. 'She's going to eat again and get well – and Ken will get well—'

'Forget that,' said Rob.

He began to make a fire, choosing a spot about ten feet away from Flicka. 'Watch her now. She's never seen a fire. Talk to her.'

'But she's smelled smoke from the house fires,' said Nell, petting the filly. 'Haven't you, baby? And the house was where *Ken* came from, so you like smoke. Anyway – she's got plenty sense – this little girl—'

Flicka's ears were pricked forward, her eyes very wide, and her whole face showed such intense curiosity and astonishment that Nell burst out laughing. The flames rose and crackled and Flicka stared, then looked around questioning, asking of the darkness, and of Nell – *what is this*?

'The important thing to decide,' said Rob, 'is whether to take a drink now, or wait until I'm in dry clothes.'

'Take it now,' said Nell promptly.

Rob took a good swig from the bottle and handed it to her. 'Want one?'

She shook her head, thinking of the night-vigil at Ken's bedside which was before her.

Rob asked her to hold the rifle while he changed his clothes.

He stood naked by the fire, rubbing himself down with the towel. The warm liquor heated his stomach, and a mood of hilarious well-being took possession of him. If it weren't for Ken – and that damned slinking beast close by—

'I'll rub your back,' said Nell. Taking the towel from him she scoured his backbone. Then, as he dressed in dry clothes, she squatted by the fire and stared at the flames.

'Rob, do you think he sees this?'

'Who?'

'The beast.'

Rob laughed. 'I told you. He attends to business. But the fire worries him more than it worries Flicka.'

'I wish you didn't have to stay here all night – you might fall asleep, and then he may eat you.'

'Now just figure it out—'

'Figure *what* out?'

'What that beast is thinking.'

'*I* don't know what he's thinking! It's only you know what the beasts are thinking. What *is* he thinking?'

'Well, there's Flicka, isn't there? And he know she's here.'

'Yes, and he knows she's a horse, and he loves horse meat.'

'Yes. Slim pickings as she is, she's still a horse. But take a look at her! That crowbar across the top of her – the ropes and the blanket and the posts on each side of her – does she look like any horse that mountain lion has ever seen before?'

Nell laughed.

'And here's a fire,' continued Rob. 'It's going to be a roaring big fire. He's never seen that before, and all wild animals are afraid of fire. Only reason Flicka isn't afraid is because she has come to have such complete confidence in

303

us that if we say it's O.K., why – all right, it's O.K. with her too. But the mountain lion, you may be sure, is puzzled and scared this minute. I don't think he'd dare come anywhere near.'

Nell was silent a moment, then she rose and picked up the poncho. 'Where're you going to fix yourself?'

'Right there at the base of the slide, about in the middle between Flicka and the fire where they'll both be under my eye. And it'll give me a back-rest. If the crittur should be loco enough to come at us, he'll have to come from the front; the hill's perpendicular right in this place behind me – if he leaped he'd leap over me.'

They arranged the poncho and blankets at the foot of the slide; and while Rob busied himself hunting about to find logs and branches to dry out by the fire, Nell stood looking up at the cliff, at the trees, at the wild flight of dark tattered clouds across the heavens. Now and then a brilliant star shone out and was instantly quenched, and suddenly the moon.

'Look, Rob! There's blood on the moon!'

Rob paused with his arms full of wood. For a moment the moon could be seen between two clouds, and it was as if a reddish veil was drawn over it. Then a cloud seemed to sweep it out of the sky.

'Forget it, Nell! Nobody's going to die! You're full of ideas—'

Nell stood watching for the moon to reappear, but it was a long dark cloud that had covered it. 'Well – I've got to go back. Kennie might wake.'

They argued again as to the division of firearms. Nell felt Rob might need the revolver because he might engage the beast at close quarters. On the other hand, if she should encounter it on the short walk back to the Green through the dark pasture, the heavy Express rifle would be little help to her.

In the end, she took the lantern in her left hand, the

loaded revolver in her right; and Rob stood watching her skip across the stones of the brook and go up the path. Soon he could see nothing but the lantern, and watched its progress as it bobbed up the path, paused at the gate, changed its direction as she walked across the Green, and finally vanished.

Rob got his shot at the lion a little before sunrise.

He had slept a good deal during the night. With his poncho and blankets making a comfortable back-rest for him at the base of the rockslide, both Flicka and the fire close enough to tend, the filly to one side of him and the fire to the other, and the loaded Express rifle on the rubber poncho beside him, he felt that he had the situation under his eye.

He got up several times during the night, threw wood on the fire, and stood for a few minutes looking around. The night had cleared and the wind died down. The reddish moon rode in the sky. The Calf Pasture, empty of every living thing except himsef and Flicka, seemed very quiet.

In the morning, thought Rob, by hook or crook they must get Flicka to the stables. And then ... I'll go after this mountain lion ... dogs ... poison or traps ... one way or the other I've got to get rid of him.

He decided on a trap. That would be the simplest, he thought. He would make a good-sized cage of aspen poles, shut half a dozen roosters in it and ring it around with heavy bear traps, properly concealed. The cackling of the roosters would attract the lion; and, prowling around the cage, he would be caught in one of the traps. Lions were not so wise nor so wary as coyotes.

It was nearly dawn and Rob was sleeping again, with his head fallen forward on his chest, when he was awakened by Flicka's neighing. Even before he had opened his eyes and put his hand on the gun he knew the neigh for a neigh of terror. He saw that her head was turned and her eyes

305

directed across the creek to the three pines. He looked over and saw the lion feeding at the carcass of the slain heifer.

Though it was a huge beast, fully the five feet three which he had estimated from the measure of its footprints, the thing that struck him was its likeness to Pauly in the curving lines of its body and the way, with feet braced forward, one paw on the skeleton, its muscular body was drawn back, pulling. The heifer's flesh ripped under the long, shining, white fangs. The wildcat's tail whipped horizontally back and forth on the earth.

Rob put the gun to his shoulder, drew a bead, and fired.

He had never shot a mountain lion before. He had heard of the extraordinary vitality of the creature; and how, even mortally wounded, sometimes carrying several bullets, they still had strength to attack and fight ferociously. He now had an opportunity to see this for himself.

As the bullet hit the lion, it leaped ten feet in the air, twisting as it curved to the earth. It landed in a ball, turned several somersaults, snarling; regained its feet again. Then, following the treeing instinct, it leaped for the nearest of the three pines. Seizing it, six or eight feet from the ground, the lion hung there a moment, giving the first signs of failing strength. Then he clawed his way rapidly up the trunk and out on the first heavy limb.

Rob had felt fairly certain of having shot him through the heart, but now began to wonder if he might have missed, or inflicted only a trifling wound.

He was lifting the gun to his shoulder for a second shot, when he saw that the lion was failing.

It slid off the branch and hit the earth fifteen feet below, stone dead.

Chapter Thirty-five

When McLaughlin said that if Ken thought Flicka was dead, he'd sleep for a month, he was not far wrong. When it was not sleep, it was delirium or stupor. The boy was most seriously ill – too ill to be taken in to Cheyenne to the hospital there. Before long, pneumonia set in, and then the doctor spent many nights in succession at the ranch, driving in to town early in the morning to attend to his practice.

Flicka, on the other hand, gained strength steadily. Soon she could bear her weight on her feet, and Gus removed the sling. She could lie down and get up; take a few steps to the creek and drink when she wanted to; and she ate her oats with a good appetite.

'Don't it beat all?' said Tim to Gus as they ate their supper in the bunk house. 'Goes to show miracles still can happen.'

'Na,' said Gus. 'It was de cold water, washin' de fever

outa her. And more dan dot, it was Ken — you tink it don't count? All night dot boy sit dere and say, Hold on, Flicka, Ay'm here wid you, Ay'm standing by, two of us to-gedder—'

Tim stared at Gus without answering while he thought it over. Gus filled his pipe. 'Sure,' said Tim finally, 'sure, that's it.'

'It's de boy, now,' said Gus slowly. 'De little feller. He's turrible sick.'

Nell hardly left Ken's bedside. Rob or Gus attended to the cooking and brought trays to the door of the sickroom. Once a day Rob took his place beside Ken and insisted on Nell's going outdoors for fifteen minutes or so.

Nell would run through the pasture to see Flicka and would stand before her, trying to read the future. How was it going to be with Flicka? Would she pull through?

The look in the filly's eyes was bright and observing; she turned her head quickly at Nell's approach; her ears were pricked; now and then she looked up the path in the direction of the house and whinnied for Ken.

Nell would fly back up the path, running as fast as she could; and would reach Ken's room breathless, red-cheeked and full of hope.

But sometimes, kneeling beside the child's bed, the sight of him made hot tears sting her eyes. It was not only the sickness of his face, the fever, the difficult breathing and dry, bluish lips, it was the utter weariness of him. It had been too much for him, this summer, this desperate striving to alter the pattern of thought upon which his life formed itself.

Rob took Howard to school on the opening date and talked to Mr Gibson about Ken. He returned to Nell, astonished and moved at what the boy had done.

'Did you read it?' he asked Nell in a low voice as they sat by the window in Ken's room '*The Story of Gypsy?*'

'No. We decided that it must be all his own. If I'd read it

308

I'd have wanted to make suggestions, and as this was really an examination paper, it didn't seem right.'

Rob handed her the paper. When he had first read it himself it had given him the strange emotion within his breast that his younger son sometimes caused.

Nell read:

Flicka is the grand-daughter of Gypsy, who was an English thoroughbred and polo mare. My father bought her when he was a West Point Cadet.

Flicka does not look like Gypsy who was pitch black, but she looks like her Sire, who is a golden chestnut. His name is Banner. Flicka's mother was named Rocket. She was the fastest horse we ever had, fast enough to win races, but it was no use, because she was loco and she came to a bad end. Flicka is not loco.

The way Rocket came to be loco was because she had a wild mustang for a father. His name was the Albino, because he was pure white, and he was a hellion, and stole mares from all the ranches. He stole Gypsy and kept her for four years, and when we got her back she had four colts with her, and one of them was Rocket.

They were so beautiful that my father kept them and tried to break them, but no luck. They wouldn't knuckle under, any of them, and he was sorry he had kept them and let them mix their blood with our horses' blood, because Banner bred them, and they had colts too, and Flicka is one of those colts.

Flicka's colour is just like Banner's (who is a registered thoroughbred) and her shape is a little bit like her mother's – and that makes her very fast, because the things that make a horse fast are long legs and a long body, and Flicka's are a little bit too long. But that is why she is so fast. She beat every other yearling.

Flicka is my horse. I am taking care of her and training her, and when she is three years old I can ride her. And if she gets gentled, she could be a race horse, because she is fast and she is not loco.

So that is 'The Story of Gypsy'.

Nell finished reading and raised her eyes to Rob's. 'Flicka – Flicka – Flicka—,' she said.

He nodded. 'Yes. That's what Gibson said. As a story about Gypsy it's a fine story about Flicka.'

Ken muttered incoherently, throwing one arm across the covers. Nell went to him to watch a moment, and to smooth the damp hair back from his forehead. He always seemed to recognize the touch of her hand, and to be eased and quieted by it.

She returned to Rob. 'What did Gibson say about it?'

'Said it was a good piece of writing. Says Ken's got a brilliant mind – asked me if I knew it—'

'What did you say?'

'I said No, I thought he was dumb; and he said sometimes brilliant people were very dumb.'

In Nell's worn and tired face the dimple of the right cheek suddenly showed. 'I didn't know Gibson was smart enough to say a thing like that,' she whispered.

'Did you know it, Nell – that Ken is brilliant?'

'I suspected it.'

'What on earth made you think that? He's always failed at everything – till this summer.'

'Well—' Nell spoke slowly, thoughtfully, 'a dreamer – you know – it's a mind that looks over the edges of things – the way Ken can do what he calls "getting into other worlds"; gets into a picture; gets into a drop of water; gets into a star – anything—'

Rob sat looking out of the window.

'What did Mr Gibson finally decide?' asked Nell.

'Said that as Ken had made a sincere effort, he would take him back into his own grade on probation.'

Rob left the room and Nell sat looking out at the Green.

The leaves of the young cottonwoods had turned to gold; and at every puff of wind a shower of them floated down with a soft rustling sound. Nell's eyes roved farther, and she suddenly realized that all the colour had gone from the world. This always happened in the fall, quite unexpectedly; and there was no more richness of the summer blues and greens and reds; the landscape became drab and seemed to shrink in size, and so would remain until the snow came and transformed it again.

In the third week of Ken's illness, his condition improved. The fever went down, his brain cleared and he recognized his father and mother. He was often restless at night. Nell, sleeping in the cot in his room, would be wakened by his voice calling 'Mother'; and would get up and go to him, to sit on the edge of the bed, holding his hand, or smoothing his hair back from his forehead until he slept again.

He never spoke of Flicka.

With no duties, no demands of any sort made upon him, and his mother beside him, day and night, he seemed very little and childish.

He said one morning, 'Don't you sleep at all, Mother?'

'Why, of course I sleep, dear, what made you think I don't?'

'Well, when I call you, you answer so quick – and in such a voice, it sounds as if you were always awake.'

'I sleep with one ear open.' Nell's dimple showed.

He looked up at her, tired but curious. 'Which ear, Mother?'

Often he was awake a long time in the night, and they had conversations. His mind roamed far afield and touched on events and themes Nell had completely forgotten.

'Mother, you know old Mrs Perkins?'

'Yes, Dear.'

'She's awful old, isn't she?'

'Yes, she's pretty old.'

311

'Mother – do you have to grow old too?'

'Of course.'

'*Like that?*'

Nell laughed.

'I don't want you to change, Mother.'

'I won't change, Kennie – not really me—'

'But your face will.'

'That'll be just a false face – like you get at the ten-cent store in Laramie at Hallowe'en'

'Really, Mother? *Really* won't you change inside? You'll be the same *you?*'

'Yes, darling—'

'Then I don't mind the false face—'

Another time he said, 'Remember when you said, Mother, there was something you'd been wanting *awful bad* ever since a few years after I was born – what was it?'

Nell did not answer right away. She wondered if she would answer at all. She lay on her side in the little cot, her face turned towards Ken. Over on the night table, a lamp was burning, turned very low.'

'Mother?'

'It was a little girl I've always wanted, Ken.'

Ken did not answer for a long time. Then he said dreamily, 'We wanted the same thing, didn't we, Mother?'

'How do you mean?'

Again he did not answer for so long that she thought he had fallen asleep, and her own eyes closed. Then she heard his weak voice, 'Do you know what *little girl* would be in Swedish, Mother?'

His eyes flew open. On the point of speaking, she held back the word. That was the nearest he had come to speaking of Flicka.

He fell asleep, but his sleep was broken and troubled. He cried out, several times, and at last she rose and slipped into her dressing gown and sat on his bedside, smoothing his hair.

Outside, a wakeful rooster was crowing, though it was only two o'clock. Ken opened his eyes and began to talk about the rooster. He was fretful and complaining.

'They're supposed to crow when something good has happened, Mother—'

'He's just a little young cockerel that hasn't learned manners yet.'

'There's *always* roosters crowing, Mother. Don't they ever stop?'

Nell bent over him. 'They crow for the morning coming.'

'But when awful things happen?'

'Still – there's a morning—'

'But if things *have died*—'

She didn't answer.

'Mother?' he insisted.

'Even then – there's a morning—'

The cockerel crowed again, his young, reedy voice like a boy's when it's changing.

Nell tried to interest Ken in the little events of ranch activity, what the men were doing, what work his father was planning, but he turned away from all this. She sensed that it was too real and too close – he could not yet bear the impact of life.

He talked about his room, his pictures, the familiar things about him and asked her what had happened to them, why they had changed so.

'Changed, Kennie?'

'Yes. Nothing's like it used to be.'

'It's you that have changed, dear – that makes everything look different.'

He twisted his head around to look, first of all, at the picture to the right of the bed, the tiny naked boy being held in the water among the ducklings; the man in embroidered suspenders playing a flute, the woman in gay peasant dress; and then the one to the left, the mother

313

holding a new baby in her arms to show it to the two children. But neither picture seemed of the slightest worth or interest. Something had gone out of them.

His eyes dwelled longer on the picture at the end of the room, and the verse in the corner, which said:

> Intreat me not to leave thee,
> Nor to return from following thee.

This picture too had changed, but in a different way. Before, he had felt something mysterious about it which he couldn't understand. Now he understood. He closed his eyes and didn't want to look at it.

Nell was waiting for just the right moment to tell him that Mr Gibson would take him back in his class; that the polo ponies had been sold for a good price; and, most of all, that Flicka was alive and getting stronger all the time. But Rodney Scott said,

'Let him wander a while yet. He's getting stronger. When he's a little farther along he'll begin to show interest and that will be time enough.'

They were seated after dinner one evening before the fire in the living room. Ken was asleep. With the colder weather Rob had filled the fireplace with logs, and the flames roared up the chimney.

They discussed at length the change that Ken's possession of Flicka had effected in him; just why they had given him the colt; just what his failings had been.

Between talk there were long silences, in which the fire held their gaze and they could sit comfortably, thinking but not speaking.

After one such silence Nell said suddenly, 'There's one thing that's been puzzling me. Why did Ken begin to dream at night all at once? And terrible dreams – he used never to dream at all.'

The doctor's eyes turned to her quickly. 'That's

interesting – but when you come to think of it not surprising.'

'Why?'

'All that stream of fantasy which used to pour out freely as day-dreams – it had to go somewhere when it was shut off. So, forced to find new channels, it invaded his sleep.'

Nell's face was alight with interest. 'So *that's* why he never dreamed at night.'

Dr Scott nodded. 'Yes. It's a pretty serious business – making a practical thinker and performer out of a day-dreamer. It's something that psychiatrists often have to do – or try to do. Mostly they fail. Day-dreaming is as potent and seductive as morphine. Once you've got the habit, it's got *you*. Lots of children do it; I think it's quite rare that it's understood or recognized in childhood when, perhaps, something could be done about it. Mostly it goes on into adult life – perhaps all life long. When doctors or psychiatrists get it to deal with, it's the *results* of it they see; inefficiency, failure, dishonesty, inability to cope with life, and then's it's usually too late to correct the habit. Here's a case where someone recognized it and applied some of the methods of modern psychology—'

'Applied just a little old-fashioned common sense,' interrupted Nell.

Rodney Scott smiled his boyish smile. 'Between you and me, they're about the same thing – and I think old-fashioned common sense is still ahead— Anyway, that's what you did, and the result has taken this boy through most of the great experience of life: falling in love; bliss; despair; sacrifice; death. If you could do that to every day-dreamer, you could probably cure them all.'

Nell sighed. 'We didn't plan to do all that. It just happened so.'

When the doctor rose to go Nell said, 'You know he still thinks Rob shot Flicka. Shouldn't I tell him the truth?'

Rodney hesitated. 'Sometimes good news is as much of

a shock as bad. He seems to have put everything out of his mind.'

'But perhaps *that's why* he won't think of anything real. Because he thinks she's dead.'

Rodney said, 'I'll leave that to your intuition, Mother. When you feel the right moment has come, and you have the impulse to tell him, do it.'

Nell told him in his sleep. Over and over again, standing at his bedside, she leaned down and said very softly, 'Did you know, darling, that Flicka is alive and getting better all the time?'

Ken was so accustomed to her voice and to her moving about him that it never woke him.

The first heavy snow of the winter came; and out on the Saddle Back the grass was covered; and the little colts, dressed in their shaggy coats of fur, whimpered because when they tried to graze, instead of the grass which now for the most part they lived on, their lips could find nothing but icy, tasteless, white stuff.

Banner told them that their babyhood was over, that now they would have to fight for their living. He showed them how. Standing beside one forlorn little fellow, the big stallion pawed vigorously at the snow until a space was cleared and the grass could be seen beneath. The little colt reached under Banner's arching neck and nibbled at the grass. Banner cleared some more grass for him, urging him to use his own little hoofs; and presently the lesson was learned and all the small ones copied their Sire and went about pawing at the snow.

Fine weather came again; three long weeks of Indian summer, during which Ken gained strength rapidly.

One day while Nell was cleaning his room he asked her, 'Whereabouts is Flicka?'

'She's down in the pasture, dear – we didn't move her, she was doing so well down there. Would you like to see her?'

After a long pause he said wearily, 'Oh, I don't know—'

Nell carefully dusted the objects on the chest of drawers. She turned to glance at Ken. 'You never thought that she had been shot, dear, did you?'

Ken hesitated, then said in a rather confused manner, 'I don't know exactly, I had so many dreams, I didn't know what was true and what was a dream— I did think that she had been shot— I heard a big shot—'

'That was the wildcat your father shot at down in the pasture that night.'

'Did he get him?' asked Ken with his first show of interest.

'Not that shot that you heard, but he got him at sunrise next morning. Your dad spent the whole night in the pasture there beside Flicka, so that the wildcat couldn't touch her.'

Ken, staring out the window, was visualizing this, and his face had a slight, smiling interest.

'Wouldn't you like to see her?' ventured Nell again; but Ken turned his face away and repeated listlessly, 'Oh, I don't know—'

With the doctor's consent, Ken was taken out for a short drive in the car, but it tired him greatly. There was too much for his eyes to see, too much for his lungs to breathe, and far too much to think about. He didn't want to go again for a long time.

'It's as if he's lost heart,' said Rob uneasily to Nell.

Some days later, when there had been a light fall of snow, and the whole world was an etching in brown and white, Rob wrapped the boy up, and telling Nell that there was something out on one of the hills he wanted to show him, drove down the road and stopped the car. Looking out of the window, they could see, a short distance away, where the range rolled up to the woods.

'Look,' said McLaughlin, pointing out of the window.

On the edge of the woods stood a great stag with a fullantlered head. Blending perfectly with the brown and white etching, he was hard to see at first. His whole body was in profile to the car, but his head was turned around to face them, held very high, the eyes in an unswerving direct gaze bent upon the car there in the road. The up-curving lines of his neck and head flowed out into the trunks and then the branches of the many-pointed antlers in indescribable beauty.

Ken's mouth fell open as he looked. The stag was absolutely motionless. The word *nobility* might have been coined to embody all that the magnificent creature expressed. Or *courage*—

McLaughlin glanced down at his son. The mouth was still open.

'How did you know he'd be here, Dad?'

'I just saw him, driving in from the highway.'

'Why does he stay so long without moving?'

'He's got a doe lying down there. He's protecting her. That's why he doesn't move.'

The boy looked a long time yet, then glanced up at his father. 'Because *she's his responsibility*?'

'Yes.'

McLaughlin started the engine, turned the car and drove towards the ranch.

Ken watched the motionless stag as long as he could see him. The boy's eyes burned; there was a choking in his throat, and all through his body a feeling as of rushing torrents.

When he could no longer see the stag, his eyes roved over the hills and woods. He did not know what had ended the cold, weary detachment and united him to the world again, he only knew that it was his own once more, that it was beautiful and alive, that he wanted to see Flicka. And he pressed his face against his father's sleeve and wept.

Late that afternoon Ken, bundled up in a heavy sweater,

slammed the house door, thudded across the Green and opened the gate. He found a new pasture; snow on the ground, bare trees, the orange glow of a real winter sunset in the sky. And Flicka—

Every day, for weeks, she had looked for him. She would stand at the corral gate with head up and ears pricked sharply; then, disappointed, whirl about with an impatient nicker and trot restlessly around the hill, then turn, point her ears, and stand listening again.

She had grown two inches in height and gave promise of being a big horse, with speed and power and fire. She had a thick, warm winter coat of long fur; there was no swelling on any of her legs. Cold mornings, she put her nose to the earth and kicked her heels in the air, or twisted her body and bucked; or galloped wildly from one end of the pasture to the other, her blonde mane and tail streaming. When snow fell, coming sometimes on a whining winter wind, she lifted her head high and sniffed at it with flaring nostrils.

Now the slamming of the ranch door caught her attention and she trotted questioningly towards the corral.

Ken's quick feet thudded across the Green, the gate rattled; and when the boy came running down the path, crying, 'Oh, Flicka! Flicka!', the neigh that rang out on the cold air was a sound the filly had never made before.

Other books by Mary O'Hara
in Mammoth

Thunderhead

Following on from
My Friend Flicka,
Thunderhead continues the story
of the McLaughlin family and their
horses at the Goose Bar Ranch. Ken
dreams of turning Flicka's colt,
Thunderhead into an unbeatable
racehorse. A moving and exciting story
of a boy and a colt growing up together.

Green Grass of Wyoming

The last of the three Flicka books, in which
the saga of the Goose Bar Ranch
reaches its peak. The McLaughlins live
through a series of dramatic incidents, and
Ken begins to grow up fast. Then
Thunderhead, the superb stallion,
roams far away into the Wyoming hills and
he is the only one in the end who can
help Ken prove himself to the world.